THE RETURN

HOUSE OF ISRAEL VOL. 1

HOUSE OF ISRAEL

VOL. 1

THE RETURN

ROBERT MARCUM

Covenant Communications, Inc.

Covenant

I dedicate this book to those who died in the holocaust, both "Jew" and "Gentile," and to those who made every effort to save them. The stories of sacrifice are too numerous to tell in these short pages. They are both astonishing and humbling, and a great lesson for those of us who live today.

Joseph Smith said, "The sacrifice required of Abraham in the offering of Isaac, shows that if a man would attain to the keys of the kingdom of an endless life, he must sacrifice all things." And the Savior reminds us that, "Greater love hath no man than this, that a man lay down his life for his friends."

PREFACE TO BOOK I

As one author states, "The principal targets of the Nazi extermination campaign were the Jews. True, Hitler started out by arresting his political enemies and murdered thousands of Communists, 'asocials,' and other non-Jews, but these groups did not pose the threat to Aryan blood that the 'parasitic' Jews did" (Mitchell G. Bard, *The Holocaust*, 21). Thus the Jewish persecution began almost the moment the Nazis came to power, even though Germany, at that time, was regarded as one of the most civilized countries in the World. Boycotts were initiated against Jews in Germany as early as 1933. In July of the same year, the citizenship of Jews who had immigrated to Germany after 1918 was canceled. A few months later Jews were denied the right to health insurance, and by 1935 signs started appearing in public places (such as stores and cafes) reading, "Jews not wanted." By 1938 every German government institution had policies denying Jews basic human rights, and the Nazi propaganda machine under Joseph Goebbels was feeding the public a steady stream of anti-Semitic propaganda, establishing the motto, "The Jews are our misfortune." In that same year, the government took away property, required Jews to sell their businesses to non-Jews, and stripped Jewish doctors and other professionals of their licenses. Next came identity cards, confiscation of passports, expelling of children from schools, and the banning of all Jews from sporting events and associations.

In 1939 things worsened significantly. On November 9 and 10, the government organized mobs that destroyed 191 synagogues and looted 7,500 shops belonging to Jews. Known as the Night of the Broken Glass, or *Kristallnacht*, it was followed by the arrest of

26,000 Jewish men, and the movement of the Jews to concentration and labor camps began in earnest. With the seizure of Austria and Czechoslovakia, the persecution widened to places outside of Germany, and with the occupation of Poland, wherein millions more of the Jewish people came under German control, Hitler's goal to eliminate the Jews became more complicated. In response, Heinrich Himmler was ordered to create a special body within his SS organization known as the *Einsatzgruppen* (special police). He gave them charge for the liquidation of all political enemies of the Third Reich. With rare individual exceptions, the Jewish people were at the top of the list.

As 1942 dawned, hundreds of thousands of Jews had been murdered, but more than 11 million still remained. On January 20 of that year, a conference was held on the shores of a Berlin Lake called the Wannsee in which the "Final Solution" for the extermination of all remaining Jews under Nazi control was put in place. After that a much more systematic approach was taken. As Bard states, "From that point until the surrender of Germany, the Nazis followed the course laid out at Wannsee and proceeded to murder approximately six million Jews as well as almost an equal number of non-Jews. And the killing continued unabated, even when the course of war turned against Germany. When every German was needed to fight; when food, oil, and transportation were in short supply, resources continued to be used to kill Jews rather than be diverted for military use" (Bard, 20).

Who really eliminated the Jews? Was it just the Nazis, or were others involved? Ordinary Germans and citizens from every other Axis country have a difficult time accepting, even today, the role of their forefathers in this extraordinary cruelty and murder of members of the human family, but such was the case. It was the ordinary citizen who "assumed positions in the bureaucracies that implemented" the final solution. "They became members of the army, the secret police, and other military and paramilitary organizations that harassed, arrested, tortured, and murdered Jews; and with all too few exceptions, they stood by and did nothing to help the Jews.

"The magnitude of the atrocities makes it easy to forget that most of the murders were carried out by individuals . . . often men with wives and children. Some Nazis were undoubtedly sociopaths, but most were not. They were typically people who sat home petting their dogs, reading bedtime stories to their children, and listening to Mozart after spending the day shooting mothers and infants" (Bard, 21).

However, there were some who did try to help the Jews, and from their efforts hundreds and even thousands of lives were saved or prolonged. Heroic acts by such people have given them a place in Jewish history as "Righteous Persons." Oskar Schindler is probably the most well-known because of the movie *Schindler's List*, but such men as Raoul Wallenberg and Chiune Sigahara also did a great work in trying to help the Jewish people. Wallenberg died for his efforts, and Sigahara's diplomatic career was ruined.

In a few instances, whole towns tried to protect the Jews who lived among them, but these were the exceptions, not the rule. The French town of Le Chambon-sur-Lignon is the most noted exception.

What did the United States government know and what did it do to stop such murderous conduct? It knew a great deal but did little. It is a part of our history, and the history of many other nations, that we assented to the atrocities simply by closing our eyes to them. As Bard states, "It is hard to believe the press did not make the murder of millions of Jews a bigger story and stimulate government efforts to rescue. The truth is that many reports of what was happening did appear, but they were often buried deep in newspapers and were written in a way that detracted from their credibility. Though the Allies had plenty of evidence to prove the mass murder of Jews, the press and general public found the reports hard to believe. It simply was not possible to believe that hundreds of thousands of people could be murdered in a single place" (Bard, 22).

World War II became the backdrop for survival of the Jewish nation. Out of it came a people tried and tested in the furnace of affliction, a people ready to fight for their lives, for a homeland where their destiny was determined by the strength of their arms and the iron of their will. Though their prophetic return was hampered by the political games of nations, the greed and blood lust of men, and the false traditions of religionists, the holocaust left them no choice. More than any other factor, it sets the stage for the return of the Jewish people to Israel.

What you will read in this book is part fiction, part fact. Most of the characters are fictional, but many of their stories are based on real events. There are chapter notes at the end of the book that will give you a more in-depth understanding of what transpired in history, but for the most part the story speaks for itself. There are not chapter notes for every chapter; instead, the designation "See Chapter Notes" at the end of a chapter indicates there are notes available at the back of the book.

Please understand that I am a writer of fiction, not of history. My obsession is simply to tell a good story based on history as I have come to see it.

PART ONE
THE SURVIVORS

CHAPTER 1

Hannah sat in the wheelchair breathing in the fresh spring air, the field of daisies stretching before her like an artist's canvas painted in bright yellows and greens. It had been a long time since she had seen anything so lovely.

She adjusted her thin body in the chair; she was still too frail to handle one position too long; the bones of her legs, arms, and hips were not fully covered by the protective muscle and fat most humans carry. When brought to this hospital, she had weighed a mere 75 pounds—a walking skeleton. The concentration camp known as Ravensbrück had taken its toll.

Hannah shuddered, the thoughts of the last four years of her life rushing in on her like a flood of filthy water that stained the bright yellow-and-green canvas before her. Closing her eyes tightly, she gripped the arms of the wheelchair with all her strength, forcing the vivid, muddy images back into the dark corners of her mind, refusing to let them overwhelm her again. She felt exhausted and weak from the exertion it took, and as her head fell limp, her chin came to rest against her chest. Would she ever be free of the horror?

"Hannah? Are you all right?"

The voice was that of one of the nuns who acted as nurses. Sister Martha had been assigned to care for Hannah for the last three months. At first Hannah had been leery of Martha, unable to believe that any German, especially a Christian, could do other than hate her. It was a fear bred into her over four years of prisons, camps, and vile treatment perpetrated on millions by the Third Reich's policy to eliminate what they called the Jewish plague. A policy that had forced her to watch her parents, along with a hundred other Warsaw Ghetto Jews, dig trenches—along the edge of which they were then lined up and shot, their bodies falling back into their graves like limp piles of human garbage. A policy that tore her two sisters away from her as starvation slowly emaciated their bodies, death crawling inside them like a voracious beast and destroying their lives months before they stopped breathing.

Tears sprang to Hannah's eyes like water from a flooding faucet, cascading down her cheeks and wetting the front of her gown. She cried a lot lately, something she hadn't done since Esther had died and she had been forced to survive on her own. She lifted her hand and wiped them away. "Yes, I am fine," she replied stiffly to Sister Martha's solicitous query. "I want to go inside." She grabbed the wheels and tried to turn the chair in the grass but had only strength enough to make it partway.

"I'll do that," Martha said, grabbing the handles at the back and reaching down to release the brake. "You're still recovering, Hannah. You must not try to do too much too soon." Martha's concern was genuine, but that only made it grate on Hannah even more. Here she was getting sympathy for her condition from a Christian nun, a representative of so many other so-called Christians who had either participated in the killing or stood idly by and let it happen.

Martha turned the chair and started up the slight rise toward the hospital. There were others sitting about the grassy lawns—some men, some women—all trying to recuperate from a war that had taken the lives of millions. Hannah knew that the hospital housed Americans, Brits, Germans, Poles, Hungarians, and Jews alike, all wounded in some way by a war that had mauled Europe like some huge animal playing with its kill. Most of the men in the hospital were soldiers. There was a German wing and an Allied wing; citizens of countries who still followed or believed in the German cause were housed with the Germans. With the loss of the war, there weren't many former allies of the Germans who still *wanted* to be known as their friends, but it seemed a wiser choice to keep them separate from the Americans, French, and British. Better to have former believers in the German Reich complain about their accommodations than to have the war rekindled by putting enemies in the same rooms.

Despite the fact that the surrender had been official for weeks and the armies had stopped shooting at one another, the hatred still smoldered like hot coals inside many hearts. Just yesterday Hannah had seen an American amputee attack a German as they sat sunning on the porch of the hospital after a rainy morning. The German had lost his hand during the war but not his pride. He had made some derogatory remark about the "American Jew-lovers," causing the one-legged soldier from the United States to lunge, grab, and pummel him nearly to unconsciousness in spite of his handicap. Two orderlies had been hard-pressed to pull him off before he killed the German. The incident had gratified Hannah and she intended to thank the American if the opportunity presented itself.

Hannah's wheelchair reached the stairs and two orderlies joined them as if Martha had planned it all ahead of time. Each was about to take an arm of the chair and lift Hannah to the top of the steps, but she put up her hand and stopped them, then stood and went up the steps on her own. Slowly, but alone. She then continued into the building, leaving Martha to thank the orderlies, then hurry after her.

"What would you like for dinner this evening, Hannah?" Martha asked, her smile evident in her voice.

One thing Hannah had discovered was that there was no shortage of food at the hospital. Though the menu offering was limited, the portions were more than adequate, and you could request more if you wanted. Hannah had spent the first two weeks of her stay sleeping eighty percent of the time, unable to eat much—her stomach so shrunken, her body so decimated, that taking more than the smallest portion would have caused her distended stomach more discomfort than it had already suffered. She had watched some of the others attack the orderlies as food was brought into the room. They reminded Hannah of a pack of starving wolves who were suddenly aware of the smell of fresh meat. They had fought over the food like animals, pummeling each other, screaming, cursing, and generally fighting for every morsel as if there would be no more. They shoved the food into their mouths, swallowing it whole before it could be snatched by another, then tried to rip more from the clutches of those around them. Though the nuns had told them they could eat all they wanted, the primal instinct for survival developed in the camps simply did not allow them to believe or to wait. When it came to food, the camps had taught them they had few friends. They had also learned, early on, that promises made by those in authority were seldom kept.

Hannah remembered her first day at Ravensbrück. They were taken into a building, told to strip, and were promised hot showers. After being on the crowded, fetid trains for more than ten days, all quickly discarded their clothes, eager to feel that hot liquid mingled with soap washing over their bodies. When the guards told them to throw their clothes into stacks because they would be given fresh ones, they were excited, even cheerful. At last, relief had come.

There had been no showers, no soap, not even water. Instead, they were forced to stand naked as a battle-ax of a woman sheared off their hair like sheep, both on their heads and between their legs, then tossed them clothes that were in worse shape than their own and told them to reclothe. When one woman questioned this procedure, she had been beaten bloody with a metal pipe; when another refused to cooperate, she had been whipped with a stick as thick as a man's wrist. Frightened into submission, the rest had obeyed, only to find their clothes infested with lice the size of a woman's fingernail and the material so thin they were nothing more than a sheet of paper against the cold winter air.

Then came the next promise as they were lined up and told there would be food and blankets. Few believed it by then, their hope only momentarily rekindled when they smelled the sweet odor of potatoes, cabbage, and beef as they trudged across the frozen ground to their barracks. That hope had been dashed when the servers' ladles revealed nothing more than a murky broth. A female guard stood next to the servers and picked out any pieces of solid matter that might have eluded their earlier sifting. Hannah had wanted to use a club on the woman as she tossed each small piece between her mocking lips.

Yes, Hannah understood the fight for food because of empty promises. After places like Ravensbrück, all Jews understood. A rotting potato found near the kitchen, or a piece of molding bread clutched in the hand of the weak or dying had come to mean survival, and the promises of better things by those in authority were not to be trusted. Given the freedom of the hospital, the freedom to take what you wanted without being beaten, was like setting a nearly starved wild beast free inside a chicken coop.

But Hannah was glad she had been too weak to join the fight. Some had eaten too much too soon, their stomachs unable to even begin to digest what they had swallowed whole. All had suffered, and a few had died. Ironically, it still did not stop them from attacking the food trays when they appeared, the lessons of the concentration camps ingrained in them like the filth they were forced to live in. Better to die from a full stomach than from an empty one.

She forced the thoughts away, the pain of it nearly unbearable. Would she ever be able to think of those days without such horrible pain?

Hannah turned and sat down on her bed as soon as she reached it. She was walking more each day but it still seemed to take a good deal of effort. Her feet were like boards under her, the nerves dead because of constant cold and frostbite. She had lost two toes, the little ones of each foot, but the feeling was beginning to return, a slight tingling sensation in the flesh.

As she leaned against the bed, she glanced up at the window near its head, only to see her reflection there. When she had first been given a mirror, the shock had nearly killed her. A grizzly apparition had stared back at her. Her skin had been gray and sallow, her long, curly hair nothing but tufts of stiff bristles sticking out where the guards had neglected to sheer it clear to her scalp. She was grateful that her hair was starting to fill out nicely, so that large, round, empty eyes were not all that stared back at her, but she still wasn't herself. Would she—could she—ever be? Would that empty look in her eyes ever go away?

Hannah lay back on the bed. How had she ever survived the long, grueling workdays and the hours of standing in lines to be counted, relieve herself at the toilet, or receive the daily ration of broth and bread made more of sawdust than flour? Of the ten thousand Jews who had come to Ravensbrück with her, only one thousand had stayed alive. Then, when the Germans had decided to move them further into the heartland of Germany as the Allies forced them from mile after mile of previously conquered territory, less than ten percent had lived through the nearly two weeks aboard hot, locked trains with no sanitation and nothing more than a morsel of cheese to put in their mouths.

Hannah remembered how crowded it was in their car at first, and how more and more space was available as the dead were removed each morning, tossed into shallow graves or simply discarded along the tracks—the soldiers were too afraid for their own lives to do more. After only a few days it had become obvious to Hannah that they were prisoners without a home, the train going first west, then east, then west again as if unable to find a safe haven. She remembered the distant sound of howitzers and explosions and then the strafing of the train itself by the enemies of Germany, which finally brought it to a metal-grinding halt as it derailed and sent them all crashing into a farmer's plowed field. Of those remaining in her car, only twenty had survived to crawl between the bodies of the dead to reach the hole that had been blown in the far end of the train car. Others, though still alive, had been too weak to get free themselves and stayed behind. Hannah had watched from a hundred yards as the planes came back and dropped their bombs, obliterating what remained. That was when Hannah had lain down to die. That was when she had given up. If even the allies hated them, they had no hope. They would simply be taken back to their camps and the pain would go on. She had closed her eyes and let the darkness that she had fought so hard to keep away creep up her numb legs and into her heart.

When she opened her eyes to take one last look at the sun she had seen so little of for the last few years of her life, she found herself staring up into the faces of two strangers.

"Is she dead?" the one had asked the other.

"Same as!" the other responded. "Look at her!" He had said it in disbelief. "Look what them filthy krauts has done to her!" Her eyes had adjusted to see him standing over her. "Medic!" he had screamed. It was then she realized she was hearing English, one of several languages her father had insisted she and her sisters study. They had relatives in America they corresponded with and had even visited on occasion. The new enemy had come! But she was too tired to run, too tired to even move.

"Shoot me."

The voice seemed small, a strange croaking sound that could hardly be heard.

"Please . . ." the voice said, "don't . . . don't take me . . . back."

"She said somethin', Billy," one of the soldiers said. "Did ya hear it? She is alive. Medic!" he hollered.

It was then Hannah realized the voice demanding death was her own.

The soldier had kneeled down. "Don't worry lady; we ain't takin' ya back! We got help comin', so you just hang on, you hear?"

Hannah forced a wry smile. Another promise. Just another promise. Surely pain would follow.

Then the soldier had put a canteen to her lips and helped her drink. The liquid had been sweet as honey, cascading down her parched throat, cool and wonderful. She had grabbed it, gulped it, let it run over her face and neck as she tried to get more. She had not tasted water for so long! She had seen early on in the camps that the water was contaminated, that it was the cause of so many getting dysentery, and she had avoided it like the plague it was. Only when she was on work detail and they were fed by the nearby farmers or allowed to drink from a fresh-water spring or well did she drink, otherwise relying only on the boiled broth and horribly watered-down but hot coffee to replenish her body fluids. Now here was real water! Fresh and wonderful! She drank it all.

"Man, she was thirsty!" one soldier had said.

"Yeah!" the other had responded angrily. "Ain't no wonder lookin' at her! They plain starved these folks, that's all! Look at 'em. Nearly dead from it! Nothing but bones walking around! Makes me sick! If I get my hands on them that done this . . ."

Hannah saw the soldier clench his fists, his jaw rock solid with hate and anger. It was then she knew she was safe.

* * *

"Do you want anything to eat, Hannah?" Martha's voice brought her out of her thoughts.

"Some bread . . . with butter, please." Hannah knew it was only an hour until mealtime, but she couldn't get enough fresh bread, and whenever Martha offered something she asked for it.

Martha gave a knowing smile and turned to leave. As she did, Hannah wanted to thank her but couldn't. The words simply wouldn't come yet. Her bitter heart refused to let them. Someday, before she left the hospital, she would find a way. Martha was not like the other Germans. She did not hate Hannah and Hannah knew it, but she was German and Christian and . . .

She saw the soldier at the door. Martha stopped. He asked a question and both looked in her direction; then he turned and came her way. As he got closer she realized he looked vaguely familiar, but she couldn't place him. He wore an American uniform but with a different insignia on his shoulder, and he had a set of wings on his lapel. He smiled as he reached the end of her bed and she gathered the blankets around her still-wretched body so that he could not see how ugly she was.

"Hannah." He smiled. "How are you?" He asked it in Hebrew.

She tried to place him, the face, the features, so familiar and yet . . . and the voice . . .

"The last time I saw you, you were trying to force mud cakes down my throat," he said, his eyes laughing.

Her heart skipped a beat. "Max! Max Herzog? Is . . . is that you?"

He smiled and came up to the side of the bed as she leaned forward to get a better look.

"Yes, little Hannah, it's me."

She grabbed for him, nearly falling from the bed as his strong arms wrapped themselves around her and pulled her safely to him. Her tears flowed freely then as she clung tightly to his strong shoulders and melted into his arms. She was home again! At last! She was home again!

See Chapter Notes

CHAPTER 2

Max watched as Hannah ate the last of her food. She looked so frail, like a porcelain doll that would break if one gripped it too firmly. The last time he had seen her was in New York. They were cousins and both had been present for the marriage of Max's brother Chaim. Hannah and her three lovely sisters had come with their parents from Poland. Chaim had gone to Warsaw for a year to study with a noted rabbi there and had fallen in love with the rabbi's daughter. The marriage had been of one rabbinical family to another, Max's father being one of the prominent rabbis of New York. According to Rabbi Moshe Gruen, Rabbi of Warsaw, it was a marriage made by God himself. New York was where the young couple would live. Hannah and her family had come to witness the event and renew relationships with her only uncle's family.

Hannah shoved the tray aside, nearly off the edge of the bed. Max stood quickly, picked it up, and set it on a nearby table.

"Tell me more, Max. I must hear it all!" she said exuberantly.

They discussed his family and his brother's wife, and two children whom Hannah had never seen. Shortly after Hannah and her family had returned to Poland from the United States, the war had broken out in Europe and they had lost all contact with Hannah's family. Max felt an empty spot in the pit of his stomach. If only they had all stayed in New York! But Hannah's father and the rabbi felt obligated to return. Things had been getting worse in Poland for years—pogroms, special taxes against Jews, then the ghettos. Their consciences simply wouldn't let them walk away to safety while others suffered. The decision had cost both men their lives along with the rest of their families, except for Hannah. She was the only survivor that Max had been able to find. Of twenty people, only she was still alive.

"What is the matter, Max?" Hannah said, seeing the sad look in his eyes.

"I was just thinking . . ." Max said. "It doesn't matter . . ." He tried to put it aside with the wave of his hand.

"No, I want to know. What is it?" she persisted.

He looked at her large eyes, her shrunken body. She had been through so much! "Your father . . . if only he hadn't . . ." His voice trailed off as he sat on the edge of the bed and took her hand.

"If only he hadn't left New York?" she said.

He nodded, his eyes on their clasped hands. Hers were so thin, nothing more than skin stretched over bone.

"Yes, I cursed him more than once for that." She forced a smile. "But my father saved at least a hundred lives before he was killed. He helped them escape to a center that took refugees to Palestine. That is why they shot them like they did." The pain was etched in the lines of her face as the memory came surging back like waves in a stormy sea.

"I'm sorry," Max said. "I don't mean to dredge up such horrible . . ."

She squeezed his hand. "No, it is better to talk of these things. Maybe they will stop haunting me at night if I . . . if we can talk about them." She took a deep breath. "When we returned to our home, it was less easy to ignore the anti-Semitism all around us. Even before Hitler and his army conquered our country . . . well, you know what it was like. Everyone blamed us for something, believed we were trying to ruin the country. Everything that could be done to make our lives miserable was done. It was much worse when we got back, frightfully worse. My father and Rabbi Dallich immediately began getting as many out of Poland as they could. He made contact with the Israeli underground organization in Czechoslovakia and made arrangements. As the first people began quietly leaving their homes on the first leg of a journey we hoped would lead them to Palestine, Hitler came to Poland and our way to freedom was cut off. Father had planned to take us out in only a few more weeks. Instead, they came to our door and imprisoned Father and Mother. My sisters and I were away shopping at the time. When we returned, they were gone. We rushed to the police station, only to see them standing . . ."

The tears sprang to her eyes, and her shoulders began shaking with sorrow. "They shot them, Max. I watched them die."

He took her in his arms again and held her close until the sobs subsided and she could get control.

Using a hanky to blow her nose, she continued. "I took my sisters and we fled back to the house. I grabbed everything of value I could and shoved it in a suitcase. My sisters were in shock, unable to help, but I forced them, pushed them, to get some warm clothes together. It was winter and I knew we would need all the warm clothing and bedding we could carry. By the time dark enveloped the city, we were on the outskirts, heading south. My father had told me where to go, how to find those who were helping with the escape. The trouble was, I didn't have the necessary papers. I didn't know how to get them, what to do to get past the patrols I knew would surely be on the roads. So we stayed in the hills. The first night we found a barn to sleep in, but when we awoke the next morning . . ." A sad look filled her eyes, "the farmer had turned us in. The police took us back. They imprisoned us, interrogated us, beat us, trying to get us to tell where others were, where they had gone. Thankfully, my father had not told my sisters. Only I had the secret." Her jaw hardened. "They beat me near to death . . . but I didn't tell them." She pulled up the sleeve covering her left arm. As she ran her hand over the flesh, Max saw the irregularity, a bump in the bone. "He broke my arm with a hammer when I refused to tell and spit blood on his boots!" Her eyes flared with hatred. "If I could have killed him, I would have! Such men should have to go through the same punishments! They should have their arms broken, they . . ." She grabbed a hold of his coat and put her head against his shoulder, sobbing. "They killed Millie because I wouldn't tell. They beat her to death, Max! I know it! It was my fault!" she sobbed. "I . . ."

Max held her again. Would she ever be the same? Could such memories, such horrors, ever leave her? She had been so happy, with a wit as sharp as his father's razor! So much fun! They had ruined her life, butchered her family! Oh how he hoped they would be made to pay!

Long moments passed before she regained control. When she finally lay back against her pillow, he could see that she was exhausted. He must leave.

"I have to get back to Frankfurt," Max said.

She grabbed his hand firmly as if to prevent his leaving. He smiled as comforting a smile as he could muster. "I'll be back, Hannah. I promise."

She tried to smile back. Another promise. So many had been broken, but she had to believe this one. She forced her head to move up and down, used all her will to lessen the hold on his hand, to let him slide free of her iron grip.

He leaned over and kissed her on the forehead. "I promise." He paused. "I am glad you survived, Hannah. So very glad!"

He turned and walked away. She watched until he had left the long hall and disappeared. Slipping off her bed as quickly as her frail condition allowed, she struggled to the window and peered out, hoping to get a last look at him. She saw nothing but darkness. She stayed a moment more, then went back to the bed and snuggled down into the covers after turning off the light on the wall above her. Moments later she fell into a deep sleep—the first she had had in nearly four years.

See Chapter Notes

CHAPTER 3

Max came again two Sundays later. Hannah had received three letters from him, and it had made a world of difference. She was eating much better and finally gaining weight. He had given her hope.

When he appeared and she saw that he had a friend with him, she quickly pulled covers over her and refused to come out.

"Hannah, please," Max begged, "he won't bite, I promise." He laughed.

"No!" Hannah said adamantly, appalled that he would bring anyone to see her in this condition. "I don't know this man, and he doesn't know me."

"He knows all about you!" Max said.

Great, Hannah thought. "No," she said again just as firmly.

"Maybe I'd better wait outside," a voice said. "If she doesn't think . . ."

The voice was appealing, deep, but soft and pleasant, Hannah thought. She lowered the blanket to the edge of her nose, then up again. Handsome, light complexion, blue eyes. "Who are you?" she demanded.

"Ephraim Daniels," the voice returned.

"Ephraim. A Jewish name?"

The pleasant voice laughed. "Sorry, the house of Judah doesn't claim me. I belong to Joseph."

The sheet came down to the bridge of her nose again, her eyes searching his, curious. "Joseph?"

"It's a long story I'll share with you sometime." He smiled. *His teeth are as white as snow,* she thought! *No one can have teeth that white.* His jaw was square and his nose aquiline. From the looks of him he was better than six feet tall, thin but with broad shoulders. She, on the other hand, was shorter at five-feet-five, normally stout, with dark hair and eyes, and a face round as the sun. How could two such opposites even discuss the weather without a fight? The sheet went back up.

"Go away," she said. "A lady doesn't meet a gentleman while she is in her pajamas. Especially a Jewish lady."

Both men laughed lightly and in her mind she could see his eyes dancing. "Yes, of course, you're right," said Max's friend. "I'll wait outside until you've dressed."

"Can't dress. No clothes," she said.

"Oh, well how about these?" came the reply.

She lowered the sheet again. Max and his friend held a skirt and blouse up for her to see. Her eyes went big. She hadn't seen anything like them for so long! They were beautiful! A soft wool skirt and a silk blouse in a beige color. Without thinking, she dropped the sheet and grabbed them both with a single swipe of her hand. They felt so wonderful against her fingers, her face, her arms. "Get!" she said, waving her hand. Ephraim immediately fled toward the door, but Max seemed to hesitate. "You too, Max. Go on. I'll be with you in a few minutes!" She grinned. "I suppose you brought some other things? Underclothes . . ."

Max pointed at the sack on the end of the bed as he fled for the door, grinning from ear to ear. "Yeah, in the sack!" He nearly fell over as he tried to keep running backwards. "Uh, nice to see you're feeling better today!"

She ignored him, already grabbing for the sack and quickly dumping the underclothes on the bed.

"I hope they fit!" yelled Ephraim from the door. "Your sizes . . . well, we just sorta guessed at 'em."

"Out with you!" she yelled back, happiness in her voice. She scrambled from the bed, suddenly realizing that the other patients were watching her, their eyes even more bulbous than usual.

"New clothes!" one said in mournful envy.

"Look at those," said another. "They must be sooo soft!"

"They'll make you look like a new woman," said another, cackling. "Something you could use."

"Can I feel them?" asked the girl in the next bed.

Hannah pulled them to herself reflexively; then she relented. She wasn't in the camps anymore; this girl wouldn't . . . couldn't steal them from her. She handed the blouse to the girl and let her touch it, then pulled the curtain so she could undress.

"How does it feel?" asked one of the girls in another bed.

"Let me," said another. Voices from every bed, all wanting to get closer. Hannah heard them shuffling down the aisle, moving close enough to get a good look, to touch them.

Surely they would have the blouse in shreds before she could even wear it, Hannah thought. Without thinking, she shoved back the curtain and grabbed for the blouse, then closed it again to the loud murmurs and grasping hands of others. Ignoring them, she quickly put on her underclothes, the white slip, the skirt and blouse. She had never felt anything so wonderful. Their underclothes had been taken from them at Ravensbrück, and she had forgotten how wonderful, how . . . how secure they made her feel. When she was finished, she sat back on the edge of the bed and ran her hands over the blouse as if caressing a new baby's soft skin. How wonderful, she thought. Surely, there is no more magnificent piece of clothing in the entire world.

She shoved back the curtain to ooh's and aah's. "You look wonderful!" said the girl in the next bed. You must feel . . ."

Hannah nodded quickly. "Like I died and went to heaven!" She laughed lightly, still caressing the blouse.

"Yeah, a real sight," said one of the hard cases from Auschwitz. "They will especially admire your hair," she said cynically.

Hannah turned to see her reflection in the window. Her hand flew to her hair. It was still short, uneven, stiff. Grabbing a brush, she quickly began working it over. The girl in the next bed watched, then reached inside a bag she had and pulled out a small case of lipstick. "Here," she said, "use some." She grinned. "That American is worth a little primping."

Hannah smiled her thanks while wondering how such a thing had happened. Where had the lipstick come from? There had been no other visitors, to anyone.

"Red Cross, remember?" the girl said.

The packages from America! Hers lay unopened under her pillow.

She smiled at the girl. She didn't know her very well. Her name was Tappuah and she, too, was from Poland. Other than that, they had little in common, and their conversations were usually short. No one wanted to say much about the past. It hurt too badly.

"Here," yelled another, "I have some rouge." The woman was in another bed at the far side of the room. Hannah was about to say she had found her own but thought better of it. The woman wanted to give, be a part of the excitement. She closed the box and put it back under the pillow, then, though still weak, quickly moved to receive the small case of rouge. Another handed her an eyeliner pencil, another a small container with body powder inside. As she received each item, Hannah grappled with what to say. Ravensbrück had taught them all to stay free of caring for others except those who were family or close friends. It was hard enough to care for self and family—if you had any—let alone for others, and even harder to watch someone you cared for die. So many had died! Hannah looked around the room, a sudden realization hitting her in the heart. For the first time in months—and for many, probably even years—they were starting to let themselves care again.

"Thank you," she said to all of them.

Each nodded, then watched her use their little items to improve her still battle-worn face. When she was finished, there were head shakes of approval. Even the hardened prisoner from Auschwitz had a wry smile on her face. "Not bad for a little Polish girl!" she said gruffly, then lay down and turned her back to them. Showing they cared would take longer for some than for others.

Hannah took a deep breath. She felt tired yet exhilarated, her return to humanity staring back at her from the glass of the window. Maybe she could survive this . . . maybe . . . maybe there was still a chance for a decent, happy life. Just maybe.

She started from the room, then remembered she had no shoes. Standing still, looking at her feet, she wondered what to do. Then Martha stood in front of her, a pair of black oxfords in her hands and a smile on her face. "I outgrew them years ago."

Again Hannah was speechless. They looked the right size, but . . .

She cleared her throat. "Thank you, Martha," she said, taking them. She lifted her foot by bending her knee in front of her and slipping the shoe on. Perfect. She quickly had the other in place. Then she took a deep breath and walked from the room, hearing the excited chatter behind her.

"Nothing does more for recovery than a prince bearing gifts," Martha said to herself in German. "I think our little Hannah will make it now." She turned to see the others gathered around the window nearest the garden area where Hannah was to meet her friends. Even the hard-nosed woman from Auschwitz couldn't keep away. Martha chuckled. "Hasn't done *them* any harm, either." She clapped her hands. "Back to your beds, ladies, time for dinner!" It was a call that usually got everyone's attention. Not this time. "Ah well," Martha said to herself. "We'll feed the spirit first and take care of the flesh later." She turned and went from the room. There was a better window in the next ward.

* * *

Hannah caught her breath at the bottom of the stairs that led from the veranda. She had worked hard all week to strengthen herself and had been successful. But it was still tiring.

She saw Max and Ephraim Daniels sitting on the grass under a tree fifty feet to her left. They noticed her and stood, walking quickly in her direction.

"You look great, my Polish cousin!" Max said genuinely, taking her by the hands and giving her the once-over. "Better than even before the war."

Hannah blushed. "In that case I must have been ugly enough to stop a train," she quipped.

Max laughed while Ephraim gazed in admiration.

"He's right. You make our little purchases look very good."

Hannah had learned to read the eyes of others. Unable to understand the language of some of the guards who had been at Ravensbrück, she had used the eyes to determine what they really wanted. Others had never learned this art and had nearly been beaten to death for it, unable to understand what commands the guards were giving. In Ephraim's eyes she saw genuine admiration and it made her tingle from head to foot.

He offered his arm. "Come, you do look a little tired. We can sit under the tree. Max hasn't told me nearly enough about you."

She took the arm and leaned on it. She was a little weak, but she wondered if it was all due to her health or if some was from her racing heart. She didn't notice the pleased look on Max's face as the three of them walked the short distance and sat down under the tree.

Ephraim glanced toward the hospital. "It seems we have enough chaperones for a school of young ladies." He smiled.

Hannah looked up to see the window of her ward crowded with faces. She waved and all waved back. "They want me to introduce them to Max," she said.

"Umm. The hard-nosed one with the granite jaw seems to be his type," Ephraim teased.

"Rachel. Yes, Rachel could keep him in line, one way or the other." She smiled.

"Thanks guys," Max responded, "but I am already taken."

Hannah glanced at him quizzically. "A girlfriend then?"

"English girl I met while stationed at Devonshire, waiting for the invasion." He was already pulling his wallet from his pocket and quickly removed a somewhat tattered picture from it. "Her name is Anna."

"Jewish, I hope," Hannah said.

"Yeah, a refugee from the Netherlands. She has a few horror stories of her own, but she escaped the camps. Came to England on a small fishing boat packed with her family and thirty others."

"I'm glad to hear that some were spared the worst." Hannah handed back the picture. "She's lovely Max, and I am sure she'll make a good wife."

"Yeah, I'll know in another week."

Hannah didn't understand and her face showed it.

"I'm being shipped back to England. We fly-boys are pretty well finished around here. Except for guys like Ephraim. He makes up for three of the best of us. Got more kills than the rest of our group put together."

"Then why stick me behind a desk?" Ephraim responded with an edge in his voice. Hannah could tell he was not happy with his assignment.

"What kind of a desk? I mean, what do they have you doing?" she asked.

"Chasing Nazis who haven't gotten the message," Ephraim said.

It was obvious Hannah didn't understand.

"I like to fly, that's all. I live for it, breathe it, eat it, sleep in my plane more than I do in my bed. Grounding me to do this intelligence crap is not my idea of a good time."

"There are no more Germans to shoot down, Ephraim. The war is over, here," Max said.

"There is still one in the Pacific. I've asked for a transfer but this intelligence stuff is delaying it."

Hannah could see that he was frustrated.

"Stopping the Russians is just as important."

"Yeah. If we hadn't let 'em in there in the first place, we wouldn't have this problem. That's a mistake that'll ruin this country for years to come."

"The Russians? What have they got to do with anything?" Hannah asked.

Max told her about how Germany had been defeated and how the political maneuvering had held back the allies and allowed the Russians to take Berlin. Now they were trying to claim it and everything east of it as their own. "They even want part of your country," Max finished.

"Hitler gave it to them," Hannah said. "They were as bad as the Germans in their treatment of my people." It made her shudder. She immediately saw that getting rid of Hitler wasn't really the end. There was still Stalin. She rubbed her arms to get rid of the goose bumps. "Stalin can have it. I never want to see it again!"

Both men glanced at each other with understanding. Intelligence reports were beginning to come in and the Nazis and Poles had killed more than a million Jews—probably many more when the final figures were penciled in by the bean counters.

"What Nazis do you chase?" she asked.

"They call themselves Werewolves." Ephraim answered. "They are a rather loose underground movement made up of people who still believe that the Third Reich can rise out of the ashes and conquer the world. They've set off a few terrorist bombs and assassinated a few of their own countrymen they feel are too quick to help us dismantle the Nazi war machine. Now they're concentrating on disrupting our supply lines, hitting trains carrying troops, that sort of thing. A sort of resistance movement meant to give them time to regroup, I suppose. It won't happen."

"Werewolf. A good name for them. Do you know what it really means?" Hannah asked.

"Mythology has it that they were men who could change their appearance at will, roaming the countryside to rid it of the weak."

"Yes, chameleons. You never know but what your next-door neighbor might be one. Are there many of them?" Hannah asked.

"Any is too many."

"You will never get them all," Hannah said.

"No, I don't think so either, but we've already gotten a few, and we'll get enough to turn this country around. But there will always be Nazis here. Beliefs about the Aryan race and the need to cleanse the earth of everyone else run deep, clear back to the tribes that first wandered through this part of the world." Ephraim paused, his eyes searching hers.

"Those responsible for what happened to you weren't just in the German high command or even at the camps. Many of the German people believed the garbage Hitler dished out, and they still believe it. Jews still have a hard time, will for years to come." Ephraim looked down at the grass and started pulling at it.

Hannah forced herself to her feet and walked a short distance away, her back to them. She folded her arms across her chest. "It will never end for us. We must leave Europe. We must leave soon."

The two men looked at each other but said nothing. After a few minutes Hannah turned back. "You should stay and hunt the Werewolves, Mr. Ephraim Daniels," she said firmly. "Shoot them down like you would a Nazi pilot!"

Ephraim was in awe of her pluck. No wonder this little lady had survived the camps. "Yeah, I guess one battle is as important as the other."

"More so," she said. "Just not as easy. Werewolves are animals of the night. They come out only when they think they cannot be seen. During the light of day they hide, but the mythology says that they watch for opportunities to strike down one or two or dozens of their perceived enemies. These men who call themselves after such an animal must be poisoned before they can accomplish the harmful intents of their miserable hearts."

Ephraim gave a wry smile. "You wanna help?"

Hannah was shocked by the question and yet pleased by it at the same time. If she could help destroy such people, she would.

"What do I have to do?" she asked firmly.

"Whoa! Wait a minute. I was just kidding," Ephraim said.

"But I am not," Hannah replied seriously. "What can I do to bring such vermin to an end?"

Ephraim was stunned by the hatred he could feel emanating from her. Hatred that turned her will to iron. "I . . . uh . . . I don't know. I . . ." he glanced at Max for help but could see he wasn't going to get any. "I'll . . . uh . . . I'll check. Maybe . . ."

She stooped down in front of him. "Yes, do that, Ephraim Daniels. It would give me and many others in this place great pleasure to kill a Werewolf. We want the world to be free of such animals."

Ephraim looked into her eyes, felt the touch of her hand on his arm, knew that this was a woman few men would be able to match when it came to spirit and determination. *Maybe* . . . He dismissed the thought. It was too dangerous, but he still found himself giving her a reassuring nod. He would check into it.

"Now, Ephraim Daniels, tell me what you meant when you said you were of Joseph?" Hannah said, sitting down in front of him, her legs pulled back under her, hiding them. At her present weight of less than ninety pounds, her legs were skinnier than those of a wooden scarecrow, and she didn't want to scare off this American. Not yet.

Max laughed lightly as Ephraim looked his way as if seeking approval. "Go ahead; she won't believe you either."

"Thanks for that vote of confidence," Ephraim said with a twisted smile.

Max only shrugged.

"Ever hear of the Mormons?" Ephraim asked Hannah.

"Never. Possibly another name for Werewolves?" she teased.

Max chuckled under his breath.

"Cute. Very cute." He smiled wryly. "A religion founded in America," Ephraim replied, ignoring his friend.

"Oh, Christian I suppose," she answered rather coldly.

"Absolutely, but we don't believe in the same Christ, in the same things as most Christians. In fact, most Christian sects call us a cult and refuse us entrance into their circle. Even call us non-Christian."

That piqued her interest.

"We call ourselves restorationists and don't claim any real connection to Catholics or Protestants. In other words, we're not break-offs of those churches, and we don't carry the same baggage they do."

"They're like Jews." Max smiled. "Consider us family."

Hannah was confused and let her face show it.

"Jacob had twelve sons," Ephraim said. "Judah was only one of them. Joseph was another. You descend from one, I from the other."

"You are a descendant of Joseph?" she asked with an unbelieving tone. "None of Joseph's seed lasted past the Assyrian captivity. Only Judah survived."

"Max here tells me that even your Jewish Talmud says their bondage didn't last forever and that after they were freed they went north. Ever wonder what happened to them?" Ephraim smiled.

She hadn't, but he had her full attention. "I suppose you're going to tell me."

He glanced at the sun. It was just above the trees to the west. They didn't have much time. "Let's just say they were dispersed among the north lands and now some of them have been found again."

He suddenly interrupted himself.

"The train. We have to catch it, but I'd like to finish the story. How about next week?" Standing, he removed a small book from his pocket and handed it to her. The cover was well worn as were the pages. "Like I said, we're Christians, but not like the ones who guarded your prisons and used Christ as an excuse to butcher your people. You're Israel, Hannah, and we're more interested in saving Israel than in decimating her numbers." He looked at Max. "We better get going."

Max nodded and stood as Ephraim extended his hand to Hannah, helping her up. "Well, how about it? Can I come back?" he asked.

"How can I say no. You bring expensive gifts, fascinating fairy tales, and kill Werewolves. A Jewish woman's knight in shining armor, I think," she teased, a long-absent blush touching her cheeks.

"You don't know the half of it," he said, stepping back and bowing low. "Until next time then." He straightened and kissed her hand gently as he looked into her eyes. "Read the book. It will tell you about Joseph and Judah." He turned and walked toward the gate.

"Crazy, isn't he?" Max said.

Hannah watched Ephraim, then glanced at the book. "Yes, but aren't all Americans?" She smiled.

"You've got a point."

"What book is this?"

"Let's just say it isn't the Talmud, and good little Jewish girls probably won't read it." He smiled.

"I stopped being a good little Jewish girl years ago," she replied. Her family had always been true to Judaism, orthodox in their observance, but liberal orthodox. Though they celebrated Passover, they also danced the modern dances and believed that women were more than chattels. She had read the Talmud, studied the Torah, and gone to the university. At least until the Polish people had forced them out of such places.

She looked at the book, then stuck it in one of her skirt's deep pockets. "We'll see," she replied.

They faced each other and she put her arms around him. "Thank you for finding me, Max. You saved my life. Until you came . . . I . . . I had nothing to live for. I wish you could stay. I . . ."

"I've written my parents in New York. They'll write soon. After that, if you like, we'll get you to the States. I promise."

"Is it better there, Max?"

"Yeah, we have our bigots, but this place makes 'em look innocent as newborn babes."

She laughed lightly, the dimples in her cheeks faintly visible. He touched her chin with a finger. "You're getting more beautiful every day."

"Thanks to your new clothes and," she glanced up at the windows to see a few faces still looking their way, "them."

He looked at her quizzically.

"You don't think this pink in my cheeks is natural, do you?"

"Ahh, a group project, eh?" He pinched her cheek. "But they do look rosier than when you joined us. Just so you know, Ephraim does that to all Jewish girls."

"I'll bet," she replied. Her brow wrinkled. "I have heard from soldiers here that American soldiers cannot . . . what is the word? "

"Fraternize? He's with me and you are my family."

"And once you leave for England?"

"Exceptions are granted, especially in the case of survivors of German brutality. Visiting the hospital, giving you aide for your survival." He shrugged. "All part of the greater war effort," He paused, kissing her on the check before taking her hand and walking her toward the veranda steps. "You're my family. I've asked that he watch out for you. I don't know a better man or one I trust more than Ephraim Daniels."

"Yes, I know. It's in his eyes," she said. "I can see it in his eyes. I've learned to read a lot from a person's eyes over the last few years."

They said good-bye and Max trotted to catch up with his friend. Hannah waved at the two of them as they walked through the gate. They waved back.

Hannah turned and started up the stairs, one hand on the rail. It had been a wonderful day, but she was so tired she could hardly stand. She must get her rest, work harder at getting rid of the skinny legs and that tired-all-over feeling. After all, Ephraim Daniels was coming back in a week.

And there were Werewolves to hunt. Both gave her something to look forward to.

See Chapter Notes

CHAPTER 4

Hannah spent the week fretting about whether or not Ephraim Daniels would actually come, while she worked hard to gorge herself, to put weight on her camp-ravished body. She was somewhat successful, gaining nearly twelve pounds and requiring less rouge on her still somewhat sunken cheeks.

Though she tried to get everyone to understand that Ephraim was a friend of the family, even she was having a hard time seeing it that way. As a result, his upcoming visit was having considerable effect not only on her but the rest of the women in her ward. It seemed that the hopeless spirit that followed them around like ghosts in a graveyard had dispelled like smoke in a brisk wind. Nearly everyone had decided that makeup might be a good idea, along with brushed hair. With such healing came a price—at least to the hospital. Everyone was a good deal hungrier, all begged for different clothes, and Tappuah, a former pianist with the Polish national orchestra, even asked for a piano! Martha had performed another miracle, an upright suddenly appearing in the outer waiting room on Wednesday morning. Tappuah had played all day, drawing crowds from every wing of the giant hospital.

It amazed Hannah what one rooster in the hen house could really do!

She pushed the thought away. A friend of the family was *not* a rooster in the hen house! It was a hard concept to deal with.

She rubbed her forehead. The ache was back. From the moment she had tried reading Ephraim's book, she knew she would need glasses. It had taken a good deal of effort to keep the words from blurring together, even though distances didn't seem to bother her.

But she had kept trying and had found parts of the book intriguing, until she saw that it was just another book about the Christian Messiah. After that it had been difficult, nearly impossible, to keep going, especially with her head splitting in half. The only motivation to read a few more pages was that she knew Ephraim Daniels would ask her opinion. She only hoped he wouldn't be too disappointed with what she had to tell him.

The thought made her nervous.

She asked the nurse what time it was.

"Nearly 10:00 A.M.," Martha responded with a smile. "The train from Frankfurt should be arriving about now."

Hannah stood, smoothed the skirt given her a week ago, and glanced at herself in the mirror lying on her end table.

"He won't come."

Hannah turned to face the woman in the bed across from her. The hard-nosed survivor of Auschwitz had been the only one who hadn't seemed to respond positively to all that happened. Hannah sat on the edge of her own bed, angry but with a bit of a knot in her stomach. What if he didn't come? The thought made the knot grow to the size of a tennis ball. She looked in the mirror a second time. Why *would* he come? She felt a moment of despair, then stiffened her back with resolve.

"He'll come," she said evenly, placing the mirror on the end table after one last poke at her still unruly hair.

"Won't come," responded the woman.

Her name was Rachel Steinman. Hannah had asked the others about her but little information was forthcoming. Another survivor of Auschwitz said that rumor had it that before the war Rachel had been the sole heir to one of Germany's richest families. It had been taken from her by betrayal, and she had been sent to the camp with the rest of the Berlin Jews. Over a hundred and seventy thousand of that city entered the camps. Less than a thousand of them left alive.

Hannah also knew Rachel had once been beautiful and could be again if she tried, but she didn't seem to care to get well, to start her life again. But then, starting over was a daunting prospect for all of them. In the camp you lived only out of the instinct for survival, but when you came through it and found you had nothing to survive for—no family, no home, nothing—it was hard not to just let yourself die. Hannah wondered if it was even harder for the rich. Maybe, but it shouldn't be. They had all suffered; they had all survived. All but Rachel had given up self-pity.

Hannah, her arms folded across her waist, turned and looked at Rachel. "Isn't it time you stopped feeling sorry for yourself?"

Rachel's empty eyes were unreadable, emotionless—dead. That was it. Rachel was walking, but inside, inside she had quit. Another victim. It made Hannah mad.

"Look around you, Rachel. Do you really think you have reason to feel sorry for yourself? That you had it worse than the rest of us, that we don't understand how tough it was and how horrible it is to be without what we left behind?

"Look at Edith," Hannah went on firmly.

Rachel didn't move but her eyes went to her lap. Hannah went to the edge of the bed and grabbed her jaw, forcing it in the direction of Edith who stood only a few feet away. "Look at her! She lost an eye to a butcher's whip. I don't see any part of you missing." She let go of Rachel's jaw with a twist of her hand. "And Misha. They beat her until she lost her child. Did you lose a child, Rachel? A husband? We've suffered, just like you! And we're not giving up! What gives you the right to sit there and quit? Nothing!"

The room was quiet. Hannah ran her hand through her stubbly hair, regaining control. She was afraid to look at the others as she realized all that she had said. Had she scratched away at old wounds, made them worse with her anger? She bit her lip against the thought.

She took a deep breath. "You . . . you can't give up, Rachel," Hannah said. "You can't let this wickedness beat you. None of us can, not now, not when we are free, when we can fight back."

Rachel turned slightly and looked into Hannah's eyes, a sudden flash of anger finally forcing her to fight back. "You are fools, all of you! Do you think they are going to let you win? How long will we be free before they butcher us again? No, I will not live just to be killed slowly all over again. I will not bring children into this world just to have them crushed as we have been crushed! Look at us!" She waved her hand from person to person around the room. "All of you.

Look at you! Look at me! What do you see? The Nazis made animals of us! What good is an animal? Does your American friend want an animal for a wife?"

Hannah slapped her. "We are not animals! We are human beings! Do you hear me?" The words were even, measured. There was no anger, only firm determination and hard will. Rachel was stunned, her eyes blinking as if she was just waking from a bad dream. Slowly, her finger went to her mouth and found blood there as Hannah turned and went back to her bed, quickly picking up her robe and folding it, then her pajamas. The others were whispering to each other, wondering what would come next, their eyes boring holes through her back. She didn't care. It had to be said. It was time for all of them to quit feeling sorry for themselves. "If we give up, the Nazis win," She said. "I will not let the Nazis win. Do you understand, Rachel? I will fight their kind with every bone in my body this time. They will never take me back to the camps! Never! And when I have children, I will teach them to fight just as hard. There will be no more giving up around me! Ever!"

She placed her folded clothes in the small dresser she shared with a girl named Zohar in the next bed. Before the camps, Hannah had never been one to say much, had always remained in the background—the sweet little Jewish girl, daughter of Chaim and Ruth Gruen, the one who would make a good wife someday because she would never talk back to her husband. That had changed. That Hannah Gruen had died in the camps. It was one thing she did not regret.

Noise from the window broke the quiet mood in the room and several rushed to see what was going on. "There are soldiers! Americans!" Misha said. "Look," Tappuah said. "It is Hannah's new boyfriend, and he brought others with him!"

"He isn't my boyfriend!" Hannah said. "He is just a friend of the family, that's all." The last part of the statement was barely audible.

"Hey, ladies!" It was Ephraim's voice and Hannah walked to the window, her heart in her throat.

"Shhh," she smiled. "You will have the nurses sending you away."

Ephraim took off his hat and bowed. "Your wish is my command, m'lady. Your knight and his fellows have come to entertain you."

"Isn't this against the rules?"

"Our commanding officer says it is our duty to visit the ill and try to give them soup for the soul," Ephraim answered, while turning to the man standing next to him. "Right, Wally?"

The other man grinned. "His exact words!" he said.

Hannah grinned as a sudden flurry of action developed behind her. Chatter and excitement filled the room with its healing presence as each scurried to make herself look presentable. Hope had returned, the hard but necessary words to Rachel fleeing out the windows like dried dandelion blossoms blown away by the wind. Hannah was relieved.

She turned back to Ephraim. "Any of these knights have tarnished armor?"

He looked at the others who got the meaning and shook their heads in the negative. "God-fearin' boys, one and all. We bring words of comfort, nothing more."

"Give us ten minutes," Hannah said, turning back to her own mirror to check her hair.

"Are they Jews?" one of the girls asked, furtively.

"Who cares!" said another. "They're men!" There was laughter.

"But the law . . ." said the first. "My father . . ." It was Zohar, the quiet, shy girl next to Hannah.

"You're not going to marry them!" said another, her eyes rolling.

"But they are Gentiles . . ." Zohar responded, a bit anguished.

"Zohar!" Misha exclaimed while rolling her eyes.

Hannah raised a finger to her lips, shushing Misha while going to Zohar and helping her brush out her hair. "We don't know that they aren't Jewish, Zohar, at least not all of them. Let's go and see, shall we? Besides, they are only here to brighten our day. We may never see them again." Even as she said it, Hannah secretly hoped she was wrong.

Zohar brightened. "Yes, you're right. There are Jews in America. Surely some of them came to help."

Hannah was touched by something inside Zohar she couldn't describe. Was it innocence, and if it were, how could such a thing be? If anything died in the camps, it was innocence.

Zohar reminded Hannah of her sister Esther—clean, pure, innocent Esther. The one whose cheeks were always scarlet in the presence of men—shy, tongue-tied Esther.

But Esther was dead, her very innocence draining her of strength. She hadn't been able to understand what was happening to them, why others hated her so. She seemed to walk around in a stupor all the time, her body finally unwilling to go on. She had lay down in the road, her eyes glazing, her ears refusing to hear Hannah's pleading to keep moving. The guard . . .

Hannah shook her head, dispelling the thought. She would take better care of Zohar. If such innocence had survived, it needed to be nurtured. It was something few had anymore.

Quickly, all but Rachel were ready. Hannah took Zohar's hand, every eye on her. "Well, ladies, shall we?" Hannah said, forcing a slight smile on her face. She felt tired but excited. She needed to see Ephraim Daniels again, needed to know that there really was hope. They all needed it. All needed to see that look in the eyes of a man that said they were worth something!

She looked at the little group of struggling girls. Still thin with short hair and legs as skinny as needles! A sudden fear washed over her. What if these men saw . . . what if they turned away? No! It would not happen. Ephraim had accepted her; surely such a man would not bring others who would hurt them!

The heads nodded with excitement. Hannah turned and started for the door, then stopped at Rachel's bed. "Come, Rachel," she said. "As soon as you're ready, come and join us."

Rachel's tough countenance had softened some and the hardness in her eyes seemed to be gone, but her only movement was the blink of her eyes and a hard swallow. Somehow she looked younger, a tough woman in a child's body. Hannah could only wonder if what she had said had done any good at all.

No matter. There was Zohar and Misha and the others. And there was Ephraim Daniels. She turned and walked to the door.

See Chapter Notes

CHAPTER 5

Ephraim and Hannah walked along the bank of the river, the sun low in the western sky. Haze sat atop the landscape as if someone had pulled a blanket over it. Ephraim had explained that people were burning and tearing down buildings that had been all but destroyed by the war, trying to go on with their lives. Knowing that, Hannah figured it was a haze that would last for some time.

"One thing I'll say for you, Ephraim Daniels; you know how to throw a party," Hannah said, smiling.

Ephraim laughed lightly as he looked back and up the hillside toward the hospital. He could still hear the sound of the music as it blared from the record player he had purchased from a German who needed blankets more than he needed music. Things were getting worse in Frankfurt. They had buried most of the dead now and that stench was gone, but more and more people were flooding into the city every day. Proud people who didn't want charity. Thus, the trade for the record player and half a dozen records featuring big bands from the United States. "Just doing our duty." He smiled. "Amazing though, what a little Glen Miller can do for morale."

Hannah smiled. The girls were unsure at first. As she had suspected, they were afraid their appearance would chase these young men into the bushes screaming; when it hadn't, they relaxed a little. Then another problem had arisen. Some of them had come from conservative Jewish backgrounds and knew little about the dances the music represented. The young man called Wally had grabbed Misha and shown them all how to do it, and the smiles had turned to laughter. Ephraim had prepared the soldiers well for what they would see and their happy-go-lucky, genuine acceptance of it pushed the barriers quickly aside. The party had burgeoned, bringing more guests to the veranda until nearly everyone in the hospital was enjoying a good time.

"Nothing like a little dancing to put color in a person's cheeks," Ephraim said.

She laughed lightly. He was right. The look of all of them had improved. The only trouble was that most of them were exhausted after only one time around the veranda. "Our lack of stamina is showing."

"Talk is good, too. Give 'em a chance to know that the world can still be a good place."

She nodded. When they left the group, most were simply visiting and eating the food the nurses had quickly prepared.

"Wally is quite taken with Misha," Ephraim said.

Hannah's brow wrinkled. "I know." She glanced back. It reminded Ephraim of the look on his mother's face when his younger brother wandered off. It was obvious Hannah had become the mother hen of this little group. He could see it in the way she watched over them, the way they glanced her way, looking for some sort of approval.

"Wally is a good Jewish kid, and he understands the rules, both military and moral. She'll be okay."

Hannah's heart raced with gratitude. "Jewish?"

"Umm. Very orthodox. At least as orthodox as you can get in the Bronx. Some of the others are as well." He shrugged. "Max knew 'em, so I knew 'em. Jew or otherwise, they all have good hearts and wanted to come."

"Yes, well, he'd better not try anything with her or I'll break his arm."

Ephraim laughed again. "Yes, I'll bet you would."

"How are things going in Frankfurt?" she asked, changing the subject.

He didn't answer immediately, his face getting serious. "We're being transferred to Berlin. The Russians have finally been forced to keep their agreement."

Her heart raced a little. Berlin was much farther away. "Agreement?" she asked, covering her feelings.

"Each of the allies has a part of Berlin as their administrative zone. The Russians took the city in April but kept it to themselves. Butchered, raped, pillaged, hauled away anything that wasn't tied down while they kept the rest of us at bay. Now that there is nothing left but starving thousands, they've opened the roads."

The edge in his voice told her Ephraim was not fond of Russians, but then neither was she. They had persecuted her people for generations, so much so that many had fled to Palestine in the first and second aliyahs. Such people were the ones who now made up the core of the Jewish settlements in Palestine and tried so hard to save the rest of them.

"And your intelligence work?"

"It's hard to kill Hitler."

She looked at him quizzically. "What do you mean? I thought he was dead. A report just the other day came to us that he must surely—"

"It's the things he stood for that are hard to kill."

They stopped and peered across the river's drifting waters. His statement made Hannah's heart race even more as she realized what such a thing meant for her people. It was a long moment before either of them spoke.

"The other leaders, what has happened to them? Will they at least be punished?" she asked.

"Many have disappeared, but we did get some of the big fish. Himmler was captured by the British and committed suicide. Goebbels killed his wife and kids, then himself. We have Speers, Hess, Goering, and a bunch of others. They'll all be tried."

"Killing them will never be enough."

Ephraim agreed. Mass murderers could never pay enough for the number of lives they took. That's why God needed a hell.

"What will you do, Hannah? You're well enough to leave the hospital, or nearly so. Where will you go?"

Hannah hadn't given it a lot of thought. A day at a time was about all she could handle right now. "I don't know. I have no reason to go back to Poland. No Jew will be welcome there. Staying here in Germany is out of the question. And most other European countries either participated in the war against us or harbor some of the same feelings. Trying to live among them . . . I don't think I could do it even if I thought they would let me. Max says I should go to America. Though I think things are better there, I want to settle where I know I belong, where I am not just a wanderer who is looking for a home. Does that make sense?"

He smiled, not only to let her know it did make sense but to cover up his own disappointment. He was beginning to like Hannah Gruen more than he should. The Church was too important for him to marry outside of it. Would she join? He couldn't depend on that and must keep his feelings in check. Then there was the nonfraternization policy. He was getting close to crossing the line as it was. If he wanted to fly again, he had to keep his record clean.

"May we sit down? My legs are a bit tired."

He nodded, noticing that she still pulled her legs under her, embarrassed. He let it go. "How long were you in Ravensbrück?" he asked, changing the subject.

"I . . . I'm not sure. Two years I think."

Two years! How had she survived so long under such conditions?

"It was a work camp but several different things were done. The political prisoners did sewing, printing of propaganda—the easy things. They had it much better than we Jews. Our group built roads no matter the weather, worked on railroads, and dug endless holes that seemed to mean nothing. A few were selected to go five miles to the rail head where there was a warehouse for sorting food, mostly fresh vegetables. Some were caught eating or stealing it for barter at the camp; other's weren't. I was lucky that way and it kept my sister and I alive longer than many others. Even the politicals didn't get fresh vegetables like they wanted, but they did have fresh bread—the real thing—and we slipped over to their barracks and traded for it when we thought it was safe. We survived that way until this past winter; then they stopped bringing vegetables. Without the extra food, . . . that was when my sister died."

She lay her forehead on her knees, trying to shut out the thoughts. "It is another reason to leave Europe; there are too many bad memories here."

Ephraim couldn't imagine what it would be like to be homeless, let alone to be without a country. For the first time it dawned on him that many more were destined to die because they had no place to go. Though relief organizations were doing their best, their resources would be depleted by winter, and there would be thousands, even millions, without shelter, food, or sanitary conditions. He did not want Hannah to become one of those statistics, not after what she had already survived.

He pointed across the river. "See those people?"

Hannah had seen them from her hospital window. The numbers had been growing daily. Now there was a steady stream of people walking along the road on the opposite bank. A few carried bundles flung over a shoulder, some had carts filled with goods, most had little or nothing.

"All Europe is in flux, Hannah. The war displaced millions; many of them are Jews, many are not. All have no place to go, so they wander looking for food, trying to find someone who will help them. It is an overwhelming movement of needy people who don't have homes anymore. Sooner or later you will be forced to join them, and if you do not find a place where you can survive the coming winter, your condition will rival that of the camps."

There was a sad silence between them as they stared at the mass of humanity on the far side of the river.

"You know, we never really believed that this would all happen until it was too late. Even when they forced us into ghettos, too many would not believe. Only when stories about the exterminations at Treblinka and Auschwitz filtered into Warsaw did we finally decide it was real. Now here I am. I have lost everything dear to me because I did not believe; many died because they refused to believe. I have learned my lesson. I believe you, Ephraim, and because I believe you, I must go to Palestine. It is the only place where I will ever be safe."

He nodded. "Your best chance is through Italy. They say the Jewish brigade is there and helping your people."

"What is this Jewish brigade?"

Stories and rumors were flying all over Europe about the brigade. He thought she might have heard.

"The Jews offered to provide men for the allied war effort. At first the British fought the idea, but when things got desperate, they started enlisting men. Finally, they gave them a separate brigade. They've ended up helping retake Italy. They're just now mopping things up. Rumor has it that they have set up camps for refugees, mostly Jews. At this point the British commanders aren't fighting it much, but the time will come when they will cut it off."

"Cut it off? Why would they do that?"

"Because they will come to realize just how many of your people have the same wish you do—they want to go to Palestine—and letting more than a few thousand in will upset their Arab friends. The Brits are not keen on that. They need the oil, and the Middle East is their last real colonial strength."

"Surely they will not let such things get in the way of my people having a home. Not after this!"

"I pray to God every night you're right, but if you're not, they'll try to close the doors and you'd best be out of the country before they do." He sighed. "They wouldn't let your people out of Europe at the beginning of the war, Hannah, and they knew what that would mean. Why should they change now?"

"Because the rest of the world has seen and still sees the results. Surely your government will not let them get away with this."

"Don't depend on my country. We turned a blind eye in '38 and '39, just like everyone else. Even now Congress is slow to accept what we're telling them. And don't forget, we're still fighting a war in the Pacific. We need all the troops we can muster to finish it. Don't wait for help from my country, Hannah. I don't think it will come. Not anytime soon."

Another long silence. "We are not ready to travel. Not yet."

She thought she sensed some relief.

"When you are, let me know. I'll do what I can."

Her mind grasped for something to change the subject. "I read some of your book."

"And?" He smiled.

"I am still reading, but it is difficult. My eyes . . . the pages are very blurred and my head aches when trying to see things up close."

He believed her. It was common among the survivors, their diet so poor that some even went blind.

"Any part you liked?"

She thought about it a moment. "And he shall lift up an ensign to the nations from far, and will hiss unto them from the ends of the earth; and behold they shall come with speed swiftly." She smiled at the curious look on his face. "Isaiah," she said. "It is nearly the same in the Bible. I know the Bible. My father made us memorize many passages, especially those having to do with the return to Israel."

"Then you haven't totally given up on God."

She pulled her knees up under her chin and wrapped her arms around her legs so that the skirt covered them. "Is there a reason to go on believing?" she asked sincerely. "Is not what has happened to my people a witness against His existence?"

"Isaiah against the sight of my own eyes. I'll stick with Isaiah."

She lifted her chin and looked at him in disbelief; then she put her chin back on her knees. "Are all Americans such fools?" she asked.

He smiled. "A Frenchman I've gotten to know pretty well said something similar the other day. He said, 'Ephraim, you seem like an intelligent man. Don't you think it is a little foolish to believe in God? Especially now.'"

"And you answered this Frenchman in what way?"

"I told him I was flattered and that I thought he was also very intelligent. But I thought it was more a matter of faith than intelligence. Sometimes, we just have to realize we're not as smart as we think we are and trust that God is still in control."

"And you can believe in this God now? You can believe that He wanted all this to happen? That He was in control?" The frustrated anger was evident in her voice, but she did a good job of controlling it.

"He didn't want it to, just didn't stop it, that's all. Just like He didn't stop the last war and the hundreds of wars before that. Man's cruelty to man has always challenged faith." He paused, gauging his next words. "Blaming God is easy, Hannah. Holding onto faith . . . now that is hard. Especially now."

"Then you also find it difficult."

He nodded. "I've never been so challenged. I find myself confronted with the age-old question I hadn't ever really given much thought until I visited Dachau and saw pictures of Belsen—If God is God, why does He allow suffering? Only a monster would let this happen."

"And your conclusion?"

"My faith tells me He cares, that He isn't a monster, so there must be another explanation." He picked out a tall piece of grass, pulled it free, and sucked on it. "I'm not sure, Hannah, but I think He's trying to make more of us than a painless life will allow."

She gave him a crooked, disbelieving smile. "A better life after death—pearly gates and streets paved with gold. The Christian tradition. I'd rather have my father, my mother, my sisters. God can keep His golden streets," she said stiffly.

"The question is would your father agree now that he is with God? Has it occurred to you that you might be the only one really miserable? That you are the one walking blind and it is your blindness that causes you pain?"

Hannah wasn't sure what to say, a sudden flood of emotions roiling within her. She shook her head adamantly. "This is foolishness. My father would—"

"Are you sure?" Ephraim said sincerely.

"This is not about an afterlife, it is about . . ." she was suddenly confused. "It is about His cruelty."

He waited a moment. He didn't want to hurt her and wondered if he should just let it go. No, it needed to be said.

"It's all a matter of perspective, Hannah. I believe there is much more to the afterlife than you do, much more than the Judeo-Christian traditions say there is. There are great things in store for us if we pass the test of faith here. There are a lot of Jews who passed it with flying colors, as well as a lot of Christians, Muslims, Hindus, and millions who starve to death every day. What about them? They existed before Hitler screwed up the world. Does God love them? If so, why didn't He stop the starvation, the brutality for them? Is your belief so shallow that it only wavers when it gets personal? I believe He has always been the same mindful, loving Deity who knew exactly what they were going through. He comforted them, when they allowed Him to do so, and taught them what He could in their situation, but He also ushered them into a life after death where they are given more, mostly because their actions under fire showed that they deserved it."

"But isn't their death a victory for the wicked who have brutalized them?" she said.

"Only if you consider staying here a victory. Isn't it like the war itself? You win a battle, maybe many battles, but eventually you lose the war. Hitler lost two wars, the physical and the spiritual one."

"Then Hitler burns. Not a totally unpleasant thought, but not enough."

"You want to *watch* him burn, is that it?"

"A reasonable request under the circumstances, don't you think?"

"For someone left behind, but I can't see your father wasting the time. In my way of thinking, he's probably too busy doing other things far more important that mortal limitations had always prevented. Besides, for Hitler it is more than heat; it is facing what he has become and cannot change. It is discovering exactly what his failure to choose good instead of evil has cost him. I believe it is revealed to a person at death what they did wrong on earth, and how that conduct will bring untold suffering you and I can't even begin to understand. Mortal limitations just don't allow it."

She couldn't help the smile. "You would have been a master of the yeshiva."

He didn't understand and it showed.

"In the yeshiva, students study in pairs, arguing, discussing the Talmud, defending their interpretation. You would do well."

He smiled. "I'll take that as a compliment. I think."

"You are a very strange man, Ephraim Daniels. What you tell me . . . I want to believe, but what has happened makes it difficult. Your belief in a life after death that offers my father a great reward for his sacrifice . . . I want to believe this, but I cannot fathom it or its opposite. How could Hitler be punished enough in such a place? And the others who helped him, how can it be justice when they continue to live and breathe and have children and enjoy the fruits of this world after such wickedness? God should pay them now," she said, firmly.

"It seems to me that any pain caused to a Hitler by death, trials, or even losing the war, when compared to what he did to others, would be woefully small and even insignificant. How can taking a man's life be justice enough for taking millions of lives? No, the payment has to be far worse than that. It has to be the kind of pain only God can hand out, where death cannot intervene or prevent that pain. That's what Hitler is experiencing now, and he won't be free from it until he has paid for every last crime that a just God requires."

He took a deep breath. "You probably don't want to hear this, Hannah, but part of faith is to trust that God will mete out justice and mercy, where and when deserved. The desire to play God because we don't think He's doing the kind of job we would like is contrary to faith and, in my view, a bit egotistical."

"Egotistical? How can it be egotistical to want justice?"

"It isn't. It is egotistical to believe that our justice would be better than His. God is all knowing. Doesn't that mean that He has a better view of what ought to be done and when? You assume that death by firing squad is better justice than what God might do to them when they pass through death's door.

"I have met some of the leaders of the Nazi movement as they've been arrested and will meet more before this is finished. We will hold trials and we will judge them according to the laws of humanity. Many will not accept that judgement. They will feel no sorrow and will bare their breast in defiant challenge to shoot them. Others will recognize the horrible things they have done and will suffer a good deal of pain. Has justice been satisfied in both cases? In either case? By human standards, maybe. By God's standard, probably not. He will exact a good deal more than man can possibly require. Frankly, I would rather let God handle it. That way I know it will be done right."

Hannah was silent. She had never thought of these things before, her self-absorption and bitterness preventing it.

"This is what your book tells you?" she asked.

He tossed the piece of grass aside. "More or less. I don't pretend to understand all the doctrinal nuances; I am not sure that I am even interpreting it right. But something inside . . . well, I think it fits with what I see happening to good people for bad reasons."

Your God is not the God of Moses and Abraham," she said softly.

He glanced at his watch. "Actually, He is, but that's a subject for another time," he said, getting to his feet. "I gotta catch a ride back to Frankfurt. I leave for Berlin early in the morning." He extended a hand and pulled her up, putting them only inches apart. "Seeing things through God's eyes takes faith, not good eyesight."

He placed her hand through his arm. "Walk me back to the hospital?"

Hannah only nodded, her head spinning with what she had been told. They were at the bottom of the veranda steps before she knew it. He pulled her over until they were out of the view of the others. He couldn't help himself. Stepping even closer, he reached under her chin and lifted her face to look up into his. "You are a wonder, Hannah.

More beautiful than the lilies of the field. I love being with you even if you haven't read much of my book." He smiled.

She couldn't help smiling back, even though her heart had stopped beating and no air moved through her lungs. When he kissed her gently on the lips, she was so weak in the knees she thought surely she'd fall as he turned to leave. "I'll be back," he said it loudly enough that only she alone could hear. "I don't know how soon, but you can depend on it."

She watched the others gather round Ephraim like a magnet as he made his way toward the gate. As he and his friends disappeared down the street, her heart ached. It was if a light entered her life when he was around, and it was suddenly darker when he left.

She turned and walked up the steps. Seeing him again would come sooner than she thought.

* * *

Hannah sat alone on the veranda, her chair pulled up under the light next to the door. Ephraim's small book lay in her hands, his words bouncing around in her head.

She had tried to remember the teachings of her father, his quotes from the Talmud. One that stuck out in her mind was a quote by Rabbi Yaakov: "This world is the antechamber that leads to the next world. Prepare in the antechamber so you can enter the banquet hall."

Ephraim said mortality was a test, and so did the Talmud.

Rabbi Yaakov also said, "Better one hour in repentance and good deeds in this world than all the life in the world to come. And better one hour of tranquility in the world to come than all the life of this world."

That, too, agreed with Ephraim Daniels.

Her father had spent his life saving others, had even died trying to do so. Surely, his life is better now than if he had remained. She had been too bitter to allow it.

Of course, there were stark differences. Her father had always believed and taught her and her sisters that the soul is part of God's essence. The ultimate goal was to become part of God, to experience that closeness forever. Her father described it as the unimaginable pleasure of being with God. Though a pleasing thought, Hannah had always wondered if that was all God wanted. If His purpose in sending mankind to earth in the first place was to grow, learn, and improve, wouldn't He want that for them in the next life as well? Ephraim Daniels thought so.

A God that gave man a chance to become something more than spirits totally reliant upon the presence of God for anything at all intrigued Hannah. Could her father, even now, be progressing toward the greater rewards of eternity because of his success here, and did Hitler's kind always deny themselves such opportunities? It was a punishment of significance when laid side by side with a heaven where little would be done to recompense evil, as her father seemed to believe when alive. The very thing Hitler had thought to deny her father and millions of others was instead granted and added to over and over. It was a pleasant thought.

Hannah looked at Ephraim's book. The thought suddenly occurred to her that her father would not be pleased with her holding it. That brought a smile, remembering the day when she had brought some books home from the university that talked about Marxism. Marx didn't have much use for God and her father had been incensed. He had tossed the book out the window into the rain-filled street and refused to let her go after it. If Ephraim Daniels was right, her father would not do such a thing to this book.

And what would her father think of Ephraim? If he were alive, he would be appalled. Ephraim was not a Jew. Jewish women did not fraternize with gentile men. She smiled again. If Ephraim really were of Joseph, she wondered how her father would react. Would he accept him as a member of the House of Israel as Ephraim considered himself? Would her father consider them a good match?

For the first time her thoughts of her missing family were pleasant ones. She could bear missing them knowing that God was pleased with them and they were busy and happy.

A tear sprang to the corner of her eye and trickled down her cheek, a warm feeling caressing her heart like a gentle hand. She would see them again. She must live so as to warrant such a blessing.

"You seem deep in thought," the voice spoke in German.

Hannah looked up to see Sister Martha in the doorway. "Just wondering about some things my American friend told me."

"May I join you?" Martha asked.

Hannah nodded.

Martha pulled a chair over and sat down. With the nun's habit, it was hard to tell how old Martha was, but Hannah guessed at about thirty-five or forty. Her features were typically Aryan with blue eyes and a tuft of blond hair showing on her forehead just below the white cloth of the habit. She was maybe five feet, mostly torso with short legs carrying a normally stocky body, now thinning due to war and rationing.

"You should be asleep, Sister Martha."

"And you, but it is hard to sleep these days, don't you think?" Her forehead wrinkled some.

Hannah nodded. "Is the worst over?"

"May God grant that it be so." She crossed herself without thought.

"May governments grant it too."

Martha smiled. "Yes, I think it may come quicker if men will do what God asks of them."

There was silence between them for a while and Hannah had a chance to notice how calm the night air was, how devoid of the usual taint of smoke. The smell of grass and flowers mingled with the odor of the nearby river. It was wonderful.

"I am sorry," Martha said, a serious look filling her countenance. "You have been treated horribly and what I must tell you will only make things bad for you again." She looked away from Hannah. "Tomorrow a new administrator will come. I do not know him, but I have been told that because the hospital is now in the Russian sector, they have appointed him. They say he is a communist but a new one."

"Then he was probably a Nazi," Hannah gasped.

"He claims to have been a Democratic Socialist. It is very amazing how fast such people changed their politics when the allies came. Now you find no Nazis and enough Democratic Socialists to populate all of Europe with them."

"Why are they allowed to do such a thing?"

"Records are destroyed, bribes are paid. They say that the allies will accept a letter of character reference from former Jews or partisans or other anti-Nazis. Such a letter carries too much weight and is difficult to validate."

"Who would sign such a document?"

"The hungry, the greedy."

Hannah nodded, understanding. Some Jews had killed their own kind for a piece of bread. Money would make it easier.

"Our past administrator thought only of helping people; their race did not concern him. Now . . . I am afraid for you and the others. The new administrator has already sent a letter stating that those who are not seriously wounded will need to be moved out of the wards and other places found for them. The Americans are all going to other hospitals and Germans, Russians, and their kind are being brought here. It is foolish to bring them this far south, but it seems to be the way of things."

"Or the way to get rid of us," Hannah said, her brow wrinkling with concern. It would never stop. It was no longer just she who must leave but all of them. If they were ever to find peace, they must leave Europe forever.

She forced a smile. "I understand, Martha. Please do not worry yourself about it any longer. Time will tell." She stood. "Come, we had both better get some sleep." They walked inside, Hannah's arm around Martha's waist but her mind on other things. If this man intended to continue where Hitler left off, he would have a fight this time.

And he would lose.

CHAPTER 6

Hannah wrestled with sleep until five in the morning, but when she awoke she felt refreshed, like she had been sleeping for days. She listened to the quiet of the early morning as she relished once again the thought of Ephraim Daniel's kiss. The sun broke over the horizon, casting its warmth through the tall windows and across the beds and floors of the ward. Birds began the day with song, and the distant sound of muffled steps in the hall greeted an early Monday morning. Six more days until his return.

After a few more minutes of quiet, others began stirring and the hospital came slowly to life. Hannah sat on the side of her bed brushing her hair, Martha's announcement about the new administrator troubling her mind and creating an empty spot in the pit of her stomach. She had thought about what to do for several hours and had come up with only one solution; she would go to Palestine, she and anyone else who wanted to go with her. The only pain this thought gave her was that it could not include Ephraim.

The sound of someone coming through the closed doors of the ward shook her out of her thoughts and she looked up to see Martha rushing toward her.

"It is worse than I thought. He . . ."

The doors through which she had just come were suddenly thrown open. A strange man entered the room and stood stiffly at the head of the ward until all gave him their attention.

"That's him. He . . ."

"Sister Martha, would you join us please?"

The voice was that of another nun who stood at the side of the new administrator. Hannah had only seen the other nun twice since coming here. Her name was Sister Katherine. She had always busied herself in the other areas of the hospital and constantly complained about the amount of food the "Jews" were eating. Hannah had known then that this was not a woman who would befriend her.

Martha hesitated.

"Go, Sister Martha. We'll be fine." Hannah forced a smile.

Martha reluctantly stood up, straightened her back and her resolve, and walked stern-faced toward the new administrator and his ally. Hannah could see that Sister Martha would do all she could, but the opposition was formidable.

The administrator waited until Martha had fallen in behind him and Sister Katherine before speaking. Hannah gave him the once-over. He was wearing a dark suit with a tie to match. His off-colored white shirt was old and worn, but he kept it starched and pressed as best he could. His stiffness didn't come from that, however. It was obvious to Hannah that Martha's concern about him was true. He was a Nazi, and he was about to act like one.

He cleared his throat. "My name is Hans Sperling. I am in charge here now and you will do as I instruct. Today, some of you will be leaving," he said firmly in German. Though she knew the others all understood the language fairly well, Sister Katherine translated it into both German and Polish. It was apparent they wanted no misunderstandings. Hannah watched her new friend's reaction, her mind already rushing through what this sudden change of affairs would mean to each one of them. There was sickly Misha; shy Zohar, who was still near the breaking point mentally; and Edith, blind in one eye and needing surgery that would repair some of the damage to the flesh around the socket. And what about Rachel? Where would she go? Wouldn't this be a serious setback for someone so mentally fragile?

"The nuns have the list and will read it when I am finished. You will take your personal belongings and will be given ten German Reichsmarks for your travel, along with clothing and a suitcase for extra underwear and your things. Where you go is up to you, but we can no longer keep you here. The beds are needed for other patients—German patients returning from the war who need much more help than you." He emphasized the words "German" and "you," making Hannah burn inside.

"Please leave no later than tomorrow morning before breakfast." With that, he turned and left the room. His stiff walk prompted Hannah to wonder if he had a board up his trousers. The thought brought a smile to her face and she let it linger until the smile was nearly a grin. It kept her from running him down and strangling him.

Sister Katherine's reading list brought back Hannah's attention. Her name had been read. Then she heard Rachel's name, then the names of Zohar, Rachel, Edith, Misha, and Tappuah. By the time she had finished reading, it was clear that all Jews were leaving.

The room buzzed with disbelief. Even Hannah, though somewhat prepared by Sister Martha, was stunned. She watched as Sister Martha stepped next to Sister Katherine. "Are you sure? All of them? Surely Misha, Edith, and Rachel—"

"All of them," Sister Katherine replied firmly. She turned to leave, her shoulders stiff, unyielding. Hannah could not help but wonder how Ephraim's God would respond to a Sister Katherine. She had probably never killed a Jew, not with her hands at least, but she hadn't helped any either. How could a woman who professed to believe in a merciful Jesus disregard giving mercy to others? How could so many professed Christians? Hannah felt sorry for her, for all of them, then found it interesting that she could. A week ago she would have seen her as no different than the weasel who preceded her from the room.

Sister Martha was standing there, stunned. "This is wrong," she said softly, then more forcefully as she turned toward the disappearing Sister Katherine. "Do you hear me? This is wrong!" Katherine turned back long enough to give her a cold, threatening stare before disappearing.

"May God and Christ shun you forever," Sister Martha said loudly. She turned back to find all her ward staring at her in shocked disbelief. "A witch in a nun's habit," she said, frustrated. Then her face softened as she looked around the room. "I don't know what to say. I will try to get a message to the diocese in Hamburg, but it will be several days."

Hannah smiled her thanks as someone touched her on the arm, diverting her attention.

"Hannah," the voice said weakly.

Hannah turned to find Zohar staring into her eyes as if searching for answers. "I don't know what to do."

Hannah suddenly wanted to run. She hardly had the strength to work out her own difficulties and couldn't take on those of others. She stiffened with fear as the others quickly pressed in, asking, seeking an answer.

"Let her alone." The voice came from behind the others, the words loud and firm enough to stop all talk. It was as if they had all inhaled at once. The group separated like the Red Sea, and Hannah saw Rachel standing near her bed.

"We can't go home," Rachel said in German. She looked at the others. "Most of you are from Poland. That is out of the question. Ingrid, you are from Austria, I from Berlin, Misha from Holland. All from areas where they exterminated most of our people. We would be fools to go back and let them finish the job."

No one spoke, each looking at the others for some response to Rachel's sudden resurrection. Hannah was simply grateful. Taking a deep breath to control her feelings, she forced herself to speak.

"She is right," Hannah said. "We must go to Palestine."

Confused, frightened chatter filled the room. They were all like sheep at the end of a terrible storm, each looking for a shepherd to calm them and take them to a safer place. But there was no shepherd, only sheep and another storm on the way.

"It is so far away," one said.

"They won't let us go," said another.

"We can't go! Look at us . . . we . . . we're still . . . how can we make a journey like that?" said a third.

Hannah felt fear climb up her throat as she realized the enormity of the task and how helpless they all were.

"It is safe in Palestine, isn't it, Hannah?" The room went suddenly silent, all eyes turning to her. Hannah felt her throat dry up like parched soil.

"They can't hurt us anymore, can they?" continued Zohar. "Can they, Hannah? Can they hurt us?"

Hannah looked at Zohar. So fragile! The war had made her the most frightened sheep of all. She forced herself to move to the young girl and put an arm around her. "No, Zohar, they can't hurt us there." A flood of fears flowed through Hannah like ice water and it was all she could do to keep from being overwhelmed. Twelve women! All weak, without transportation, food, or any real money. How could they possibly get to Palestine?

"There are camps set up by the allies," said another woman. "I will go there. They will feed me, and they say there are hospitals with medicine."

Others nodded agreement and quickly the group broke up into two factions. Hannah knew of the camps. They were in the same places as the old, the same barracks, the same barbed wire. She exclaimed she would never go there, but those now gathering at the far end of the room ignored her, involved in their own conversation. The camp was close, another woman said, only a few miles. They could be there soon. Others would know what to do after that.

"Hannah, should we—" Zohar asked weakly.

"I will never go back to the camps!"

"Nor I," Rachel agreed. Misha and Tappuah nodded their heads. Zohar sat on the edge of the bed, an unsure look on her face.

"It will be all right, Zohar," Hannah implored, sitting next to her and putting an arm around her shoulders. "We'll find a way, I promise."

Zohar gave her a weak smile.

"Everyone is to shower," someone said. "Who knows when we'll have a chance for another. Dress, get your things together. I'll have Sister Martha bring breakfast onto the veranda. Then we will decide what to do." The voice was authoritative, full of hope and strength. Hannah cast her eyes about to see who was speaking when she realized it was her own voice. "Go, we have no time to waste," she said to her four new friends.

Misha and Tappuah grabbed towels, and Misha handed one to Zohar, then took her hand and started for the hallway. The other group had broken up and were sitting on their beds, watching. Several whispered quietly and shrugged. Hannah could see they were still so very afraid, and their fear caused atrophy.

"If any of you want to come, you are welcome," she said. All looked away or busied themselves. She felt sorry for them but there was nothing she could do. It would be difficult enough as it was. To have to force others . . . she could not even imagine.

She looked at Rachel. "Maybe they're right. Getting to Palestine is impossible." She felt a sudden urge to crawl back in bed and pull the covers over her head.

Rachel smiled. "Getting me out of the well of self-pity was impossible, Hannah. Compared to that, this will be snap." She paused, biting her lip. "Thank you for . . . for yesterday. I needed someone to . . ." She choked back the tears and lifted her head, stiffening her resolve. "I'll be okay now."

Hannah gave a weak smile in return. Rachel was tough. She had given up for a moment, but no one survived Auschwitz without an iron will. She must not let this woman down now. She took a deep breath and stood, picking up a towel.

Rachel looked relieved. "What can we do?" She ran her hand over her hair as she picked up her own towel.

"I really don't know, Rachel." Hannah said, suddenly serious. "I suppose we'll need maps, passports, travel papers . . . so many things." She started chewing her nails.

"Will your American friend help us do you think?" Rachel asked.

The thought of Ephraim gave her hope. "Yes, you are right. If anyone can get us papers, it must be the Americans. We should try."

She started walking toward the hallway. "We'd better join the others. We have a lot to do."

Rachel joined her. "I can't do this without a lot of help, Rachel; you know that. Zohar, Tappuah, Misha—they are all still very weak, and you and I can't climb a set of stairs without breathing like we had just gone up the Matterhorn."

Rachel gave a wry smile. "There is nothing but cold air and a nice view at the top of the Matterhorn. Our people wait for us in Jerusalem." Rachel forced her voice to sound confident, hopeful, but deep down she was regretting those days of refusing food and medicine. They would come back to haunt her now, but she would not be left behind, forced to wander or go back to the camps.

"Ephraim has been transferred to Berlin," Hannah said. "I'm not sure we can even get to Berlin."

"Yes, we can get there. I lived there, remember?" Rachel retorted.

Hannah nodded, a more hopeful look on her face.

Berlin. Secretly Rachel feared returning there more than anything else but knew she must do it, and if she found her father and had a chance to slit his throat . . . If there was a God, she could only hope that He would be so willing!

Rachel and Hannah were just about to enter the shower room when they heard a scream inside. Glancing at each other, they quickly flung open the door. Standing to the side with nothing on but the clothes she was born in was Zohar, her eyes fixed on a dozen suitcases standing against the wall. Her skin was paler than usual and her eyes wide as an American silver dollar.

Hannah rushed to her, grabbing a robe and flipping it around her just as the door flew open and Sister Katherine and the administrator burst in.

"What the devil is . . ." The administrator cut himself off when he remembered where he was. He glanced around furtively, making sure there were no others uncovered enough to force him from the room. When he saw that he was safe, the anger returned to his eyes and he used them to bore a hole in Hannah. "What is wrong here?" he demanded through clenched teeth.

"I don't know," Hannah responded stiffly, "but one thing is certain: this is a women's shower; and unless you are a master of deception, you are not a woman." The tone in her voice was cold and hard. It matched her hatred for this man.

The force of Hannah's ire and the snickers from others in the room turned Sperling's face several shades of red. His pride stiffened his back, as if to challenge her when Sister Katherine grabbed his arm and pulled him toward the door. "Not now!" she said. Hesitant at first, he finally turned on his heel and let her pull him from the room.

"Weasel," Rachel said. "The allies missed that one on their way through. Maybe we should . . ."

"Never mind, Rachel," Hannah said. "Zohar, what is the matter? What happened?"

Zohar slowly raised her hand and pointed at a brown suitcase with a half dozen stickers plastered to its exterior. "That . . . that belonged to my father. He took it when we went . . . when we left home."

Hannah hesitated. Could it be? She knew that the Nazis took everything from the Jews when they entered the camps, then stockpiled them. She had heard that entire warehouses had been discovered with such things stuffed inside, and that the allies had begun distributing them for use, but what was the chance of Zohar's father's case ending up here, in this place, at this moment?

She quickly grabbed it, ran to the window, and tossed it out into the yard before returning to help Zohar sit down. Hannah didn't know what the chances were or if it was the same case, but it at least reminded Zohar of the past and had to be discarded. "We'll get another," she said softly.

"He . . . he is dead," Zohar said weakly. "My father is dead. If they took his case . . ." Her voice trickled into silence.

Hannah could do nothing but hold the young girl tight as sobs caught in her throat, then wracked her small frame. Was Ephraim Daniels right? Did suffering make a difference? Did it somehow cleanse and purify the soul beyond what even the Christian penance or the ancient Jewish sacrifice could muster? Oh how she hoped that he was right!

After a few moments, Zohar wiped away her tears. "I'm all right now. I have to get ready. Father always wanted us to go to Israel. I must do as he wanted. He was going to take us there, you know. He had it all planned. He had bribed the guards with the last of our money and had hidden . . ." A sudden thought made her stop, her face showing that something important had occurred to her; then her face brightened like a lamp in a dark room. "The suitcase!" She ran to the window.

Hannah sat there, stunned. The case had nearly scared the life out of her and now she wanted it! Zohar must be sicker than Hannah thought. She fell in behind the young girl as she ran through the door and down the hall to the outer door, clutching her robe tightly around her. When Hannah caught up, Zohar was already at the suitcase and trying to release the brass clasps that held it closed. Hannah fell to her knees by Zohar and grabbed the girls arms until she faced her. "Zohar, what are you doing? Are you sure—"

"Yes, yes!" She grabbed the clasps again and pushed and pried until each released and the case fell open. Staring at the interior as if looking for something, she ran her hand around the bottom and sides until her fingers seemed to find it. "There! There! I was right! It *is* father's suitcase," she said aloud.

She flipped the suitcase over and felt along its edges until she reached the hinges. With a giggle she pushed hard on both at once and something clicked. Flipping the suitcase over again, she reached inside and lifted out the bottom of the case. "Yes! See, it is here!" she said. Hannah looked inside and saw a small, flat box lying in the bottom of the case.

Hannah knew many Jews used such cases, hiding valuables from the Nazis, but the Nazis also knew of such deceptions and usually discovered such hiding places. Hannah had heard that the Germans had added millions of Reichsmarks to their war chest through such discoveries. That was why they made everyone discard their clothes and possessions. After a thorough search they would then give them to the next group that came through a camp, devoid of any valuables.

Zohar grabbed the box and quickly opened it, her nervous hands nearly dropping it as she did so. She laid the box down again and rolled back the cloth that was neatly folded inside.

The result made Hannah's breath catch in her chest.

CHAPTER 7

"I . . . I've never seen anything that beautiful," Rachel exclaimed from her leaning position behind Hannah. "It must be worth—"

"It was my mother's," Zohar whispered almost reverently.

Hannah stared at the necklace, its gold chain, rubies, and diamonds glistening in the early-morning sun. She had never seen anything so beautiful that hadn't been hanging around the neck of royalty.

"Father gave it to her when the Queen of England came to Poland for a state visit. It nearly rivaled that of the queen," she said proudly.

Hannah suddenly realized they were very visible and that others were watching from the high windows of the hospital. Some would surely come and want to know what had happened. She quickly closed the cloth around the necklace to keep prying eyes from seeing it. "Zohar, we must hide it again, quickly!"

Zohar didn't seem to hear, a confused look on her face as she tried to open the cloth again. "No, no, I remember when she left the house that night. Her dress was imported silk made of soft pinks and golds. She was . . . she was so elegant. And beautiful!"

"Zohar, we have to put it away. Now!" Hannah said.

Zohar blinked a couple of times, then glanced around her, perplexed. It was then Hannah noticed the administrator heading down the steps of the back entrance toward them.

"Put it away, Zohar, or you're going to lose it," Hannah whispered emphatically.

Zohar's eyes, fixed on the administrator, narrowed as her face hardened. She deftly put the necklace away before snapping the false panel back in place and shutting the suitcase. As they stood, the administrator caught them, grabbed the handle of the case and tried to jerk it free of Zohar's grip. The young girl held tight, her face suddenly flooding with red hate. Hannah quickly stepped between them.

"Let go, Mr. Sperling," she said firmly. "Though it seems impossible, the case belongs to Zohar's family."

The administrator sneered, jerking on the handle again. "You are right, such a thing is impossible. This is the property of Germany. I will take it and see—"

"No, you will not!" Hannah said, gripping the handle with Zohar. "You may not have learned that I have been entertaining an American army captain the last few weeks. He works in the intelligence division hunting for Nazi sympathizers. If you do not let go, I will see that he throws you in prison with the rest of the Werewolves he's capturing." Hannah's words shot at him like bullets and his hand slipped from the handle as he stepped back, confused but still somewhat defiant.

"Werewolves eat little Jews like you. Be careful when you leave this place or they'll have your bones for supper." He started away, then turned back. "I want you dirty Jews out of here by noon, do you hear me!" he shouted. "Noon!"

Hannah was too weak to move and didn't until Sperling had reentered the building.

"Werewolves?" Rachel asked.

Hannah tried to explain as they walked toward the door back to the showers. By the time she finished, they were inside.

"You knew Sperling was one of these animals?" Rachel asked.

"I guessed." Hannah forced a smile. "He knows Zohar has something in the case. Something important. He'll try to find out what it is."

"We need to move quickly and catch the noon train to Berlin. Darkness is the friend of the wolf, Hannah; it is our enemy."

They herded the others straight back to their rooms, insisting they dress quickly. Hannah tried to explain without details, afraid they might question her or drag their feet from fear. None did. All of them had experienced men like Sperling. All of them wanted to get away from him as quickly as possible, and all had a sudden and overpowering desire to go to Palestine. No matter the route nor the hardship, they simply knew it was time.

See Chapter Notes

CHAPTER 8

The trains were erratic. The stationmaster surmised it was because the Russians couldn't make up their minds whether to let the Germans rot in Berlin or feed them so they could be good communists. He thought his joke funny until he noticed he was the only one chuckling. Clearing his throat, he shuffled down the boardwalk.

The Americans had only two train lines into the city but were using them mostly for freight. Hannah and her new sisters waited until five when a freighter came in with two passenger cars attached. They crowded aboard. People sat on benches facing each other, their knees pressed together. Hannah, Rachel, and their friends stood until they reached Leipzig where several people vacated the train and they were able to get seats, Zohar in the middle.

It was hot, and the smell of old sweat and decaying clothes permeated the air. Hannah sensed the girls' fear. Boarding a German train bound for the very center of Hitler's lair was not their idea of a trip to safety.

Hannah watched the people to take her mind off her own fears. A soldier in the next bench, his uniform tattered and dirty, sat with his chin against his chest, asleep. His brown hair, long and greasy, fell down in front of his face. Returning from a prisoner of war camp? Probably.

A woman with a small child sat next to him. The child fussed, constantly asking for food. The mother, clad in her once-modern dress, now soiled from travel and tattered from wear, shushed him, anguished frustration on her face. It was obvious she had no food. Rachel watched as Misha removed a slice of bread from her pocket and gave it to the woman. The rejection was firm, the face granite.

The child screamed. Misha offered again. The woman took it. Would Germany ever get over her pride?

Hannah thought she had picked out a half-dozen camp refugees, all thin, pale, and wearing hand-me-downs like their own. Jews? Political prisoners? The starving masses maybe. All had a lost and empty look in their eyes, searching for someplace to reconnect to humanity. From Ephraim's description of what was happening in Berlin, Hannah was sure they wouldn't find much relief there.

Berlin. Were they fools? The city was starving, full of murder, rape, and banditry. There were no places to stay, and they would only add more hungry mouths to an already starving population. Fools, that's what they were, and she was the biggest fool of all.

She rubbed her head, trying to relieve the ache, then scratched a little where the dress she wore seemed to be making a rash.

The clothing they had been given was rough and worn, but clean. After the experience with the suitcase, Hannah felt sure that the dresses, coats, and shoes had probably belonged to a former concentration camp resident who had been forced to peel them off just as she had been forced to do nearly four years earlier. She had seen the reluctance in all of them but knew there was no choice. She had set the example by pulling on the one Sister Martha handed her, then watching as the others followed suit. Each took a small suitcase from the pile and packed their few belongings inside. Hannah had kept a strong grip on Zohar's case as they left, Sperling standing near the door, a smirk on his face, watching them leave. Hannah had winced at his obvious self-satisfaction from forcing them to wear the clothes of the dead and, unable to control herself any longer, she had stepped toe-to-toe with him and given him a smile. "Thank you," she had quipped.

It caught him off guard and all he could stutter was "What . . . what for?"

"Better to wear the clothes of a good Jew gone to heaven than those of a bad Nazi going to hell." She had turned and walked away, leaving him speechless. It had felt good until she began to worry that it may have only made things worse. He would surely come after them, but now he might do more than just try to steal Zohar's necklace. She would never forgive herself if her lack of control brought harm to these fragile women.

She glanced up at her own small case in the overhead storage. Her new skirt and blouse were inside. The memory of the touch and warmth of the cloth caressed her flesh. Before the rags they wore were given to them, she had been going to wear Ephraim's gift, but she was glad now that the need to lead the others had made up her mind for her. The trip would surely soil them. When they found housing in Berlin she would reconsider, once she knew she would see Ephraim Daniels again.

She had tried to form a plan in her mind but it was useless. This was a good example of the Christian saying that when the blind led the blind, both would fall into the ditch. She could only hope that Ephraim would give her hope, some direction on what they should do.

She rubbed her forehead with her hand. Would her head ever stop aching?

"You're Jews, aren't you?" The statement was said in German and came from a large man sitting across from them, two children on each side, napping. Hannah felt no animosity in the voice and simply nodded, then looked out the window.

"You shouldn't be going to Berlin. It isn't safe for Jews." There was a resonant sadness in his voice, tiredness in his face and eyes. He looked to be in his sixties, and yet the ages of his children . . . maybe they were his grandchildren.

He glanced out the window and watched the countryside slip by. "My wife was a Jew," he said softly.

Hannah felt Rachel stiffen, her whole body alert.

Hannah had known of Jewish women married to gentiles. When the Nazis had come, they felt sure they were safe but were only fooling themselves. In time, the Nazis came for them, and if their husbands or families did not denounce them, they too were taken to the camps. Hannah felt no pity for this man. He had let his wife go alone.

"You are from Berlin?" Rachel inquired stiffly.

He nodded. "We have been in Poland, looking for my wife."

"Why?" Rachel asked coldly. "You gave her to the Nazis once. Why burden yourself again?"

The man's eyes blinked and his shoulders seemed to sag even further. "She was never a burden."

The girl nearest the window stirred and whimpered. The man put a gentle hand on her head and spoke softly.

"She still has nightmares."

"How did you keep them from . . . from having to go with their mother? Their Jewish blood . . . surely they were doomed," Hannah said.

He looked out the window, a dark sadness settling on his brow. "She denounced them, said they were not hers. I was wealthy enough to manage the rest. It was amazing what money could buy in those days. Or should I say, *who* it could buy."

"But it can't buy back your wife, can it?" Rachel spat the words out.

He looked down at his daughter, his hand caressing her hair. "Few of us really believed our families would become targets for Hitler's insanity. After all, Germany's industrial base was critical to the war effort, and those of us who ran that industry felt we were safe. We were like flies who flit about the spider while he builds his web, impervious to the intent. By the time the fly realizes what is happening, he is trapped. Then the Spider attacks, slowly sucking the life from its body." He paused as if trying to handle the pain of being so blind.

"You as good as murdered her," Rachel said. The hate in her voice made Hannah cringe, and she reached over and touched Rachel's knee to calm her.

The man gave a perceptible nod but no reply.

A heavy silence settled over them, each dealing with dark memories. After long moments, Zohar closed her eyes and either went to sleep or pretended to do so. Hannah closed her own eyes and tried to make her mind shut down. It was impossible. She never could sleep on a train, or on anything that moved for that matter. But she tried just the same. Tried to keep from looking at the man for another minute.

Her thoughts turned to Ephraim, but immediately she put him out of her mind. Their lives led in opposite directions, to two different continents and ways of life. She had to keep her feelings under control. It was as simple as that. A few moments later she fell asleep.

Something moving next to her brought Hannah back, her eyelids releasing as if on springs. Sperling stood there, a large burly man at his side. She could see another of similar size and intelligence behind them.

The smile on Sperling's face was one of contempt mingled with satisfaction. Hannah had seen that smile on the faces of the guards at Ravensbrück when they were about to punish someone. She felt her blood turn to ice and sat forward in her seat as if to protect Zohar, now awake and frightened. Rachel was on her feet and about to try to swat the little spider before them, when Hannah put a hand on her leg and motioned for her to sit back down. One swipe from Sperling's bodyguard and Rachel would find herself unconscious and bleeding on the floor.

"I believe you have something that belongs to the hospital," Sperling said, glancing at the man in the seat.

Hannah noticed the seated German stiffen slightly as Sperling stepped forward to reach for the case wrapped in Zohar's arms. Hannah deftly lifted herself out of the seat and blocked the way. Better that she take the bruises than Rachel. "Do you have proof it belongs to you or the hospital, Mr. Sperling?" she asked evenly.

He gave her an evil, crooked smile. "Proof? A German needs no proof when dealing with a Jew!" he spat. The larger man stepped forward and shoved Hannah toward the window, the same look of disdain in his eyes.

"I wouldn't do that if I were you." The voice was cold, calculated, and hard. The source was the German sitting across from them.

Sperling turned to him with a challenging glare. "Stay out of this," he said in German. "Or . . ."

The German stood, towering over Sperling and matching his bodyguard inch for inch.

Sperling's friend reached for his pocket, but Hannah's newfound protector grabbed his arm, preventing it, while removing a gun from his own pocket and placing it against Sperling's ribs. "Tell your friend to back away, near the door to the car."

Sperling began to sweat and nodded slowly for his bodyguard to obey. As he did, Sperling backed against the bench across the aisle, his eyes on the Luger. It was then Rachel noticed that everyone in the car was taking a good deal of satisfaction in what was happening, even the soldier. It stiffened her back.

"You have accused this woman of taking something from you. What would it be?" the German with the Luger asked.

"A . . . a suitcase." He looked at the case on Zohar's lap. "That one."

"This seems like a lot of fuss for a beat-up old suitcase that is more in keeping with this young lady's station than yours. And why would a hospital be concerned with such a thing?" He smiled crookedly. "All that aside, the lady asked you for proof. I also would like to see your proof."

"I . . . I have no . . . The Reich . . . there is something that belongs to the Reich . . ." Sperling said weakly.

"In case you aren't paying attention, the Reich is no longer," the German said through clenched teeth. "Now get out! And if I see your miserable face near this car again, I will ventilate your already empty head!"

Sperling quickly left, the door closing automatically behind him and his bodyguards. The German watched the weasel and his friends disappear into the car behind theirs. He put his gun back in his pocket and turned to Hannah, a smile on his face. "I enjoyed that," he said. He pointed at her chair. "Please, sit down."

Hannah, a bit overwhelmed by what had just happened, went to the seat and lowered herself down. He did the same. "Hitler's greater race," he said with disdain. "Their dark uniforms matched their dark hearts." He took a deep breath. "In the beginning even I thought Hitler could save us. Our economy, our morale was in such tatters after the Great War. My father owned a fairly good-sized appliance company, but we could sell nothing and were going under quickly. Most companies were. With the Reich everything seemed to blossom. We were not only saved industrially but the country seemed to come alive again. But gradually I began to see things more clearly as good men were destroyed and replaced with men like the fool that was just here." He shook his head sadly. "Had Hitler been victorious, the world would have been turned to a black and loathsome place, filled with the cancer of hate. He and his kind would not have stopped with the annihilation of your people. Slowly, he would have killed anyone with an ounce of morality in their bones, and the black hearted would have ruled supreme. Then the battle would have been a matter of degree—evil against evil—with the most evil, the most cunning surviving."

"Then Jews were just a place to start," Rachel said bitterly.

He shrugged. "Actually, he started with good Germans who would never have agreed to getting rid of you."

"And you survived," Rachel said.

"Your assumption is wrong," the man said.

"What?"

"Those of us who stood idle . . . when they took my wife . . ." He averted his eyes from Rachel's. "Cowardice is a horrible malady. It creates a different kind of prison. Even death will give no release from such a prison. Survival, as you call it, can be hell."

Hannah had never seen such sorrow and regret in a man's face. It filled every line, consumed every pore, and made his eyes nothing but empty pools of self-loathing. She wondered why he had gone on but realized the answer was sitting by his side. Ephraim had told her how some would pay now, living in a hell of their own making. It struck her that this is what King David must have looked like after his adultery with Bathsheba and the murder of Uriah. There was no escape from this pain, now or even through death.

The German closed his eyes. Was it to sleep or just to avoid further talk and the pain that must surely accompany it? Hannah found herself feeling sorry for this man until she reminded herself that he stood idly by and let his wife go to the camps. Did he know her fate when he let her go? What kind of mind games did he have to play to salve his conscience, she wondered? Hadn't he just come to their rescue? Had his horrible act of desertion made him stronger?

Hannah thought it interesting that a picture of the future of Germany had just been played out in their little compartment; the remains of the Reich against the remains of the people who refused to cower any longer before the Sperlings of Germany. She could only wonder who would actually win Germany in the end.

The thought made her shudder with anxiety. The sooner she could flee this godforsaken land, the better.

Sleep. She needed to get some of it. But only a moment. They were almost to Berlin. She closed her eyes.

And the train pulled into the ruins of a city.

* * *

The train came to a stop in Stettiner Bahnhof and Hannah and the others gathered in the passageway to disembark.

"What is your destination?" their German protector asked.

"The American headquarters," Hannah responded.

He had not heard that the Americans had actually arrived but knew it would be west of the station. Possibly the Russian soldiers would know, but they should be very careful about the Russians. They have no pity for women, regardless of race.

He tipped his hat and started down the aisle, then returned and quietly handed her the Luger. "They say only a silver bullet can kill a Werewolf. In the case of the one who seeks your blood, I think this weapon will do." She returned his smile and shoved the gun into the deep pocket of her plain cotton dress. He turned and made his way along the passageway until he disappeared out the door, his children just in front of him. Hannah found herself wishing him peace. If men like him did not survive, even with his past weaknesses, Germany would turn into a land of howling, bloodthirsty wolves.

Her little flock gathered round her after stepping from the train. Their eyes were wide with fearful anticipation, and she felt over-whelmed by their reliance on her. Taking a deep breath, she looked up and down the boardwalk at the signs. There weren't many. The protec-tive roof that usually covered the area was gone, and the depot itself had filth and debris scattered everywhere. Allied bombs had left their mark.

After getting her bearings, she gave instructions, assigning Rachel to take Misha's hand while she and Tappuah walked with Zohar between them.

"We must find a room," Rachel reminded Hannah.

"We find Ephraim first. He'll know where we can look. We are not strong enough to just wander until we find something. Especially at night. Remember what that man said about the Russians."

Rachel nodded as they walked to the end of the boardwalk and into the station, or what was left of the station. The allied bombs had done a good deal of damage here too, and piles of rubble lay about everywhere, the roof half gone, the west wall filled with gaping holes, and the windows bare of most of their glass. They crossed the great room with difficulty, the place crowded with the homeless, the beggars, the weak and tired who had no place else to lie down. Russian soldiers, presumably sent to keep order, prowled the place looking for or making trouble. She saw them kick beggars, cursing them, forcing them to move a few feet out of their way; others stopped innocent-looking people and interrogated them, while searching through their belongings and taking anything they liked. Hannah kept one eye on Zohar and the other on the exit she wanted, praying to Ephraim's God to bring no more tests down upon their heads. The soldiers eyed them but took no real interest and let them alone. Hannah was grateful as they broke out of the stench into the fresh summer air.

Rachel gasped as she surveyed the street and city before her. "It . . . it is gone," she said in awe.

The pavement was littered with wreckage; the buildings had all suffered some destruction; most were nothing but piles of rubble spilling into the street. There were no automobiles, no trolleys— nothing. The city was empty of anything mechanical and an eerie sort of silence settled over them. She saw people, or at least remnants of people, walking the streets, their feet covered with rags instead of shoes, propelled by some invisible source, zombies looking for food. Hannah found herself seeing Ravensbrück all over again, just on a larger scale.

Rachel wet her lips and tried to swallow so she could speak. "We go that way," she said, pointing down the wide, war-torn avenue before them. "When we find a wide, open street that goes west, we take it."

She forced her legs to move and the others followed, their voices echoing in the sheer emptiness of the ruins. As they made their way around the wreckage, the absence of the constant sounds of a city was unsettling.

"Ruins," Rachel uttered. "Nothing but ruins." She stepped quickly to Hannah's side. "We can't stay here, Hannah. There is no place to stay."

"Then we'll sleep in the streets." She forced a smile. "Remember why we're here, Rachel. It is only to see if we can get what we need for the journey out of this horrible country."

Rachel nodded, then fell back with Misha. They had walked nearly a block before Hannah looked behind her and saw Sperling. Her throat went dry again as she realized the man wasn't going to give up. She wanted to run but knew there was no place to hide. They must find another way.

"I don't like this," Zohar said weakly. Her eyes filled with fear and Hannah put an arm around her, giving some comfort even though she, too, was scared.

"Look!" said Misha in a whisper tinged with fear.

Her little group seemed to hold their breath in unison as an army truck came into the street and turned toward them. Russian. Again she prayed that Ephraim's God would blind these men to their existence, at the same time hoping they would take note of Sperling and at least detain him and his two morons.

The truck seemed to slow as it approached. A soldier in the back of the truck saw them and made some comment to his buddies. Several turned and came to the side of the truck, whistling and making what Hannah knew must be crude remarks, but the truck kept going toward the depot and Hannah started breathing again.

"Rachel," Hannah said, summoning her friend to come forward, "Sperling is following us; if they try anything, we'll have to fight. Have each of the girls pick up something as a weapon—a rock, a stick, anything."

Rachel nodded.

Hannah had a sudden thought. "Wait." She took Rachel's arm while leaning toward Zohar. "Open the case and get the necklace, Zohar. Do it now."

Zohar had a curious look on her face but was nodding.

"Let me hold the case, and you release the false panel and get the necklace. Rachel, have the others tighten in around us."

Rachel signaled Misha and Tappuah as Zohar handed Hannah the suitcase. She quickly released the latches, pushed on the hinges, and released the false panel. Opening the box, she removed the necklace and handed it to Hannah before closing the case. Hannah shoved it down her dress, hoping her oversized underwear would house it without notice. For the first time in weeks she was thankful that her bosom had shrunk! Quickly putting the false bottom back in place, Zohar closed the case. It was then Rachel told them about Sperling. Everyone stopped, some glancing quickly over their shoulders. Sperling saw it and hesitated, then came on even quicker.

"Everyone knows what he is after. We make him think it is in the suitcase, but we don't give it up without a fight. Understand? It will convince him he has what he wants. The deception will give us enough time to get to the American sector."

All nodded, their faces pale but their jaws set with determination.

"Good, circle around me, facing out. Pick up something for a weapon.

The girls picked up stones and sticks. Rachel found a two-foot length of steel, spit on her hands, and grinned.

"Rachel, be careful. If they show any weapon . . ."

Rachel gave an impatient nod.

"Zohar, stay with me. Hang onto the suitcase, okay?" Zohar was pale with fright but nodded. Hannah switched the case to her right so Zohar could get a hand on the handle next to hers. Sperling tramped up to them.

Hannah knew that each heart was racing, memories of beatings looming in their minds. She wondered who would fall apart and who would rally. Though Rachel was weak physically, Hannah was grateful she was by her side. Now past her own crisis, she was proving to be the strongest in will.

Hannah felt sweat beads explode on her forehead.

Sperling gave that same wicked smile. "Now, fräulein, I will take what is mine."

"Were you ever in the camps, Sperling?"

The question caught him off guard. "No . . . I . . ."

"Then you never saw what a pack of mean, hungry women might do to a guard who looked the wrong way."

Sperling's face went pale, but then he seemed to think of something and the smile returned.

"Wilhelm, please fetch the suitcase."

The big one on the right took two steps.

"Girls," Hannah said.

They drew back to throw their stones and Wilhelm hesitated then retreated, unsure of what to do. It was then the other one pulled the gun.

Hannah remembered the Luger in her pocket but thought better of it. This man had been a professional soldier, probably SS, and trained in killing for pleasure.

The girls stood their ground, waiting, determined. Hannah was awed by the fact that they would fight if she told them to.

"He will use it," Sperling said.

Hannah hesitated for effect. Rachel took a step forward and the Luger shifted in her direction.

"No!" She forced Zohar's hand off the handle and extended the case to Sperling.

The look on Sperling's face nearly changed her mind, but she let it go.

Sperling took the case. The Luger went back in the moron's pocket, and the three men turned and started back for the depot.

"Girls, let's go," Hannah said.

They moved at a quick pace, Hannah glancing over their collective shoulders to check on Sperling now and again. He wouldn't stop until he felt he was safe; then he'd check. Hannah didn't know how long that would be, but at the corner she picked up the pace to a slow trot and the girls fell in behind.

They had to find Ephraim.

See Chapter Notes

CHAPTER 9

Ephraim, just leaving the new headquarters building, looked up to see Hannah and her new-found sisters coming across the street toward him. She hadn't noticed him yet, and he was too stunned to say anything. What on earth was she doing in Berlin? Their eyes locked and a visible wave of relief turned worry lines into the creases of a smile on her exhausted face.

"Hi," he said. "Come to do some shopping?" He smiled.

She wanted to fall into his arms but resisted. Instead, she stood there, grinning ear to ear, as the others crowded around her. "They kicked us out," she said. "We are looking for a new place to live." She quickly explained what had happened.

Anger filled his chest. The war had taken most of the best and brightest of Germany. The Nazis had seen to that by forcing the anti-Nazi intellectuals out of the country, underground, or into the work camps. They had wanted no opposition. Now that the Nazis were gone, a few of this class were returning, but most of those who survived were staying put, refusing to help a country that had chosen Hitler over humanity. Without a new base upon which to build, the allies found themselves forced to turn to those low-level Nazis who had controlled mid-to-lower-level government and knew the bureaucracy to rebuild the infrastructure. Under present conditions they had no choice but to look the other way when such people declared they had been forced into the Nazi party and had affidavits signed by a dozen others to prove it. In doing so, sometimes bad apples got into the barrel. Unfortunately, the Russians were even less particular. After all, it wasn't a big leap from Nazi to Stalinist—both needed brutal, amoral people to keep everyone in order. The Werewolves were using that to their advantage, declaring themselves Stalinists without so much as a twitch. They could then position themselves for the future while continuing to cause trouble for those they didn't want in Germany.

Ephraim's anger stemmed from helplessness. His own government still wouldn't see that Stalin was just another Hitler and that he too had his sights set on conquering the world. It was obvious to anyone in the city that the Stalinists intended on making Berlin a subservient Russian city. They had kept the other allied countries out of the city for nearly three months now, hoping they would give it up altogether. Even this morning, coming here in a large convoy, the Russians had stopped them at half a dozen checkpoints as if trying to get across the message that this was their city, and even their former partners in war would have to answer to them. It made Ephraim mad enough to spit. Trouble was he knew it would worsen. In their blind paranoia about needing Russia as an ally against Japan, the American leaders were selling out Europe to keep Stalin happy, believing they could work out any difficulties later. However, the Russians were becoming so entrenched in Germany they would be impossible to root out anytime soon.

But now was not the time to tell Hannah all that. She was here, and he'd see that she was safe. He took Hannah's suitcase. As he did, another soldier near the door of the American headquarters recognized them.

"Hey, Misha, how ya doin?" It was Wally. Misha's face turned scarlet, and it forced a giggle from the others until Wally stepped in beside Misha.

Hannah gave the young soldier a side glance that was more a scowl.

"Don't forget, his father's a Rabbi," Ephraim said quietly.

Hannah recognized his attempt to give her comfort and removed the scowl. After all, she wasn't Misha's mother.

They walked a short distance to what was left of a small park and they all collapsed on what remained of the dry, dusty grass. Ephraim gave Wally some instructions and, reluctantly, the sergeant obeyed, heading back to headquarters. Hannah and Ephraim found shade under what had been the wall of some building, no longer identifiable.

"We're going home," Hannah said.

He shook his head. "Poland isn't a good place right now, Hannah. The border is closed, the new Polish government is controlled by the Russians, and they . . . they are keeping Jews in the camps until they can move them out of the country along with other people they consider undesirable."

Hannah gave him a tolerant smile. "We're not going to Poland, Ephraim, we're going to Palestine."

Ephraim looked over her little group. "You're not ready. They aren't strong enough yet."

"You were the one who said we should go right away."

"I didn't mean in the next few days, Hannah!"

"We need papers, tickets, maps, train schedules, anything that you think might help us," she pleaded. "And if you could fly us to Marseille, . . ."

He laughed lightly. "Sorry, no flights into Marseille."

"Can you help?"

He looked at her, his eyes serious, even a little sad. She hoped the sadness had something to do with her, but shoved the thought aside. Two different directions, two different worlds—she had to remember that.

"Yeah, I think we can help. It will take a few days, but Wally and I and a few others will see what we can do. Quietly, of course. Don't want anyone thinking this is more than a mission of mercy." He grinned.

She got the message. Anti-fraternization was still in place, but there were exceptions. She felt comfortably relieved.

"Thank you. Your help is badly needed."

"You'll need a place to stay."

"Any room at the Berlin Ritz?" She smiled.

"I'll check, but until then we'll find something else."

She faced him again, her heart pounding. "Thank you."

"Don't thank me until you see what I can offer."

"We'll make do," she said laughingly. "You have to remember, these ladies aren't exactly used to all the comforts, at least not in recent history."

"Well, as you can see, Berlin won't spoil you."

She heard the motor of a truck and looked up to see Wally in the passenger seat of a troop transport pulling up. He had a self-satisfied grin on his face as he waved to Misha, who quickly got to her feet and waved back.

"Impressive," Hannah said.

"Some guys will do anything for a woman." He smiled. "No self-control whatsoever."

"I thought you said he understood the rules."

"Umm, I'll remind him. Mission of mercy and all."

Everyone gathered up their belongings and scurried to the back of the truck where Wally, Ephraim, and the driver helped them in. When everyone was settled, they worked their way through what remained of the city. As they left the center going west, more and more of the buildings were standing and the crowds of people grew.

"There are so many! How do you feed them? How do they survive?"

"We just got here, and frankly, I don't know yet how we'll do it." He paused. "Fortunately, there are signs of a new economy coming to life. The center of it is the black market. Officially, we're supposed to try and get rid of it, but unofficially we can't and wouldn't if we could. Without the black market, even more people would die."

A truck was parked nearby. They were loading bodies. Ephraim explained. "When we entered the city this morning, the first detail assigned was to get the rest of the dead buried before the place starts to crawl with disease. Be careful where you go. Even though the Russians organized the locals into burial details, there are still more, buried or half buried, in the rubble. Then there are the ones in the canals, rivers, and lakes. We'll get to them in the next few days."

"Isn't there a danger of the plague?"

"Yeah, there is, and if we don't get more food in here, picking up the dead will never end." They gripped the side rail as the truck hit a deep hole. "Many of the Werewolves made their last stand here. When it was obvious to most of the population there was no sense fighting any longer, the animals started hanging or shooting deserters and civilians, calling them unpatriotic." He pointed to a piece of rope hanging from a lamppost. "Some of them were still hanging when we got here this morning."

Hannah felt sick. She had always wanted the Germans to suffer for what they had allowed, but now that she was seeing that suffering, she was finding that revenge was not nearly as sweet as she thought.

After another ten minutes they pulled into a street still pretty much intact and stopped in front of a row of apartment buildings. American soldiers stood and sat about the staircases. There were only a few civilians. She wondered how many starving people no longer had homes to make way for the conquering armies but immediately felt guilty. The soldiers had gone through their own kind of hell to get here; many had died. Discomfort on the part of the populace who allowed such a thing was the price to be paid.

Unloading, they took the stairs up one flight, passing curious soldiers and a few civilians along the way. Ephraim knocked on the door and waited.

"You'll share this place with a couple of locals. They're Germans who resisted and had to go underground. I met them a couple of hours ago when we took over most of the rest of the building. They offered to help anyone we found who might need a place."

"Jews?"

"No, but their organization helped a lot escape."

"Uncle Emil," Rachel said.

The others looked at her curiously.

"The code name of a group who helped many get out of Berlin. My . . . my mother contacted them, but we waited too long."

"There were several groups. Most were caught and sent to the camps," Ephraim said.

The door opened and a man stood in front of them, his thin, emaciated body held up by two crutches. A woman, healthier, stood behind him."

Ephraim explained in perfect German why they were there. The couple smiled genuinely and invited them in. Hannah and her friends crowded in and shut the door. Hannah was still dealing with Ephraim's near-perfect German. He had not spoken the language in her presence and she wondered why. Surely he knew she could speak it.

"Welcome," the woman said. She pointed at a single chair. "Please, sit." Hannah looked at the others. Tired as they were, no one moved. "Thank you, but we're fine. Your husband should sit."

The gentleman smiled his thanks and let himself into the straight-backed kitchen chair, his pain obvious.

"I know you," Rachel said, looking at the old man, a smile on her face. "You are with the Berlin Philharmonic, the principal cellist."

The man seemed both surprised and pleased at the recognition. "Yes, but how . . ."

"I also played the cello. You came to my school and instructed us several times."

The woman pointed to an adjoining room. "It is large and there is another through there. Sorry there isn't any furniture, but the Russians took almost all of it."

"I'll have cots brought up for all of you, and blankets," Ephraim said in German. He turned to the older woman. "I will bring food for you as well as for them and pay you, if necessary."

"Food is enough. A gift from heaven. Thank you."

He turned to the others. "The building was still intact when we requisitioned its use, but they have no hot water and the cold is sporadic. There is no electricity either. Hopefully, we will have the problem resolved soon." He smiled.

"May I speak with you a minute?" Hannah said, taking his arm and moving toward the door. Once in the hallway, she gave him a smile. "You speak perfect German. How is that?"

"I was a missionary here before the war. It's probably the reason they stuck me behind a desk."

"Why didn't you speak it before now?"

"Because you speak better English than I do German." He grinned.

She turned her back to him, reached down her front, and retrieved the necklace. Turning back, she showed it to him.

Ephraim whistled. He had never seen anything like it. "Beautiful. How on earth . . ."

She told him. "I need an opinion on its worth."

He took it and carefully placed it in his pocket. "I'll see what I can do. Bound to be a jeweler around this rubble, pushing stuff on the black market."

She pushed her hand into the deep pocket of her skirt. "I have something else for you," she said. She handed him the Luger given to her aboard the train. "I wouldn't know what to do with it, and I don't want it around."

He looked at the weapon, a curious look on his face. She told him about their German friend's treatment of Sperling. Ephraim seemed pleased that it had happened.

"Maybe you should keep it . . . for protection."

She shook her head. "No, we are in no danger here, and having it around will only make me nervous."

"Good enough."

"Thank you for everything, Ephraim Daniels." She was tempted to give him a kiss but resisted, turned, and went back through the door, passing Wally as she did. Closing the door, she turned to the woman. "This is your house. We wish to help in any way we can."

The woman gave her a smile. "I would welcome help in the kitchen, and cleaning is still needed. We have been quite ill." She pointed to another door. "That is the bathroom. As the American said, the water is only cold, but with the soap he gave us this morning it is good enough." She glanced at her husband. "He is not well. When he has to go to the bathroom . . . "

"Get out of my way!" he said with a grin. "If you know what I mean."

The others chuckled. "We know," said Zohar, rolling her eyes. Diarrhea was a reality of life in the camps.

"What are your names?" Hannah asked.

"His is Gunther Ludwig," Rachel said.

"And I am his wife," said the lady, shooting a thankful glance at Rachel as her husband beamed under the light of recognition.

"Is it all right if we use that room? That way if others need a place, the other room can be used."

The woman nodded agreement. The room was spacious and five cots would not be crowded. Hannah opened a set of French doors off the living area that led onto a small patio. She glanced up and down the street but saw nothing that alarmed her. This was the American section of town now; only soldiers and those associated with them would be about. She felt relatively safe.

As she went back inside, there was a knock on the door and Rachel answered it. It was Wally with a military cot. Another soldier with a cot stood behind him. A half-hour later they all had something to sleep on, along with blankets, potatoes, bread, and flour. Zohar volunteered to help prepare a meal while the others took a cold shower and cleaned up. As Hannah was about to take her own shower, there was another knock at the door. It was Ephraim.

"Hi again," he smiled, handing her a folder with some papers inside. "Maps. I contacted the Jewish authorities directly connected with Palestine. They want to see you tomorrow."

It was music to Hannah's ears. "They are here?"

"I just found out they followed us in."

Her heart jumped. With the help of such people, surely they could get to Palestine quickly!

Ephraim said good-bye as he descended the stairs. Hannah turned back to her friends, repeating the good news. Amidst their excited chatter, dinner was prepared. Food had never tasted so good.

CHAPTER 10

Hannah sat on the steps leading down to the first floor, fanning herself with a page from a nearly destroyed book she had found in the hallway. Even though it was evening, the early summer heat was oppressive and she hadn't been able to sleep. She heard the door open and turned to see Rachel.

"Hi," Rachel said.

"You can't sleep either?" Hannah asked.

Rachel sat on the step next to her and took a page for her own fan.

"Are you okay? Coming home like this, finding everything changed? It must be horrible."

"I'm numb, that's all, numb clear to the bone. I could see the area where we lived from the railway station. Not very well, but I could see it. From the look of it, there isn't much left. And as we came here, the museums, the theaters—all gone, or so much so that they will have to be replaced. It is horrible."

"What about your father? I've heard you talk about your mother, but your father . . ."

"The man on the train, the one who let his wife go to the camps, he is like my father."

"He deserted you?"

"Worse—he turned us in."

Hannah looked over at her new-found friend to see if she was joking. She wasn't.

"My mother had inherited a fortune, her father a prominent indus-trialist who owned factories in the Ruhr Valley of Germany, along with many other businesses across Europe. Unfortunately, she also inherited his genetic disorder—he was a Jew. His father had fled Russia in the late 1800s when pogroms became official doctrine, and many Jews realized that after nearly five hundred years of trying, equality would never be a part of their lives unless they left the Czar's realm. Most fled to the United States, some to Palestine, but my grandfather came here where he set up a small business and began to prosper."

Hannah adjusted her position until her back was against the wall and she was looking directly at Rachel.

"It was the beginning of the industrial revolution in Germany, and grandfather contacted the Warburg family, Germany's most prominent financiers at the time—and also Jews. They treated him well and he quickly developed his small company into an industrial powerhouse. At the outbreak of World War I, he used his capital to gear up for the production of vehicles. When the war ended in such disaster and everyone was looking for someone to blame, the Jews were natural targets."

Hannah knew of the change of attitude after World War I. Before that time, much of the anti-Jewish movement was based on the evil-doing of Jews and their murder of Christ, but in the 1920s it turned into a race issue and the terms Semite, and thus anti-Semite, were coined. The propaganda of the "new" anti-Jews no longer emphasized the Jew's non-Christian beliefs but taught that Jews were inherently evil because of their genetics, and until they were eradicated the evil would remain to punish and haunt all others. At first the philosophy was absurd, but as anti-Semitic organizations and political parties proliferated, the Jews found themselves in worse straights than at any time in their history. The pogroms were no longer just regional or local but grew into national events. A Jew in Germany was the same as a Jew in Poland or Russia, and all were the cause of the ills besetting an economically impotent Europe. And until the Jews were eliminated the sickness of the society would continue to exist. Hitler was the most avid supporter of the doctrine, the camps his attempt to bring about a new Europe by ridding it of what he claimed was the cancer that had always kept it from its rightful destiny—the Jews.

"For the survival of his family, my grandfather converted to Christianity," Rachel continued. "Such a thing was acceptable to Christians then. Surely that conversion would rid the Jew of his evil tendencies and all would be well."

Rachel stopped, her eyes on Hannah. "I went to the camps a Christian, Hannah. It was there I became a Jew."

Hannah was a bit stunned by the revelation. She remembered others like Rachel housed with her at Ravensbrück. They wore their Christian crosses and kept to themselves, afraid that association with the "real thing" would make things even worse, while also waiting for someone to realize they were not Jews, not really, and to free them. She remembered being gratified when even one of these was beaten or deprived of food. She watched them come to the realization that no one was coming to their rescue, and had no pity for them when they gave up and died. Such women were caught between two worlds, accepted by neither, most put there by such men as Rachel's father. Guilt rushed through Hannah as she realized how horrible it must have been for them, for Rachel.

She took Rachel in her arms. "You survived. That's all that matters."

Rachel put her arms around her friend and accepted the offering of friendship, relieved. She would have nothing to live for if Hannah turned away.

"My grandfather should never have converted. Becoming a Lutheran only delayed the inevitable and was so wrong, anyway." She started to cry but quickly brushed the tears away.

Hannah knew the stand of the German Lutheran Church on the Jews; they adopted a clearly anti-Semitic attitude from the earliest days of the Nazi movement and did not abandon it until the end. Even when converted or partly Jewish Christians like Rachel's grandfather were affected, its stand remained hard and fast.

She also knew the attitude of the Vatican. Through the war it never reacted to the killing of the Jews. Even in 1942, when invited to sign the watered-downed "solemn resolution" of the Allies condemning Nazi crimes, the Pope refused. The Uniate Archbishop of the Greek Orthodox Church in Galicia remained silent as well, never protesting against the terrible acts of murder occurring in front of their very eyes, and the Russian Orthodox Church had assented to the Communist pogroms without much hesitation either. In fact, some members of the clergy across Eastern Europe had spread savage anti-Semitic propaganda.

Hannah shoved these thoughts aside. If she wasn't careful, she might forget the good that Christianity could do and had done, but it was hard when they had allowed so much suffering and let so many die!

"My father became a wealthy man when he found out we had Jewish blood. He used it to get rid of us, and in the process he inherited my mother's considerable wealth." Rachel laughed lightly. "Now he also has lost everything."

Hannah remembered what Ephraim had told her; the rich would be needed, Nazis or not, to rebuild Germany. If Rachel's father survived . . . She dismissed the thought. Rachel didn't need to hear such thinking right now.

Then it occurred to her. If Rachel's father found out she was alive, what would his reaction be? She could get him thrown into prison, couldn't she? And he would want to prevent that. Her stomach churned. She would have to keep Rachel close to her until they left for Palestine.

"He wasn't all bad, you know. Not at first," Rachel said. "I think he loved my mother. It's just that when Hitler took leadership, everyone in Berlin was caught up in the excitement and power of it all. Opportunity seemed to greet us at every corner. We joined the youth corp and signed documents pledging our allegiance to the führer. He even came to our school once. What a day!" she said. "So much excitement!" She was quiet for a moment. "We didn't understand then. We didn't know!" Rachel sniffed. "I was at a private school. They came to my room when they found out that I had Jewish blood. You see, they searched the background of anyone in the youth corp and they found out . . . it . . . it was the first time I knew that I was a Jew. I told them it was all a lie. When they showed me the documents, I said it was some sort of horrible mistake. It made no difference."

Hannah realized that Rachel looked much older than she really was. Instead of a woman in her thirties, Rachel must not be more than twenty, possibly even younger. How horrible it must have been for a girl her age to be so popular and well liked one day and so hated the next. *Ironic*, she thought, *here was a girl who had probably made fun of Jews, even believed some of the propaganda and assented to it, only to discover she was one of them.* At least Hannah had been prepared. She had been persecuted all of her life.

Hannah found it interesting that she didn't hate Rachel. She should hate her, but she couldn't. Maybe it was because she was just tired of hating, or maybe it was because Rachel had suffered enough. Whatever the reason, Hannah was grateful. There was enough to hate without adding Rachel to the list.

"Mother came to get me the next day," Rachel continued. "None of my friends were there to see me leave. I was no longer one of them. They hated me." Another silence. She sniffed and Hannah knew she was choking back tears. "At first I blamed it all on my mother; then I saw that she too was being spurned, despite her former position among the upper class of Berlin. Worse still, I saw my father change. It was horrible."

The statement shocked Hannah. "You mean he didn't know she was of Jewish descent, either?" Hannah asked.

"I do not know if he knew before . . . before I was dismissed from school. It wasn't until then that he began to change."

"At first my mother tried to tell me it would be all right, that father loved us and would protect us." Rachel continued. "But when my father stopped coming home, telling us that he had to stay in Hamburg and that the factories needed his attention . . . well, they had never needed such attention before," she said stiffly.

"We lived like that for more than two years. Mother and I seldom left the house. At first we listened to the broadcasts, but the news about resettlements upset her so much that we finally stopped." She sighed. "Finally, men from the gestapo came and requested that mother accompany them. Though they were civil, they made it clear she had no choice. Frightened, I tried desperately to get hold of my father, but he . . . he couldn't be found. I cried myself to sleep that night, afraid she would never return. But five long hours later, she came back. She was very frightened. We had been ordered to report to headquarters in the morning, together this time. We both knew if we did, we would be sent away. She sent me to my room to pack a suitcase with warm clothes and bring it downstairs. I didn't know it at the time, but she had already made some plans for getting us out of the country. She was crying when I came down, afraid she had waited too long, afraid that her reluctance to leave our house and her belief that her position in society, and my father's, would protect us, would now cost us dearly."

There was a long pause as Rachel tried to get her emotions under control.

"We waited until after midnight; then we left the house to walk to the train station. We hadn't gone fifty feet before a car pulled up beside us and took us into custody." She sniffed again. "The next morning we were forced into the back of open transports with dozens of others and hauled to the train station. From there it was a horrible ride to Auschwitz." Hannah heard the catch in her throat. "I saw father at the train station. I was so glad, but when I called to him he . . . he only looked away. Then, as I cried out louder, he quickly turned and walked to his car and drove away." Her voice caught; she turned into Hannah's shoulder and cried.

Hannah now understood why Rachel had declared that Ephraim would not come. Her own father had deserted her to countless days of misery. How could she possibly trust other men?

After a moment, Rachel got herself under control. "My mother was right, you know. We did wait too long. If we had only gone earlier . . . "

Hannah understood. Her family had waited too long as well. Most Jews had waited too long, believing that this, like all other periods of persecution, would pass. It had cost so many lives.

"We must leave Germany, Hannah," Rachel said. "We must leave soon. This time we cannot wait. Do you understand?"

Rachel put her face in Hannah's dress and cried, but Hannah did understand. They had no place in Europe, and waiting would only cause more misery to all of them.

She heard the door open and close downstairs, then heard someone coming up the stairs. As he reached the lower landing he looked up. It was Ephraim. He came on up and sat on the stair just below them. He looked at Rachel and saw that he was interrupting something. An apologetic look crossed his face. Hannah touched his shoulder and told him to stay, everything was fine.

"It is late," she said.

"Umm." He reached in his pocket and pulled out the necklace, handing it to her.

"It is not worth much, is it?" she said.

He shook his head. "Paste. Very good paste, but paste just the same."

Rachel grabbed the necklace and looked at it carefully. "Paste? But this cannot be!" she said in an anguished voice.

"This . . . this is supposed to get us on a ship to Palestine!"

"There isn't a great market for this sort of thing. Black-market prices won't give you a tenth of what even a good piece of paste jewelry might bring under normal conditions."

Hannah took the necklace back. "It is just as well. It holds a lot of meaning for Zohar. It would be asking a lot to make her give it up."

"There are other ways to get the money," Rachel said. She stood and left them to go back to bed.

"She makes it sound like money grows on trees around here," Ephraim said.

"If there are money trees, Rachel will find them." Hannah smiled.

"I'd best get to bed. I am in the first room at the bottom of the stairs, if you need anything." Ephraim stood.

Hannah got up as well. With her standing two steps above him, they were almost the same height, and she found herself staring directly into his eyes.

"I am sorry," he said. "I could try and find a buyer, but my guess is you're looking at a few bucks at best."

"It is better that Zohar keep it. God willing, we'll find another way."

"God willing? I thought you were mad at Him," he said, teasing.

She smiled. "It is only a saying popular to Jews, our way of placing blame. If what we want does not happen, it is His fault. God willing, we'll get to Palestine." She shrugged. "Now, if we do not make it, no one can be mad at me; it is God's fault."

His eyes smiled as he looked into her dark eyes, and she wanted him to take her in his arms and hold her, wanted him to make everything bad in her life disappear like the mist of a fall morning hit by the sun. But, in the same instant, she knew she must step away. Two different worlds, two different directions. She turned and started for the apartment door. She felt his hand touch hers, hold her fingertips, felt the fire shoot through her, the passion, felt the ache melt her heart. It was all she could do to keep going, her fingers slipping from his, the connection broken.

"Good night, Hannah Gruen," he said, still at the top of the steps.

She turned back. "Good night." She said it softly for lack of strength and while forcing herself to turn the knob and close the door between them. Leaning against it, she listened as his footsteps descended and slowly faded until she heard him open then close the door to his new quarters.

Hannah's heart was pounding, her limbs weak. Oh how she wished things could be different, that she could let him know how she felt! She needed to be held, needed to be loved and touched and told he would protect her!

She walked to the balcony and let the air cool her flushed face. Was it so wrong to want him so much? To need him?

She heard someone behind her and turned to find Misha standing at the door, pain etched in her face.

"What is it, Misha?"

"I, I don't know. Pain . . ."

Hannah quickly wrapped her arms around Misha as she went to the floor. "Misha!" she said. "Misha!"

There was no response.

She placed the girl's head in her lap and called for help. Rachel was the first to get to her.

"Get Ephraim, quickly!" Hannah said.

Rachel was already out the door.

CHAPTER 11

The hospital overflowed with the sick and dying—Berlin's civilian casualties from Hitler's need to hang on to the bitter end. Ephraim and Wally's uniforms had gotten Misha a bed and a doctor almost immediately. The American doctors and nurses were new to Berlin, and already they were overwhelmed by the ill and dying. Hannah could see it in their faces.

They waited.

Wally looked pale and sick. It was obvious he very much liked Misha. In a way it pleased Hannah to know that those kind of feelings were happening for some of them. But on the other hand, if Misha died, Wally would have his heart broken. That saddened her.

He got up and wandered down the hall to the operating room where Ephraim was standing.

The doctor had asked questions.

Had Misha had any problem like this before? Hannah had answered that she had seemed weaker than the others, and there were the pains in her chest that would come and go, but the doctors at the previous hospital had found nothing. She had never fainted.

What were her injuries from the camps?

She and Rachel looked at each other, realizing that Misha had never really said much about her treatment in the camps, but then none of them were eager to discuss that part of their past.

Had she ever been beaten?

They had both smiled at that. Everyone was beaten, Rachel had answered. The doctor had been embarrassed. "Of course. I'm sorry," he responded. Then he had disappeared into the room where Misha lay unconscious. It had been two hours since they had last seen him.

Rachel, Tappuah, and Zohar had showed up an hour ago. They sat or lay on the floor next to the walls of the hallway near the operating room where Misha was. Hannah sat with Zohar's head in her lap, stroking the young girl's hair as she looked at the others. Which of *them* also had unseen injuries that endangered their lives? Which would never have children because of what had been done to them, and which would never reach middle age because of some kind of damage done to them, making them time bombs ready to explode in an unknown moment? The thought made her shudder.

For another hour Hannah had watched as the dying came for help. There were so many!

Ephraim told her that of the dozen or so hospitals in Berlin, only two had survived the bombings sufficiently well to offer any real help. Those were so flooded with the sick that they were constantly running out of medicines and supplies. Unlike the hospital where Hannah and the others had been taken when rescued from the camps, this one was overrun with sheer numbers that overworked the limited number of doctors and nurses, and filled every bed and corridor with people simply unable to take care of themselves.

She watched as nurses had to turn away those who weren't on the edge of death. In better times such people would have found refuge here, would have been nursed back to good health. But not now. Now they were sent away to fend for themselves and to try to get well among the starving masses of the city. Some were lucky enough to leave with medicines for their ailments or bandages for their wounds and sores, but most left just as they had come.

At first Hannah had found it amazing that such people did not complain about being turned away but then realized that, like her, they simply looked around them and saw the reality of the hordes of sick and dying people. How could they complain? She found her heart aching for all of them, even though she knew that some still believed she and her friends were the enemy, knew that they had supported Hitler's destruction of her people, either actively or passively. But they had supported it just the same. It saddened her to think that it was this hate that had brought them all here, to this hospital, to suffer together, and that they still didn't understand that.

Ephraim and Wally came down the hall. Wally sat down across from them and put his head on his knees as Ephraim crouched down in front of her, his face grave. "She's still in surgery. Something about a broken rib . . . and her heart." He shook his head. "They don't know how the doctors at the last place missed it."

Hannah only nodded, her fingers caressing the hair of a still-sleeping Zohar. Rachel moved a little to her right, and Ephraim sat down next to Hannah, his back against the same wall.

"She was only a day away from the ovens," said Tappuah, who was sitting directly across from Hannah. "Just a day, that's all. We were all just a day from death."

She told them their story. Tappuah and Misha had been at Auschwitz Birkenau. Birkenau was the extermination part of the camp; the main camp held politicals and others who were used for hard labor until they were too weak to do so; then they were moved next door to Birkenau. Tappuah and Misha were to go to the ovens the morning that the Russians overran the camp and freed the prisoners. The Russians did little for the captives; there was little they could do for more than six thousand people who were nearly dead from starvation.

"Jacko beat her," Tappuah said. "Jacko did this to Misha."

"Jacko?" Ephraim asked.

"A kapo at Auschwitz. We were made to dig up a Jewish cemetery in Krakow. They were making another camp. At first it was pleasant enough. There was shade from the large trees and you could even hide once in a while behind the monuments, get a moment's rest; but then we had to dig deeper, dispose of the decaying bodies. Misha was working a little apart and found the body of a child they had killed. She refused to touch it. Jakco beat her with a shovel."

"Even now the camps kill us," Rachel lamented.

Kapos. Hannah remembered—other prisoners put in charge of inmates. They were usually not Jews but politicals who knew that doing their job well meant more food and comfort for themselves. They were often the most cruel men and women in the camps. In the ghetto they were Jews, Jews who decided to reject their heritage to survive.

"I tried to stop him. He beat me as well." Tears broke from the corners of Tappuah's eyes. "We kept working. Otherwise, we would be sent to the infirmary. No one came out of the infirmary. I used a part of my clothing to bandage my bloodied face until we got back to the barracks. It was all we could do to get Misha into our bunk." She brushed the tears off her cheek. "The next day we couldn't go to work. It was then we were told we would go to Camp B."

She told them the rest. The Russians had come. Tappuah and Misha, along with Zohar, whom they had not known before their release, had walked to a nearby village. A priest had found them a doctor and eventually they ended up in the hospital where Hannah had been taken. Their being alive was a double miracle. They had missed the ovens and their wounds had not killed them in the horribly unsanitary conditions of the camp. Even then, they had nearly died of malnutrition, and Misha had never really seemed to get well. Now they knew why.

They could only hope she could be treated.

"I had a red scarf," Zohar said, sitting up. She hadn't been asleep after all. "Mother gave it to me." Her voice had a tinge of guilt to it and Hannah wondered why.

"Why did she give it to you?" Hannah asked.

"To save my life," Zohar said it matter-of-factly, as if she was surprised Hannah didn't know instantly the purpose of the red scarf.

Rachel nodded with understanding. "The Siemens factory. It had been built next to Auschwitz to make the most of slave labor. Those who worked there wore red scarves and also a different gown, one with stripes." She looked at Zohar. "You must have worked at the factory."

"No, I didn't work. Mother told me what to do. The factory workers would have roll call after ours. I would stand for roll call with mine; then, instead of going with them, I would hide and change into the clothes and scarf of a factory worker. After that I would slip in amongst them for their roll call and then get in their food line. They ate much better than we did.

"Once they were gone I would sleep, then change into my regular clothes again and be there for roll call when my group returned. Then I would eat again. Mother told me to do it. She said it would save my life. She . . . she was right."

Hannah marveled at the genius of Zohar's mother and was sobered by her sacrifice. She wondered if Zohar felt guilty. After all, she had eaten enough food to stay alive—her mother had not. Surely she must feel some guilt for that. But then all survivors felt guilt, didn't they? You did anything to survive, and in the process you knew others would die. You grabbed the rotting potato and shoved it in your mouth before anyone could get it from you, knowing that it was them or you. Now that it was over, you felt lousy about it. It was no wonder that Zohar was so dependent on others, and so innocent. Her mother had made survival easy for her. She had never learned the ways of the camps, the brutality of the beatings, the need to grovel to guards and fight everyone else.

Hannah said a silent prayer for Zohar's mother and for all like her. There had been so few.

The doctor appeared in the hallway, surgical mask in hand. Hannah saw him first and started to get up. Ephraim beat her to it and offered a hand. She turned to face the doctor.

"How is she?" Ephraim asked.

"Alive, but barely. A broken rib has been rubbing against her heart. We've removed the rib, but there isn't much we can do for the heart. Only time will tell if it will heal itself. Right now there is a lot of internal bleeding, so we're keeping her on blood, but, well, our supply is so small that we can't give her much more."

"We can give blood," Hannah said.

He looked at them. They were healthier than most he had seen, but they still looked a bit anemic. "We'll have to run some tests to see if you have the right type, and if the blood itself is okay. If you are still anemic, we cannot use it."

Everyone nodded willingly.

"Wally and I and some of the guys can give as well," Ephraim said. "What is her blood type?"

"O positive. Pretty common. But you know the rules, Ephraim. No soldiers . . ."

"We're out of combat now, Rollo. We can make an exception."

Rollo looked concerned at what breaking the rules might mean for both of them but nodded his agreement.

Wally was first in line.

CHAPTER 12

It took nearly four hours. Rachel failed the test and couldn't give, Tappuah could only give half a pint, Zohar was the wrong type. Hannah, Wally, and Ephraim gave a pint each. When she was finished and tried to sit up, Hannah felt weak and dizzy. It took a few minutes before she could slide off the gurney.

"Are you okay?" Ephraim asked, grabbing her arm.

"Yes, just a little lightheaded."

He helped her to a chair and sat down beside her. "I hear you ladies talk about what happened to you and I want to break somebody's jaw."

Hannah laughed lightly. "You'd probably break your hand. Men like Jacko are made of stone."

"Yeah, well, I used to work in a rock quarry splittin' granite with a six-pound hammer. Jacko would be a good diversion."

"Will Misha be all right here?" Wally asked the doctor. "I mean . . . the Germans who work here, they won't . . ."

"Most are American military nurses," the doctor responded. "We rooted out the riffraff this morning. She'll be fine."

"You look a little short-handed," Hannah said.

"A little? We could fly every doctor and nurse we've got in Europe into Berlin and we'd still be short-handed," the doctor responded.

"We're not nurses, but could they use our help?"

The doctor's look bordered on astonishment. "You'd help these people after what they've done to you?"

"No, but we'd do it for the money."

"Hmm. Mercenary are we?" Ephraim chimed in.

"Realists. You don't go to Palestine on prayers alone. Besides, the shape these people are in, they won't give Rachel and me much trouble."

"Just the two of you?" the doctor asked.

She nodded. "Tappuah and Zohar aren't ready for this." She turned to Ephraim. "Zohar will help at the house. Maybe there is something else Tappuah can do."

Ephraim grinned. "You move right along."

"Palestine is a long way off. We need to get moving as soon as Misha can travel. Until then, we work."

"Hmm. There is a need for some help at the headquarters building. Answering the phone, going through papers we have confiscated. What languages—"

"She speaks Polish, German, Yiddish, and Hebrew. A little Russian, but not enough to matter unless you're desperate."

"Yeah, well, we get desperate sometimes. She can go with me at seven in the morning." He looked at his watch. "Which is already past and gone. Nearly ten." He stood. "Gotta run. We'll have her come tomorrow."

Hannah stayed put, afraid that if she stood . . . well, she just couldn't walk away from any more kisses. Her resistance level was all but nonexistent. Instead, she smiled a heart-felt thank you.

Ephraim nodded and walked away, then turned back. "Oh, the Jewish Agency. I'll pick you up at one."

Hannah nodded but had no time to reply as she hastened to steady a very unsteady Tappuah.

She glanced over her shoulder to get one last view of Ephraim as he walked down the hall, but he had already turned the corner. As she helped Tappuah to a chair, she wondered how she was ever going to get by without him.

And it scared her nearly into a faint.

CHAPTER 13

The people representing the Jewish Agency were located nearby, and Hannah and Ephraim were there in a matter of minutes. Stepping inside, Hannah felt her heart race as the sound of fluent Hebrew reached her ears. So few of her people knew that language anymore. Once again, she found herself blessing her father for his care in her education.

Ephraim asked for someone named Dov and they were quickly ushered through a long hall to an office at the back of the building. As they entered, a man stood and greeted Ephraim with a handshake.

"And you are Hannah Gruen," he said matter-of-factly. He pointed to a pair of chairs against one wall of the small room. "Please, both of you, sit."

He stood at five feet ten, with dark, grey-tinged hair receding down the middle of his round head. His rather large nose sat between two sleepy-looking eyes and presided over a small mouth and double chin. Hannah estimated him to be in his fifties, but the war had probably aged him like every other Jew.

"Ravensbrück. You were lucky. Not many walked away from Ravensbrück unless they were politicals," Dov said.

She nodded. "They were set free a few days before we were put aboard the last train."

"According to soldiers captured from your train, you were headed for Belsen but got caught in the middle of allied forces. There were so many soldiers riding on flatcars they thought your train was a troop transport."

She nodded again, her hands wringing together in her lap.

"Do you have any family left?" Dov asked.

"Possibly friends or relatives on my mother's side, but I don't think so."

He leaned forward and picked up several pieces of paper held together with a clip, then stretched them out toward her. "Our latest list of survivors. You will find your name there. See if any others you know . . ." He let his voice trail off as Hannah took the papers and began scanning through them. After folding back each page, the empty feeling in her stomach grew until it filled her midsection, and she handed the papers back to him. She had always held out hope.

"Nothing," she said. "How do you compile such a list?"

"The allied intelligence services have someone talking to every survivor they can find."

"The soldier who came to the hospital a few days after I was there. I don't remember him well, but he asked a lot of questions."

"As you can imagine, the list is not complete. There will be others. Don't give up hope." He laid it aside. "Each of the women in your group should come here and check it. If they have family, we will try to bring them together."

Hannah nodded again. She had had many talks with the others over the last few days. Tappuah or Zohar might have family, but they had not received visitors. Rachel's father might still be alive, but he was a German and Rachel wanted nothing to do with him; best to leave that unsaid. "Can you get us to Palestine?"

He shrugged. "We are trying, but for now we have camps in Germany, Austria, Yugoslavia, Italy, and southern France where—"

"No camps," she said firmly.

Dov was reaching for a cup of coffee and stopped, then sat back. "There are thousands waiting to go to Palestine, thousands more coming from Russia as well as the rest of Europe. The British have refused and continue to refuse to allow enough visas, so we are being forced to smuggle as many into Palestine as we can, but it is neither easy nor cheap, and thousands are in line before you."

Hannah stood. "Then we will find another way."

Dov glanced at Ephraim who only shrugged, a smile creasing his lips.

"Sit down," Dov said impatiently.

Hannah stayed standing. "What is your closest collection point to the ports of Italy or France, and how many people wait to leave Europe?"

"We have none in France but will shortly. Near Marseille. The brigade is rescuing many and have made camps in Italy. It is our best route for now, but the brigade may move further north at any time and—"

"How many people are in these camps?"

"I don't know, but hundreds more find the way there every day. Thousands, hundreds of thousands will eventually be there."

"And the British immigration quota?"

"The latest release is fifteen hundred, but pressure is mounting to give us more. We have asked for a hundred thousand right away but have received no answer."

"Fifteen hundred a year." Hannah could only shake her head in disbelief. "They will kill as many in those camps as the Germans did." She took a deep breath. "And the numbers you send illegally?"

"It varies. Right now the numbers are high; there is chaos. Churchill has turned somewhat of a blind eye, but pressure mounts on him from the Arabs and others. If he is not re-elected—"

"Ephraim has told me of this. How many?"

"About the same number."

"Then a year's wait is unrealistic," she said. "Do not be offended. I understand your problem. We will find another way."

"You do not understand," Dov said firmly.

Hannah couldn't control the anger. "No, you do not understand!" she said loudly. "Do you know what it is like to stay here? To go to bed each night still afraid that they will come again, in the night, and take you back to the camps? Do you understand the nightmares all of us have because we are afraid of such a thing? No, you do not! No one does who has not lived this nightmare. We must leave this place, and we must leave it soon, or we will go crazy!"

"You must wait your turn," Dov said quietly.

"Waiting condemns us to more suffering, both physical and spiritual. The women with me have hope now. Only this will keep them alive. I will not take them back to the camps and watch them die waiting to be free again."

He glanced at Ephraim. "It is obvious you have someone who could sponsor you for an American visa. Possibly . . ."

She refused to look at Ephraim, afraid doing so would tempt her beyond her ability to withstand. "Ephraim cannot sponsor all of us. I will not leave them behind." She said firmly, "We go to Palestine."

Dov took a deep breath, defeated. "The Americans are allowing us some freedom of movement in the parts of Germany they occupy, but the borders of other countries are closing quickly. They have neither the food nor the money to take more refugees, especially Jews. It will be a very difficult trip for you, and if you do not leave soon, it will be an impossible one."

Hannah stood. "Then we will leave soon."

"Even if you get to the coast. Getting the necessary papers . . . then finding passage . . ." He shook his head at the impossibility. "Unless you go aboard one of our boats . . . and you will have to wait your turn—"

"We will find a way. The British will be forced to open the doors. World public opinion . . ."

"Is not as strong as you think, and the British are not as worried about opinion as they are about saving their empire, much of which now exists in the Middle East. The Arabs could be the force that pushes them out and they know it, so they will give them what they want, and what they want is no more Jews!" He spoke with considerable frustration.

"Thank you. I know you are doing your best, but we must try. No matter what happens to us, it could never be worse than going back to the camps. Not now that we are free." She turned to leave and Ephraim stood and opened the door.

"Talk some sense into her, Captain. She will get them all killed trying to make that journey alone."

Ephraim gave him a "you must be kidding" smile and closed the door behind him. He remained silent until they were outside the building and walking back to the apartment. He knew it would do no good. Secretly, he had hoped that the agency would convince her that the United States was a good option. He should have known better. He could see how attached all of them were to her now, and how attached she was to them. As much as he would like to separate them, it was not an option.

It also gave him a glimpse of the fear she must be dealing with, the anger and paranoia. His heart ached for her, for all of them.

"I'm sorry," he said sadly.

"It is not your fault the agency . . ."

"No, I am sorry about the suffering you have been through, that you are still going through. If only our government hadn't turned a blind eye when we learned of what was happening."

"What could you have done? Could you have fought the war differently? Would diplomacy have forced Hitler to stop what he was doing or only speed it up? It is not your fault, Ephraim. It is Hitler's fault. It is the fault of the majority of the German people, and the Poles, and others in this part of the world. And it is them that I fear."

"Then how can you possibly work at the hospital? They will be everywhere."

"You will think I am a miserable person for saying this, that surely I have lost my mind, but their suffering eases mine. It even restores my faith in the just God you talk of."

"An eye for eye and a tooth for a tooth."

"Yes, I know it is macabre, but that too is what the camps have given me. I read in your book the other night about the wicked killing the wicked. What I see around me makes that a reality. If there is a God, and He does not intervene as much as we would like, at least it is comforting to know that He didn't really single us out. The war did, and war is no respecter of persons; it treats everybody the same."

She stopped and faced him. "But we must move on. Even their pain is beginning to sicken me because I know there is a life without so much of it. That just as there is extreme sorrow, there is also extreme happiness. It just isn't here, nor can it ever be here, not for us at least. We must go to Palestine because it is the only road to real happiness, to any chance at inner peace or even a full return to God."

They started walking again, both deep in thought. After a moment Ephraim spoke. "I'll see what I can do. In the meantime, get the rest of your ladies over to the Jewish Agency offices and have them check the list."

They reached the apartment to find Rachel, Zohar, and Tappuah sitting on the front steps, a half-dozen soldiers gathered around visiting.

"Ladies, back to the room," Hannah said in Polish, and though disappointed, they responded and started up the steps. Hannah turned to Ephraim.

"I keep having to say thank you. I hope you understand that I really mean it."

He glanced around, making sure other soldiers were not within earshot. "You know that I want you to stay, go to America. I . . ."

She placed a finger against his lips. "I know, and if we're not careful . . . we must be careful. My heart can't stand another breaking."

His eyes filled with the love he was feeling in his heart. It was all he could do to keep from taking her in his arms. Oh how he wanted to protect her! To heal her wounds and never let her be touched by another evil. But he couldn't. Not now. There were rules, and there was still a war, and Ephraim Daniels was still a warrior. With that he stiffened his back, stuffed his hands in his pockets, turned, and walked away. She had better leave soon. Even warriors were mortal.

See Chapter Notes

CHAPTER 14

The doctor sent word, along with an escort, that he could use Hannah's and Rachel's help. When they arrived at the hospital, they went immediately to Misha's room. She was conscious and smiled as they came through the door.

Hannah's right hand held Misha's while her left one pushed matted hair from her sick friend's forehead. "How do you feel?"

"Like a kapo has been beating on my midsection." She grimaced. "Where is Wally?" she asked. "He was here a minute ago."

"He probably went after coffee or something," Hannah said.

Misha looked at their hands to avoid eye contact. "He . . . he wants me to go to the United States. He says he can make it happen, if I want."

Hannah wanted to find him and beat some sense into him. His action could get him kicked out of the army and would do her no good unless he really meant it, but she forced a smile instead. "What does the doctor say?"

"Not to rush. I must concentrate on getting well first. It will take some time for the paperwork and—"

"He's right," Hannah said, squeezing her hand.

Wally came back into the room, beaming, coffee cup in hand. He went around the bed and took Misha's other hand in his. "You're lookin' better already," he said.

Hannah watched Misha's reaction. Wally's breaking of the rules gave her hope. She needed hope. With hope she would mend easier, better. She regretted her earlier feelings and made a mental note to thank this young man.

An American nurse approached them. "You are Hannah Gruen?" She asked it in German.

Hannah nodded.

"Then you must be Rachel." She smiled at them both. "Welcome! We can use your help. My name is Golda Spengler. I am from New York and am also a Jew. Can you come with me?"

Rachel and Hannah grinned at each other. Both had developed misgivings during the night about Hannah's request. This helped put at least some of them to rest.

Hannah kissed Misha's forehead, then looked at Wally. "Take good care of her, Wally from the Bronx."

"You better believe it," Wally smiled while glancing at Golda. She had a bit of a frown on her lips.

Hannah turned to the nurse as they left the room. "Please don't report him. He is all she has to cling to right now," Hannah said.

Golda only nodded.

"You speak German very well," Rachel said.

"It is one of the reasons I was sent here. My parents immigrated to the United States at the beginning of World War I. It was not comfortable for Jews then, either."

"What can we do?" Rachel asked.

"Have you had any experience with medicine or nursing?"

Each looked at the other, and both shook their heads at the same time.

"Then we will help you with some of the basics. You will spend the day with me. I will show you what we do and teach you how to do some of it. Come, let's get started." She turned in at the next room. "We can start here."

A man lay unconscious in the bed.

"An American soldier hurt in a bomb blast last night. Sometimes I wonder if this war will ever end." Golda stepped forward and showed them how to check the IV in the soldier's arm, how to change the old bottle for a new one, and how to make notations on the chart sitting on the end table. She also taught them about changing the bag attached to the catheter, how to take a temperature from an unconscious patient, and how to check a wound for infection. As Golda unwrapped the wound, Hannah flinched. Though she had seen much worse in the camps, she had never gotten used to such things. She supposed it was a healthy sign of her humanity still being intact.

They slipped from one room into the next. A woman lay in the bed, her body decimated from the hunger she had experienced. Golda explained her condition as extreme malnutrition in which her kidneys were failing and her heart was severely over-worked. "There isn't much to be done except give her nourishment through IVs and hope that her body will repair. If not . . . well, we will have an empty bed in a few days, maybe a few hours."

"How many will die here today?" Rachel asked.

"I don't know. I refuse to keep track. We'll save the ones we can, but as you know from what you see in the halls and waiting area, there is no end to the suffering, and the rumor is that it will only get worse." Her voice was genuinely sad and Hannah recognized Golda as a highly sensitive, caring person.

Room after room was the same; the very worst of the sick and suffering were being cared for as best as the circumstances allowed. In the process, Hannah and Rachel were shown other things they could help with; keeping medicines, bandages, and other supplies stocked in designated cabinets. They were shown where to retrieve goods sent by plane from the United States. Other nurses approached them on many occasions, asking Golda questions or reporting on various assignments or patients. It was obvious she was the head nurse.

"We have much of what we do not need and only a limited supply of things that really matter. We do the best we can."

The waiting area revealed other volunteers talking to people who had come for help. "These ladies are instructed to ask particular questions. The process filters out those who have come only for food or shelter. We send them to other places." She looked away.

"Where can they go?" Hannah asked.

"The black market, or to the Russian sector. They have all the food anyway."

"But the Americans don't feed them?"

"Not yet, but we're trying to get the supplies that are needed. It will be an endless process and there will never be enough, but we will try."

"Why?"

Golda didn't understand. "Why what?"

"Why do you try to feed them? It is the Germans' turn to starve." Rachel paused. "Have you been to the Jewish section of this city?"

Golda looked confused. "No, of course not. I—"

"Nazis took the houses. Germans—probably some of them that wait for you to call their name and heal their illness or feed them— drove our people into the streets and watched as they were hauled off to concentration camps. Then they moved in like a herd of vultures, stealing our furniture, our food, everything we owned. They ate well on the spoils of war. Now their inhumanity catches up to them, their crimes come home to roost. It is they who did this to themselves—not the Americans, not the Russians, not the Jews. It is they who should suffer the consequences. I will not get in their way or take their lives as they tried to take mine, but I will not help them either. Your General Eisenhower and your President Truman are right in their treatment of such people. They killed thousands of your soldiers. To let them get away with it without pain will only increase the chances of it happening again. A little suffering makes one think twice."

"And if your people are also caught in this net? Would you refuse help to them as well?"

Rachel didn't respond, unsure of what to say. They hadn't gone hungry since their release, and she assumed that all Jews were being taken care of.

"Jews are Germans. The government has made no distinction. They starve here along with all others. And children, should they starve children?" asked Golda.

"They starved *our* children."

Hannah knew the argument was getting out of hand and Rachel was about to make an enemy they did not need.

"Stop it, both of you! There are no answers to this," Hannah said. "War is not so easily placed in neat little packages that allow us the pleasure of always being right."

"But human suffering is always wrong," Golda interjected.

"Turning the other cheek is a nice philosophy," Hannah said, "until it is your cheek they slap again and again and then put a gun to your head because slapping doesn't seem to be enough to satisfy their lust for blood. For you it is easy to look at the Germans and have pity. For us it is not so easy."

She turned to Rachel. "And you, if we must learn anything from the camps, it is that to make men suffer in such a way, or even be happy that they do, is immoral. If we become the next generation of kapos, we are no better than those who beat us with sticks and tore us apart with their horrible words. If humanity is not to become a kingdom of kapos, we must resist any desire to be like them."

She turned back to Golda. "Let's help who we can and not worry about who we can't, okay?"

Golda, stunned by the fiery spirit in front of her, only nodded, then started for the nurses' station. Giving them a notebook and pen, she instructed them to begin resupplying cabinets and to make a list of all items used and where they were put.

"You are right," said Golda. "We should concentrate on the living. Thank you for reminding me." She turned to aide a nearby nurse struggling to help a patient too weak to get up from the floor.

Hannah hoped they had not lost a friend.

* * *

Hannah, finished with her duties for the day, rested in the war-weary chair next to a sleeping Misha's bed.

For the first time in a long time, Hannah was comfortably tired. The work of the day had been hectic but very satisfying. It was good to be busy again, doing something beyond the job of day-to-day survival. She closed her eyes against the dim light in the room and let herself float in the luxury of quiet peace.

Wally had spent most of the day with Misha, and when Hannah had looked in on them, she had witnessed the healing power of a special kind of relationship. She knew Misha would be in good hands if Wally didn't give up on her, but she was concerned about what might happen if Wally left before Misha was released, and she and the others were out of touch on their way to Palestine. She couldn't stand the thought of Misha here alone.

Misha awoke. Hannah stood and took her friend's hand, rubbing the back of it with her thumb. "Hello again," she said.

Misha smiled. "Where . . ." She looked around the room, a sudden fear in her eyes.

"He had to attend to some duties. He'll be back."

She relaxed. "I'm still a bit tired. Will you stay . . . until he comes?"

Hannah nodded. "He'll stay the night and watch after you."

Misha smiled, then her eyes grew worried. "Hannah, will . . . will this get him in trouble?"

"No, no, don't worry. Wally is smart enough to handle this properly."

Misha breathed relief as her eyes filled with tears. "Hannah, I . . . I love you."

Hannah's throat tightened and no words would come. She blinked hard to keep the tears from flowing and could only squeeze her young friend's hand and give a slight nod. Misha closed her eyes and went back to sleep.

Hannah wiped away a tear from her cheek, then sat back down and shut her own eyes. After a few minutes she was under control again. It was then she realized that Rachel still hadn't finished her duties. What could be taking so long?

A tired Golda passed in front of the door, saw Hannah, and stopped.

"How is she doing?" Golda asked.

"Much better."

"Umm, that young soldier, he does wonders for her." She leaned against the door-jamb.

"Golda, what is it like in the United States?"

"If you're wondering whether or not your friend will be happy there, the answer is yes. If her soldier can make it happen."

"Can he?"

"There is a rumor that they are reconsidering the non-fraternization policy. Once that's out of the way, they'll establish a method for GIs to take a young lady home to mother." She smiled.

"Could it change before winter?"

"I doubt it." Golda's face saddened. "And nothing is worth the pain that will come with winter."

"Can he get her out of the country before then?"

She shrugged. "Does she have other family in the States who could sponsor her?"

Hannah shook her head in the negative.

"It will be more difficult, but with Ephraim pulling a few strings it is possible. Wally can help, but it would be better for her if he were only in the background." She paused. "Do you have family there?"

Hannah nodded.

"Ephraim could get you out, Hannah."

"I know, but the others. I can't leave them behind and none of them have sponsors. Maybe I will come later, after I get them to Palestine."

"Well, I know one man who would be very pleased."

Hannah blushed. "You know him pretty well."

"Yes, he used to come around once in a while when we were stationed in England." She smiled. "He seems to be a bit distracted."

"I . . . I am sorry. I . . ." Hannah stumbled.

"Don't be. Ephraim was never in love with me, and my father wouldn't understand if I married anybody but a Jew."

"Mmm. I had a father like that."

Golda found another chair and they talked about their families for more than an hour. Golda's family was orthodox, her father a kosher deli owner in Manhattan. She had five brothers and two sisters, all involved in the war effort in one way or another. Hannah told her about her life before the camps. She was glad to dwell on good memories and thankful Golda didn't ask about the last few years.

"What do you know about Ephraim?" Hannah asked.

"Not much. You know as well as I do that he doesn't talk about himself. Idaho farm boy; raised potatoes, cows, and horses while his dad flew a mail plane between some town in Idaho and Salt Lake City, Utah. He's Mormon clear through but considers Jews part of the family. Strange idea nowadays, but that's what makes Ephraim Daniels special, I suppose."

"What do you know about Mormons?"

"I didn't know anything until Ephraim asked me to dance one night. After that, the subject seemed to come up quite often. All I can say is if they are all like Ephraim, they're a Christian of a different kind."

Hannah nodded as Wally bounced into the room, said hello, and sauntered to Misha's bedside. Golda stood, Hannah with her. "I hope your intentions are honorable, Sergeant," Golda said.

"Yes ma'am," he beamed.

"I'll see you busted if they aren't," Golda responded with a smile in her eyes. "Come on, Hannah. One of the soldiers can run us home."

Hannah nodded as she looked at Wally. "You'll be around tonight?"

"Yes ma'am. All night."

"Thank you."

They left the room and were on their way out of the hospital when she remembered Rachel. "Oh, Rachel . . ."

"Not to worry. I saw her leave when you two finished up. I tried to get her to let someone take her, but she said she'd walk. You need to talk to that one. She's tough, but a woman alone in Berlin these days is just asking for trouble."

Hannah nodded, fear tightening like a fist around her stomach and giving her a sudden urge to hurry home.

CHAPTER 15

Rachel had been watching the house for more than an hour, the memories flowing like warm honey. It seemed like a lifetime ago.

She stayed in the dark recesses of a bombed-out building across the street, examining the house more closely. The allied bombers had been kind to the place, removing only the front facade of stone around the entry and breaking a few windows, all of which had been boarded up again. The house looked deserted and scavengers seemed to ignore it, moving past quickly as if it held some sort of curse. She supposed in a way it did.

She had left the hospital and come through the Russian sector, being careful to avoid any soldiers. As she entered war-torn Prenzlauerberg she kept to the shadows, ducking inside empty door-ways whenever she saw or heard soldiers. It was now early evening. She was tired, hungry, but determined. They needed money.

She waited. Was it empty? Was her father still alive? If so, was he here, or would he return? Her stomach churned with fear. He had turned her in once; would he do it again?

Shaking her head, she tried to dislodge the thoughts. Palestine would never become a reality if she didn't try. Her parents had taken great care in building their safe room. Not even the servants had known of its existence. Surely there would be something left. Her mother had a good deal of jewelry; her father had always kept cash and some gold in the safe. They felt the valuables room was safer than the banks. They had been right, but if it had been found as well, if her father or others had removed everything, . . . She had to know.

Working her way around the block of deserted and destroyed houses, she came in at the rear of her family's home. After a twenty-

minute wait in the yard of a neighboring house, she worked up
enough strength and courage to step out of the shadows, climb the
wall, and let herself down into the ample backyard of the home she
had known since childhood. Though things had deteriorated, everything on this side of the place looked intact. No bombs had blown
holes in the roof or walls; no tanks had been through tearing up
courtyards and gardens. But no gardener had trimmed the trees and
no water had been sprinkled on the lawns and flower gardens, either.

Quickly crossing the backyard, the sun on her back, she tried to
lift the cellar door and found it locked. A bit frightened, she ducked
under a shrub, then saw the broken basement window. Skittering to
it, she quickly reached in and turned the latch, lifted the window, and
crawled in, letting herself down to the floor. She didn't move, her
heart pounding hard enough she was sure it could be heard through
the thick stone walls of the house by every Russian soldier within a
mile. As her eyes adjusted, she saw that very little had changed except
that the discarded items they had left there two years earlier were
covered with a thicker layer of dust.

She listened for footsteps upstairs but heard nothing. Working her
way to the wooden staircase, she started up, cringing as each creak of
the old wood was magnified by the stillness. When she reached the
top, she opened the door carefully and was grateful that the hinges
squeaked at a lower decibel level than the sound of her own breathing.

She entered from under the wide, winding stairs leading to the
second level, surprised to see the elegant French chandelier still
hanging over their expensive oriental rug where it spread across
parquet floors. She wondered why the Russians, who had looted the
city rather efficiently, had left it intact.

The answer made her mouth dry. Her father was either still alive,
protected by the Russians and a part of the new order of things, or
the Russians themselves had taken up residence. She nearly turned
and ran back the way she had come, but stayed put instead, listening
even more intently to the sounds of the house. She could hear the
distant voices in the street, but there was no other sound. Whoever
lived here was out. For how long was the question. She must hurry.

She crossed the entry and entered her father's darkened drawing
room, then his study. Her father had smoked expensive cigars since

she was a child, and the smell of them mingled with his cologne, hung in the air. Resisting any thought of him, she went to the bookcase behind his desk and pulled out a copy of *Homer's Iliad* in German and found the false panel she was looking for. Quickly pushing it left, she reached inside and pulled a lever. The bookcase snapped open and with a slight pull allowed her entrance.

Inside she found a switch for the light and flipped it on. The lights did not respond. She flipped them again. Nothing. The power was off. There were no windows. Candles. Her father kept several in a drawer. She returned to his desk and found several, along with matches.

Lighting two, she reentered the valuables room and stuck the candles in holders on the shelf. The safe was directly in front of her, but she ignored it for the moment. Instead, she retrieved a key from a small box hidden behind another false panel and shoved it in a barely visible hole near the floor. As she turned it, the panel of the wall slid upward, revealing a series of shelves with metal boxes housed on each. Opening the first, she found it empty. The second was also empty, except for her mother's diamond-studded locket. She undid the pin, then pinned the locket to the underside of her underwear. It would be safe there for now.

She reached for the other boxes. No cash. No securities. Nothing. He had taken it all. Still, she was not anxious. Removing the last box on the top shelf, she lifted the lid. Empty. But she quickly pulled the silk material away from the inside to reveal a series of numbers written on metal. He had not erased them, but then why should he? The only other people who even knew what they meant were dead to him. He had nothing to fear.

Retrieving a pencil and paper, she quickly wrote down the numbers before putting everything back in place and closing the cabinet.

Kneeling in front of the safe, she paused a moment to try to remember the combination. She dialed the knob to 27, then back to 15, then around to 38 and tried the latch. Nothing. She thought again. The last two numbers, did she have them backwards? She tried. This time the handle moved and she pulled the door open. Grabbing the closest candle, she shined it into the dark recess of the safe and peered at the items on the shelf. There was an expensive black box, which she opened to find a medal—the Nazi award for extraordinary service to the führer. She quickly closed it and shoved it aside with disdain. He had probably received it for cleaning his house of Jews.

There were envelopes and papers and she quickly rifled through them, unsure of what she was looking for. She found birth certificates, outdated passports for her and her mother, ownership papers for the house here and the one in Finland. They were still in the name of her mother. Good. She grabbed a file folder and shoved them inside before looking through what was left.

Pictures. She discarded any of her father and shoved the rest in the folder. Contracts for servants, gardeners, and others. She discarded them.

Then she saw the envelope leaning against the side of the safe wall. Removing and opening it, she pulled free the papers inside: a letter from Hitler himself commending her father for his allegiance to the Reich, then asking for renewed determination in hard times. The date was 1944 and the Reich was losing the war.

Another letter, from Himmler this time. It referred to a list of businessmen, with a request for her father to write a letter about their loyalty. In these times, Himmler said, we must rid Germany of all those, no matter their station, who would not stand with the Reich at all costs.

The next two sheets were the list. Two dozen names, many of whom Rachel had known, were placed in two columns on the two separate pages. A red pencil had been used to make notations such as "Questionable" and "Completely loyal." She recognized the scrawl as that of her father, but wondered why it had never been returned to Himmler. She went back to the letter. April 30. The Reich had surrendered only a few days later. She thanked the God of Israel that he hadn't turned the list back to the butcher of the SS, but cringed at the knowledge that her father had not stopped making life and death judgements of others so casually. The man had become a monster.

The last sheet was a letter from a man familiar to Rachel, by the name of Gustav Krupp von Bohlen und Halbach. Krupp was the head of one of the biggest industrial complexes in Germany and possibly all the world. From the tone of the letter, it was obvious Krupp was having second thoughts about the Reich. Krupp went on:

Your presence at our meeting in Strasbourg was deeply appreciated. You know what Hitler has done to us, and to you. His bumbling has cost us millions, and the Reich is near destruction, and Germany in danger of losing her position in the world. His suicide reveals to us the real Hitler, devoid of the strength of character needed to bring about the Reich as it could have been.

Her father, ever the survivor, playing both sides of the fence. While prepared to give Himmler a list of those he considered disloyal to the Reich, he had been meeting with some of them. Just in case.

She looked at the date on the letter. May. Rachel felt the bitterness of the letter and derived a good deal of satisfaction from it. Krupp, her father, and other businessmen had thrown their considerable wealth behind the Reich and used their factories to produce the massive war machine that Hitler used in his fight for world domination. They had built factories next to the camps, including Auschwitz, to avail themselves of cheap slave labor, thereby increasing their profits. Now they, too, were finding that their führer was nothing more than an inept and bumbling little man, a mad coward unable to face responsibility for his own crimes. Yes, it gave her a good deal of satisfaction.

Krupp continued:

However, we are still believers in the doctrine, as we know you are, and know that someday we can help reestablish the Reich through the hands of greater men who must and will survive this temporary setback.

You know of the promises we have made to Bormann and the others. We are relatively safe here, but they are not. If the Reich is to ever flourish again, they must be protected. Though they have used our accounts to send the SS monies into foreign accounts for the present, it will do them no good if they cannot be free of allied prisons or worse. They must go into hiding so as to continue to lead our cause.

Rachel knew what at least a portion of the SS monies were: the Nazis had "nationalized" Jewish assets, plundered Jewish homes, and stolen everything from gold rings to gold teeth from Jewish bodies. The wealth that had suddenly come to the SS must have been beyond their wildest imaginations, plunder from millions of Jews. Had that been their intent from the very beginning? It made Rachel sick to her stomach to realize that the Jewish ability to make and conserve money had made them an even more inviting target. She shook it off and continued reading:

I remind you of the decision of the Strasbourg Conference wherein we, as businessmen, have promised the party that we will lodge the less prominent party leaders as "technical experts" in our various German enterprises and government entities. There the Nazi ethos can continue to have influence and prepare for the return of the Reich at a future date, where they will be prepared to serve and facilitate returning leaders. The party apparatus has already prepared the necessary documents for new identities, and those we wish to preserve at any level have been given instructions on how to proceed. When they come to you, to any of us, we must use every influence, every contact, every ploy to find a place for them.

Rachel thought of that little weasel Sperling and knew that in at least one case the "less prominent" Nazis were receiving the help promised. If this was the type of human being they wished to preserve for a Fourth Reich, the world was in store for an even more degenerate war. It made her skin crawl.

She continued reading:

Obviously, Bormann is our choice to lead us into a new future. Others have been selected to assist him, but they cannot do so here; they are too well known. Therefore, their escape to places of refuge is essential. You have offered assistance and your name has been given to them as one of several contacts. It is a task I know you will do well, even at the risk of your own life, as you have always been loyal to the party and its goals. You know the routes, the contacts in Rome. FH has made it clear that his office and his facility will respond to our every need. It is a pleasure to take advantage of the Church's charitable nature. Such fools never learn.

If prison or execution at the hands of the führer's enemies is our destiny, it will be a sacrifice sure to bear fruit in the rise of the Fourth Reich. Keep us informed about Zhukov and his plans. We promise that once this is over we will all help you rebuild your life in a new world.
Heil Hitler,
GK

After putting the letter down, Rachel rubbed the goose bumps on her arms. Was such a thing possible? Could Martin Bormann escape? Could such a horrible machine of death and destruction as the SS survive to ruin the world again? She shuddered at the thought.

With shaking hands she shoved the letter and the other papers back in the envelope and placed them in her folder. She had to get these to Ephraim Daniels.

She must leave. With sweat breaking out of every pore, she quickly closed the safe, blew out the candles, and left the room. Pushing the lever to close the door, she quickly replaced the *Iliad* on the shelf and the candles in the drawer with the matches.

Her heart was pounding and she sat down in the desk chair to catch her breath, her knees weak from the revelations contained in the envelope. As she sat there she pulled opened the top desk drawer and peered inside. Pens, writing paper, the usual, except for the small manilla envelope near the back. She pulled it out and could tell there was something bulky inside. Bending back the clasp, she opened the flap and shook the envelope. A ring fell into the palm of her hand. It was her mother's wedding ring.

But her mother had been wearing it when they were sent away. How could that be? How had her father obtained it?

She heard someone enter the front door. She held her breath as she quickly put everything away, slipped her mother's ring on her index finger, and grabbed the folder before standing against the wall behind the door.

She forced her breathing to slow, trying to concentrate on what she could hear. Voices, two men in the entry, but she could not hear them clearly. She took a deep breath and held it while peeking through the crack of the door. She had a direct line of sight through the drawing room and into the entry but could only see the arm of a man dressed in what she thought must be a business suit. He seemed to be talking to someone at his side, but she couldn't see who it was. The language was German.

She looked again. The man had moved, his back to her. Her breath caught in her chest and she ducked back as he turned to come this way. She couldn't move, frozen with fear and disbelief. Though gray with age and slumped of shoulder, it was her father!

* * *

The floor creaked; then there was the lifting of a lid and the sound of scissors cutting. When she heard him striking a lighter, she knew he had retrieved a cigar from the fancy box her mother had given him for his thirty-fifth birthday. The smell of the tobacco carried through the room as she heard the same ceremony repeated and the "thank you" of the second man in the room.

Her knees were shaking so badly she thought surely he could hear them knocking together.

"Then your plans are going well?" her father inquired. His voice seemed tired. Old. Almost a different voice altogether.

"Yes," the other man replied with a genuinely pleased tone. Rachel noticed the accent now. It was definitely a Russian speaking German. "Thanks to your help, we have dismantled many factories in an amazingly short period of time. Your German women are nearly as strong as our own. The most important of these factories are being shipped to mother Russia; the others will find a scrap heap somewhere so as to do no further harm to our union. You understand this is necessary. Reparations, a lesson to be learned by your people . . . All of it is necessary." He sounded almost apologetic while being arrogant.

"And when do I leave for Moscow?"

"It will take some time for your factory to arrive. There is no hurry. Maybe two weeks."

"And until then I am still under your *protection?*"

"Do I sense bitterness, Mein Herr? You forget. You are lucky to be alive, but we need you." He laughed. "Especially now, when you and your factories are needed to rebuild our countries and make mother Russia even greater than your failed Reich."

Rachel could not see her father but knew he must be boiling inside. He had hated the communists long before he turned on her, her mother, and the rest of the Jewish nation. Even Rachel's heart raced with anger, though for different reasons. Stalin was just another Hitler, Zhukov nothing more than Himmler in a different uniform. It sickened her to think of what still might lie ahead for her and her people.

"Now, to the matter at hand. You know that there were large amounts of . . . ah . . . treasures taken from my people and brought back to Germany. We have found many of them but know that many more exist. Possibly you have some information about such things or know who does have such information."

"You have already found The Gold of King Priam, the Treasure of Troy excavated by Schliemann in 1872, Hitler's paintings at the bunker in Freidrickshain, not to mention emptying our museums, churches, homes, and banks. What more could there be?" Her father's voice was stiff with controlled rage and Rachel took a peek to see if he was about to ring the Russian's neck. He wasn't moving, and the Russian stood impatient just a few feet away. Her father must have a very important reason for resisting.

"Yes, yes, we have searched all these, but it is obvious your man Hitler socked more away. And what of the property of the Jews? Surely there was a great fortune to be had in that harvest?"

Her father seemed to relax, gain control again. "To my knowledge no such fortune exists. Every cent was spent on the war. Every last cent!"

"Come now, comrade. Hundreds of millions of Reichsmarks worth of Jewish wealth cannot have all been used up." The tone was beseeching but irritated. The tone of a frustrated man who was trying to find something he lusted for but could not seem to put his greedy hands on.

Her father sighed, his way of getting control. "Our economy was one of war, comrade Zhukov. We had no trade with most of the other great powers; therefore we had no income. What was taken from the Jews was fed into the mouth of a most hungry lion—the lion of war."

Zhukov! The great Russian general, liberator of Germany from the Fascists but no better than them! That is who this man was! No wonder her father controlled himself. The Russians would skin him alive if he so much as touched Zhukov.

"It is too bad. With the wealth of the Jews we would have had to take less from you Germans," he said coldly.

"Is that all, General? It has been a long day and, as you know, my health—"

"Yes, yes of course. I know your doctor has given you orders, but if you hear—"

"I will be the first to notify you. I am sure we could work something out, could we not?"

Zhukov's laugh was that of a fellow conspirator. "As always, comrade Bauer. As always. We will make a rich communist out of you."

"Yes, I am sure you will," her father replied. "I assume guards will still be posted?"

"Only for your protection, comrade. If the Americans could get their hands on you . . . "

"Thank you, General. I am sure you only have my best interests at heart."

Rachel felt sick. Such sugarcoating by two men who obviously would just as soon shoot the other was more than she could stand.

The voices dimmed and Rachel looked through the crack to see both men leave the drawing room.

Rachel felt the adrenalin give way, her head spinning, her limbs weak with the fatigue of fear and confusion. She waited a few minutes to regain mobility, listened intently, took a deep breath, and started across the drawing room. She must get out of this house before it became her tomb.

When she reached the door to the entry, she put an ear to it, listening, before opening it just a crack and looking for any sign of someone. When she saw that it was empty, she quickly crossed to the basement door. She closed it carefully behind her and descended the steps. She was crossing to the window when someone stepped out of the shadows.

"Hello, Rachel," her father said.

Rachel nearly fainted but fought it off. He would see no weakness in her. She turned to face him. "Retrieving a bottle of mother's expensive wine?" she said cynically.

"You should be more careful. The dust of the cellar has left footprints on the floors where you walked, and on the carpet. If Zhukov were half as intelligent as he thinks he is—"

"Ah, Zhukov. Your new bed partner. You prostitute yourself way too cheaply, Father. Even more cheaply than when you slept with Hitler." The anger, hate and frustration welled up in her like vomit. She could do nothing but spit it out, hit him where she thought it might hurt him the worst—in his disloyalty to the Reich, for which he had given her and her mother up.

Her father weakly shook his head. "I don't suppose it would do any good to tell you I have regretted . . ."

"Don't!" She automatically dropped the folder and slapped her hands over her ears.

"Very well," he said, stooping to pick up the folder. She held her breath as he opened the flap and thumbed through the items she had gleaned.

"I see you remember how to get into the valuables room." He pulled out Krupp's envelope, looked at it, then put it back, "and the safe."

"I thought I would gather my inheritance before you spent it all. Obviously I was too late."

His face showed age beyond his years, his eyelids heavy. She wondered if he was on medication of some kind or just worn out. He opened the envelope with the letters and map and checked the contents before closing the flap and setting it aside. "I suppose you have seen what it contains," he said.

"Your rich friends are as mad as you are. Your plans can never work. Humanity will hunt all of you down and hang you as the butchers you are."

"Humanity is not as involved as you are, Leibshein. Even the allies turn a blind eye. They need us too badly."

"Need you? You can't be serious."

"The Russians exploit us, and the Americans and the English need our expertise, afraid Europe will never recover from the economic devastation. As distasteful as it is to some, they keep us in place, allowing us a good deal of latitude on whom we use in our factories. Of course, they expect that we will pour the profits back into reconstruction or reparation."

"But your friends offer you as the sacrificial lamb, leave you wounded and bleeding for Stalin's animals to feed on."

"It is no sacrifice; it is an honor."

"The honor of thieves and murderers. It is blasphemous to use the word in connection with such men."

He handed the folder and its remaining contents to her. "None of that will be of much good. What was left in the family accounts was moved to Switzerland months ago, and the home in Finland was given to the Reich the day you and your mother . . . I suppose it has been confiscated by the Finnish government now."

"So sacrificing us wasn't enough to purify you from the stench of us."

"It was my gift. They did not require it."

"And mother and I, were we your gift to the Reich as well?"

He shook his head adamantly. "I cannot expect you to understand."

For the first time Rachel did understand. "Your Messiah requires sacrifice. Human sacrifice. Men, women, children, all just blood sacrifice; Mother and I were your offering to your new gods."

Her father blinked several times, his face filled with confusion. "I . . . I don't understand . . . "

"Your party god is false, Father; its prophet impotent; your offering in vain. They have not given you salvation but degradation and death. You sacrificed us for nothing!"

She turned and started for the window, leaving him stunned at the remark. She was starting to climb when he grabbed her from behind. "Please wait."

Rachel struggled and he let go. "I won't hurt you, I promise, but you have to understand! It is important that you know . . . I . . . I did love you and your mother."

Something broke inside her and she slapped him as hard as she could. He stumbled to the side, his hand touching his jaw as if shocked by the power of the blow, looking even older and more fragile than before. But Rachel's anger overflowed, uncontrollable. She dropped the envelope, stepped into him, hitting him again, then again, until he fell to the floor under her blows. Overwhelmed, he could not fight back, and she stood over him, hatred shooting from her eyes.

"There is some of your love, Father! I hope you die from it just as my mother did!" Picking up the envelope, she turned to the window, tears erupting from the corners of her eyes and down her cheeks, blinding her. She groped for the edge of the window casing and pulled herself out and onto the lawn She was sobbing, her chest wracked with pain, but she was determined she must get away from him. She grabbed the folder and started for the wall. Moments later she was on the other side, running. She never looked back.

See Chapter Notes

CHAPTER 16

Hannah paced in front of the staircase outside their apartment building. Zohar and Tappuah sat on the stairs. Soldiers were scarce at the moment, most of them off doing their duty somewhere. She had tried to get hold of Ephraim, but he had been detained at a meeting in the British sector.

Panic was close to overwhelming her. Rachel had become more dear to her in the last few days than any woman she had ever known outside her family. If something happened to her now . . . after all Rachel had suffered . . . Hannah would never forgive herself for not keeping track of her.

"She went home, I know it," Zohar said from the steps.

Hannah turned to her. "How do you know, Zohar? Did she say something to you?"

Zohar shrugged. "No, it's just . . . well, it is what I would do."

"Rachel asked Misha's boyfriend about a place called Prenzelburg or something like that," said Tappuah. "He said it was in the Russian sector."

Hannah wanted to ask Tappuah why she hadn't told her this sooner, then remembered Tappuah was the last one to come back from the Jewish Agency, arriving only a few moments ago.

"Her home is in the Russian sector," Hannah said softly.

"I told you, she went home. If we go there, we'll find her." Zohar stood as if the problem were solved; now all that was needed was a short walk across town. Once again Hannah found herself admiring Zohar's innocence.

"You're right, Zohar, but we can't go right now. The border between the Americans and the Russians is closed. When Ephraim or Wally comes, maybe then."

Zohar shrugged lightly and sat back down. "Yes, that would be better. They do have a truck."

A vehicle of some kind turned into the street and drew closer. Hannah relaxed when she saw that the soldiers were American.

"It's Rachel!" Tappuah said, jumping up and down. "It's Rachel! Look!"

Hannah joined Zohar and Tappuah as they stepped in front of the jeep and brought it to a halt. All the soldiers except one seemed pleased at the reception. He sat stoned faced in the front passenger seat.

Rachel looked exhausted, beaten, fearful. She didn't move, her eyes looking into the distance.

The stone-faced soldier, a man of medium height with a dark, ruddy complexion, stepped from the vehicle. Though Hannah did not know the marks of command decorating the American uniform, it was obvious this one was important. She used a hand to move her girls back as the soldier helped Rachel from the jeep.

"Rachel, are you all right?" Hannah asked.

Rachel allowed Hannah to take her in her arms, laying her head against her shoulder, but said nothing.

"She was in the Russian sector. She came running up the street toward our border post when she was stopped by the Russians. There wasn't much we could do but point our guns and tell 'em to keep her in the open."

"I hope no one was hurt," Hannah said.

"No ma'am, but it was a standoff for awhile. They asked her questions, lots of 'em, and took some sort of folder she had with her. The whole thing nearly blew up in our faces when she fought to get it back." His stony expression turned into a smile. "She's a feisty one." The smile left as quickly as it had come. "The Russian of equal rank and I worked it out. She cost us about ten packs of cigarettes, the folder another two packs."

Hannah smiled. Cigarettes were gold in Berlin and it was no small price. "She is worth it."

"Don't know about that ma'am, but she hollered at us, said she knew an Ephraim Daniels, Army Air Force pilot. That sealed it for us. Captain Daniels pulled a German convoy off our backs at Remagen."

He turned back to the jeep. "Keep her outta the East part of Berlin. Odds are she won't be so lucky again. Tell Captain Daniels that Colonel Petrie came calling. Tell him we're even." He grinned.

Hannah nodded as the soldier gave his driver orders to get moving. The girls separated as the four men, two sitting in the backseat and heavily armed, drove away.

"Are you all right Rachel?" Hannah asked a second time.

Rachel only nodded, turned, and went slowly up the stairs, clutching the folder to her chest, then disappearing through the door. Hannah caught up to her, giving her support, the others on her heels. When they got to the apartment the old woman helped Rachel sit on the dilapidated chair. Hannah sat on the edge of the table while Zohar and Tappuah found a place on the floor with their backs against the wall. No one spoke, all fearing the worst.

Rachel cleared her throat. "I . . . I am sorry, Hannah . . . I tried . . ."

Hannah knelt down and took her hands. The tears flowed freely then, and over the next hour Rachel slowly told them all that had happened.

She handed Hannah the folder. "Father says none of it is worth much, but the account numbers may have some funds in them. She reached down the front of her dress and unbuttoned the broach. "This may bring something."

Hannah took it. "You . . . you went there to get money?" She was overwhelmed and wrapped an arm around her friend. "Nothing is worth what might have happened to you, Rachel. Nothing!"

"Hannah is right," Zohar said. "Next to her, we need you the most."

Rachel gave a small laugh and turned to Zohar. "Thank you."

Hannah dropped the broach inside the folder. Time for those things later. "You need some rest, Rachel. Come, a shower, then to bed with you."

While Rachel showered, soup was prepared, and Hannah retired to the small patio to think things through. They needed money and the broach could help, though black market prices would bring them only a minute portion of what an item was actually worth, even one as beautiful as the broach. They would need more. Their work at the hospital would give them something, but it would never be enough. Her mind went over other options, but most of them would be illegal or immoral.

She went back inside, her head aching.

Rachel was at the table, slowly stirring her soup. The others sat about eating and visiting. With Misha's recovery and Rachel's return, the black cloud seemed to be lifting.

"Rachel, you have done a wonderful thing, but the locket is your mother's. Are you sure— "

Rachel touched Hannah's arm. "I'm sure." She paused. "There was more in my father's safe." She quietly told her about the envelope and the letters.

"We must tell Ephraim," Hannah said when Rachel finished.

Rachel's grip tightened on Hannah's arm. "How much would such information be worth to the allies?"

Hannah grinned. "You are a devious one, aren't you?"

"How much?"

"We'll have to find out."

A knock on the door interrupted their conversation. Zohar answered it and Wally stood in the opening. The look on his face made Hannah's heart stop, but she forced herself to her feet.

"What is it, Wally?"

"He stared at his feet in dreadful silence.

"Wally, you're scaring me. What is it?"

"Misha, she's . . . she's gone." With that he turned and went down the steps, the echo of his empty footsteps ringing in Hannah's ears.

Suddenly, the black cloud had returned.

CHAPTER 17

The doctor said it had been a blood clot lodged in her brain that had cost Misha her life. Hannah knew better; it had been a kapo's beating. It had been Hitler and Himmler and the Nazis and the Germans. All of them. How could one win against those kind of odds? Well, mostly one didn't.

They must escape. Before it was too late for the rest of them.

Ephraim and Wally managed to get a coffin. It now sat on the back of Ephraim's commandeered jeep, and their little group made their way along the road to the burial ground of the city.

Rachel had told them about it. Her family had a place, she said, a crypt, with places for her and her parents. They should take Misha there.

Thankfully, it was in the American sector and Ephraim had gotten permission to requisition it, making it allied property—unusual, but not unheard of in the dark days of Berlin, and it prevented Rachel's father from ever being buried there. In that alone there was a good deal of satisfaction. For all of them.

They entered the cemetery to find that, like the rest of Berlin, the allied bombers had visited. Large craters were cut in the earth, tombs and crypts destroyed. In the distance Hannah could see workers in masks continuing to rebury the dead.

"We came here first. Most of the dead have been reburied, but as you can see it is not an easy task," Ephraim said.

"How many do you think died in this city?" Hannah asked.

"Millions," he said sadly. "And it's not over yet."

They worked their way around rubble and along the cobbled paths until they came to Rachel's family crypt. Rachel let out a muffled cry when she saw the door was open. She rushed inside. There were two rooms. To the right she and her parents were to be buried, with room for Rachel's husband had there been one. On the left was another room. There had been burials there, but the coffins were gone.

"My grandparents," she said mournfully. "They didn't even let dead Jews rest in peace." She sat down, tired and frustrated. Hannah stood next to her as Wally, Ephraim, and two other soldiers who had come along to help protect their little band removed the casket and brought it inside. As they came through the door, Rachel stood and directed them to the niche where she would have lain if things had been different. The casket was slipped into the niche. Normally, a marble stone would have been placed over the opening and cemented in, but such luxuries could not be afforded now.

All of them knelt down and began to weep. The traditional Jewish mourning period could not be observed here, but the grief was genuine, the tears real. All of them truly missed Misha. She had been one of them, a survivor, but now she was gone.

After nearly an hour, Hannah signaled all to rise and was about to pass by the casket one more time when Ephraim took hold of her hand. "Would you mind if I . . . well, if I said a prayer?"

Hannah's face softened as she looked into his eyes. They, like her own, were red from crying, but there was something solid and firm behind them. She simply squeezed his hand and nodded.

He stepped forward and faced them. "When I think about it, some of you might not believe what I am about to tell you, but blame that on the messenger, not on the message. I never was much good at funerals. So difficult to know what to say. I remember when my dad died and people by the hundreds came to express their sorrow. I couldn't find the words to tell them it was okay. Dad was in a better place. And as much as he loved all of us, he wasn't about to turn around and come back.

"This is a nice place, Rachel, kind of representative of what death is like. You pass from the outside world into this room and everything is different, almost peaceful. That's the way it is for Misha. She's just in another room. Except her room is much better than this, with endless possibilities. She walked through a door that frightens us when it shouldn't, because it holds a better life. She's with loved ones who preceded her in time and have been waiting for her arrival ever since. Her spirit is strong, healthy, and happy. She continues to learn, grow, and discover the wonders of eternity. Though all of us will miss her she is only a step away and will be happy to greet us when we too enter that realm. I don't know what you think about death, but that's how I believe it is. When we're finished here on earth, it opens a door that offers a lot of promise."

He bowed his head, his hat in his hands in front of him. All of them took the hint and closed their eyes as well.

"Father in Heaven. By the power of the priesthood vested in me, I dedicate this place of burial for Misha Celivic, that her remains might be protected from the elements and from the depredations of men, that this might be a safe resting place until she comes forth in the resurrection of the just to inherit a kingdom prepared for her from the foundations of the world, and I do it in the name of the Messiah, Amen."

Zohar was standing next to Hannah, her head against Hannah's chest and arms around Hannah's waist. Tears dripped off her cheeks, but she looked much more at peace than Hannah had seen her since they met. There was something in what Ephraim had said. Not just truths, but a feeling . . . a comfort she had felt when he talked of his book or his beliefs. She felt calm, whereas before she had felt out of sorts, even angry. Was it him, his comfortable, confident manner, or was it more than that?

After a moment of drying wet eyes, the small group began to file out into the sunshine of a summer day.

Wally closed the door and latched it firmly before placing a rather ominous lock in the proper location and snapping it shut.

"We've got a welder coming later today to seal it securely. Until then, Wally will stick around," Ephraim said. They started back toward the main gate.

Rachel stepped in beside Ephraim and put an arm through his. "I enjoyed your blessing; I only wish it had come before my grandparents . . . before they were taken away."

"It's a formality we do when we can, but God is mindful of their remains, just like He is mindful of Misha's. He'll keep track of what is needed when it comes time to reunite body and spirit."

"Your God has a great memory," Rachel said.

Ephraim chuckled. "Yes, among other traits. God remembers perfectly."

"Will He remember all this?" Hannah asked.

"Probably with a flood of emotions we can't even begin to comprehend."

They reached the gate and Zohar broke away from Hannah to jump in the back of the jeep. Tappuah joined her. "Captain, should I run 'em home?" asked the driver.

Ephraim nodded. "We'll stay on this street. Pick us up when you can."

The soldier nodded, then drove away with Zohar and Tappuah. He seemed elated.

"Tell me, Captain Daniels, how many Nazis have you rounded up and what will be done to them?" Rachel asked.

Ephraim glanced curiously at the girl hanging on to his left arm. "Not enough, and as much as the evil in me wants to dispatch them without a trial, they'll get one. To do less puts us in the same class as they are."

"How many do you suspect there are for whom you would like to have trials?"

"The really sadistic ones, the ones who murdered, plundered, and gassed millions, are estimated to be about a hundred thousand, probably more."

"And you have captured how many, a thousand?" Rachel continued.

"At this point, less."

"What would it be worth to the allies to know where many of the rest may be hiding or how they plan to escape?"

"We know where a lot of 'em are hiding. They have new identities." He glanced at a man hurriedly moving down the other side of the street. "For all I know, that's one of 'em. You'd be surprised how quickly they changed their colors, their names, and, in some regards at least, their allegiances."

Rachel and Hannah were both amazed and disappointed in Ephraim's answer. "Then you know they may even be working for you, for the British and the Russians."

"Yeah, we know," he said. Hannah sensed the distaste in his voice.

"And why do you allow this?" Rachel asked.

"Because they were so well prepared with their new identities that we are having difficulty identifying who is who. It is as if everyone has always been against Hitler, were closet democrats, and fought the Nazis as a part of the resistance. They protect and vouch for one another, forge documents, and lie through their teeth about the last twelve years, but until we can question every last one of them and check out every story they give us, there isn't much we can do. As you can imagine, it's a slow process—imperfect at best—and one we don't have the manpower to accomplish."

"What if you had information that could speed up the process?" Rachel asked.

Ephraim stopped, facing her. "What is this all about, Rachel? What are you telling me? What information?"

"My father was one of them. I saw some letters from friends of his that I think may be worth something to you. There was also a list, most of which I can remember, detailing who is helping them.

"The worst are dead, or we already have them," Ephraim said. "Hitler, Goebbels, and Himmler all are dead. We have Goring, Ribbentropp, Speer, Doenitz, and a dozen others."

"The new Reich considers them all failures. As far as they are concerned, you can have them. Do you have Martin Bormann?"

"Uh, not yet. Are you telling me you know where he is?"

"I'll tell you this much: those who survived this ordeal consider him the next führer, and they will do everything they can to protect him." She paused. "I may be able to help you find him and some of the others." She smiled. "For a price."

He smiled lightly. "How much?"

"Four tickets on a ship to Palestine, along with the necessary documents to permit our entrance and some cash to get us started once there."

Ephraim started walking again, both women putting their arms through his. "Did you know about this, Hannah Gruen?"

Hannah glanced over at Rachel. "I know what she has is very important. Believe me, it is a fair price."

"Cheap, actually," Ephraim replied, "but I can't guarantee you'll get it. The Brits are getting very hard-nosed about Palestine. They have come to understand just how many of you there are and what letting you into Palestine would mean for them. Greedy, cold-hearted beggars, but they'll have to agree to this just the same."

"We are only four, remind them of that," Hannah said.

"And you can provide the identity papers," Rachel added.

He nodded, his mind turning over all the angles. "I'll talk to my superiors."

"Do it soon, Captain," Rachel said. "My father knows that I have his papers."

Ephraim looked concerned. "He'll warn the others."

"The Russians have him under house arrest. His conspirators are not in Berlin and getting them a message will be difficult, but not impossible. The sooner we have an answer, the quicker you can begin rounding up his friends. I would start watching him immediately, if it is possible."

"You will need to give me something to verify what you are saying is true."

Rachel thought a moment. "I will tell you this: there was a conference held in Strasbourg recently. The Krupps, my father, Fritz Thyssen, Kurt von Schroeder, and the heads of I.G. Farben were all present. See if they were in Strasbourg around the month of August last year."

"Your father was among them?" The light seemed to come on. He had never really thought about Rachel's last name. "Bauer. Rudolf Bauer! The industrialist. I'd heard he sent his wife and child to the camps! Sorry, Rachel, I didn't realize . . ."

She went on. "Then you have also heard he cooperates with the Russians."

"He hasn't a lot of choice. They've nationalized his factories, along with a few dozen others. Most were dismantled and sent to Russia under the guise of reparations."

"Yes, I know. He is supposed to go to Moscow in a few weeks to help them put them together again. I can almost guarantee he will disappear by then. He has nearly as much hatred for communists as he does for Jews.

"What about the factories of Krupp, Farben, and Thyssen?" Rachel asked.

"Some are in the Russian sector and have experienced the same fate as your father. Most are in our sector, England's, or that managed by

France. The Russians have been demanding that we send most of the production from such plants to them, again as reparations." His voice sounded frustrated, but he couldn't help it. "Over the last two months they have annexed land worth seven billion dollars, given another chunk of prime real estate worth two billion to Poland, dismantled everything from plants to wash basins and toilets, and sent them back home to the tune of another four or five billion—and they still want more. If this keeps up, no Germany will be left to administer."

"They are worse thieves than the fascists," Hannah said. "You should stop them."

"Unfortunately, our leaders were sucked in by Stalin. We signed agreements early on that have us in a noose now. Washington is finally beginning to see the light and our generals are starting to throw up roadblocks, but for many things it is too late."

"I have always wanted to see the Germans suffer for what they let happen, not only to us but to everyone who opposed them, but now I fear that a more frightening menace will rise from the ashes of this war and the world will suffer an even worse fate," Hannah said.

Rachel looked at her with disbelief. "Communism is not fascism, Hannah. Many Jews believe in the socialist principles espoused by Marx and Lenin. You know as well as I do that the kibbutz system of Jewish Palestine is set up on Marxist principles. And look at what the communists have done since coming here. The government is beginning to function again, there is electricity, they offer more food than the other three sectors put together. They have reestablished schools and the university, while the other allies do nothing but watch." She glanced at Ephraim as if looking for an argument. He gave none.

"The principles Marx espoused are not what Stalin forces upon these people. There is only choice as long as you choose what they say must be. You know that their shock troops, the SND, are already trying to intimidate those who lead democratic parties and force them to be quiet and do it their way. And the university you speak of is nothing more than a school in communist theory. Every course must have as its base Lenin's unique brand of Marxist theory. The students will soon realize what is happening to them and rebel. And what is the food for? Where does it come from? Why does it suddenly appear when the communists who control government want to influence the people against something the Americans or the British are trying to do? It is nothing more than a bribe, and the communists are no more than fascists of a different color." Rachel turned on Ephraim. "And you. Your government does nothing to help the new democratic organizations trying to get a foothold. You tell them to make their wishes known to the people; then you do nothing to protect them from the SND. Already three democratic leaders have been threatened, and one has completely disappeared. If you do not do something soon, the communists will take Berlin from you as easily as a mongrel dog steals a bone."

"Do you know why the Germans let Hitler get away with what he did?" Ephraim asked the question without animosity. He could see that it caught Hannah off guard.

"I'll tell you why: they are used to being taken care of. It is time to see if they have learned anything from being passive."

"And if they have not?"

"Then they'll get what they deserve. Another despot, more wars and bloodshed."

"And if some choose to fight? How can they defend themselves from the Russian armies that even you Americans fear?" Hannah asked.

"If the Russians don't honor their choice, we will try to help, but they must fight first."

"Another war," Hannah said.

"Maybe, but I don't think so. The Russians are a lot of bluff. They tried to keep us out of this city. We were patient about it for two months, but when push came to shove, they backed off. They know we have weapons that would put them out of business in a matter of hours. That has a tendency to even the playing field."

"But you have given them so much," Rachel said.

"Yeah, more than most of us who work here wanted to give, believe me, but we're still fighting a war in the Pacific, and our leaders believe we still need Stalin a bit longer. Personally, I think we should put the clamps on."

The jeep pulled up alongside them.

"I have one other question about German industry," Rachel said.

"Shoot," Ephraim responded.

The slang of the Americans tickled Rachel and she couldn't help but smile. It had taken her some time to understand that "shoot" meant to go ahead, or that "you bet" meant you were right or some such. "Their financial condition, what is it?" Rachel asked.

"Broke. All of 'em."

"And begging you to fund their restructuring," Hannah chimed in.

"Yes, but how else can they rebuild?" asked Ephraim.

"Never mind for now," said Rachel. "Just know that they are not so broke as you may think. Are you willing to check out the Strasbourg conference?"

"Yeah, we'll check it out."

They jumped into the jeep and continued their trip back to the complex. As they arrived, a soldier dressed in a beat-up German uniform was visiting with one of the military policemen who was checking papers. Ephraim could tell that the lad had been through a lot because of the war, but also that his face was freshly bruised and his lip bleeding. Then he noticed an American soldier standing a distance away, another MP questioning him. The flesh around his eye was already swelling and turning a dark blue. Ephraim wondered what was going on and said so when the jeep came to a halt next to where the four men stood.

"Joseph? Joseph Echardt. Is that you?" Rachel stepped from the jeep, her eyes glued to the face of the young German sergeant.

"Rachel Bauer. You are a sight for sore eyes," the soldier said, grinning through swollen lips.

Rachel put her arms around Joseph and held him close. Joseph, though embarrassed because of the presence of American soldiers, still put his arms around Rachel and returned the affection. As they pulled back, Ephraim cleared his throat and spoke in English.

"What happened here?" Ephraim said.

"It is my fault, American commander," the German said in clear English. "My presence means only trouble, only fighting."

"The war is over, son. Sergeant . . ." Ephraim glanced at the MP's name on his uniform. ". . . Deckert, shed some light on this for me, will you?"

Deckert looked at the American with the black eye. "It seems corporal Harmon there took offense at this German soldier coming around looking for Rachel. A little name calling led to a few punches, and real quick we had ourselves a first-rate boxing match."

"Who won?" Ephraim smiled.

"Pretty much a draw, Captain."

"Put Harmon on report and give him extra duty for the next month as a reminder that we're here on a peaceful mission," Ephraim said. Soldiers were fighting all the time, usually brawls in the new bars and brothels that were springing up all over the city and usually with Russians. Letting the men pick on wayward Germans wasn't the same and could lead to vigilantism. Instructions from the Kommadatura, the committee made up of the four different allied countries, was to leave the returning Germans alone unless they were known Nazis and on the blacklist. All but the Russians were doing their best, at least in principle. The communists considered anyone in a German uniform a fascist and roughed them up to force them out of their sector.

"Yes, sir." The MP turned and signaled for his partner to bring Harmon along and they headed down the street.

"How did you know I was here?" Rachel asked Joseph.

"I saw you near your father's house. You were running away and reached the Russian-American gate before I could catch you." He looked away. "The Russians have never taken a liking to us, so I stayed back. Later, after I got out of the Russian sector, I asked the Americans at the guard station if they knew where you had been taken. They told me to come here."

Rachel touched his bruised face and he grimaced. "Come, let's take care of you," Rachel said, leading him up the steps. They disappeared through the door.

"This could be trouble," Ephraim said.

"His uniform is Wehrmacht, regular army. He was probably not involved in atrocities," Hannah said hopefully.

"We've got reports of civilian atrocities under Wehrmacht commanders. We know what units they led and we are holding all soldiers accountable."

"Were these atrocities against Jews?" Hannah asked, a sadness in her voice.

"At the end of the war, the SS needed help emptying the eastern camps. Units of the Wehrmacht were involved. Then there were villages in Greece . . . men, women, children."

He turned toward his jeep. "I need to get to a meeting. I'll let you know."

"And the information Rachel gave you?" Hannah asked.

"The meeting I'm going to is the place to bring it up." He smiled. "You look very good today, Hannah Gruen." He had started the vehicle and was gone before Hannah could chase away the blush.

CHAPTER 18

Joseph and Rachel sat on the small balcony, their backs propped against the wall. Rachel had spent the last hour telling Joseph about her father's betrayal, the camps, her survival, and the desire to go to Palestine. She and Joseph had known each other since they were twelve years old and Joseph had always been someone she could talk to, except at the end when she had been run out of school. Of all her friends, he was the one she had expected to come and at least say good-bye, but he didn't. Then, once she was home, she had hoped every day that he would come to the house. He never did.

"When we were at school and it was discovered I was a Jew, why didn't you come?"

Joseph stared at the wrecked building across the street. Everything was so foreign to him. It was like living in a nightmare that never ended. "I was afraid. It is no excuse, but it is the truth."

"But I thought of all people, you would not desert me." There was a bitter edge to her voice she couldn't help. He had deserted her, and they had been close. Most thought they would surely marry. Now she was confused about those feelings. She couldn't be as angry as she thought she would be, and yet she couldn't forgive him either.

"I am sorry. I have been sorry every day of my life since then." He stood, brushed off his pants from habit because it made no difference to cleanliness, and stood at the rail. "When the Americans set us free and told us to go home, I had to go through Bergen Belsen. I had heard of the camps, but I refused to believe. I stopped at a village nearby to beg food and ran into a soldier I knew two years ago. He had been transferred to work in the camps. He was sitting in the middle of the road, mumbling senselessly about . . . about what he had done. I could not get him to move, though I tried. He just sat there, rocking back and forth and speaking gibberish. He had lost his mind. Then I knew all the stories were true."

"Did you go into the camp?" she asked softly.

He nodded sadly. "Even though the dead are all buried now there are still skeletons in the furnaces and the gas chambers. It made me sick to my stomach and I retched until nothing was left. And the smell . . . dear God, the smell of death hung in the air like . . . like a cloud!" He bit his lip, turning to face her, blinking to try to keep the tears from flowing again. "I thought of you, Rachel. I thought of how horrible it must have been for you, and I swore I would kill your father for what he had brought upon you. I left Belsen and came to Berlin as quickly as my weak condition would allow. When I found a pistol I could buy on the black market for the gold watch my father gave me, I went to your father's house." He stooped down, looking straight into her eyes. "That is when I saw you. I could not believe my eyes. I thought I was dreaming. By the time it dawned on me that it was not a dream, you were already too far ahead for me to catch."

"You would have killed him?" she whispered.

"I would have tried."

"He is not worth it, Joseph. Forget him," Rachel said.

"You saw him that day?"

She nodded. "He is still a believer. Fanatically so. He will never change." Her words were caustic.

There was silence between them for a time before Joseph sat back down beside her. "What happened to us, Rachel? What happened to the dreams of a better world with Germany as benevolent fatherland? Everything seemed so good at first!"

Rachel thought back to those days. It had started out innocently, but then, slowly, like an insipid cancer, the gospel of hate crept through society until they were too sick to be healed without radical surgery.

"Germany is sick, Joseph. Sick and dying. She stinks of it and the whole world retches at her stench."

"Then we must save her," Joseph said in anguish. "We must." He slammed his palm down on the rail in frustration.

"The communists are trying. If you wish to help, they will surely take you under their wing."

"The communists?" He said it with obvious disbelief. "I have seen what the communists do when they take over. If the communists are not stopped, the sickness will spread from the body of Germany to her spirit."

"You sound like Ephraim Daniels," she said.

"The American commander. Then Ephraim Daniels is a wise man. Believe me, Rachel, the Stalinists will finish what Hitler could not."

There was a feeling in his words that gave Rachel the chills, and she knew there was something behind them besides an adversity toward Marxist theory. "What happened?" she asked, placing a hand over his.

He took a deep breath, gripping her fingers in his. "When I first entered the army three years ago, I was sent to the eastern front. At the battle of Leningrad I was captured and sent to a prisoner of war camp near Moscow. They put most of the prisoners on trains headed for Siberia where they would work in mines and factories. Later, I was told by a Russian that none would ever return.

"A few of us were kept in the camp near Moscow. We were guinea pigs for the Communists who believed that with proper—shall we say, treatments—they could make anyone a believer."

"I do not understand," Rachel said.

Joseph rubbed his forehead as if it ached. "The Stalinists believe that you can manipulate the mind. They experimented on us. Electro-shock therapy, hours without sleep while pounding our minds with endless Marxist-Leninist theory. Torture to force us to get in line and follow, be disciplined, become believers. We broke, we cried, we swore we were believers. They broke us down and then tried to rebuild us after their own image. I decided early on that I would never survive if I did not play their game, let them think they were winning, act the part."

"You were always a good actor. You could fool all of us with your sudden sicknesses, your stories."

"It was a command performance. If I failed, they would beat me to death."

"But now you are here, alive. How did you get free?"

"After a year they were convinced that two of us were changed enough to put their experiment to the test. They let us out, gave us apartments, secretly watching our every move. We had duties in party headquarters, and we were tested to see if we would run."

"A controlled experiment," she said.

"Psychology, sociology, psychoanalysis, all the social sciences were brought to bear on us, brought together to find out if the mind could be absolutely changed, reworked, re-engineered."

"But if you knew you were being tested, it would be no test at all. You could fool them."

"It was not that easy. It was like walking through a minefield. It drove me more crazy than any of the indoctrination or torture. By the second month I couldn't sleep for worrying about what I had done that day. I would go over everything time and again, making sure I had not made a mistake. Then there was the fear of the knock on the door, of being hauled away and put on one of those trains because they knew. I wished that I had not fooled them, that they had been successful, and that I was nothing but the mindless automaton they wanted. I realized my time was running out and I had to escape.

"It was another month before my chance came. There was a guard who was about my size and build at the door to the apartment complex. Under the pretense of illness, I induced him into coming up. I knocked him unconscious and changed clothes with him, took his papers, and left the city. There was a troop train going to the front. I caught it. By then I knew Russian well and was able to pass for one of them. It took two months of fighting Germans without hitting any, running for my life when they broke through and wanted to kill me, until the chance came. It was a bloody battle. The dead were everywhere. When it was finished, I was wounded but able to switch into a German uniform, then crawl toward the German trenches. At sunup stretcher bearers came and hauled the few wounded off the field. I was back."

"And they sent you to a hospital?"

He laughed lightly. "It was only six months ago. They needed everybody that could even move a trigger finger. I was stuck back in the line the next day. We were routed and slowly forced west in retreat. Then my unit was sent south to fight the Americans. It was there I was captured."

"When was that?"

"Five months ago. I've been in a prisoner of war camp since."

"And they let you go?"

"I was not on any of their lists. Others were. They stayed. Some were taken to prison. All SS were held. They consider them the butchers. The Wehrmacht, the Flying Corp, all the fighting machinery had names on their lists, but men like me, men of low rank, they let go."

She squeezed his hand. "I am glad you are safe, Joseph. How about the others, our old friends? Have you heard what has happened to them?"

"I went past some of their homes, past my own home; they are all empty, deserted, destroyed. I found Gerta searching the rubble. I hardly recognized her."

Gerta. The most beautiful of their circle, and the most proud. It had been Gerta who had immediately denounced Rachel at the school. She felt both satisfaction and sadness. There was a part of her that still demanded—even needed—revenge, but there was another part, the part that had been tortured and beaten and nearly destroyed, that was beginning to feel sorrow again. Sorrow even for Gerta. She wondered how the spoiled daughter of a rich landowner could ever survive in these harsh conditions. Ironic. Not being a Jew had only delayed her suffering.

"And you do not know what happened to your parents?"

"Mother died just after you were taken away. She had always been sickly. Father was working at the plant when it was bombed by the Americans or the British—who knows for sure? Gerta said he was never found."

Rachel knew there were no brothers or sisters. His mother had contracted her illness shortly after Joseph's birth. There had been no more children.

Rachel felt like she was in a dream. She had loved Joseph since they were small, but she had put him out of her mind when he had deserted her, and now here they were, together again. And yet it was not the same. It would never be the same. Though their lives and the lives of many others had been closely intertwined for so long, there was nothing now but threads, pieces of beaten tapestry from which the beauty and luster had faded, then disappeared.

"Where are you staying?" she asked, getting to her feet.

"The cellar of what was my father's house." He joined her.

"And how do you survive?"

"The Americans gave us occupation currency when they freed us. I have a little left." He shrugged. "I have a strong back. There is work for men with strong backs."

They left through the apartment and said their good-byes on the steps. "It was good to see you again." She smiled.

"And you. When will you leave for Palestine?"

"No more than a month, maybe less." She stared at the ground.

"Can I see you again?" he asked.

She looked into his eyes. She wanted to say yes, but something inside kept her from it. "There are some things better left in the past," she responded.

There was disappointment in his eyes, mingled with understanding. He turned and walked down the street, his shoulders slumped with the weight of the past. Some of the weight she was sure he didn't ask for and didn't deserve. She realized that she was part of that weight, part of what he carried and needed to get rid of.

"Joseph," she said.

He turned back.

"I work at the hospital in the American sector. You will need medicine for your wounds."

He smiled, waved, and moved on, his gait a little quicker, his shoulders less slumped.

For the first time Rachel felt some of her own weight blow away in the late summer wind. She closed her eyes and relished the moment. She had forgotten that such feelings even existed.

Tappuah descended the steps with a bounce in her gait, gave Rachel a smiling hello, and started down the street.

"Where are you going?" Rachel asked.

"Gunther, our resident cellist who is allowing us to sleep in his house, has made arrangements for me to use the piano at the officer's club. I am going to practice." She waved.

"Be careful, and don't be gone after dark," Rachel called after her friend.

Tappuah didn't turn back but smiled. Rachel and Hannah were like mother hens, scurrying about, trying to keep the flock together. She was grateful for their concern but she was a big girl, probably the oldest of the group, and fully capable of taking care of herself. She was nowhere near the Russian sector, and the Americans were much more humane to women. Sure, they would try to pick her up—secretly, she would be offended if they did not—but they would not force themselves on her. Anyone who did would immediately be taken into custody by the American military police and given a few days in a cell to cool down. If they did worse to the women, they would be court martialed and imprisoned. Everyone knew the rules.

She and Gunther had become friends. The old gentleman was truly an artist; their discussions of music were long and very enjoyable to Tappuah. She loved music nearly as much as she loved life, and to be able to get back to it again gave her an excitement she had not felt since her last concert in Warsaw.

She came into Kurfursten Damm with its hustle and bustle. As the center of the burgeoning black market, every sort of transaction was taking place. Soldiers were trading food and cigarettes for jewelry, Nazi souvenirs, and anything else of value. They had nylon stockings, perfumes, cosmetics, and other items that might help them pick up German women. It was the one thing that saddened Tappuah—women selling themselves for nothing more than a pair of silk stockings or a pack of cigarettes. Their virtue had become their most sellable commodity.

A GI sidled up to her and gave his pitch; she smiled and waved a hand of dismissal. She kept her eyes straight ahead, her gait even but quick.

After a few moments' walk and three more proposals for a good time, the bustle turned into a wasteland as she approached the center of the city. Groups of people were at work cleaning up the rubble and hauling it away, filling craters in the streets, and trying to make a way clear for streetcars to run again. She hoped it would be soon. It was a long walk from their quarters in Dahlem to the theater. She turned left and walked into the street where the officers club was. The military policeman stopped her at the door, then checked the note Gunther had gotten for her. He motioned her on and she entered the reception area of the Berlin Theater. She had heard of this place and knew it had once been one of the finest halls in Berlin. The Americans had requisitioned it immediately for their officers to use because it was still in fairly good condition. Then they had hired workmen to begin rebuilding and refurbishing it for use. As she walked through the reception area and into the great hall, she observed a dozen men working on different projects. The most notable was the cleaning of carpet and walls, and the repair of the roof at the far end of the building.

She entered the concert hall to find little damage. Chairs of dark red cloth sat in their rows ready for the next audience, and there was a stage at the far end, the gold curtains drawn to the fully open position. She could see that the music stands and chairs were in place in the orchestra pit, but the players had finished for the day and a single individual sat at a table going over some music and papers. He was about average height, his hair blond with a grey tint around the ears. His beard and moustache were appropriately cared for, and he wore spectacles on the end of his nose. She walked to his table and introduced herself.

The man sat back in his chair, removing his spectacles as he did. "Yes, Gunther discussed you with me. You are welcome to use the piano." He glanced at the grand piano to his left. "It is one of the few very good ones that survived the bombs."

"You must be Andrik Mendel."

He nodded, his lips turning at the corners of his mouth in a slight smile, his cold blue eyes glinting even in the dim light.

"Gunther says you are a great conductor, that you will bring the very best music back to Germany," she said.

"Gunther is too kind, but music is my love, my only love really," he responded. "You had better do your playing. Another is coming soon to help me with a new score we are putting together." He leaned forward and scanned his music as Tappuah went to the stage, then to the piano.

She sat, her hands shaking with excitement. Taking a deep breath, she placed her fingers on the keys and began playing something simple, allowing herself the luxury of warming to the joy of the sound that erupted from the instrument. The hall was suddenly filled with the music she had learned to love, the notes coming back to her memory as if they had never left, her fingers automatically gliding over the keys, pouncing on some and gently caressing others. She went to more difficult pieces from Bach, Beethoven, and Tchaikovsky. She played something from all the great composers until her arms ached so terribly she simply could not go on.

Letting the last sounds of the piano drift away to the far corners of the hall, she finally lifted her fingers reverently from the keys. The applause came from two sets of hands and she turned to give a slight bow, a grin spreading quickly across her face. She looked up to see Andrik standing, a pleased look on his face. Next to him was Ephraim Daniels.

She stood up and walked to the steps, then down to where the two men stood. Ephraim offered her a chair and the three of them sat down.

"Gunther did not tell me you were so very talented," Andrik said with genuine appreciation.

"Now *you* are being too kind. I made many mistakes, but with time . . . may I come again tomorrow?"

"Yes, of course, but it will need to be before noon. The Americans will open it for their officers after that time."

She nodded. "I will come at nine then."

"How would you like to give a concert?" Ephraim asked.

The proposal took her breath away. "Me? Thank you; it is very flattering. But I will need weeks to go over the music, relearn it well enough to play in front of others."

"I'll give you ten days," Ephraim said seriously. "A group of American congressmen is coming to Berlin. They need to hear you along with Andrik and the orchestra."

"Andrik I am sure is ready, but— "

"You can be ready," Andrik said. "I will help if you want."

Tappuah was overwhelmed. "But why me?"

"Because you are the best we have heard, and because the congress is debating a bill to support a return of your people to Palestine. The British are lobbying that we get in line behind them and support their decision to keep immigration at present levels. We need to convince them that saving your people is a worthwhile endeavor." Ephraim smiled.

Tappuah looked at Andrik, confused. "My people? But, I did not know you were Jewish."

"I am not, but I was a part of an underground operation that fought Hitler and survived. We saved several hundred Jews from the gas chambers by creating false documents they used to get out of the country. I think the Americans see me as a good ambassador for continued support of your cause."

"That is why you know Gunther," she said.

He nodded. "I believe in a homeland for your people, and I am willing to use my talents to help that happen." He leaned forward, shoving some papers across the table. "That is the music of Beethoven's piano concerto number one. Do you know it?"

"Of course, but—"

"Do you know all of it?"

"Once, yes, I knew all of it. It was the last piece I played at a concert in Warsaw just . . . just before they took us to the camps. I . . . it has very bad memories attached to it. Can we pick another?"

Andrik sat back. "Of course, but take the music. Try it tomorrow. If you cannot do it, I will have another piece with me. I would also like you to do Mozart's piano concerto number twenty-one in C major; then there are several you could do with the orchestra."

Tappuah was overwhelmed. "In ten days?"

"How much can you be ready for?" Andrik said, smiling.

It suddenly dawned on her that she had been set up. Gunther's encouragement to come today was no coincidence. She turned to Ephraim. "You arranged this with Gunther, didn't you," she said firmly with a pleased edge to her voice.

Ephraim smiled. "I heard you play at the hospital before you came to Berlin. Your ability stuck with me, and when Andrik said they needed a good pianist . . ." He sat back. "But in fairness to Gunther, his discussions with you about music sold him. He knew you had talent."

Tappuah looked at the music in front of her. "Very well, I will play. This piece, maybe not, but I will play."

Both men sat up, very pleased at her decision.

"The piano is yours whenever you need it, except in the evenings when the Americans use the building."

She gathered the music and stood. "Then I will begin now," she said.

The two men stood and Ephraim touched her arm as she turned to go back to the stage. "I have one more request," he said sheepishly.

She waited.

"Tomorrow is Sunday. Can you play any Christian hymns?"

* * *

That afternoon Ephraim, Wally, and those under their command laid out their plans for watching the Bauer residence. Dressed as beggars, they would work the houses and ruins around the Bauer house until they could find a spot from which to keep an eye on things both back and front. It took until six o'clock to find the spots they wanted and move in what they needed. They knew Bauer was still around because three Russian infantrymen watched the front door while two guarded the back.

Two other men from intelligence spelled them at six-thirty, and Ephraim was grateful. He had just enough time to get ready, then he would pick up Hannah at seven-thirty for a private dinner. He knew he was walking a fine line between being charitable to a friend's cousin and carrying on a romance, but he could not help himself. Besides, he had a buffer. She'd be heading for Palestine soon. With caution and the buffer, nothing serious would happen.

Why then did he feel disappointed?

See Chapter Notes

CHAPTER 19

Rachel and Hannah headed back to the hospital in the afternoon. The routine was the same and it seemed like there were more people in need than ever.

"More refugees coming in from Poland and Hungary," Golda said. "We are in for a horrible winter."

They worked to help make people comfortable, exhausting themselves in the service of others who were suffering. Hannah met half a dozen Jews who had been released from the camps after gaining some of their health back but who still needed medicines and attention. After helping them as best as she could, she gave them the address of the Jewish Agency offices and sent them on their way. One had said she also had been at Ravensbrück, but Hannah did not recognize her. Three were out of Bergen Belsen and were healthier than the others. They had been captured late in the war and had not deteriorated as badly, but both had been tortured and their wounds had become infected. The others had been interned at Neuengamme. It was one Hannah had never heard of and it made her wonder how many more there had been.

Hannah was restocking supplies when Rachel found her and announced she was going home. Joseph had come to the hospital for new bandages, and he would walk her back to their apartment.

Later, as the sun was about to set and Hannah was leaving the building, Ephraim pulled up in his jeep.

"You look like you could use a ride." He smiled.

Hannah climbed in and slid down to rest her head against the seat. He put the machine in gear and they headed back to Dahlem.

"Any news?"

"Uh-huh," he said. "The Russians are screaming about a shooting between our soldiers and theirs. Two of their men were killed. When we refused to turn the MPs over to them, they walked out of an important session of the Kommandatura. General Clay was in no mood to discuss other issues. I have some time with him tomorrow." He shifted gears. "I've had our people check a few things out. Rachel was right about the meeting in Strassborg." He smiled at her. "Hungry?"

"Always," she responded.

He turned the jeep into an unfamiliar street, moving it deftly through the rubble and finally stopped at a building she did not recognize. "This will be a church after tomorrow, but for tonight it will be a restaurant."

They climbed the stairs to the front porch. Ephraim removed a key from his pocket and unlocked the door, ushering her inside. The place had been stripped clean of everything except a desk and two chairs standing in the room to their left.

Hannah saw that the desk had been set with real plates, silverware, and cloth napkins neatly in place. There was bread, sausage, vegetables, and a chocolate cake all prepared for their use.

"You've been busy," Hannah grinned. She felt her mouth salivate. It was hard, even now, not to tear into such wonderful food. She had been deprived so long that she could not help wanting to devour everything she saw that was edible. Even after these many months, it took a good deal of self-control.

He reached in his pocket and pulled out some matches, struck one, and lit a candle sitting between the two plates. "There aren't many places for a candlelight dinner." He pulled out a chair for her before seating himself in the chair behind the desk.

He handed her the vegetables and they began filling their plates. "You know we're only complicating matters," Hannah said softly.

"The future will take care of itself, Hannah. Right now, let's just enjoy the time we have, okay?" He gently brushed her hand.

He was right. Life was too short and the future too uncertain to miss moments of happiness. Who knew what tomorrow held? Wasn't it still possible that the Germans could rise up again, throw all of them back into the camps? She shuddered at the thought, which came unbidden.

While they ate, they talked of their families, their lives before the war, the amusing events of childhood, and the differences between growing up on a farm in Idaho and in the city of Warsaw. They avoided the subject of the war and the camps, but Hannah did want to know what it was like to fly a plane. From the way Ephraim's eyes lit up, Hannah knew it really was his first love.

"I would like to fly someday," she said.

"I'll see what I can do," he replied.

There was a comfortable silence between them as Ephraim cut the cake and put a generous piece on each of their plates. Then he pulled a small candle from the drawer and stuck it in Hannah's piece of cake before lighting it.

"Happy birthday," he said, kissing her on the cheek.

She had forgotten. Completely, totally forgotten. "But how . . . how did you know?"

He moved his chair around the desk and next to hers. "Max told me before he left. Gave me instructions to see that you got this gift." He pulled a package from the same drawer the candle had been in. She went to grab it but he pulled it back. "You have to make a wish and blow out the candle first."

"A wish?"

"An American tradition. Humor me."

She closed her eyes and made her wish, then blew out the single candle. As she turned to face him, he took her chin in his hand and gently kissed her. "That's from Max."

She chuckled. "Max would never kiss me like that."

"True, but if I include him, it gives me one more opportunity and makes me feel a little better about breaking the rules." He kissed her again, this time more passionately. Her hand moved to the back of his neck and she pulled him to her. When their lips parted, she leaned her head on his shoulder and held him tight, feeling his warmth, never wanting to let him go. Finally, he pulled gently back and lifted the present between them. "You'd better open this," he said, flushed.

Smiling, she took the gift with some reluctance and tore away the paper. Inside was a shoe box with a new pair of shoes. A note was stuffed in one which she quickly unfolded and read.

Hannah, I noticed you needed these. Hope they fit. Shalom and happy birthday. I hope we can celebrate the next one in New York. Love, Max.

She felt warm all over and quickly positioned herself to exchange the old shoes she had been given at the hospital for the new ones. They were a perfect fit. "Where did Max get a pair of new shoes?"

"The black market in Frankfurt is a bit more sophisticated than this one," Ephraim said, "but . . ." he pulled a pair of glasses from his pocket and handed them to her. "Try these."

She put the glasses on, but they blurred her vision. "I am sorry . . ."

"Not to worry." He pulled out another pair, then three more from the desk drawer. She tried on two more pair before she found the ones that worked. "Amazing!" she said, staring at him. "You aren't nearly as good looking as I thought!"

He laughed. "Maybe I should take those and . . ."

She pulled away from his outstretched hand. "Not on your life."

"Do you think you can stand to look at me then?"

"I'll try."

"Good, because you will need those to read these." He pulled another package from under the desk and handed it to her. It was a plain yellow envelope bulging with its contents. "Sorry, no time to wrap it. I only received them tonight."

She undid the clasp and pulled back the flap. Reaching inside, she pulled out a packet of documents with a rubber band around them. She noted they were written in English and couldn't read them very well.

"What are these?"

"Those are passes that can be used on trains anywhere in Europe." He grinned.

Hannah was speechless as she quickly shuffled through the passes to verify his words.

"But how . . . how did you get them so quickly? I mean, you didn't know . . . you said you were told nothing."

"I lied," he grinned. "You need to have more faith in Rachel, Hannah. Her information is worth a few pieces of paper that will transport you south. The rest I can't guarantee. The British will have to decide whether or not to let you into Palestine, but this is the least our government can do, and my commanding officer thinks so too."

With a yelp of joy, she threw her arms around his neck, their chairs nearly toppling over backwards. While struggling for balance, she kissed him hard. "Thank you," she murmured, her face against his.

"You're welcome," he said. "If you need anything else . . . well, for another one of those—"

She kissed him again, this time more tenderly, all her cautions suddenly melting away as gratitude and love overwhelmed her. She hadn't felt this way since . . . no, she had never felt this way.

He drew her closer, extending the kiss, his strong arms enfolding her against his warm body. She melted into him, refusing to back away, the tingle exciting her clear to the bone. When the kiss had taken their breath away, she laid her head on his shoulder.

"I think I'm in love with you, Hannah," he whispered softly in her ear. "Kind of ironic, isn't it? I've just given you the passes that will take you right out of my life at the moment I most want you to stay."

Tears sprang to Hannah's eyes. They were words she never thought she'd hear again, feelings she never dreamed she'd feel. So much had died inside her at Ravensbrück! So much!

Ephraim felt her chest catch in a sob and held her tighter. She wanted him to never let go, wanted to find a way to work out how they could spend their lives with one another, but knew that would only make parting more heartbreaking.

After a few minutes, she pushed herself away, pulling her knees up and hugging them against her chest. "I love you too, Ephraim, but . . ."

Ephraim got up and helped her to her feet, then took her in his arms, holding her close. He knew it would end with them living on two separate continents. He also knew he shouldn't even be considering a relationship with someone outside his faith. It would never work. But he was falling in love, and he couldn't seem to stop the fall. Even though he knew she was starting to think seriously about God again, had even seen her reaction in the cemetery, he knew she was a long way from conversion.

For the longest time they held each other, then kissed one more time before beginning to put away the dishes and food. Being with Hannah felt so comfortable that he dreaded even these moments to end, and the thought of letting her go made him shudder.

But he pushed the thought away. There was still time to be together. Though he knew it would make any separation harder, he couldn't hold back his feelings. He loved her. He could only pray that when it came time to say good-bye, he could pull away and she would understand.

They walked in silence until they reached his jeep. Once they were both in their seats, he started the vehicle. Turning on the lights, he pulled into the nearly empty street. After driving several blocks and reaching Kurfursten Damm Street where they were to turn right, Ephraim turned left.

"Where are we going?" she asked.

"Oh, just to make a couple of deliveries," he said.

They spent five minutes in travel before he pulled up in front of a two-story house. A young boy emerged from the shadows and scrambled to the jeep as if he had been waiting. Ephraim stopped only long enough for the boy to reach under the tarp in the back of the jeep, remove a hefty box, and quickly take it into the house. Not a word was said.

As they drove away, Hannah glanced back over her shoulder to see half a dozen others emerge and begin removing items from the box.

"Food?"

Ephraim only smiled as he turned right, then left again. Ephraim pulled up in front of a bombed-out building, and a man limped to the jeep and removed a second box. Ephraim had to wait a moment before moving on. The man slid the box toward the steps until another emerged from the wreckage and helped him lift and carry the box up the stairs and into the dark, half-destroyed building.

"Franz Zehlendorf. He knew Von Staufenberg and several of the other generals who tried to assassinate Hitler; in fact, he was one of Staufenberg's aides at the end. He knows things most people don't and is helping us locate Goering. He has to eat but he can't work, so we help out here and there."

"Someone actually tried to get rid of Hitler?" asked Hannah incredulously.

"We knew they were trying, even made contact with a couple of 'em, made a deal if they got Hitler out of the way." He paused, his face sad. "But the man had the luck of the Irish. Take Von Staufenberg, for example. He put his bomb under the table where Hitler was seated. When he left the room, he didn't realize there was a very heavy oak panel between the bomb and Hitler, which deflected most of the blow. Several others were killed, and Hitler was injured but still kicking. Von Staufenberg called the others who were in on the plot and told them the deed was done, and they started to make their plans to take over; then word got out that Hitler had survived and everybody scrambled for cover. Von Staufenberg and others took the brunt of Hitler's fury and were killed. Franz was tortured and spent the rest of the war in a concentration camp—he had a strong back and they needed laborers. He helped dig underground tunnels at Berga, along with captured GIs, misfits, and the like. They were trying to move their armaments factories underground. We got here first."

"And Franz, how did he escape?"

"In April the Nazis marched their prisoners south. It was a march designed to promote death. Little food and water, circuitous routes over hazardous terrain. On a break, Franz and a couple of others went into the trees to urinate and just kept going. The soldiers guarding them were old guys, home-guard types who were as tired as their prisoners. They didn't follow. The escapees found shelter in a farmer's haystack, too weak to go any further. The next morning, Franz's companions were dead. He was close to following when the farmer found him and fed him. After regaining his strength, Franz came home. He showed up at our headquarters yesterday."

"And the boy? The first delivery?"

"It isn't the boy; it's his mother. She was one of the clerks in the chancellery. Right now she's going through documents we think are important but don't have enough knowledge to know for sure. A lot of them are in German shorthand that only someone with her skills can understand. We found out this afternoon that she has tuberculosis. The box had medicines and food for the German doctor and his family who are taking care of her."

The next stop was fifteen minutes away. The house was small and Hannah could tell from the dim light through a broken window that only a candle was burning for light. This time Ephraim pulled up and shut off the jeep. "A lot of these people are only beginning to accept what really happened to people considered enemies of the state. They refused to believe it, to their everlasting shame they refused. But now they try to help where they can."

"But surely a man in the position of Franz Zehlendorf would have known."

"Yeah, Franz knew; it was one of the reasons he helped Von Staufenberg. Though Von Staufenberg's motives were less noble, he knew they couldn't win the war as long as Hitler kept meddling, over-ruling his generals and overextending his troops. However, they both had the right idea, and both would have ended the death camps.

"And this place? Who lives here?"

He got out of the jeep and went around, taking her hand. "His name is Krueger, Leo Krueger. He was interned in the Ghetto at Theresienstadt." After Ephraim retrieved a box of groceries, they approached the door and Ephraim knocked lightly.

"I have never heard of this city," Hannah said.

"It is the German name. You probably know it as Terezin."

"Yes, this city I know," she said. She remembered her father being told about Terezin early in the war—1941 as she remembered. It had been advertised as a gift Hitler would give the Jews. Admission rights were sold to privileged Jews in Germany and Poland. She had known a woman at Ravensbrück who had been sent there from Terezin. It had all been a hoax. As soon as they arrived they were stripped of everything, and the fortress fortified by the Prussians in the 1700s had become their prison.

The door opened and a hunched man with nearly silver hair stood in the opening. Hannah could not see his face clearly because the candlelight was at his back, but she guessed it was worn and creased from hardship and pain.

"Ah, Ephraim Daniels, my friend. Come in, come in," he said. The voice was warm and friendly, even inviting. Hannah got the distinct impression that, though the body of this man had deterio-rated in the camps, his spirit had survived, strong and vibrant.

They stepped past Leo Krueger into the comfortable room. A candle sat in the middle of the table and several books lay open around it. Hannah felt the warmth of a fire in the fireplace and noticed wood, which had been gleaned from bombed-out houses and buildings, stacked in a corner. There were several chairs around the table and a mattress with blankets and a pillow on the floor near the fireplace.

"Leo, this is Hannah Gruen, survivor of Ravensbrück," Ephraim said.

Leo extended a hand and took Hannah's. He kissed it lightly, then enfolded it in both of his. "Ravensbrück," he said reverently. "I hear horrible stories of Ravensbrück."

"And I of Terezin," Hannah replied.

He smiled. "Terezin was paradise compared to the camps; we both know it."

"Then you were sent from Terezin," Hannah said.

"Few remained at Terezin long unless they were of some reputation in the world. The Nazis didn't know what to do with those, afraid prominent world leaders might inquire after them. They survived longer, but eventually, when they also were forgotten, they followed the rest of us. Please, sit down." He pointed at the chairs around the table. "Hannah, take the chair nearest the fire. Warm yourself."

They sat down and the warmth from the fire immediately crept up Hannah's legs and into the rest of her. "You must spend all day finding wood. There is so little left."

Leo glanced at Ephraim. "A friend pays some of the children to do it. We are all grateful."

He went through the box, handling each item gently, as if it might break. He grinned when he found a small package and began unwrapping it. "You were successful!"

Ephraim nodded, smiling. "A friend of mine stationed in Paris sent them."

Hannah was beginning to realize why Ephraim had suddenly shown up at the hospital with his cousin. Helping others was a deeply ingrained part of his soul. If he wasn't helping, he wasn't happy.

Leo pulled the first artist chalk from the tissue, then another and another until he had a full set lying on the table. He touched each gently, mixing the dusts of different colors together in his fingers. "How . . . how can I thank you, my friend?"

"We've already discussed that."

Leo looked at Hannah. "This is the woman?"

"It is." Ephraim grinned at Hannah's bewilderment.

"I am an artist, Hannah Gruen. Your captain here wants me to make a portrait of you."

Hannah flushed and was near tears at the same time. "A . . . a portrait! But . . . I am not . . ." Her hand went automatically to her hair. "Surely not now, not tonight."

Leo and Ephraim both chuckled. "No, another day, when there is natural light. Come then," Leo said. He squinted a little in the dim light as he looked closer at her. "You are a beautiful woman, Hannah. It will be an honor to put what I see on paper."

Hannah turned an even deeper red, her face burning. Suddenly, the fire seemed awfully warm. "Tomorrow" was all she could muster.

He reached for a large envelope standing against the wall and opened the flap, pulling out several pictures. "I returned to Terezin before the Russians forced us further west. We hid our paintings in the walls, at least the ones unacceptable to the Nazis. Some of them were still there." He handed her a picture that made her skin crawl with goose bumps. It was the picture of a crowd of gaunt men and women in a room, lying on the floor or leaning against the walls. Some were sleeping, others simply staring into space. They looked so very tired, worn out, and lost. She understood this picture. She had seen it in thousands of faces, knew what they were feeling.

"They are waiting to be deported," she said softly.

"Yes, one of my last sketches at Terezin. I was sitting against the wall on this side of the room."

Each person depicted in the painting seemed to be avoiding contact with the others, as if each had to be alone while they awaited their fate without hope. It made Hannah ache inside. A tear suddenly reached the corner of her eyes. All the horrors of being ripped from everything she had known suddenly came back to her: the loneliness, the realization that no one could stop what was about to happen, no one could change it, that you had absolutely no control of your fate. She had to remove her new glasses as Ephraim handed her his handkerchief. Replacing the glasses, she laid the picture down on the table, then gently ran her fingers over the outlines of each person in the picture. "Where were you taken?" she asked.

"Auschwitz, Sachshausen, then Mathhausen. I was released from there."

"And these people?"

"To my knowledge, none survived Auschwitz."

"The world must see such paintings," Hannah said softly.

"This envelope contains the paintings hidden at Terezin as well."

"We've given instructions to search other camps under our control," Ephraim said.

Hannah only nodded, her eyes on the picture in front of her. Though it moved her to tears, it seemed to give her a sort of peace, as if these lost souls were reaching back from death to tell her they were all right.

Leo pulled a small piece of tissue paper from his envelope. "I found this in the section of Terezin where they kept the children."

Hannah took it and saw that on it was a poem written in Hebrew. She read it aloud.

I am a Jew
by Franta Bass
I am a Jew and will be a Jew forever.
Even if I die from hunger,
Never will I submit.
I will always fight for my people,
on my honor.
I will never be ashamed of them,
I give my word.

I am proud of my people,
how dignified they are.
Even though I am suppressed,
I will always come back to life.

"Did you know her?" Hannah asked.

"Yes. In the ghetto we could move about easily and had much free time. It is quite different than the camps. We secretly taught the children languages, literature, and art. And we had many who could do it very well. She was one of my students. It is why I searched the house where I knew she lived."

"We had such things at Warsaw as well. May I copy this?"

He nodded. "Of course. If you have paper, we can use these new charcoals."

"I have paper and a pencil," Ephraim said. He pulled a small pad from his inside pocket, along with a pencil. She quickly jotted down the words, then handed the original back to Leo.

"What will you do now?" she asked him.

"Return to my homeland, Czechoslovakia." He glanced at Ephraim. "My friend and I see eye to eye on many things except our politics. I am a communist. He is not."

"But the communists are as bad as the fascists," Hannah said.

"The Stalinists are not the only communists, my dear."

"You should come to Palestine," Hannah said.

"Maybe someday. I understand that there are many socialists there, that they have the Kibbutz and run it on socialist principles. Commendable. But my home is in Czechoslovakia."

Ephraim could see that his friend was tiring. "We should go. I'll bring Hannah by in a day or two."

They stood and Leo shuffled to the door and said good-bye. As they walked to the jeep, Hannah put her arm through Ephraim's and snuggled in. "Thank you."

"He is remarkable. There is something inside, something different . . ."

"His soul is not as marred as the rest of us. Possibly his art, the ability to express and testify of what happened helped him hang on to his dignity. That drawing is a testimony, Ephraim. It and all others like it should be gathered and used as evidence, somehow, without ruining them."

"We've taken photographs of the ones we've found." They were at the jeep and he helped her in. A few minutes later, they were driving through the streets toward the apartment building. "Thank you for the glasses; they make a very nice difference," she said, then continued. "How did you meet him?"

"He was in Frankfurt but moved here a few weeks ago. He showed up at headquarters this morning to welcome us." He pulled the jeep to the curb in front of their building. Half a dozen soldiers with rifles were positioned in the street. A nightly occurrence for the peace of mind of the American military who were the primary citizens of the place.

They got out of the jeep and started up the steps, separately. As they reached the top of the stairs where there were no prying eyes, she turned into him and put her arms around his waist, laying her head against his chest. "I love you, Ephraim Daniels, and it is breaking my heart."

He wrapped his arms around her and held her tight. "I know," he said softly in her ear.

They held one another, neither having the strength or desire to pull away, but neither knowing what to do to change the inevitable.

"We have a saying among my people," Hannah said. "Next year, Jerusalem." She looked into his eyes. "Come to Jerusalem, Ephraim Daniels. Please, come to Jerusalem." She broke away and quickly disappeared through the door to her apartment, tears spilling down her cheeks.

Ephraim sat down on the steps and removed his hat. Jerusalem was a long way from his home in the United States. A long way.

See Chapter Notes

CHAPTER 20

When Hannah, Rachel, Tappuah, and Zohar arrived at the theater, they found workmen still repairing the place, but few others were about. It was eight o'clock in the morning and only hungry Berliners were hanging around the side door where food scraps were usually placed in large garbage bins before being hauled to a dump outside the city.

Ephraim waited at the door to the main hall, greeted the girls, and showed them a room near the entertainment hall where the church meeting was to be held. There was an upright piano and a music stand to act as a podium, with half a dozen chairs behind it facing another hundred chairs in neat rows that filled the rest of the space. Two soldiers and a young man who looked to be a local Berliner were preparing something that included bread at a small table in the front corner near a large window. Hannah and the girls recognized the soldiers as two of those who had come to the hospital with Ephraim the day before they were forced to come to Berlin. They remembered Zohar and Tappuah by name. It immediately helped them relax a little to see familiar faces.

The boy was introduced as Max Eifelmann, a Berliner whose family lived in the Russian sector. He wore the normal attire of Berliners these days—ragged, stained clothes—but his face, arms, and hands were freshly washed, and his hair was combed straight back from his forehead. He was missing the starving, gaunt look of most Berliners, and his cheerful countenance told Hannah he was probably another one of Ephraim's charity cases.

Ephraim had given Tappuah a hymnal in which he had marked the hymns to be played, and she had studied them the evening before.

They were of little challenge to her ability, but she was still nervous, afraid she might make a mistake and ruin Ephraim's meeting. Hannah and Tappuah had read the words and found their message varied and interesting. One was about being thankful for a prophet, another about the sweetness of prayer, a third about Jesus and his suffering in Jerusalem, and a fourth told the story of a wayfaring man of grief who was comforted.

"Would you like to play prelude music while people come? It helps maintain reverence," Ephraim whispered.

Tappuah nodded, stepped to the piano, and played the pieces Ephraim had assigned her. She found them beautiful and comforting to her nerves. After a moment she was immersed in the notes and sounds from the piano.

"They are beautiful pieces," Hannah said.

Ephraim nodded. "When you're ready, you, Rachel, and Zohar can find a seat here on the front row. Save one for Tappuah as well. She'll want to sit where she can see the speaker when she isn't playing."

People began arriving and many went out of their way to greet each other and Ephraim. In between arriving groups, Hannah managed to get close enough to Ephraim to ask questions that were nagging at her.

"What kind of meeting is this? Should we . . . how should we act?"

"It is what we call a sacrament meeting." He explained the process.

"This sacrament is for members only. We should not be here," she said.

"You see these people? I can guarantee you that only a few of them are members of our Church. Some are Lutheran, some Catholic, some are atheists who are just curious or were simply hopeful of food and drink. They are all welcome. Some partake of the sacrament, some don't. It is up to them. Enjoy the talks, enjoy the music, and decide about the rest."

A man entered the door and quickly greeted many people while working his way to Ephraim.

"Brother Daniels," he said in German while shaking Ephraim's hand.

"President Rausch, good to see you have made it safely from Frankfurt. I assume you will preside. Do you wish also to conduct?"

The man nodded and the two of them went toward the front of the room, discussing several other matters and leaving Hannah confused. A moment later Ephraim returned and explained.

"Brother Rausch is acting mission president for our Church. He is a native German who has served the Church very well through the war and held things together beyond what I would have thought possible." He pointed to several soldiers coming through the door. "Most of the military men you see here now are all former missionaries to Germany, like I was. They know many of these people from the time they spent here before war broke out with Poland. Some of them barely escaped prior to Hitler's shutting down the railways to mobilize the troops. Had they been caught . . . well, we hate to think about that."

"How many missionaries did you have here before the war?"

"One hundred seventy-five," Ephraim answered.

"And they all escaped?"

"Yes. It is time to start." He saw her to her seat and took one at the front next to the man he called President Rausch.

People continued to arrive even through the greeting by the mission president and the first song, which Tappuah played expertly as Ephraim led. Though Hannah and her friends did not know the words to "We Thank Thee, O God, for a Prophet," the voices of the others echoed through the half-ruined building and spread into the street. It was a wonderful song of hope and gratitude. She had thought at first that the prophet they were singing about was one of the Old Testament prophets, but as she listened to the words, she realized they were singing of a modern prophet. She remembered what Ephraim had told her about Joseph Smith and others who had followed him.

The prayer was given by an old gentleman sitting on the first row. It was simple, heartfelt, and humble. Hannah felt goose bumps on her skin.

When the mission president stood, he discussed several business items and included thanks to the soldiers present for getting the building and for their generosity in helping members of the Berlin branch. He then announced that something called the Relief Society was organized and asked for sustaining votes of several women who were in the group. They would be set apart after the meeting. He excused someone called the branch president who was traveling out of the city in an attempt to bring potatoes from the French zone. There was some excited but whispered discussion about that and the announcement that the apostles had sent a letter indicating that aide was being sent from the States as soon as President Smith could arrange it with the U.S. Government. Disappointment showed when he told them it could not possibly arrive before early spring of the coming year.

He then gave words of encouragement, and several matters were discussed about the growing numbers coming into Berlin from other areas. Priesthood leaders, in conjunction with members of the military, were making arrangements for some more housing and temporary camps around the city. The people in the room were instructed where to take new refugees so that they could get the help needed. By the time the business was finished, Hannah realized two things: Ephraim Daniels' charity cases extended far beyond what she had thought, and his church was very busy taking care of their own. She was overwhelmed by the feeling these people had for one another and knew that each was doing their best to take care of others.

"Now, brothers and sisters, we know all of you are not members of our faith. Know that we will do our best to help you as well. Brothers Sorensen, Luftganz, and Miner will be at the door to this building to get your names and give you instructions. However, it is not a handout. There is work to do, and we hope you will be willing to pitch in and give us a hand. That way no one goes hungry or cold this winter." Rausch smiled.

Hannah noticed that no one left.

The sacrament song came next, and the emblems were prepared and passed. Hannah did not partake, nor did her three friends. She noticed that others also did not partake, but that those who did, did so very reverently. As the water was passed, a thought struck her. How many of these people had been Nazis? How many had persecuted her people?

It gave her a cold chill and she tried to shake it off. Hitler had deceived even the very best of Berlin if he had succeeded with these people.

After the sacrament was finished, President Rausch announced that he and Ephraim Daniels would speak.

President Rausch's talk dealt with prayer, and he used quotes from the Book of Mormon and the Bible to support his ideas. It made Hannah realize that the Mormon way of praying was very different from her own—very personal. They thought of God as a real being to whom they could talk and who would respond.

"I know all of you feel you have prayed but that you haven't been heard. I want you to know that you have. God's answer, though difficult, is simple; as a people, Germany chose a path that would lead us to this place, and though God knew it would end in such a way, he let us suffer the consequences of our choices. In the Book of Mormon, the people of Zeniff, Noah, and Limhi did exactly the same thing. They chose a bad king; they chose not to listen to Abinadi, God's prophet. The consequence was bondage and heavy burdens. Thus it is with us. We must now handle our burdens and pray God will make them light." He closed with his testimony and sat down.

Ephraim stood at the music-stand pulpit. It seemed so short for his six-foot frame. She marveled again at how handsome he was. He thanked President Rausch for his words, then turned to Tappuah and thanked her as well. He then told the congregation about the four of them, who they were, and what they had been through.

"There was another. Her name was Misha. We buried her two days ago. The camps took her even after months of release." He then used his scriptures to teach from the Isaiah chapters about Judah and Joseph, how they were eternally connected, what the responsibility of one was to the other, and how important each was to the house of Israel.

"Some might continue to believe that the Jews are getting what they deserved when they crucified Christ. Anyone in this room who thinks that is the way of it, does not understand the scriptures and is an enemy to all that the Savior stood for. It is an evil tradition in some who profess Christianity, a tradition that even some in our Church hold, that the Jews must be punished for killing Christ. Certainly, the chief priests and other leaders of Judaism wanted him dead because of greed for power and money, and they were successful in bringing that about. But all Jews were not responsible. Like the high priest and his inner circle of powerful followers, Hitler, Himmler, and others became the Antichrist and once again tried to destroy all that the Savior stood for. Can we believe that our Lord would condone such atrocities? Or can we believe that He would support and sustain such men? No, we cannot!"

He grew even more serious. "I know that some of you in this room believed in the Nazi movement. Like some Jews of Jesus' day, you were deceived by evil and conspiring men. There is no longer room for justifying such belief. We know what they have done. We have seen the camps; we see what their evil has brought upon the world. The few have brought about the destruction of the many. Because of Hitler and his lieutenants, all Germans have lost everything. It is you in this room, all of you who survived, who must be vigilant and never let this happen again."

He changed the subject to baptism and its importance, then to something he called the gift of the Holy Ghost. He was a gifted speaker and held the audience spellbound for nearly forty minutes. Then he bore his testimony of Christ and sat down.

Ephraim's final words burned themselves deep into Hannah's heart, and she did not hear President Rausch's closing remarks. Ephraim really did know; and because he knew, she knew. She could talk around it all she wanted, she could avoid doing anything about it, she could fight the feelings, but she could not deny them. In her heart she felt a solid reality she had never felt before: Ephraim Daniels' God lived, and Jesus was the Messiah.

The last words of the hymn bounced around the hall as tears came to her eyes and flowed down her cheeks. She quickly wiped them away but then noticed Zohar was sobbing next to her. She put an arm around her young friend and held her close as she tried to deal with her own feelings. She loved Ephraim. Surely, that must be why she felt what she did. There could be no other explanation, could there? This Holy Ghost he spoke of was foreign to anything she understood, and she could not believe that something other than her own emotions were burning inside her. Mysticism was beyond reality, and this Holy Ghost was mystical, unknown to her senses. It was hard enough to face reality; to think of dealing with something she could neither see, feel, nor hear was something she could not handle right now.

A woman stood and offered another humble prayer. Hannah noted that though these people had nothing, this woman spent most of her prayer thanking God for His blessings—life, daily bread, and clothing to keep warm. Her only request was that all might have peace of mind about the past.

The prayer was ended and people stood, shook hands, visited with one another, and began to file into another room where some boxes of food and other items awaited them.

Hannah watched as many people went out of their way to thank Ephraim for his words and to shake hands with him and President Rausch. It was obvious that both were highly thought of—even loved—for the words they spoke, even though Ephraim's had been to chasten.

Someone tapped her on the shoulder, and she turned to find several women who introduced themselves and thanked her for coming. They were sorry for what had happened and wished they could go back and make things different. They hoped to see her again. Hannah noted that her friends were also surrounded by people wanting to find out more about them and what had happened. She noticed that a man had cornered Tappuah, and she seemed to be enjoying his attention.

"How are you doing?" Ephraim whispered near her ear.

"Fine," she said, somewhat distracted. "Who is the man with Tappuah?"

"Andrik Mendel."

Tappuah had come back to the apartment after meeting Andrik, eager and excited to tell Hannah about his invitation. They had spent an hour discussing her fears and the challenge of what must be done. Hannah had never seen Tappuah so alive and happy.

"Tappuah tells me he was in the Resistance," she said.

Ephraim continued to greet people but managed to slip in an answer. "Yeah. Hitler would give Andrik's performance a standing ovation on Saturday night, then unsuspectingly curse the man's resistance organization the rest of the week."

"Gunther and his wife were some of his people?"

He nodded. "I have to check out a piece of property with President Rausch for a couple of hours."

"The house we visited . . ."

"Yeah, that house. Too bad, huh? No more candle-lit dinners."
He grinned.

"Will I see you later?" she asked, facing him, her arms folded.

"Probably about sundown. You remember that meeting I told you
about with General Clay? Well, it is this afternoon. They should give
me some answers about Rachel's information."

"I'll be waiting." She smiled as he clasped her hand in his and softly
pressed it before turning to the door to catch up with President Rausch.

As Hannah watched him go, another woman introduced herself.
Yet she had a hard time taking her eyes off him until he disappeared
through the door. She faced the short lady in front of her, her mind
racing to catch up to the words the little woman had already spoken.

"I'm sorry," Hannah said. "What did you say?"

The eyes smiled and the question was asked again. Over the next
half-hour Hannah repeated a condensed version of her story a dozen
times, as did the others, until the crowd began to disperse. Hannah
saw many things in their eyes: anger, sorrow, sadness. But one thing
was always there—they had known and they felt the heavy burden of
guilt for it. Hannah never asked, nor did Rachel and the others, but
the question that burned in all of them was, why? Why had such
good people ignored what was happening? She supposed the answer
lay in the comment of one of the few younger men attending the
meeting, a soldier of the Wehrmacht who had come back alive but on
crutches.

"They lied. Deep down we knew they were lying, but we refused
to believe that they would do such things. It seemed . . . well, beyond
humanity. No one would do something like that."

Was it their innocence that prevented action? Naïveté? Fear?
Maybe all three. To Hannah it didn't seem to matter anymore. She
was tired of trying to find reason.

They were walking the few blocks home when Zohar pulled a
small, worn leaflet from her pocket. "The boy that was in the
building at first, he gave me this. His name is Max."

Hannah took it. It was in German and read:

*Soldiers on the Home Front! Soldiers on all fronts! The führer has
promised you that 1942 will be decisive, and this time he will stop at*

nothing to keep his promise. He will send you by the thousands into the fires in order to finish the crime he started. By the thousands your wives and children will become widows and orphans. And for nothing!

"What did he tell you about this?" Hannah asked.

"A member of the Church printed hundreds of those on different subjects in Hamburg. Without knowledge of this Church or anyone else, he and two of his friends would stuff them in mailboxes and hang them in public places. See the sentence asking them to pass it on?" Zohar said.

Rachel took the leaflet and read the last part aloud:

The European Awakening has begun. In reply to the laughable, audacious contention of the Axis propagandists that in a month or so the U.S. has already been badly damaged by the Japanese attack and that 'Roosevelt's dream of having a say on the continent of Europe is nothing more than a dream,' American air, land, and sea forces have now taken up positions in the north of Ireland, Berlin, and Rome. Tokyo may try to veil the dimensions of this landing and may gloss over it with sneering gestures, but time will tell who spoke the truth.

"At least someone tried to stop the Germans," Tappuah said.

"Max said there were three boys involved, and when they caught them, they brought them here to Berlin for trial before the Volksgerichtshof."

"The Blood Court," Rachel said softly. "Hitler controlled it personally. They had no chance of walking away from that tribunal. They almost always rendered the death sentence."

"The leader was beheaded, the other two imprisoned."

"If two of them did not die, they were very lucky."

"And Max kept this leaflet all that time?" Hannah asked.

Zohar thought a moment before going on. "I . . . I think Max is ashamed he is still alive. He wishes he had done something to fight Hitler. I think his cowardice haunts him."

Hannah remembered Ephraim's comment to her and Rachel. The Germans had been passive long enough. They must learn to fight for freedom, for survival. He was right. Even good people must learn to fight evil.

"One of the women said her neighbor was a Jew, and also a member of this Church. He was taken to Theiresenstadt and has never returned," Tappuah said.

"Many of their members have been killed," Zohar added. "Max's parents were killed in the bombing, and all those who were at the meeting have lost their homes."

"Their husbands are gone, many of the women have been ravished, and yet . . . they have hope," Hannah said. She let her gaze follow other homeless people passing them on the street or sifting through the piles of rubble for food and other treasure. "These are different. They seem empty, lifeless. They have been through the same challenges but they have lost all hope."

The four of them walked for a while without speaking, each deep in her own thoughts. When they came to the small lakes along Kurfursten Damm street they noticed that all of the bodies and other debris had finally been removed from the water, leaving the lake's surface calm and serene.

"I want to go back to their meeting," Zohar said matter-of-factly.

No one answered, but Hannah knew they all felt the same. There was peace in Ephraim's Church, and there was hope. It was something they all needed.

* * *

Ephraim and Wally picked Hannah up later in the day and they made more deliveries. When they arrived back at the apartment, Rachel and Joseph were sitting on the porch, talking. Joseph stood and came to attention as Ephraim got out of the jeep.

"At ease, young man," Ephraim said with a smile. "You aren't in the army anymore, and there is no need for formalities."

Joseph looked sheepish.

"I took the liberty of checking our 'most wanted' list for your name," Ephraim said more seriously, while glancing quickly at Rachel, noting that she seemed to hold her breath. "My friends here will be glad to know you are clean."

Everyone relaxed.

"I wish to work, Herr captain," Joseph said softly.

Ephraim measured his man. "My Church has purchased a new building near here. It needs some work. All we can promise you is two good meals a day and temporary shelter."

Out of habit, Joseph clicked his heels together as if coming to attention and executed an automatic salute; then he saw Ephraim's eyebrows lift and got the message. He extended a hand to shake instead. "I will work for you," he said in broken English, his face smiling.

Ephraim pulled a small notepad from his pocket and wrote down President Rausch's name and the address of the new building, then handed it to the young German. "See this man and tell him I sent you. He'll put you to work."

Joseph thanked him again, and Ephraim, Wally, and Hannah slipped past him and Rachel.

"You will like working with this President Rausch," Rachel said.

"You know him?"

She told him about going to the meeting.

"I am not a religious man, but if they let me work, I will believe in their God," Joseph said.

"They won't expect that," Rachel said. "They are different. They give without asking anything in return, especially allegiance to their Church."

They sat back down on the steps. Joseph glanced at the soldiers guarding the street. They still made him a bit nervous after the experience of yesterday. "Are you still Christian?" Joseph asked.

"I am confused. The things I heard in Ephraim's church today reminded me of my former beliefs, and he has told Hannah many things she has shared with us that I like, but I am a Jew now. It is hard to be both."

Joseph stood as if to leave.

"You were a Lutheran before the war. Do you still believe?" Rachel asked.

"In Lutheranism? No. . . . In God?" He took a deep breath. "I have many questions I do not have time to answer. Now I just try to survive and find a new life."

The door opened and Ephraim came down the steps. He handed Joseph some clothes. "These should fit. No sense you making yourself a target for Russian soldiers too drunk to see the difference between a German army uniform and one from the SS." He turned and went back inside. Joseph was stunned and only blurted out a thank you after the door had closed.

Rachel chuckled at the look on her friend's face. "Don't try to figure him out, Joseph. Just be grateful you know him and show your appreciation by working hard."

Joseph nodded and turned to leave, then turned back. "I will find a place to take a bath. Maybe I will need my bandages redone again tomorrow." He smiled.

Rachel nodded agreement and watched him walk down the street. She was glad he had survived.

See Chapter Notes

CHAPTER 21

Ephraim was back on duty early Monday morning. Bauer's house had been busy all day Sunday and his crew had picked up half a dozen Nazis with new identity papers provided by Bauer. They expected there would be more today.

By noon they noted that Bauer had had two guests. Both were dressed in business suits. Neither were pictures on their most-wanted list, but Ephraim had both men followed. The first was picked up entering a house near Havel Lake. He gave no resistance because he was at his sister's place and there were children. On top of that, Ephraim's people said he just looked plain beat.

Wally followed the second man to a small beer hall near the Brandenburg Gate. It was a dirty little place, but one that did a healthy business. He entered the building but soon came out with another man at his side. They went to a dark corner and the first man gave the second some papers. When the two men separated, Wally decided he would follow the second. He let him get a few blocks away, then stuck a gun in the Nazi's ribs. Wally asked for papers and the man bolted. Quick and tough, Wally had the man on the ground before he had gone three steps, pummeled him a few more times than was really necessary, then stuck some cuffs on him. On returning him to the interrogation room, they discovered they had a midlevel Nazi by the name of Steglitz under wraps. He had been an undersecretary in the chancellery under Bormann and had papers to get him hired back at his old job as soon as the dust settled. Their audacity was unmatched in the known world. Or was it stupidity?

Now Wally had returned and it was late in the afternoon. A man had entered Bauer's house but had not come out.

"Maybe he's going to stay the night," Wally said. He was sitting in the shadows of a room on the second story of a partially bombed-out building a hundred yards across and east of Bauer's place.

There was a long pause in their conversation as they watched a few people passing through the street. There weren't many, however, as Bauer's Russian guards scared them off. Ephraim watched them come into the street, see the uniforms, then turn around and hurriedly go back the way they had come. Especially women.

"Are you going to send Hannah home to your mom and dad?" Wally asked.

"Why do you ask?" Ephraim said, his eyes still on Bauer's place.

"You're breaking the rules on fraternization, Captain. You wouldn't if you didn't feel pretty strongly about her," Wally said.

Ephraim didn't respond for a minute. He did love Hannah, but love wasn't enough, was it? "Do you remember how we came to be friends?"

"You mean in England? Yeah, I remember. The Mormon and the Rabbi's son. Neither of us drank, smoked, or fooled around with women. A few others joined up with us and we've held together ever since."

"Living your religion was important to you, Wally. As important as living mine is to me. Do you remember what you told me you liked most about Misha when you met her, other than she was going to be pretty again?"

Wally was getting the picture. "Yeah, I said I was glad she was Jewish. I'd get stoned if I took home a Catholic. But . . . well, I'm a Rabbi's son. It's expected that I marry Jewish."

"Why?"

"Well, because . . . because a Catholic or a Protestant . . . they don't understand saying kadish, or kosher food, or going to synagogue . . . and well, they're Gentiles, and . . ." Wally shifted uncomfortably.

"Jews should marry Jews." Ephraim finished Wally's sentence.

"But you're different. You're practically Jewish, and Hannah isn't the daughter of a rabbi."

Ephraim laughed lightly. "We might both be Jacob's descendants, but our religions are very different."

"But Hannah . . ." Wally swore. "Eph, you're a fool if you let religion get in the way of marrying her."

"I am a fool if religion isn't a factor. It would be better for both of us, and especially for our kids, if I became a Jew or if she became a Mormon than to split our home down the middle and hope the kids know on which side to find their religion. My bet is that they would be so confused they'd forget religion altogether. Neither Hannah nor I want that. No, better to have a broken heart than a broken home. This way fewer people get hurt."

"She went to church with you. She'll convert," Wally said weakly. Then smiling, he added, "You know that book of yours? You might try getting her to read that," Wally said.

"You read it and you're still Jewish," Ephraim responded.

Yeah, well, I . . . uh . . ." He paused. "I liked the book, Eph. It helped me understand a lot of things. I'll even be a better Jew for it," Wally said.

"That's something." Ephraim smiled. "I love you like a brother, Wally, and someday I'm gonna drown you in a font or know the reason why."

Wally laughed but made no reply.

Ephraim peered through the hole. The Russian guards had moved about a bit, but nothing else looked amiss. He picked up the short-wave field radio and checked with the two guys they had around back. Nothing moving.

"Hannah has the book."

"And?"

"She's reading."

"You two will make it. I know it. Give her a chance, pal." Wally stood and moved to where he could see Bauer's place better.

"I am, Wally. I am."

There was a long silence between them, each occupied with his own thoughts. Just talking about this made Ephraim ache all over. He was finding out how love challenged faith, how it made you start to think that maybe, just maybe, your case was different than anyone else's, that you could make it work even if ninety percent of those who married outside the Church really struggled. He found himself using excuses and talking himself into going ahead because he was sure she would convert once they were married. Wouldn't she? It was possible wasn't it? Hannah wasn't a rabbi's daughter, she had no family to hold her, and she was disillusioned with Judaism; surely he could convince her.

Dang. He was doing it again.

"She's going to Palestine." He didn't intend to say it out loud; he just did. But it was what he always said when he got close to justifying what he was feeling about Hannah. His escape from feeling trapped.

"What?" Wally asked, turning his eyes away from Bauer's place.

"Palestine. She's going to Palestine, and nothing is going to change that. Even if I could, I wouldn't change it. The others depend on her. To take Hannah from them would be like taking the mother away from baby birds just breaking out of the shell."

"Rachel could handle it," Wally said.

"Rachel is tough, but even she looks to Hannah."

"Then she can come to the States after she gets 'em to Palestine," Wally said with frustration.

So much for that argument. Wally was right—a detour via Palestine shouldn't keep them apart.

Another silence. Ephraim found himself hoping Bauer would make a move just to get his mind off of Hannah. He was weakening and he didn't like how it made him feel.

"Maybe we're going about this wrong, Captain," Wally said.

"What?"

"The longer we wait, the better chance Bauer has of knowing he's being watched and taking steps to elude us. Maybe we should go on the offensive."

"I suppose you have an idea to back up that proposal."

Wally smiled. "Patience, my friend. I'll think it through tonight and lay it out for you in the morning."

"How long have you been working on this brainstorm?" Ephraim asked.

He glanced at his watch. "All of three minutes. Brainstorms are like that."

"I can hardly wait." Ephraim paused. "We can't make a move like that until we meet with General Clay tomorrow. Anything from our stoolie in the Russian sector?"

"I'm supposed to meet with him in the morning. He says he has stuff worth a couple cartons of cigarettes."

"Sounds interesting," Ephraim said

"Well, well, what have we here?" Wally said, leaning forward a little. Ephraim peered through the hole. A man had stepped to the door and a guard was checking his papers.

"Your turn to follow," Wally said.

"Got it." Ephraim stood and left the room, working his way down the pile of rubble that used to be a staircase. Though difficult to get down, it was also difficult for anyone to sneak up on them. A little inconvenience for some peace of mind was a good trade-off.

He went to the back of the house and jumped out through a window. Working his way around front, he watched from the corner of the building. He didn't have to wait long. The man came out, gave a bow of deference to the guards, tossed them a pack of cigarettes to share, and hurried into the street. He walked past Ephraim, who busied himself searching the garbage heap around him. When the man was fifty feet away, Ephraim hurried around the side of the building and took a parallel course.

The man never looked back, never seemed to suspect that he might be followed. Half an hour later he was entering the same beer hall Wally had watched the night before. After fifteen minutes and no sign of his quarry, Ephraim was about to go inside when he saw a familiar face come out of the beer hall. He couldn't place the man at first, but then he realized he had seen him at their own headquarters building. Some sort of worker in documents. Just a coincidence? The courier also stepped out of the entrance to the beer hall, took something from the document man, and then the two men left in different directions. Ephraim debated only a moment before falling in a hundred feet behind the document worker.

Rachel had said the SS was placing midlevel Nazis inside the temporary allied governments under false identities. Apparently this was one of them and he was providing something important to Bauer's people. Forgeries? Certificates? Maybe blank forms that could be used for forgeries.

They didn't go back to headquarters. It was late in the day and the place would be closed. Instead, the man led him through the rubble to the west until they neared the outskirts of town. As dusk was about to disappear into darkness, Ephraim found himself in a street with no buildings left standing higher than basement level and no one to follow. His quarry had disappeared.

Ephraim sat down on the stone steps of a bombed-out building and let his eyes wander across the rubble. There were several dozen people going through the piles of debris one brick at a time in search of food, wood, clothing, and anything else they could find, but the man in the dark trousers and faded, soiled, white shirt wasn't among them.

He noticed that like most other apartment buildings, these had had steps that led down to basement apartments, half a dozen of which were cleared of rubble. People were desperate for shelter, and Ephraim was sure his quarry had disappeared into one of those stairwells, his place of refuge. Nothing to do but wait and watch.

He rubbed the overnight growth on his chin. The one part of his disguise he kind of liked was letting his whiskers go unshaven. It reminded him of day after day of flying in which there was hardly enough time to sleep, and the five o'clock shadow was neglected. He looked at himself. What he didn't like was the filthy clothes. Though they had been washed to rid them of lice, they had quickly picked up plenty of grime, which mingled with the sweat created by the summer heat. As a result, he looked like every other Berliner.

An old woman walked by, her left arm dragging a piece of canvas tarp. Tucked under her right arm was a book of some kind, and her pockets bulged with other treasures recovered. She stopped in front of him and asked a question in German.

"Nein," he said gruffly in the same language. "I have no money for your book. Go away!"

"Ah," she said, spitting to her side. "Your accent gives you away! You are no Berliner. Possibly one of those running from Stalin, then? One of those Nazi pigs who did this to us? You animals burned our books, and look what you did to our homes! You should be shot for it!" She cursed him and strode away, ranting at him and the world in general.

"Hey!" he yelled after her in German. "How much do you want for your miserable book?" He said it gruffly for the sake of his disguise, while pulling a few American dollars from his pocket.

She saw the bills and her lips quickly changed from a curse to a smile. American dollars were uncommon and worth a great deal more than any other currency right now, and from the look in her eyes she knew it. Seconds later, the bills were gone with her thanks, and he held the book in his hand.

He opened it and turned through the pages to find it was written in English. *The American Cowboy.* He couldn't help but laugh. He had come all the way to Germany to buy a book about the American cowboy.

He watched a man working his way around the rubble, his uniform that of the Wehrmacht. Common. There were thousands of those around Berlin. Wanderers, looking for homes and family that didn't exist anymore; recent releases from prisoner-of-war camps with that blank, defeated look in their eyes. Most of them just boys— Himmler's last-ditch effort to try to raise any army to push back the Allies and save the Reich. Knowing what he knew now, Ephraim had come to the conclusion that the Nazi leaders had simply thrown more bodies into the breach in hopes of buying enough time for them to try to save their own skins.

The soldier looked both ways, slipped down a set of steps, and disappeared. Ephraim's senses sharpened. He waited. Shortly, the soldier came out again, stuffing some papers in his pocket. He made note of the stairwell. Unless he missed his guess, documents were being passed on from there. Or created.

It was near midnight before Ephraim started back. He had a handgun in his pocket as a deterrent to those who might want to rob a beggar for even a small scrap of food. When he hit the street where the black market was located, he found it still thriving. People by the hundreds milled around, looking for bargains, trading items, trying to sell things they had discovered during the day. Here cigarettes were king, the currency of the new economy. Soldiers were trying to sell rifles for food; children were hawking books, clothes, shoes, jewelry, and a hundred other items for chocolate, bread, eggs, vegetables, and milk brought here by soldiers in the uniforms of four different armies who had either pilfered it from stores or had purchased it from PX centers set up for their use. Much to Ephraim's chagrin, even American soldiers were starting to make fortunes off the starving population of a dead city.

A jeep with four MPs pulled up to the curb and broke up a brawl. Ephraim watched until they were finished, then presented his credentials, briefly explaining his attire and what he had been up to, sensing that they regarded him as some sort of nut. "I could use a ride back to my apartment," he said.

"Yes sir," the MP said.

Moments later he was in the jeep and on his way home. Making a mental note to put the documents handler under surveillance, he let his mind drift. It was late. He was asleep before they reached his apartment.

*　*　*

Joseph watched as the jeep left the curb. He could swear the man in the beggar's clothes was Captain Daniels. He shrugged. It could not be.

He wandered, musing over the last twenty-four hours. He had just lost his house. Returning to the place where he had grown up and where he'd been staying the last couple of nights, he had found it inhabited by five other men who refused him entrance and threw stones at him until he had run out of range. He touched the cut on his forehead. It had stopped bleeding, but he could feel the crease in his flesh. Good reason to return to the hospital tomorrow.

He still had the clothes given to him by the American captain. He had wanted to bathe before wearing them, but because he had spent last night trying to find a place to sleep, there had been no chance for a bath. This morning he had gone to the address the captain had given him and had spent the day helping clear a house of debris and begin repairs. He recognized the home as that of a former Nazi leader by the name of Hoss and told the Church leader named Rausch it was not a good place for God-fearing people to have meetings. Rausch had only smiled, put an arm around Joseph's shoulder, and told him not to worry. God was used to chasing the devil out of such places. Joseph had wanted to say that God had taken his sweet time getting rid of such devils over the last five years but decided not to. He supposed that sometimes it took even God a little time when there were so many to get rid of.

He had enjoyed working with Rausch and half a dozen others of his church. They were friendly and kind, and he had eaten better than he had in weeks—soup that actually contained more than a few pieces of cabbage. He patted his stomach, the food still warming him. He would be sure to go back tomorrow.

He made his way through some trees to his new home, a burned-out tank with its tracks missing and its gun badly misshapen. Not exactly roomy, but at least it would keep rain out and offer some safety. Turning, he stared across the dark waters of Lake Havel. He longed for a bath, but was it safe and clean enough? He knew that the visible bodies had all been removed, but there might be others beneath the surface, and even though the lake was a freshwater lake and the cold liquid flowed through in a natural cleansing process, there might still be the danger of disease.

But a bath!

He decided to chance it. It was near his new quarters, and though it was late, the darkness would keep his intent hidden and reduce the chance of being jumped by drunks, or worse.

He climbed inside his new home and removed from his pockets the bread, cheese, and half bar of soap he had brought with him. On his way here he had rummaged through the ruins of a number of buildings and found several silver spoons and a nice silk scarf he had then traded for the food and soap. He put the bread and cheese in the magazine of the tank's cannon, closed it, then climbed back out, soap and captain Daniels' new clothes in hand. Walking the short distance to the water, he sat down and began taking his beatup shoes off his feet. He could not see their holes in the dark but knew they were nearly through to his skin and would not last the winter. He must find a way to get something else before cold set in or he'd have no toes by spring. He stopped a minute and listened. Nothing but silence. Quickly he stripped off the rank, grimy clothes and slipped silently into the water. Though cold, it felt wonderful as he dunked himself and then began scrubbing away the filth.

When he was finished, he had used practically all the soap; he was shivering and quickly moved onto the shore. He rubbed the water off as best as he could with the palm of each hand, then unwrapped the clean clothes. He didn't expect to find underwear but there it was, along with a new pair of heavy wool socks, pants, and a shirt. He slipped them on, enjoying the ecstacy of cleanliness and the warmth of the new clothes as they soaked up the remaining water on his skin and quickly heated it.

He grabbed the old clothes and tossed them against the tank tread before sitting down and letting himself relax. His eyes closed and he thanked God for this little comfort. Then he pulled on the socks.

At the moment he was about to get to his feet, the cold steel of a gun barrel pressed against the back of his neck and he froze.

"You! What are you doing here?" His clothes made him look American, that was for sure, but why would a Russian demand to know what he was doing when it was the Russian who was out of his sector? The smell of liquor and the slur in the voice were probably the answer: the man was drunk and didn't know where he was.

Slowly, Joseph turned his head to look directly up at his captor. He could not see the face, but he could see the barrel and knew that drunks with a gun in their hand were as dangerous as old, sweating dynamite. Mishandling could cause death.

"What can I do for you, soldier?" he asked in fluent Russian. He wasn't surprised that an armed Russian was in the American sector at this time of night. The Russians were having a hard time accepting the boundaries established after the Americans arrived and sneaked in nightly to steal and find women, who were now smart enough to avoid the Russian sector, especially at night.

Rumor had it that the Americans were about fed up with it and had started putting Russian soldiers in jail for a day or two before dumping them back in their own sector. This usually got the soldier another couple of days discipline or worse from his own commander, thus curtailing further crossings of the border.

The man's threatening posture didn't change. "Whiskey, do you have any whiskey?"

Joseph nodded slowly while reaching into his pocket as if to retrieve something. He lifted an empty hand toward his captor, hopeful that the dark and the drunk's blurred vision would cover his deception and give him a chance.

The soldier reached for what he thought was a bottle, and the barrel of the rifle slipped to the left. Joseph grabbed it, then jerked the gun even farther to the left, sending the soldier flying headfirst into the side of the tank against which Joseph had been sitting. The sound of skull against metal made Joseph flinch, but he was quickly on his feet as the soldier fell to the ground. Turning him over, Joseph checked for a pulse. It was still strong, though there was a cut about the same size as his own in the man's head. Such is life, Joseph thought. Especially in Berlin.

He searched the body, found a few cigarettes he could use for trading, a set of identity papers written in Russian, and a new wax candle with a box of matches. He took all of it and placed the items on the tank before dragging the unconscious soldier back to the road where he would be found and dealt with. He thought about keeping the rifle but decided against it. A German caught with a gun was harshly dealt with, and he neither needed nor wanted the grief.

He returned to the tank and climbed inside, closing the lid and locking it shut. He lit the candle, removed his bread and cheese, and ate a small portion while going through the Russian's papers. He had learned to read Russian pretty well, could speak it like a native, and saw quickly that the papers might be valuable if he ever wanted to forage in the Russian sector again. He would have to have a uniform, but there were enough drunks like the one outside that he could readily obtain one if needed.

The soldier's name was Feodor Antonov and he was the equivalent of the German army's second-to-lowest rank. There were no letters from family or girlfriend and nothing to indicate he was more than just another grunt sent out by the generals to do the dirty work and, in the case of the Russians, to act like he loved every minute of it.

The last paper in the wallet was a letter from his commanding officer containing orders to take effect the next day. He was being sent back to Russia. For him the war was over.

It angered Joseph, and impulsively he put the paper over the candle and let it burn. He shoved the other papers back in the document case and placed it in a crack of the turret until they were out of sight but still reachable. The soldier would have a devil of a time explaining the loss of his papers. Maybe such a loss would get him a few months duty in the Berlin he had helped create. This would serve him right.

Joseph blew out the candle and lay down, trying to get comfortable on the rags he had found the night before. Closing his eyes, he willed himself to sleep. He would return to the Mormon building tomorrow for work and the hot meals, but it was only temporary. He needed to start looking for something else. There was always the cleanup of the streets and the rebuilding, which would be endless, but with winter approaching it would be cold and offer little reward. Possibly he could find something at the hospital where Rachel worked, or her American friend, Captain Daniels, might know of something. He would try to talk to both of them tomorrow.

He tossed and turned, trying to get comfortable with his thoughts more than with his hard bed. Finally he got up, removed the documents from their hiding place, opened the turret door, and slipped into the cool night. He went to the street and found the drunk Russian still lying where he had been laid. He shoved the papers back into his pocket.

"Sorry about the trouble you will have because of the one I burned, but at least you can go home. No sense both of us freezing to death this winter." He went back to his bed and snuggled down. A moment later he was fast asleep.

See Chapter Notes

CHAPTER 22

Hannah didn't see Ephraim until late Tuesday morning. She was sitting on the balcony reading to Rachel from Ephraim's book when she saw him pull up in his jeep and turn off the key. She yelled to him as he jumped to the sidewalk.

"Hey, soldier, are you looking for someone?"

He looked up and smiled that great smile. "Yeah, Hannah Gruen. Do you know her?"

"I might. What do you want with her?"

"Well, I might have a solution to her immigration problems." He grinned.

She put the book on the chair, grabbed Rachel's folder, and dashed through the apartment to the door, then down the steps, Rachel on her heels.

"Do you think . . . I mean, would they really agree to help us?" Rachel asked as she grabbed Hannah and stopped her at the bottom of the steps.

She thought of telling Rachel about the tickets but decided there wasn't time. She had kept them hidden, waiting until they had everything they needed before breaking the news to the others, afraid that it would only break their spirit to have tickets that gave them nothing more than a free ride around Europe where things were as bad or worse than they were here. She opened the door to the outside. "Let's find out, shall we?" she said.

He was back in the jeep, the engine running. "Hop in."

Rachel jumped in the back as Hannah took the front passenger seat.

"Where are we going?" Hannah asked.

"To meet someone." He pulled away from the curb and glanced over his shoulder at Rachel. "What you have to say had better be good, young lady. These men don't like being toyed with."

Rachel seemed to pale a little bit but nodded vigorously, reassuring Ephraim. Her dread mounted as they went past the Pariserplatz, the plaza next to the Brandenburg Gate, which had been pretty much the center of activity during the war years. They passed what had been the famous Adlon Hotel, then the deserted and wrecked American Embassy just across from the destroyed French Embassy. She did glance up to see that Wilhelmstrasse street was completely destroyed. Hindenburg's old palace, which Ribentropp had taken over, was gone. The Foreign Office, where the announcement was made every time Germany broke another treaty, was nothing but a burned-out set of walls; and Goebbel's propaganda ministry, where he had lied to everyone and had convinced Germany the Reich was their Messiah, was nothing more than a mess of twisted steel and fallen stone. Across the street was the Chancellery, the place where the war strategies had been laid out, where lies and decisions about the deaths of millions of innocent people had taken place as easily as dining on roast duck. It angered her.

Millions butchered. Millions more broken and maimed. Homes in ashes and ruins, all because of what took place in this street as Hitler and his attack dogs acted like maniacal gods. Well, now it was her turn. If she could stop a few of them, if what she knew could bring some to justice, she would do it. If she could buy freedom for herself and her friends with her information, she would; but if not, she'd give it to the allies anyway. Another Reich could never be allowed.

They stopped in front of the Brandenburg Gate and Wally hopped in beside Rachel with a quick hello.

"Did you get it?" Ephraim asked.

"Yup," was all Wally said, but he carried a thick folder of material and Rachel could see it was Russian writing. "Got something else, too." Wally grinned. "For an extra carton of cigarettes, he threw in an autopsy report belonging to Adolph Hitler."

Ephraim nearly tipped the jeep over as he jerked the wheel trying to look Wally in the eye. "You're kidding?"

"No sir," Wally said, "but if you're going to kill all of us, I'll keep the rest to myself!"

"Sorry," Ephraim said, staring straight ahead. "So what have you got?"

"It seems the bodies were removed by the Russians two months ago. They've even done an autopsy. The crap put out by the Russians about Hitler poisoning himself was propaganda, an attempt to make him look less the hero. He blew half his skull away with a pistol."

"And this is supposed to be more heroic?"

"Morbid, isn't it?" Wally added.

"You're sure?" Ephraim asked. "There is no chance they're feeding us bad information, setting us up or something?"

"Not a chance. This source is as good as gold, and I've got the original reports right here." He revealed the folder in his hand. "Signed by a guy by the name of Krayevski, Chief Physician of the Russian army or something."

"Of what value is such information to you? As long as he is dead, that is all that matters, isn't it?" Hannah asked.

"From time to time General Zhukov needs to be reminded he hasn't been telling us the truth and that we know it and have ways of knowing more. It keeps him off balance and open to suggestions he might not otherwise consider," Ephraim said.

"The information you gave us is better than the autopsy," Wally added. "We've been accusing them of harboring Nazis for months; now we have proof."

"But it is only my word, I—"

"We've been watching your father's place, Rachel," Ephraim continued. "There have been a dozen guests in the last forty-eight hours. We've picked 'em all up as soon as they came out of the Russian sector. No major players, but we've gotten to a number of midlevel officials: two out of the chancellery run by Bormann, a half-dozen out of Himmler's home office, two former workers at Bergen Belsen, and two who worked in the Special Sections department of the Reichsbank."

"People from the Reichsbank?" Hannah asked.

"It is a bit curious, isn't it?" Ephraim answered.

"But the men you have captured say nothing?" Hannah quizzed.

"Not yet."

Rachel glanced at Hannah and gave her a slight smile. Maybe their information was worth more than they thought.

They pulled up in front of American headquarters in Dahlem, and Ephraim shut off the motor.

"General Lucius Clay of the United States is commander of the American zone. We'll be in his office. His guest for the next few days is the British Deputy Military Governor—Lieutenant-General Sir Ronald Weeks. Weeks is the typical stiff-upper-lip, live-by-the-rules, professional soldier that the Brits have been putting out since they first became an empire."

Hannah felt limp. "He has come to see us?"

"Not exactly. He's here on other business, but when General Clay found out what you wanted and that I had verified your knowledge about the Strasbourg Conference, he wanted a command performance for Weeks." He paused. "But let me warn you. Weeks is hardnose. You will have to be convincing, even direct, or he'll brush you off."

"How comforting," Hannah said dryly.

He grinned. "C'mon," he said, climbing out of the jeep. "Time to get this over."

Hannah climbed out of the jeep and took Rachel by the hand, holding tightly as they walked toward the building, then passed security inside. Hannah's emotions were mixed. This was their chance, their way to a new life in Palestine. But it was also the way that would separate her from Ephraim. Somehow, the dream wasn't what it used to be.

* * *

The two generals and several others sat in chairs at a table facing a large map at the far end of the room. Ephraim's nervous party was behind the men and stood to one side of the door until they were announced by Clay's assistant. Clay glanced at them, nodded to his assistant, then concentrated on what was being said.

"Without better cooperation from the Russians, we could lose up to fifty percent of the civilians over the next six months."

"Then we'll just have to get their cooperation," Clay said stiffly. "Get it on the agenda for the next meeting of the Kommandatura."

"He won't take kindly to it, sir, especially with the deaths of his soldiers still giving him heartburn."

"Zhukov doesn't give a hoot for two men caught stealing and trying to use their weapons on Americans. Everyone here knows he'll probably have their entire families sent to Siberia for their stupidity. What he wants is that stoolie Markgraf to receive official status as police commissar from all the members of the Kommandatura, and he thinks this will better his chances."

"That may be true, general, but he still has his orders from Moscow. He isn't going to give us any more cooperation until Stalin says so. Stalin has millions of his own people to feed this winter and intends to do it with German food, regardless of how many die here."

"I should remind you, general," another said, "we can't afford to upset Stalin. He's nearly committed to declaring war on Japan, and the President would not want that to change."

General Clay swore. "Then how do we feed these people?"

"We ship in more food," said another. "They might not get steak and potatoes, but they will eat."

"We won't have enough," said the first. "We're feeding half of Europe right now and our food supplies are stretched to the limit." There was real frustration in his voice.

"All right. Thank you gentlemen. Ben, get it on the agenda and keep it there until we see some movement from the Russians." He turned to the only British officer in the room. "Ron, tell your prime minister that they had better start applying some pressure to Stalin or be prepared to bury another half of the survivors before spring. I'll do the same with President Truman."

It suddenly dawned on Rachel how big the allied problems were. The war was over, the Americans wanted their men home and were wondering why they should pay through the nose to provide for a people who didn't like them and weren't even going to say thank you. The immigration problems of four women probably seemed very small to them, with Germany literally disintegrating around them and the Russians waiting to pick up half of Europe if they weren't careful.

Why should they give her what she wanted? Why should they care if a few more Nazis were rounded up or not? In their eyes, what

she was about to offer probably amounted to a one on a scale of zero
to ten. She nearly turned around and walked out, then took a deep
breath. No, too much was at stake. She would just have to be
convincing, forceful.

Funny, she thought, before the camp she would never have tried
something like this. Even before Hannah made her wake up and quit
feeling sorry for herself, she would not have tried. She supposed the
camps had made her refuse to quit. After all, what could these men
do to her that the camps hadn't? Telling these men what she knew
would be a piece of cake compared to a single day at Auschwitz.

Several men stood and walked out. Three greeted Ephraim as they
left. One stopped to talk.

"How ya doin', Eph?" the man asked.

"Up to now, I was fine."

"Mmm. Clay's had a bad day, so has Weeks—ornery as a couple
chained dogs. Watch yourself," he grinned.

"Thanks a bunch, Dal." Ephraim forced a smile and Dal laughed
as he exited the office.

The assistant told them to take seats and Ephraim led the way,
pulling out chairs for each and allowing them to sit across the table
from the two generals. Hannah felt faint. Rachel felt determined.

"This is Colonel Mackland, head of Intelligence," Ephraim said
to the man at the end of the table. He rose slightly and smiled before
sitting back down.

Mackland handed identical sheets to General Clay and Deputy-
Governor Weeks, who quickly read them. Probably refreshing their
memories about who these two women dressed in rags could possibly
be, Hannah thought. Now she wished she'd taken the time to change
into her new skirt and blouse.

"Captain, welcome. Your reputation precedes you. I understand
they're giving you a medal in a few days."

Ephraim went red. "Thank you sir, but like I told Colonel
Mackland— "

"Never mind the modesty, Captain. You get the medal whether
you like it or not. Every town needs a hero, even Hibbard, Idaho,"
Clay responded.

"Yes sir."

Clay looked up. "Which one of you survived Ravensbrück, which Auschwitz?" he asked softly.

Hannah told him.

"It must have been hell," Clay said.

"Hell would be easy after the camps," Rachel responded without emotion.

"We're told you have some information for us," Clay stated.

"What guarantees will you give us?" Rachel asked, just as emotionless.

"Your request to go to Palestine . . . it is very difficult. There are so many survivors who want this," said Weeks.

The words were condescending and made Hannah mad. She tried to bite her tongue but then remembered what Ephraim had told them. *Don't let them put you off.* "And you aren't exactly rushing to open the way, are you General?" Hannah remarked. She saw the smile at the corner of Ephraim's mouth, and his dancing eyes made her glad she had been direct. That helped her relax.

"We can't—"

"Can't or won't?" Hannah broke in. "There are several hundred thousand people who are still in those miserable camps because of your policy. If you condemn Hitler, why do you continue to do his work for him?" She saw both generals flinch, but Weeks also stiffened.

"Now see here . . ."

"Whoa, let's not get the cart before the horse, shall we?" Clay said, trying to smile. "You'll get your guarantees if you can give us something worthwhile, won't they Ron?" He stared down Weeks who only nodded, his flushed face pushing sweat onto his forehead.

"Was the information about Strasbourg correct or wasn't it?" Rachel asked.

"It was, but we haven't any idea what the meeting was about."

"The industrialists who have survived with their companies intact are, with possible rare exceptions, Nazis. They used slave labor to increase their profits while providing what was needed for Hitler's war machine, and, like Hitler, they did all of this from a distance, refusing to involve themselves in the misery and death that they were causing. They are criminals and should be treated like criminals. Are you willing to do so, or are they going to be left free, regardless of what I tell you?"

Both men glanced at each other, as if determining the other's position.

"Germany must be rebuilt. Industry is essential to that. But if we find they have committed crimes against humanity, they will be tried."

"You have seen Auschwitz. You know that I.G. Farben had a factory there."

Mackland leaned forward. "We know, and their managers are being questioned. We also know of other such factories and are investigating them, but you are right, they distanced themselves from operations enough that it will be difficult to prove their complicity. The SS controlled the camps, and the industrialists claim they had nothing to do with what went on there. In fact, they show records that indicate the people who worked in their factories were fed when at work and, in some instances, were even paid."

Hannah smiled. "And you believe them?"

"They have produced witnesses," Mackland responded. "Affidavits, receipts for foodstuffs, clothing; they have covered their trail very well. We do not like it. If we had our choice, we'd throw the lot of them in Spandau prison and let them rot, but democracies run on laws, and we are here to uphold those laws; otherwise, we become Nazis ourselves."

"Give us something we can prove, Miss Bauer, and we will nail their stinking hides to the wall," Clay said. "But it must be provable in a court of law."

"According to the letter I have, the group of industrialists at Strasbourg decided they would offer financial help to selected Nazis and help them relocate with new identities, if necessary. They believe in the Reich and think that given enough time, and by saving the right people, it can re-emerge and continue its work. My father has been left behind to see that those still caught in Germany receive the help they need to either get out of the country or to disappear within it."

"You can prove this?"

Opening the folder, she removed the letter to her father from Krupp and shoved it across the table to Clay. He read it and pushed it to Weeks.

"They've selected Bormann. That proves he is still alive," Clay said.

"My father and his friends blame the Nazi leadership for the failure of the Reich. Apparently, they do not have such feelings about Bormann. They will get him and others they trust out of the country to protect them. You already know that they have begun providing new identities for others, such as those Captain Daniels has found leaving my father's house, so that they can infiltrate whatever government you leave behind. They think they can return their leaders to Germany eventually and do it all over again."

"What men, Captain?" Clay questioned.

"We've been watching Bauer's house. We've picked up more than a dozen midlevel Nazis based on Rachel's information about her father. They all have well-forged documents, but none have any that would get them out of the country. They're staying, melting into the soup. Planning for a revival is my guess, just as that letter indicates."

"Only the most recognizable are to be taken out of the country," Weeks added, his eyes on the letter. "They're fools."

"That is what many said after the first world war," Hannah added. "Do not underestimate these men—especially the wealthy ones, Deputy Governor. They have an insatiable desire for power, and the riches to bring it about. Without these men, Hitler would never have come to power. They made him, paid for him, prepared his war machine. They think they can do it again. This time they must be stopped."

"How do they intend to get the top members of the party out of the country, and where can they go?" Weeks asked. "It is ludicrous to believe that any kind of shadow government can survive in a foreign country. Ridiculous."

"There are a hundred thousand Nazis, true believers, who will try, Deputy Governor, probably more. How many have you rounded up? Are you so sure that, given enough time, they cannot raise up another Hitler?" Ephraim asked, a bit frustrated.

Weeks flashed Ephraim a cold look but didn't answer as Colonel Mackland gave a similar look to his young captain, then sat forward and quickly spoke. "Bormann is probably out of the country by now."

"Unless he is resting in some prisoner of war camp because his new identity wasn't as good as it should have been," Wally said. "Himmler comes to mind."

Clay nodded but saw that the two women were in the dark. "Himmler had a false passport under the name of Heinrich Hetzinger. He shaved his moustache and wore a black eye patch. The only mistake was taking the identity of a major in the Gestapo. We rounded all of those boys up. He got caught in the net."

"But committed suicide," Hannah reminded them.

"Later. But yes, that's what happened."

"Himmler was not part of this. He was in disfavor," Rachel said adamantly. "He, Goering, Ribbentropp, even Hitler, would not have received help from these people. They failed. There is no room for them in the new order."

"Maybe," Weeks said, ever the pessimist.

"Where was he arrested?" Rachel asked.

"Up north. They think he was headed for Sweden."

She shook her head adamantly. "The route mentioned in my father's envelope goes through Rome. You will note that the letter to my father says the Church there has seemed to find its charitable nature again. The contact is a man with the initials F. H. If you watch my father, he will lead you to him; I am sure of it. He will not put up with the Russians much longer. It is not in his nature."

Colonel Mackland was writing furiously. "We should increase our watch along the Italian border," he said.

Clay nodded. He trusted his Intelligence leader and his staff but knew that watching the borders of Germany and Austria to the south would be like trying to keep a sieve from leaking water.

Rachel spoke. "Also at Strasbourg it was decided that Hitler could not win and that their assets and the assets of the Reich were at risk. Arrangements were made to get what still remained in Germany out of the country."

"I knew those beggars weren't broke," Weeks said stiffly.

"My mother and I spent many hours together when we were found out to be Jews. She told me many things about my grandfather's businesses and how they operated. Until my father became the managing director, all assets were kept inside Germany. It was a patriotic gesture by my grandfather and then by my mother, but father felt differently, especially once the Reich began to obsess him. He transferred much of the money into numbered accounts in banks located in Sweden and Switzerland. My mother signed papers authorizing the action but insisted that the accounts be in all of our names."

"Then he sold you out?" Clay asked angrily.

"He brought documents for mother to sign dissolving some companies and creating others. She said it was an attempt to hide them from Germany's enemies. She didn't agree with it, but I could tell he had left her no choice. Now I believe that he may have been threatening her with the camps," she said coldly.

Hannah saw the look on Ephraim's face. She had never seen such a cold, determined set to his jaw. Rachel's father would pay for his treatment of his family; Ephraim would see to that.

"Cloaking," Wally said almost to himself.

Hannah saw Clay give Mackland a quick look. It was obvious this was not the first they had heard of what Wally said. "You know of this cloaking?" she asked.

Mackland looked at Clay again, who gave him a slight nod.

"It is the process of hiding your holdings by the use of dummy corporations. If I may go to the board, sir, I think I can illustrate what I mean." With a nod from General Clay Colonel Mackland went to a small chalkboard attached to the wall.

"After World War I, the Versailles Treaty forbade Germany any kind of significant armed force. Their humiliation was more than they could stand, so prominent government and economic leaders put their heads together and came up with a way to circumvent the treaty."

He drew a square and wrote Krupp Corp in it; then he drew three more squares below it and connected them to the first with lines. On the next level he drew eight boxes and connected two to each box on the second line and also connected them by lines to each other.

Inside the three boxes on the second tier he wrote Sweden, Switzerland, and Spain.

"These are the banks Krupp used for his cloak. The accounts are put under the names of dummy companies to which Krupp has no visible attachment. Those dummy corporations then use their assets, placed there by Krupp through a series of transactions that masked where they came from, to buy stock in the foreign companies listed in these last eight boxes. He kept buying until he had controlling interest. His dummy corporations then had control of eight foreign companies."

"But how did that help Germany?" Ephraim asked.

Mackland pointed to the first box, which had the company name of Bofors written inside it. "Bofors is a Swedish steel and munitions factory. Krupp used it to develop experimental guns and ammunition. Because he controlled the stock, and thus the company, he was able to pass that information on to the German Ministry of Defense before World War II."

"In other words, it allowed them to develop new weaponry without having it taken away by inspections teams from the allies between the world wars. We think many of the effective hand weapons used in War II were developed by Bofors. He did the same thing with the rest of these companies; one developed submarines, another airplanes, another tanks."

"But they caught him," Clay smiled.

"Yes, and the Swedes passed an antidummy law in 1934, but it didn't do much good in the long run. Though Krupp was forced to sell his stock in his Swedish companies, he sold them to friends who continued to control what the companies did and continued to aide Germany. They just became more efficient, that's all. We figure that nearly half a billion dollars in German company assets were invested in foreign countries, and much of it put together the war machine that was ready for Hitler's use when he came to power. They continued to operate through the war, though we have been successful in shutting some of them down." He dropped the chalk in the slot at the bottom of the board and returned to his seat. "Your story is very plausible, Miss Bauer, because we know it took place on a much larger scale than most people realize, and it is very difficult to trace. We recently confiscated the Krupp company records and we are making some headway, but I don't believe we'll ever really know the extent of their cloaking activities."

"My father purchased stock in a company in Sweden called Siderus Smit. It is an armament factory. He also purchased an Austrian company that made ball bearings," Rachel said. "My mother had to sign the papers."

Colonel Mackland nodded. "Siderus Smit builds tanks, and the manufacture of ball bearings was crucial to the war machine. It fits."

General Clay spoke. "They rake in the profits from other legitimate deals their conglomerates put together and use creative bookkeeping to subsidize the Reich with cash laundered and sent back to Germany until they can come out in the open. Brilliant, isn't it?" He said it with disgust in his voice and his brow furrowed. He obviously was frustrated with the whole issue and how to fix it. Stopping cloaking was not like capturing a city. You couldn't just surround it and beat it into submission. "Miss Bauer, I think you have more to tell us."

"My father's companies are many. I can give you their names and account numbers, but not until we have your guarantee that we will be allowed to go to Palestine legally," Rachel said. On the surface she looked tough, formidable; inside, she was a mess of nerves.

Clay looked at Weeks who glanced down at the letter in front of them.

"We will provide the necessary papers; the Americans will provide what you need to get to a port in France or Italy."

"You will also give us enough money for the passage," Rachel said firmly.

"Very well," Weeks agreed.

Rachel smiled at Hannah, then sat back in her chair. "I do not wish to offend, but it must be in writing."

Clay and Weeks both hardened their jaws.

Colonel Mackland came to the rescue. "One of our people can have something in a few minutes, General, if you will allow me to see to it." He was already standing as General Clay nodded. "In return, Rachel will sign a document turning her papers over to us. She will also agree never to speak of these things again to anyone."

Rachel hesitated, thinking. "If you shove this under the rug, General, no paper will keep me from talking. I promise you."

"You are a hard case," General Clay said, staring at Rachel.

"The camps teach you many things about survival. One of them is to trust no one who gives you promises."

Clay only nodded. "Go ahead, Colonel Mackland. Both papers, please."

"You are only escaping to another war," Weeks added. "Palestine will erupt within the year."

"And whose side will the British be on this time?" Hannah asked.

Weeks leaned forward, fire in his eyes at her accusation. "We protect your people as best we can. They fight us tooth and nail for it."

"If the protection you give to our people still languishing in Hitler's camps because you refuse them a home is indicative of what you mean, I understand their fight. It is no wonder, Mr. Weeks, that your empire shrinks like leather in a hot oven. No one can trust you."

Weeks went red again but said nothing as Colonel Mackland returned with a document in hand. He handed it to Clay, who seemed to be enjoying Weeks' discomfort. The general struck Hannah as a man who didn't like what the Brits were doing, but his duty prevented him from saying so in front of present company. He took the paper from his aide, read it, and handed it to Rachel. "Is that what you wanted?"

Rachel looked at it but could not read English well and handed it to Ephraim who read it out loud. It outlined very well what was promised and had two lines for the signatures of Weeks and Clay, along with two lines for witnesses. The two generals signed; then Colonel Mackland and Ephraim added their names as witnesses. It was given to Rachel, who gave it to Hannah to put in the folder they had brought with them.

The second document was brought in, read, and signed by Rachel alone.

Rachel asked for a piece of paper and wrote down the names of the companies her mother had told her about, then gave them the account numbers she had taken from her father's house. When she had finished, she shoved the paper to General Clay, who looked it over and seemed a bit shocked. "Two of these companies are in the United States," he said.

Rachel only smiled. "I think you will find them ignorant of their involvement. Mother said that a dummy company that they and you thought to be Russian was used to send materials to Siderus Smit."

Clay handed it to Mackland, who looked at it and paled. "But this company . . . in Philadelphia . . . I know this company. It is one of the biggest in the States."

"And one where we consistently had trouble getting our orders filled," Clay said. "Russia was in a worse fix than we were. We thought they should get their parts first." He swore. "You're telling me that all that time it was the Germans who were receiving 'em?" He shook his head. "I hope to high heaven you are wrong."

Weeks reached for the paper and Mackland handed it to him. There were no English companies on the paper, and his face showed a bit too much arrogant relief.

"My father was small compared to Krupp, Thyssen, and the others," Rachel said. "Mother thought they probably had companies in every nation in the world." The relieved look fled from Weeks' face. Rachel continued. "These same companies have been used to send their money out of Germany. They may claim they are broke, but they are not."

"Trying to avoid reparations," Wally mumbled.

"It gets worse," Rachel said. "The Nazis are using these same company accounts to send the SS monies, once controlled by Himmler but finally controlled by Bormann, out of Germany as well."

"We have received hundreds of reports about the loss of Jewish assets, companies, houses, and everything in them—money, jewelry . . ." Ephraim paused, glancing at Rachel and Hannah. "We have good evidence that the Nazis even removed gold fillings from the teeth of the dead, forced other prisoners to melt them into gold bars, then sent them to a secret section of the Reichsbank here in Berlin."

General Clay muttered an oath. "Colonel Mackland, start with Bauer's companies. Freeze their assets. Find out from the Treasury in Washington if we have any names of companies controlled by the other industrialists, especially Krupp, and have them do the same. Fill them in on Miss Bauer's revelations and get them cracking on every German company we know of. Secretary Biddle has always wanted to sink his teeth into Krupp's hide. Now's the time."

Mackland wrote it down. "Yes sir, but it won't be easy. Banks that would involve themselves with the Nazis are not about to let us look at their accounts willingly. We will need absolute proof that the accounts contain monies taken through murder or some other criminal activity, and even then it would take years to litigate and force the banks to give up the funds."

"One other thing," Wally said. "We . . . uh . . . have a contact in the Russian sector. He turned over to me some records of the Reichsbank this morning." He shoved the folder across the table to General Clay. "You will see that there are large discrepancies in what they had a few weeks ago and what was found in their vault. Very large discrepancies. And the Russians didn't find it, either. Our contact guarantees it. He was present when the vault was opened by the Russians, and it was empty as Coney Island on a winter day."

"Which adds credence to Miss Bauer's story. Do any of the bank officials have an explanation of these so-called discrepancies?" Weeks asked.

"Not yet, no sir."

"Does your Russian contact have any idea of the extent of this discrepancy?" Clay asked.

"Two billion Reichsmarks," Wally responded.

Clay whistled and Weeks sat back, amazed by the figure. "And this is sitting in some bank account in Switzerland?" Clay asked.

"Or Sweden, or Spain and Argentina," Ephraim said.

Clay stood and went to the window. "If we can prove the industrialists were involved in all this, we can break their conglomerates into small pieces and force them to pay reparations to the people they used. This young lady's letter will help, but we need more."

"Sir, that will mean we will have to try them," Mackland said. "Without their help Germany may never recover—"

"Excuse me, Colonel Mackland, but it may actually speed up a recovery. The conglomerates have only their own interests at heart. We now know those interests include a private agenda to bring back the Reich. They will drag their feet and manipulate the system to get what they want. If we can force them to sell to men we know have no such agenda, it will help the recovery, not hinder it," Wally said. "The best thing for the likes of these kind of men is a trial; then let them spend the rest of their lives cooling their heels in places like Auschwitz!"

Mackland had no answer.

"I only hope the politicians agree with you," Clay said, turning to Mackland. "Let's get crackin' Colonel! These murdering thieves need to be stopped, and I don't give a hoot if it takes into the next century—they need to pay for their crimes with cold, hard cash as well as prison terms! And the next time one of those slimy thieves tells me he's broke, remind me to wring his neck."

"Yes sir," Mackland said.

"Captain Daniels, I want you to stay on this young lady's father. He'll show us their underground if we let him. It may not be wise to pick up everyone he helps just yet. Stop them on some pretext and get their names and addresses. We'll round them up later. Clear?"

"Clear," Ephraim said, then looked at his boss. "But I'll need more men."

Mackland nodded.

"Daniels, you keep Colonel Mackland and myself well informed. If you need anything, you'll get it." He stood. "Short of giving these ladies a plane, work out a way to get them to Marseille and first-class passage to Palestine."

"Done," Ephraim said, giving Hannah a quick glance.

Clay turned to Weeks. "How long before you have the proper papers to get them into Palestine?"

"A few days." He looked at Ephraim. "Contact my aide. He'll send someone by with the proper forms and to get pictures." He stood as well.

Hannah knew it was an invitation to leave, but she was so stunned by what had happened she couldn't pull herself out of the chair.

Clay reached across the table and took her hand, helping her up. "Ladies, this has been a real pleasure, but it has to be our little secret. If word got out we were shipping refugees out of the country in exchange for information, everybody in town would be knocking on our door with stories that would match this one. Only trouble is, most of 'em wouldn't have a lick of truth to 'em, and we'd be chasing mirages for the next decade. Also, you've heard some highly classified stuff flying around this room; we'd appreciate it if you'd keep a lid on it."

"Thank you, General," Rachel said. "As long as we get to Palestine, you will have nothing to worry about."

Clay laughed. "Never met a woman as hard-nosed as you. You'll get what you've been promised, won't they, Ron?" He turned to face the British Deputy Military Governor who only nodded, already working on filling a pipe he had produced from his case.

General Clay turned to Hannah. "Good luck in your new country."

"Thank you sir, and thanks for seeing us. I know what little we told you before wasn't much incentive."

"You mean about Strasbourg." He looked at Ephraim. "Slim, but the captain verified it then vouched for you—with his career. His word is good as gold around here. Captain." He shook Ephraim's hand, and then he and Weeks turned to other business as the doors opened and five soldiers joined them. Ephraim guided his two charges out of the office and into the main hall with Wally following. Rachel and Hannah grabbed each other and hugged as they danced around in a circle. Other soldiers waiting to see the generals stopped and stared, and Ephraim and Wally moved the two women along as best they could until they were outside.

Rachel and Wally climbed in the backseat but Hannah turned to Ephraim. "Thank you."

"You're welcome, but it was Rachel—"

"Your career. You put it on the line, remember?"

"Not much to put there. I'm going back to flying in a few weeks, either fighters in Japan or a mail run in Palestine. Or do you folks still send letters by camel?" He smiled at the shocked look on her face.

"You can do this? You *would* do this?"

"Oh, there are still a few details you and I need to work out, but I like my options."

She put her arms around his waist and kissed him. "I like your options, too," she said.

"Hey, you two, I'm as big a romantic as anyone, but you're gathering a crowd," Wally said.

Hannah looked around to see grinning soldiers looking their way. "Oh, dear," she said, blushing. "I have gotten you into trouble for sure." She pulled away and jumped into the seat of the jeep.

He handed her his hanky and she dried the tears on her cheeks as he started the vehicle. "Where to?" he said softly.

"It's time we told the others."

He smiled, seeming relieved. "Well, if the response is anything like the one I got last night, I'm all for it."

She poked him in the ribs with a doubled-up fist. "I'll see that it isn't."

"What are you two talking about?" Rachel asked, a bit perturbed that she hadn't been informed of something that seemed very important.

Hannah told her about the tickets. "I was going to tell everyone at dinner tonight, but now is even better."

Rachel threw her arms around Ephraim's neck from the rear and kissed the back of his head, nearly choking him in the process.

The soldiers standing about laughed and the one called Dal yelled, "Hey Eph, I thought you Mormons were done with polygamy!"

The laughter grew as Ephraim threw the jeep in gear and started away.

"You believe in polygamy?" Hannah asked, confused.

He laughed. "Nope, but if I did, I couldn't think of two better wives."

"I'll share him," said Rachel, verbally jabbing at Hannah.

Hannah laughed with them, her heart filled with as much joy as she could remember. Ephraim would come to Israel. They would be happy. Out of the ashes of her life, new blossoms were exploding into bloom. Only months ago she wanted just one thing—to die. Now life had come back into her burned-out soul, and the past seemed nothing but a dark tunnel through which she had passed and was quickly fading into the recesses of that part of her mind that locked up ugliness.

She reached over and put her hand on Ephraim's arm as she blinked away the tears of joy. He had saved her, heart and soul. She wanted nothing more than to be one with him, to marry, have children, and grow old watching them grow up to be like their father. Was it possible? It was within reach, but she knew what he meant when he said they would need to work out a few things. One was where they would live; the other was religion. Could there be compromise?

She glanced over at Ephraim. On Israel? Yes. On religion. No.

Could she give up her faith, become a Christian?

It was the one question she still couldn't answer.

See Chapter Notes

CHAPTER 23

Ephraim was at the office and about to head for Bauer's residence to join Wally when things erupted at headquarters. There had been a gunfight at the dividing line between their sector and that of the Russians; four men had been killed: one American, three Russians. The reaction was typical for Zhukov who shut down his entire sector to any transportation from the allied sectors while he rounded up anyone from there and booted them out. The administrative offices were in the Russian sector and there were a lot of American GIs and Germans who worked for them who suddenly found themselves being driven out like cattle.

In an emergency meeting of the Kommandatura, Zhukov had ranted for an hour and demanded that the American GIs involved and still alive be turned over to him for trial and punishment. Evidence showed that the Russians had come into the American sector and were in the process of robbing a German black marketeer of his day's income. They had refused to stop when challenged by American MPs, then had started shooting. Zhukov called it a pack of lies and walked out. It wasn't the first time and wouldn't be the last. Ephraim was getting sick of the Russian attempts to bully and suspected that their incursions were attempts at intimidation, or worse.

Ephraim had been called in to a meeting in General Clay's office. One of his aides was explaining what had happened.

"Our MPs were fully within their rights." He handed the general a stack of papers. "Those are signed affidavits of German eyewitnesses who will testify that the Russians were both drunk and stealing, that they fired first, killing one of our men, before we gave a deadly response."

The General looked at the papers, his face grim. It was another of Zhukov's tactics to get something. This time it wouldn't work. "What's happening on the line?" he asked.

"No one is being allowed entrance into the Russian sector. They're throwing up a few more walls and their patrols of the city itself have increased tenfold. We hear they're locking up anyone still on their side of the line."

"We have four men in there, at Bauer's place," Ephraim said.

"In uniform?"

"No sir, which could be worse if they are looking for an issue."

Clay swore. "Get to them, Captain. Get them out of there."

"Yes sir," he said, leaving the room.

Ephraim was in his own office when one of the four men rushed in. Ephraim was relieved at first, but when he saw the look on the lieutenant's face, the knot in his stomach tightened. "Where's Wally and the others?"

The lieutenant caught his breath. "They didn't make it. The Russians have them."

Ephraim felt like throwing up.

* * *

Joseph was in the middle of removing the broken glass from windows on the second floor when he saw Captain Daniels pull up in his jeep. He watched as the captain spoke to President Rausch, who pointed toward Joseph. The captain looked up, thanked the president, and started for the porch. Joseph thought for sure he was in trouble.

"Have you got a minute?" Ephraim yelled from the ground.

Joseph gulped but nodded that he did, then quickly climbed inside and went downstairs, meeting the captain in the entrance area.

"President Rausch says you are doing a fine job," Ephraim said.

"He is a good man, and the work is good for me, not to mention the food," he answered. His heart was racing, but he was hiding it well. One thing he had learned in Russia was to act a good part.

"Rachel tells me you've been to Russia and know the language."

He nodded but said nothing, afraid this part of his background might have come back to haunt him. The Americans were losing their love for the Russians. Was his association now a problem?

"Could you pass for a Russian soldier?"

Joseph looked at him curiously. "I was one, once. Yes, I could do it."

"We've got a problem and we need your help," Ephraim said.

"Tell me, please," Joseph said in passable English.

"The men we had watching Bauer's place were captured by the Russians this morning." He told him the situation. "We don't know if their true identities have been discovered or not, but we need to find out."

"And you want me to go into the Russian sector and see if they are still alive?"

"They're alive all right. The Russians may be amoral, but they're not stupid. If they find out that my friends are more than beggars, they'll declare them spies, then try to make a deal that will give themselves considerable advantage."

"And you will make such a deal?"

"The Russians always start ridiculously high, but we'll come to terms."

"But the Russians would never do this. Their soldiers would rot in your prisons before they would make a deal for their lives."

"That's why they'll never last long. They don't care about their people."

Joseph shrugged it off as if it did not matter to him, but inside he was strongly impressed. "I will help you." He wished now that he had kept the Russian papers he had taken off the drunk last night, and the uniform also, but he hadn't. Another would have to be provided. "I will need papers and a uniform."

Ephraim turned and started from the house. "Come on. They'll have both ready for you when we get to headquarters."

Joseph put down his tools and followed. "You knew I would say yes?"

"Rachel vouched for you; that's enough for me."

Joseph hesitated; the words reached his ears, but his mind was unable to process them correctly. "Rachel vouched for me?"

"Yeah." Ephraim smiled back at Joseph. He could see that Rachel's approval meant a lot to him. "I'll tell you what, Joseph; you help us with this, and I'll take the two of you to the officers' club for dinner."

Joseph didn't believe him. "This is not possible. The American soldiers would not like to eat with a German soldier."

"You save a couple GIs and I think they'll make an exception." He hopped in the jeep and started the engine as Joseph climbed in the passenger side. The sky was bright with late afternoon sunshine and seemed especially beautiful to Joseph.

"By the way, you'll have a companion on this little journey," Ephraim said.

"You have another German?"

"Nope, just me," Ephraim smiled. "Just me."

"It is enough," Joseph said.

He decided he liked this American captain. He liked him a lot.

Now he must concentrate on keeping them both alive.

CHAPTER 24

Ephraim felt a bit pinched in the uniform and the hat felt tight enough to shut off circulation to the brain. He adjusted it as they approached the building used by the Russians as a holding prison.

They had been able to get back into the Russian Sector by going through the French sector where the Russians weren't so rambunctious about security. Joseph had received some flack from the soldier at the crossing but had handled it well. Rachel's friend had guts and the ability to use cold calculation when it was needed. Ephraim had been pleased to see it. They would need every ounce of bluster and bluff they could both muster to get inside the Russian prison, and if they were caught . . . well, the Russians would have two more chips to throw in the fire. General Clay would not be happy.

Ephraim and Mackland had decided to keep this little operation to themselves. Better to go ahead and make their apologies later than have the general face a court martial for giving orders even the President of the United States might not issue.

Joseph, seasoned by personal experience with Russia's most adept interrogators, told Ephraim never to make eye contact unless he was directly confronted by an officer of higher rank than they were. It was this arrogance of the Russian military that would be a dead give away if they didn't exhibit it. After hearing what little Russian Ephraim knew, Joseph also told him to keep a stern face and tight lip. No sense getting shot because he said the wrong thing at the right time, or vice versa.

They both wore the uniform and trappings of Russian colonels of the NKVD, the Russian intelligence organization, with forged papers to match. Ephraim's name was Arkady Dutyetov and Joseph was Colonel Alexei Bruganov. Neither man existed, though their uniforms belonged to two similar men who had been killed in the last battle for Berlin, their bodies buried but not quite deep enough to keep scavengers from stripping them of their clothes and putting them to good use in the black market. Americans loved Russian souvenirs nearly as much as they liked German ones, and uniforms were particularly prized.

Joseph also carried a letter supposedly signed by Zhukov himself giving them permission to interrogate all prisoners and remove those who may be valuable for negotiations with the Allies. A forgery, but a good one.

They saluted several soldiers guarding the building, walked up the steps and entered.

"Remember," Joseph said under his breath, "I talk, you nod a lot."

"Da," Ephraim responded, using one of the half-dozen Russian words he knew.

The building was the old Reich's museum—large, spacious and missing half its roof. There were large open areas left and right but the back of the building was intact. Joseph had been told by the captain's intelligence officers that they had sealed up the windows of rooms in that area and put in steel doors for holding prisoners. It was where they needed to go.

Joseph walked directly to the desk where a soldier had a mess of papers spread out before him to complete. Two other men waited for the signatures but were not officers and Joseph ignored them, saluting sharply. Ephraim followed suit.

"Comrade, I am Colonel Bruganov of the NKVD," Joseph handed the soldier at the desk his papers. "This is Colonel Dutyetov." Ephraim handed his papers over while secretly holding his breath. They were as good as forgeries got, but were they good enough?

The soldier took the papers, eyed them, looked up at his visitors, eyed the papers again, sat back, stared at them through lazy eyes for what seemed like ages to Ephraim then leaned forward and handed them back. "What is it you want Colonel?" The voice was mechanical, as if they were simply another problem he'd just as soon have move on, and the quicker the better.

Joseph bent over to eye level. "Your attitude about matters important to mother Russia are duly noted, comrade," he said stiffly, "and
button up your uniform before I have you replaced by someone with
a little Russian pride." He stood straight as the man hurriedly
buttoned his uniform and brightened his countenance.

Joseph handed him the letter from Zhukov. It was read and the
soldier quickly got to his feet and started barking orders. Three
soldiers carrying rifles appeared front and center. "These men will
escort you to the prisoners, then to the interrogation room."

Joseph only nodded stiffly, his eyes cold and hard. Ephraim found
himself looking at a side of Joseph he had never seen before. But then
Joseph's experience in Russia had created this man before him and it
was giving him the ability to pull off something that no one else
could. It made Ephraim simultaneously shudder and give thanks.

Two of the soldiers started toward the prison area and Joseph
and Ephraim fell in behind them, the third at Joseph's side.
Ephraim thought he could feel the relief of the desk sergeant as they
walked away.

"Do you have anyone besides Germans here?" Joseph asked.

"Yes sir, in cell one," the soldier responded.

"Then we go there first," Joseph said.

Ephraim did not understand much but stayed in step and tried to
play the uncommunicative interrogator ready to bully his adversaries
into submission. It was a hard part to play but he gave it his best shot.

An order was given to the two soldiers and they stopped in front
of a door. The soldier at Joseph's side quickly unlatched the door and
pulled it open. The other two stepped in and barked several orders in
broken English. Ephraim sensed some movement in the dimly lit
room but couldn't see faces.

"Step aside," Joseph said sternly. He entered the room with
authority and Ephraim did the same. Their eyes adjusted and they
found themselves looking into the eyes of Wally and his two men.
Wally stifled a smile as he saw that Ephraim and Joseph were wearing
Russian uniforms.

Stepping closer, Joseph looked them over authoritatively. "You
wear beggar's clothes, but you are Americans," he said in broken
English.

Wally lifted his dog tags, "That's right, and if you don't let us outta here real soon . . ."

The slap came quick and hard from Joseph, landing a blow across Wally's face. Wally reacted, but then stopped himself when he saw the Russians behind them raise their guns to where he could look directly down their barrels.

"We will decide when you will leave, and on what terms. Is that understood?" Joseph said coldly in adequate English.

Wally wiped the blood from his lip. "Yeah, understood."

He turned to the soldier who had opened the door. "Bring him," he said, reverting to Russian again.

Wally was grabbed by the two with guns and manhandled from the room. With all backs turned, Ephraim threw a quick wink in the direction of the other two, along with a smile. They responded in kind.

The interrogation room was several doors away but they were soon inside where Joseph ordered the guards to leave them alone as he began removing his coat. Ephraim followed suit.

With smirks of pleasure arising from Wally's discomfort, the guards left, shutting the door with a clang. Wally stood, grinning, but Joseph shoved him back in his seat while he looked around the room carefully, then at the door. Going back to Wally he leaned down and spoke in his ear. "They listen. They always listen."

Joseph signaled to Ephraim who pulled out his pen and pad. Joseph had forewarned them that their conversation would be monitored somehow so Ephraim had written out a series of statements and questions they knew would be needed. As Joseph began speaking loudly like an NKVD man laying the ground-work for a long series of interrogations, Ephraim showed the first written question to Wally.

Are we the first to interrogate you? the words on the notepad asked.

Wall nodded in the affirmative.

Ephraim turned to the next sheet. *Any other Americans you know of?*

Wally shook his head in the negative.

Another sheet was turned. *We'll interrogate you, then we will tell them we're taking you out of here and by train to Moscow. We have a letter from Zhukov giving us full authority.*

Wally nodded agreement, then signaled for the paper and pencil, quickly writing something down for Ephraim to see.

They said someone would be here today. I don't think they were talking about you.

Ephraim nodded as he showed it to Joseph, then he went to the next page with its already prepared message. *The interrogation by Joseph will be intense; just go with the flow.*

Wally looked at Joseph as he continued through his initial spiel for the benefit of any who might be listening in the adjoining room. The look on Wally's face was one of befuddlement, as if he couldn't put Joseph in this part. Ephraim had a ready answer. He flipped to the next page of his pad.

He was interned in Russia once. He went through this crap for a year.

Wally nodded, his look turning to one of admiration.

Ephraim gave Joseph a nod and the interrogation began. Ephraim watched during the next fifteen minutes as Joseph went so effectively from a soft-spoken fellow soldier to a hard-nosed, vicious attack dog that it made Wally start to sweat. It gave Ephraim an eye-opening look at what the Russian intelligence service was like and how they could break a person with a relentless barrage of words and brow-beating. Even *he* was glad when Joseph came to his last threats.

"I see that you will need convincing, comrade," Joseph said stiffly. "Possibly a trip to Moscow will help you give us what we want."

"I don't know what you want," Wally said without any kind of emotion.

"You are a spy. We want a confession, in writing. When we have it you can return to your imperialist stooges on the other side of Berlin." He paused.

Ephraim showed Wally another sheet. *Make him mad.*

Wally spat in Joseph's direction. "You can shove your confession where the sun don't shine," he said angrily.

Joseph blew up, barking something first at Wally then at Ephraim. Ephraim got the impression from Joseph's hand signals that he was to slap something, then knock Wally to the floor. He looked at his friend apologetically, then smacked him on the side of the chin. Wally spun out of his chair and hit the floor with a grunt. Joseph turned to the door and called for the guards, then ordered them to take Wally back to his cell and prepare all three men for travel. The plan was that he would demand a truck and they would haul them off in the direction of Moscow, then switch courses and end up in the American sector through Brandenburg gate where Mackland waited their arrival with a contingent of soldiers in case any Russians tried to stop them.

The soldiers grabbed Wally shoving him roughly down the hall to the door of his cell while Joseph barked more orders at the wide-eyed soldier attending the desk. He was scrambling to get their truck as the guards appeared with the three Americans. They brought out a set of shackles for each and had them in place when the desk soldier yelled that the truck would be out front immediately.

Half a dozen other guards stood about watching the action unfold. One of them stepped up to Ephraim and uttered something in Russian. Ephraim had no idea what was said and only grunted a response. The soldier pressed him with what sounded like a question. Ephraim grunted again but felt his stomach tie in a knot as sweat formed on his forehead.

Joseph rescued him with an order to the soldier plying Ephraim. The soldier jerked to action, quickly moving into a position to put his guns in Wally's ribs and prod him toward the exit.

The shackle keys were handed to Joseph who stuck them in his pocket and followed their captives down the long hall. Soldiers stood about eyeing them curiously, most with laughter in their eyes at the predicament of the Americans. Joseph glared at the desk soldier and gave him one last order that Ephraim did not understand. The entire place changed as the order was repeated and soldiers immediately started disappearing or coming to attention. The desk soldier quickly walked to Joseph and handed him his original papers and several others.

They were outside heading down the steps as the truck pulled up in front. The driver waited while the three Americans were put in the back and four guards climbed in with them. Joseph made it a point to pull down the tarp covering the back of the vehicle and signaled to Ephraim to tie it in place. He stepped close enough to Ephraim to whisper instructions.

"We sit in front. You next to the driver. When we're in the clear, you open the door and get rid of him, then drive."

Ephraim nodded.

As they were getting in the truck, Ephraim noticed a car pull up behind them and two soldiers get out. They were dressed in uniforms exactly like theirs and were eyeing them curiously. Ephraim hesitated and Joseph pushed him.

"Get in. They're NKVD," he said coldly. "And they are not acting."

Ephraim was quickly inside and Joseph calmly ordered the driver to go, when someone yelled an order from the direction of the car. The driver looked in his rearview mirror and seemed confused, glanced at Joseph, got another order and seemed even more confused. Joseph repeated it as he slammed his own door shut. The driver put the vehicle in gear as a soldier stepped in front of the vehicle and another was suddenly on the side board, giving an order. It was obvious he wanted ID.

With cold determination Joseph stared him down and said something that made him wince. Joseph handed the man the letter from Zhukov and shook it at him while speaking firmly. The man was a bit pale but stood his ground, took the letter and read it. He stepped down, saying something that Ephraim took as an order to stay put.

Joseph watched through the rearview mirror as the NKVD officer finished the letter, then studied their identity papers. After a moment he went up the stairs and disappeared inside the building.

Joseph spoke kindly to the driver, who nodded and got out and headed for the rear of the truck.

"I know this kind of man. He does not know us, and even though I told him we were only recently assigned under special orders from Moscow he will check it out. He out-ranks me so I cannot intimidate him. We are in trouble I think."

Ephraim slid over into the driver's seat. "Then it's time we left."

He started the engine, threw the transmission in gear, and pushed on the gas. The soldiers blocking their way stood their ground for a split second then jumped out of the way. Ephraim looked back. No one moved, no one tried to come after them, or even raised a gun to try and stop them.

"Russian military initiative," Joseph smiled. "They can do nothing unless they are told."

They were out of the square and headed into a side street when Ephraim looked again and saw the NKVD officer standing on the steps yelling orders. Soldiers were suddenly running for vehicles. They had their initiative and would pursue.

Ephraim saw the bombed-out building in front and to the right of them. Only part of one wall was still attached, letting it lean toward the center of the street as if it would come down at any moment. He shoved the truck into low, jerked the wheel, and rammed the front right fender against the building while pushing on the gas. Sparks flew and the impact threw him and Joseph forward but the heavy truck rolled on and they were quickly free of the wall as it shuddered, tipped, then fell into the street. Brick after brick fell, blocking the road behind them. Ephraim used the rearview mirror to watch the first of their pursuers slam on his brakes as their vehicle was hit by the last of the four-story building's upper-front wall.

"I think that should give us enough time," he said.

They drove quickly back the way they had come, avoiding main streets and ending up near the checkpoint for the French sector. Ephraim pulled up and quickly got out of the vehicle along with Joseph. Opening the tarp at the back, Joseph gave orders in Russian and the three guards jumped to the ground. His next command brought some shrugs, but they slung their rifles over their shoulders and walked back down the street.

"What did you tell them?"

Joseph shrugged. "That we were going to shoot the Americans and did not need their help."

"And they believed you?" Wally asked.

"They are machines, brainwashed by fear. If they disobey an order they can be shot so they do not fight the system. It is Stalin's Russia." He spat on the sidewalk, then seemed to get pale. "Excuse me," he said quickly moving away. Ephraim grimaced as Joseph heaved up his guts. After he was through he returned. "Come, we need to change."

It was as if throwing up were just part of the deal and it made Ephraim smile. The man had been hard as a rock even though he was a mass of nerves on the inside. The guy had what Wally would call moxy.

"Hey, Joseph," Wally said. "You saved our bacon, thanks."

"You are welcome, but it was the captain's good driving that kept us all free." Joseph said without a smile, his face still a bit pale.

"Yeah, well, I'm still aching from his right hook, so I'll thank him later," Wally grinned.

"That love tap wouldn't have bothered you if you didn't have such a glass jaw."

All of them laughed as they quickly removed the Russian uniforms and tossed them into the back of the truck, then dressed in the American ones, and started the short walk to the French checkpoint. They presented their papers and had no trouble getting through and were soon at the meeting place just inside the French sector where Mackland waited.

"Any trouble?" Mackland asked.

"Let's just say they know they've been hoodwinked," Ephraim said. "They will raise a ruckus in the Kommadatura tomorrow, sir."

"General Clay sent word to Russian headquarters asking about any Americans captured and was told they had none. They lied and they know we caught 'em. They opened this can of worms and we'll feed it to 'em."

I'm beginning to think we have traded one Nazi for another," Wally said.

"The Stalinists are like the Nazis, you cannot let them intimidate or they will not stop. If they see you are soft they will hit you, bully you, until you submit to them. Better to defend yourself against a bully. Even if he blacks your eye, he knows he cannot shove you around," Joseph said.

Mackland liked Joseph's fire. "How would you like a full-time job, Joseph?"

"If it has food at the end of the day, I am willing," Joseph answered.

"You won't go hungry." Mackland turned to Ephraim. "Put him to work on those Russian messages we've intercepted and see what he can make of them."

Ephraim nodded. Mackland was a hardnose sometimes but he treated men well, especially those that showed incentive and determination.

"We have embarrassed them, Colonel," Wally said. "They'll tighten up security and we won't get back to Bauer's place any time soon."

Mackland's brow wrinkled.

"There is always their forger, sir," Ephraim said.

The captain's right, Colonel," Wally said. "Everyone Bauer sees gets connected to the forger. If we watch him we'll catch most of Bauer's contacts, and he lives in our sector."

"Mmm, I wonder if he knows about the escape route we were told about?" Mackland said.

"I doubt it, sir. That's Bauer's domain."

"Then we must have Bauer."

"Yes sir," Ephraim said.

"And the forger?" Wally asked. "He is probably former SS and we ought to pick him up."

"When you're ready to move in on Bauer, not before."

"Yes sir," Wally said with a grin.

Mackland got back in his jeep and started the engine. Ephraim hopped in next to him with Wally and Joseph in the back. The other two members of Wally's team got in a second jeep driven by MPs. They crossed the French and British sectors to the American one.

By the time they were back at headquarters Ephraim had an idea.

Now all he needed was Rachel's help.

See Chapter Notes

CHAPTER 25

Wally and five soldiers entered the forger's office in the American headquarters building and made a quiet arrest. They kept him under lock and key in the same building while Ephraim, Rachel, Joseph, and two others carried out the rest of Ephraim's plan, including the delivery of a message to Rachel's father.

Half an hour later she and Joseph walked down the street toward the house. They were both in tattered clothes and both carried their own papers. Joseph also carried Ephraim's military-issue forty-five stuffed between his belt and his backbone, his beat up coat covering it.

The guards noticed them and one stepped directly in front of them, his rifle sending the message to go no further.

"This is Herr Bauer's daughter," Joseph said in Russian. "I am her husband. You can tell him we are here or we can tell him ourselves." His fluent Russian only added to the guard's confusion. He finally stepped aside and jerked his head toward the door.

They ascended the steps as Joseph put his arm around Rachel's waist. "Ready?"

"Yes," she said, in nervous confirmation.

Joseph knocked. A moment later the door opened and her father stood there in the afternoon sun. He didn't seem surprised to see Rachel but didn't fully recognize Joseph. He waved them in then closed the door.

"I thought you might come back," he said to Rachel. "Who is this?"

"Joseph," Rachel said.

The light of recognition came to her father's eyes. "Ah, yes, Joseph. I thought you were dead. The eastern front."

Joseph reached behind his back and pulled out the weapon. He let his arm hang to his side.

"You have come to shoot me?" her father smirked.

"After what you did to Rachel and her mother, shooting is too good for you," Joseph said coldly.

Bauer looked at his daughter. "You have something else in mind then."

"I gave your papers to the Americans. They have arrested Krupp and some of the others. They will serve long prison sentences."

"I have no intention of spending the rest of my life in Spandau prison."

"We have your forger. He was arrested this morning," Rachel said. There was a flicker of fear in his eyes. "He has told us much about your intention to escape, about the underground railroad through Italy. You will get nowhere."

A bead of sweat broke out on Bauer's forehead. He shook it off. "The little man doesn't know these things." He tried to sound confident.

"The Americans sent me with this message. If you will testify against Krupp and the others, if you will tell them more about the escape route and help them round up others, they will . . ." She hesitated. At first she had told Ephraim she would never deliver such a message. For her father to go free after what he had done to her mother would be insane! But Hannah had helped her understand. More lives would be saved, worse men would be convicted, imprisoned. She had finally agreed.

"It is hard for you to say," he said, a wry smile on his lips.

She lifted her head. "They will let you go free after you serve two years in prison."

"Only two years?" He laughed. "How considerate of them."

"They will not let you escape. You will either go to Moscow or you will cooperate with them. It should be an easy choice for a man who hates communists nearly as much as he hates Jews," Rachel said.

"You won't last a month in Moscow, Herr Bauer. I have been there, I know them. They will use you, then send you to Siberia. It is where they send anyone no longer useful to them," Joseph added.

Bauer's face seemed to sag with sadness. Joseph had never seen the man look so horrible. He could not be more than fifty and yet he looked eighty.

"And how do they expect me to get to them? I am under house arrest by the Russians who expect to take me to Moscow soon to rebuild my factories there. Those guards are here to keep me in more than to keep others out."

"Bribe them, kill them, get them drunk and slither away like the snake you are. They do not care how you do it, but if you are still alive when you try, they will keep their bargain," said Rachel.

"And you trust them?"

"After what you did to us I never thought I could trust another human being again, but two people have given me hope. One of them is an American. He has been watching this house, picking up Nazis who come here to get help. He hates your kind almost as much as I do, but he is a man of his word."

Bauer looked at Joseph. "You know this man?"

"She is right. You can trust him."

Bauer sat down on the steps that led upstairs. "Tell your friend that I will meet him at the beer house next to the Brandenburg gate. Tonight. Eight P.M."

Rachel moved to the door, then turned back. "Do not play games with them. They will hang Krupp or they will hang you. It is your choice." She left and Joseph followed. They never looked back.

* * *

As Ephraim waited in the German black-market beer house, he watched those who came and went and wondered how many were Nazis who had gotten away with murder. Maybe when Bauer arrived he could point out a few.

He breathed deeply. He was getting cynical, negative, black-hearted. He hated this business and could only hope new orders would come in soon and he'd be back flying and knocking Japs out of the air; finish off the war in the Pacific where Hitler's Japanese allies continued to hang on by the skin of their teeth.

Then he thought of Hannah. He supposed he could put up with this job a little longer. At least until he got her on her way. When the fighting was over, he would join her in Jerusalem. He had meant that.

He glanced at his watch. It was nearly eight-thirty. Maybe Bauer had changed his mind.

* * *

Bauer was only a few blocks away, wearing stolen clothes from one of his Nazi visitors now lying unconscious on the floor of Bauer's study. After the sun began setting, he had walked away in the deepening shadows without even a second glance from his Russian guard. By the time his unconscious visitor recovered he hoped to be across the line separating the Russians and the Americans.

He reached the border crossing as the last rays of the sun disappeared behind the horizon. His papers were forged, his identity that of a nondescript German Jew by the name of Hans Glitner, a former worker in his wife's factory and most recently a resident of Dachau concentration camp. When it was his turn he presented his papers to the Russian guard who looked them over with a scowl and compared his face with the picture.

"Your business among the Americans?" the guard asked flatly.

"I work for your government but live in the French sector. It is quicker to go this way."

The guard's face remained impassive. "For whom do you work?"

"The department of political affairs, Comrade Sutsov." Bauer knew Sutsov. The Russian had taken bribes to accept several of Bauer's Nazi friends into offices under his direction, but he had not forewarned Sutsov of his decision to leave the Russian sector and defect to the Americans for obvious reasons. Sutsov might hide a few midlevel Nazis for trinkets of gold and diamonds, but he would not aide the escape of a man General Zhukov was planning to send to Moscow.

The Russian guard eyed the papers again, compared the picture, then handed them back to Bauer. "You are free to go," he said, with a sharp jerk of his head.

Bauer wanted to dab the sweat from his brow but thought better of it, shoved the paperwork in his pocket and walked across the square to the American Sector where he went through a similar process.

"What is your business here?" the American soldier asked, taking the forged paperwork.

Bauer gave them the same answer he had given to the Russians.

"Are you carrying any weapons?" the soldier asked.

"Nein," Bauer responded.

"Stand over there just the same. Let's have a look."

Bauer moved to where he was told and the soldier patted him down. "Sorry, sir, but things are getting a bit sticky with the Russians these days."

Bauer only nodded. He endured the humiliation of the search, received his papers back and started away when he noticed two men near the wall of the closest building. Both seemed to be watching him but looked away when his eyes fell upon them. Americans? Russians? Possibly criminals looking him over to determine if he was a good target? He lengthened his stride and walked briskly in the direction of his meeting place with the Americans. He heard no footsteps following and started breathing easier, though a nagging sense of something he couldn't quite put his thumb on lingered. He was not a popular man with the Americans, and the Russians would like him even less once they discovered he had removed himself from their sphere of influence. Even his Nazi friends would not like him if they found out what he was up to. So many enemies, and so few friends. His pace quickened. Over the next ten minutes he stopped occasionally, listened, heard nothing unusual in the dark streets, and, except for beggars trying to find a place to spend the night, saw nothing that concerned him. He relaxed as he turned a corner and saw the nearly ruined Brandenburg Gate and the beer house next door. He looked at his pocket watch. Nearly quarter of nine. He was late. He should go in, but didn't. He was changing everything if he met with Daniels. Everything.

He sat down on the steps of a bombed-out building and pulled out one of his cigars. Nearly his last one. Biting off the end he spat it on the ground then ignited a match on the concrete step and lit the cigar. He would have little chance for such a small pleasure in the near future. Spandau prison offered few such luxuries.

He thought back to the events that had led him like a mouse behind the Pied Piper to this place. He had been a believer in Hitler and his plans for a greater Germany. This could never change, but in his overzealous support he had betrayed his family.

At the time he had believed the propaganda. Hitler himself had praised him for his sacrifice and promised him that Germany would someday be free of the tainted blood of the Jews so that a pure master race could rise up to lead the world for a thousand years. The nightmares about what he had done to his wife and Rachel had been eased only by alcohol and by others telling him constantly that he was the best among them, that his sacrifice set an example for all to follow. Few had.

When Rachel had come to the house that had all changed. He had been forced to face what he had done without the illegitimate reinforcement of others. It had been a horrible revelation. Three times since then he had put a gun to his head to be rid of the anguish he felt but had been unable to pull the trigger. He was not only a traitor—he was a coward. Possibly helping the Americans would at least take the edge off the pain, even help Rachel understand that he knew now. Knew that he had been wrong.

He stood. Rachel would never understand. There was no understanding of such betrayal. No, it would do nothing for his relationship with Rachel. That was gone in the fires of those horrible places he had refused to believe existed for fear they would drive him absolutely mad! He would pay in hell for what he had done, but possibly he would not have to pay so long if he helped the Americans. He could do a good deal of damage to the underground network, possibly even destroy it, and Krupp would die in prison if Bauer told even a tenth of what he knew. Millions of dollars were housed in bank accounts in Norway, Switzerland, and Argentina and he knew how to get his hands on every single one of them. The fourth Reich wouldn't have a prayer without those funds.

He was tired. So very tired. It had all crumbled to ashes and those who continued to believe that it would rise again were only deluding themselves. Hitler was gone, Himmler buried, Goebbels in hell. Bormann did not have the charisma of the Fuhrer, the evil mind of Himmler, nor the silver tongue of Goebbels. Bauer knew that all Bormann wanted was to survive and live the life of a rich man in Argentina. Krupp and the others were too blind to see it, so they would give him the money. He would never give it back. Unless Bauer stopped him.

Yes, he was tired.

He knocked the hot ashes off the end of the cigar and then pinched it until there was no fire before sticking it back in his pocket. Standing, he took a deep breath and started for the beer house.

He saw the movement in the shadows to his left, then to his right, and it made his heart race but he kept a steady pace. He was only feet from the front door and the safety of the interior. No one would be foolish enough to jump him here, not with a half a dozen Americans lounging about the entrance. Besides, he hadn't been followed. He was sure of it.

He pushed open the door and went inside, taking a deep breath in an attempt to get rid of the nagging feeling of danger. But wasn't such a feeling normal? After all, he *was* in danger. He was about to go to prison.

His eyes scanned the poorly lit bar for an American in uniform. There was only one. He sat in the corner of the room, his back to the wall. Bauer walked to the table. "Captain, I am Rolf Bauer. I assume this chair is reserved for me."

Ephraim nodded and Bauer sat down.

"My daughter says you can be trusted."

"She doesn't know me that well."

Bauer smiled. "She is a good judge of character, believe me."

"Mmm, do I sense some regret?" Ephraim asked.

"Only that the Reich did not survive. I paid a high price for it."

"Would you like something to drink?" Ephraim asked.

"A beer would be nice."

Ephraim called a waiter and Bauer ordered.

"Tell me about the escape route."

"You do not waste time."

"I want to know if you're worth what I've offered." Ephraim glanced up as two men came through the door.

"I know enough to close the door on such a place, but I have a price."

"Rachel told you; two years and you're free."

Bauer received his beer and Ephraim threw an American dollar on the table. The clerk thanked him and left. Bauer took a drink. "I ask only that I live long enough to see Krupp and Bormann hang. After that I do not care."

"An attempt at penance?"

"Call it what you like. I also ask something for my daughter."

Ephraim saw the two men take beers and sit at a table against the wall fifteen feet away. There was something about them he didn't like.

"Time to go," he said, pushing his chair away from the table and rising.

"I haven't finished . . ."

Ephraim leaned down. "You were followed, Bauer. Get up!"

Bauer stood and turned around. Ephraim took the position between Bauer and the two men. Wally was at the bar in civilian clothes and two others at a table on the other side of the room. He gave them a signal with his eyes and Wally reached for his weapon.

It was too late.

The two men stood, one pulling an automatic weapon from inside a bag on the floor. Ephraim reached at the small of his back and retrieved his weapon but Bauer shoved him away, placing his body between the assailants and Ephraim.

A ribbon of bullets emitted from the black barrel, cutting Bauer down like they were cutting up a tree. Wally fired, killing the assailant where he stood as the second man emptied his own weapon into Bauer's lifeless frame before he was hit in the chest and knocked to the floor like a puppet whose strings had been cut.

Ephraim went to Bauer and turned him over. He checked for a pulse. Nothing.

Wally checked one of the assailants. Pulling up a sleeve he found the tattoo of the SS Deathhead squad. "Nazis," he spat as he shoved the arm aside.

"They must have followed him. When they saw he was meeting with us they decided to be rid of him."

Wally only nodded. "Makes you wonder what he knew, what they were afraid of."

"My bet is a good deal more than we'll ever find out from anyone else."

It seemed the Werewolves still had teeth.

* * *

In the next twenty-four hours the American Army was able to round up nearly a hundred more Nazis using false IDs made by the forger. The fool had kept a list, probably to make sure their names were registered at the American document center at which he worked so there would be no question as to their authenticity. The roundups would continue for at least another week. Ephraim figured they would get several hundred more.

Krupp and several other industrialists were arrested, interrogated, and either put under house arrest or in jail. General Clay started feeling the heat from such a move before the day ended and Ephraim seriously doubted many like Krupp would ever see the inside of a prison. The trail of the money from the Reichsbank went cold with Bauer's death. Thanks to Rachel, Colonel Mackland's intelligence people knew where it was, but couldn't get at it without someone letting them inside accounts other than Bauer's. Krupp and the others refused to cooperate, under any circumstances. Ephraim figured it would be years before any of the money came back to Germany or to the Jews from whom most of it was taken. He could only hope that stiff reprisals would be waged against the industrialists, forcing them to give it back out of their own company pockets. The way things were going he knew it was doubtful.

He wanted out of this dirty business and dealing with dirty people. He walked into Mackland's office two days after Bauer's death wanting to know the status of his request for transfer to the Pacific Theater. Mackland tried to convince him he was needed here but Ephraim didn't let it go. Either get it done or he'd appeal directly to General Clay. Mackland knew he meant it this time and didn't balk.

Bauer was buried the next day. Rachel had refused him burial in the family crypt, so he was to be buried with Berlin's poor in a mass grave. At the last minute Rachel softened, selling her mother's brooch to buy a plot in the cemetery. A coffin was provided and Bauer was buried with only Rachel and her friends present. It had been necessary for Rachel to finally let go of the hate.

Berlin was beginning to rebuild and by the tenth of July the streets were cleared and the city prepared for the visit of American dignitaries. There would be a concert, and Tappuah and the newly organized orchestra under the direction of Andrik Mendel would be center stage. It was only a day away.

CHAPTER 26

Andrik watched in continued awe as Tappuah finished the last piece and then lifted her fingers ceremoniously from the keys. She played with her heart and soul, and Andrik felt like he was hearing it all for the first time. When she was finished he was both amazed and speechless.

She turned to face him, a broad smile and the deep flush of satisfaction covering her round face. He had begun noticing how beautiful she was the first day they met, but the more she played the more beautiful she seemed to become and it was hard for him to take his eyes off her.

"Well?" she asked when he said nothing.

He cleared his throat. "Horrible," he said, trying to fake a frown.

The look of horror on her face elicited a broad grin from him.

"Andrik! If you do not quit doing this to me, I . . . I . . . ."

"Yes, Tappuah, you will what?" he asked evenly.

She lifted her chin in mock arrogance. "I will never play for you again."

He smiled as he stood and went to the edge of the stage, his arms extended to help her down. The once-attached stairs had mysteriously disappeared and Andrik figured they had been stolen either for firewood, for cooking, or by the allies for some purpose only they and God knew. "You would deny me the one joy of my miserable life?" he said seriously.

She stood and stepped to him. He lowered her down and they remained close to one another for a brief moment before he turned back to his work. "There was a bit of hesitation between notes." He brought over his copy of the music and pointed at the place with his pencil. "Here."

She was still looking at him but let her eyes fall to the music long enough to see what he meant before staring at him again. "Yes, I know. I will take care of it. Andrik, will you kiss me?"

He was a bit startled by the directness of the request but more so by the fact that he wanted to, very much.

He put his arms around her waist and kissed her lightly on the lips. She held him close and kissed him back, once then twice, then a third time but with more passion. He found himself giving in to the waves of heat that rolled over him. He was in a sea pushed by a wild storm and it was all he could do to keep from drowning in wild reverie.

She placed her head against his shoulder as he held her to him. "This is an unexpected pleasure," he said.

"Mmm. I want to marry you."

He pulled back, looking into her eyes to see if she was serious. "Marry? That's even more sudden than the kiss," he smiled.

"Do you want to marry me?"

He didn't know what to say. Did he? Or was it just his hormones? "I . . . I don't know," he said softly.

"Marry me anyway," she said. "I will make you very happy."

He laughed lightly. This was happening so fast, catching him so completely off guard, that he actually found himself wanting to do it but fearful of it at the same time!

He stepped back and pushed himself up onto the stage into a sitting position, his legs dangling. He ran his fingers through his long hair, unsure of what to say. She folded her arms across her stomach, a coy grin on her lips, waiting. Tappuah was a girl who had always been direct and who knew what she wanted and how to get it. In the camps she had been forced to suppress that trait but relished its return. She wanted Andrik. Wanted him now, and knew they could make it work because they both had the same passion for music, were both temperamental, and both had a passion for life that would carry them through days of darkness to those when the sun would shine bright.

"I am not a Jew," Andrik said quietly.

"I will take you anyway," she responded.

"I can't leave Germany. This is my home. This is where I stay."

"Then I will stay with you," she countered, stepping forward, facing him, one hand on his knee. "I ask only that you give me children, a home, and a chance to play my music to audiences all over the world, not necessarily in that order."

He couldn't help but smile. "You are using me to forward your career, give you posterity, and house you. I will be nothing but a slave."

"But I will love you in return," she said coquettishly. "Few men will be able to claim such a devoted wife."

"Why me?" he asked softly.

"Why not?"

"I'm serious, Tappuah. I am German, you are Jewish. It seems to me that you would hate . . ."

She pushed a finger to his lips. "You resisted, Andrik. You saved Jews instead of turning them in. That alone is enough to make me love you. You are honorable, strong, passionate. I see these qualities and I want to possess them before another does." She looked down. "It is I that may not be the prize, not you."

He lifted her chin so that their eyes met. "Is that why you push so hard? You are afraid you are not desirable? That you may never find someone who can love you?"

She looked down again.

He slipped from the stage, their bodies against each other. He wrapped his arms around her. "You do not need to worry on that account. You feed a fire in me that burns hot enough to consume us both."

"But you . . . you do not love me," she said.

"I . . . I don't know what I feel, Tappuah. Only time . . ."

She backed away. "Time will change nothing. Either you love me or you don't." Turning she ran from the room.

Andrik sat there wondering what had just happened. In a moment he'd had the chance to marry a woman who gave him sleepless nights and had let her slip away because of his inbred aversion to spontaneity. He jumped from the stage and ran after her.

As he came into the street he found himself in the middle of a summer rainstorm and was immediately soaked through to the skin, but he hardly noticed. Looking left and right he saw her running down the rain-pummeled street toward the apartment complex. He yelled after her but she did not hear or refused to listen. In long strides he nearly caught up when his shoes slipped on the slick stones of the street, his legs flying out from under him. He landed on his back with a crunch that took his breath away and put a hard ache in the lower part of his back.

"Andrik!" Tappuah yelled as she saw him fall. Quickly she ran back and knelt by his side. "Andrik, are you all right?!"

He saw the fear in her eyes and knew instantly that her feelings for him were more than just those of insecurity, even as pain forced him to grimace.

"I . . ." He tried to catch his breath, force the words out. "I . . ."

She lifted his head to her lap, kissing his forehead as the rain washed over them.

"You love me, don't you?" She grinned. "I knew you loved me!" She kissed him on the forehead again.

He put up a hand so that she would stop long enough for him to try and get up. When he was on his knees and facing her he took her head in his hands and kissed her. "Yes, I love you," he said. "Will you marry me?"

"Not on your life!" she said. Then with a laugh she kissed him again, then flung her arms around him and held him tight. "I love you, Andrik." she said. "I really do love you."

CHAPTER 27

They pulled up to the gate, Ephraim flashed his ID, and they were let through. Hannah saw the sign, "Flughafen Templehof." Airport Templehof. What was he doing?

He had picked her up at the apartment complex saying only that he had something he wanted to show her. Now here they were, passing through rows of bombed-out buildings and onto the tarmac of Tempelhof. What was it that he wanted her to see here?

Several large planes with bullet-riddled bodies slumbered to their left as if trying to recuperate and become whole again. Next to them sat a dozen fighters, their sleek torsos glinting in the sun and ready for more service if called on. They passed all of them, stopping at a small building at the far end of the hangars. He shut off the jeep and came around to help her out.

"Wait!" he said, barely able to contain his excitement. "Stay right there." He signaled with his hand as he backed toward the building. She stopped in her tracks as he began opening the large doors. A moment later Hannah peered into the dark shadow of the hangar at the nose of an old biplane. Excited, Ephraim took her hand and quickly led her inside. As her eyes adjusted she could see the plane was in mint condition, bright yellow in color with black markings of the regime prior to the Nazis.

"World War One. A collector's item. Goering had it restored and used to fly it around the country before we controlled the skies with faster fighters and bombers. By some act of God it survived the bombing of this place. Can you believe it?"

Hannah couldn't help but smile at his excitement, but couldn't resist the urge to tease either. "It is very old, Ephraim," she said with a worried tone in her voice. Surely it would never get off the ground.

Ephraim's face grew serious as he looked at the plane then at her. "No, really, it's in fine shape . . . it . . ."

"But look how heavy the wings look, and the tires they are worn so thin," she said mournfully.

"What? No, no, these are different tires, they . . ."

"And the propeller, it has only two pieces to it! Surely that is not enough . . ." She grinned as he ran to the front of the plane, then realized he had been taken.

He turned and came slowly toward her. "You deserve a good spanking." He lunged to grab her arm, but she was too quick for him. Dodging left and right, laughing as she escaped, then pounding him on the chest playfully as he caught her and swung her around in his arms, holding her tight. He kissed her lightly, then smiled. "You said once you would like to try flying."

"Yes, I did, but I'll need a pilot. Do you know anyone who might know how to fly an old plane like this?"

He took her hand and started for the plane. "No, but I'll give it a try." He stood on the wing and reached inside, picking some things from off the front seat and handing them to her. She saw that it was the old-style leather helmet with a pair of goggles and a heavy wool scarf of yellow. She quickly put hers on while Ephraim did the same with another set from the rear seat. He then gave her instructions on how to pull the prop, climb in her seat, and fasten herself in.

"Can you do it?" he asked.

She flexed a muscle. "Strong as an ox," she said going around to the front of the plane. He climbed inside, adjusted several switches, and gave her the okay. She pulled on the propeller with all her strength, then jumped back when it caught. The motor coughed and sputtered to life as she worked a wide circle and climbed aboard. As she fastened herself in the harness, Ephraim worked on the engine until it purred. Slowly they moved out of the hangar and onto the tarmac, and a few minutes later were rushing down the runway at takeoff speed. She turned a bit to look back at him and saw that he was speaking into a headset.

When he was finished he yelled, "A Goering addition, along with a bigger, more modern engine." She only nodded, knowing the wind would carry her words away as soon as she spoke them. She turned back as they sped over the remains of buildings at the end of the runway. A moment later she looked down on Dahlem and recognized the Luftwaffe building, then their apartment complex. She felt the plane bank right, go lower and come back across the complex at rooftop elevation. It took her breath away and she closed her eyes briefly; afraid they might ram the poor apartment building. Then she forced them open and glanced down to see Rachel and Zohar standing in the street, waving frantically. She wondered if Ephraim had forewarned them.

He did a complete circle and headed south; in moments the city disappeared behind them and the green of the country stretched out in the distance. They flew over towns and villages, some completely destroyed, some without a single building damaged. She saw farmers working their fields, and people traveling the roads by cart and bicycle. Even from here they looked haggard and worn, a mass of humanity trying to find where they belonged. It saddened Hannah.

Fifteen minutes later they were circling a large field once used for landings, and a moment later they were settling down on the soft grass. Hannah grabbed the side of the plane as they bumped, left the ground momentarily, then settled down and came to a stop at the far end of the field after turning back, facing the way they had come. The propeller came to a halt as Hannah removed her gear, then turned to Ephraim, curious about why they were here. In response to her look he reached down and pulled out a basket.

"Another picnic," he said. They were quickly out of the plane and walking toward a line of trees nearby. As they got closer she could see that a stream ran through the trees and that nothing but farmland stretched beyond it.

"Where are we?" she asked.

"South of Remagen. We used this field for a while. Over there," he pointed to some buildings at the far end of the runway field, "was where we parked the planes for refueling. I lived for two weeks in a tent to the left of the old headquarters shack. I came down here to get away, calm my nerves, find a little peace."

He led her down a path until they came to a spot of grass along the edge of the stream. They sat down, the picnic basket between them.

"Thank you," she said. "This is wonderful."

"I like picnics," he smiled in return.

The singing of the birds seemed loud and Hannah realized she hadn't heard any in Berlin since going there. She wondered if they would ever return.

Though the warm sun radiated through the trees, shade insulated them from its burn. A more idyllic setting certainly could not exist, Hannah thought. It made the war seem so far away, the sorrow and pain of displacement momentarily kept at bay.

"Where did you fly to from here?" she asked.

"Wherever troops needed air cover, or we flew against a few left-over fighters of the Luftwaffe who tried to knock down our bombers when they'd come over from France and England."

"Does it seem like a dream to you?" she asked.

"More all the time. You?"

"Yes, and for this I thank your God."

"He's your God, too, Hannah."

"Yes, I know, but I still find it necessary to distinguish between old and new."

He pulled the sandwiches he had purchased at the officers club from the picnic basket, along with a jar of pickles, some boiled eggs, and a bottle of fresh water. He handed her one of the waxed-paper-wrapped sandwiches and they ate, enjoying the peace of the afternoon and each other's company.

"How do you like flying?" Ephraim asked as he peeled away the shell of an egg and dropped it into the waxed paper wrapping.

"It is very peaceful and yet exciting at the same time. Yes, I like it very much."

"I thought you might." He handed her the egg, then peeled one for himself. They washed it all down by drinking from the same bottle of water.

"I went to Leo's," Hannah said, after putting things back in the basket. "He finished the portrait." She removed the picture from her pocket. She had gone to the black market where she had found a simple wood frame with glass still intact. She handed it to him.

He admired the work. It was Hannah and it was different than Leo's past works. This was full of light instead of dark colors. "You are a beautiful woman, Hannah Gruen."

She leaned forward and put her hand to the side of his face, then kissed him. "I love you, Ephraim. I love you for what you have done for me, for what you have given all of us, but most of all I love you for saving my soul."

"I . . ."

She put her finger to his lips. "Shh. I have something I need to say. My faith in your God, your Messiah, is still weak but it is growing. I just need time, Ephraim. Just give me a little time."

He took her hand and kissed it. "I haven't always believed what I believe, Hannah. Like everyone else I had to find out for myself. It took a lot of study, hours of prayer, even some fasting, but I did find out. Knowing what it takes, I can wait while you work it out. Okay?"

Hannah lay back and Ephraim stretched out next to her, his hands behind his head. After a few moments of watching the light filter through the trees, he lifted himself to an elbow and looked at Hannah, who turned her head toward him. She watched as a mischievous look crossed his face and lit up his eyes. "What are you thinking, Ephraim Daniels? Whatever it is I don't like it!"

"It's awfully hot out here, don't you think?" he said. He glanced at the creek even as he reached out and grabbed her arm.

"Oh no you don't!" she said, quickly getting to her knees and trying to pull free. "If you want to take a swim, be my guest but not me!"

He was up as she pulled her hand free and backed away, jumping behind a tree and keeping it between them as he tried to get hold of her again. He feinted left, then jumped right when she took the bait. He had her in his arms, kicking and pounding on him as he marched down the bank and into the water.

"Don't you do it, Ephraim! I warn you!" she laughed and growled as she tried to break free.

A moment later, still clutched tightly in his arms, she found herself nearly submerged in deep, cold water that took her breath away. She held tight to his neck as he tried to dunk her, pulling hard and making him lose his balance. Suddenly he stumbled and both of them went under. She kicked free and grabbed his head and pushed down, holding him until she got her balance and pushed herself across the water to the bank. He came up, shaking his head and spraying water for several feet around him. He saw her grasping for the shore and quickly lunged after her, catching a leg and pulling her screaming back into the water where he gripped her one more time in his arms.

"Prepare for submersion, dear girl," he said.

"Don't you dare!" she said, threatening. The smile and laugh did little to drive the warning more than skin deep and he lifted her high before throwing her into the middle of the stream, her playful scream suddenly cut off by the sudden rush of water over her face and mouth. She came up sputtering and spewing forth water, a red glare to her eyes. "You!" she said, coming after him. He dodged left and right, backed up, laughing, warding her off, but she was not to be denied. Grabbing his hand she twisted his fingers and pushed up on his arm hard enough that he threw himself back to get away. Trying to get his balance in the deep water gave Hannah the chance to over-take him. She shoved his head down for the second time and held him down long enough to thrust herself toward shore. When he came up she was scrambling up the bank. She made it this time and was sitting on the grass by the blanket when he stumbled out and threw himself on the ground next to her. Rolling on his back, he spread his arms to the side. "I give up." he said. "You win."

"You're crazy, do you know that?" she said playfully. "Look at us, we're soaking wet!"

"Ah, but don't you feel refreshed!" he said.

She laughed, lying back beside him. "Refreshed? Cold, that is what I feel!"

He got to his feet. "Come on then, I have just the ticket." He started for the field, picking up the blanket and basket as he did. She got to her feet, her dress clinging to her and dripping water as she ran to catch up.

"Surely we're not getting in the plane. We'll freeze to death."

"Nope, *on it!* The wings, up there!" He pointed. "See how the sun hits them? No warmer place than that. I know. I've used plane wings to dry off more than once."

They reached the plane and he helped her climb up. He was right, the metal was hot to the touch and as she lay her wet body on it she felt the warmth travel through her almost immediately.

"Ohh, that feels good!" she said, as he found a spot close by.

"The best!" he said.

A few minutes later, the heat sucked from the wing beneath them, they slid to the left to find more. Over the next twenty minutes they shifted three times and were nearly dry.

"How many girls have joined you for such delicious entertainment?" she asked.

"Well, let me think." He started counting on his fingers. He sighed. "Alas, only one."

"I'm honored."

"Only one besides you," he teased.

She slugged him on the shoulder.

"Ouch." He shifted positions, his face to the sky. She lifted to one elbow and looked over at him. "You're nearly dry," she said.

"You too. Wanna go in for another swim?" He grinned.

"Let's save some of the fun for another day, shall we?"

"If you insist." He paused, staring at her. "I like your hair frizzy like that. Very chic."

Her hand went immediately to her hair. It wasn't frizzy at all. Her hair had grown a good deal in the last few weeks and it was naturally curly. It now clung in matted curls to her scalp. She ruffled it, letting the wind finish drying it out. "You're not a bit funny, you know."

"Do you still love me?"

She looked down at him but gave no answer.

"Well, do you?" he asked.

"I'm thinking." She smiled, then lay down on her back again, staring at the sky. There were a few clouds but mostly there was blue. Deep and wonderful blue. "Thank you for a wonderful day."

"You're welcome."

They lay silent, the sun warming them and drying the last few spots of water from their clothes.

"I meant what I said the other day, about Jerusalem," Ephraim said.

She turned on her side, an arm tucked under her head. "I know, but I will go wherever you want, Ephraim; you know that, don't you?"

He nodded. "We should make millions with my new airline. We can live in both places. We'll teach our kids to be cowboys *and* camel jockeys."

She laughed.

"How many?" he asked.

"How many what?"

"Kids."

"That's easy. At least a dozen."

He grinned. "All boys, of course."

"Of course. Twelve sons. Like Jacob."

He sat up. "Come on. We'd better get going."

He slid off the upper wing and onto the fuselage, then helped her do the same. A moment later he lifted her to the ground. She found herself standing close to him. He raised her chin with his index finger so that she could see into his eyes. Then he kissed her. She wrapped her arms around his neck and responded to the love she felt through the soft and gentle strength of his arms. As he pulled slowly away, softly kissing her cheeks, then her lips again, tears came to her eyes and dropped gently down her face. How could one person love another so much?

She lay her head against his shoulder and they remained in each other's arms for long moments before Ephraim pulled back, brushing the tears from her cheeks. He kissed her gently on the lips once more before taking her hand and helping her into the seat of the plane.

It was then they heard the voices and turned to see two men coming from the trees. They were older men, dressed in farmer's clothes and carrying implements of their trade. They noticed Hannah and Ephraim and nervously started to move away.

"Wait," Ephraim said in German. "You do not need to leave. In fact, if you like I will take you each for a ride."

They were both shocked by the offer and one of them backed away, fear filling his face. "No, no," he said. "Birds were meant to fly, not men!"

Ephraim held back the chuckle and turned to the second. "You, how about you, would you like to go up in Goering's plane?"

"Goering? This is his . . . this is the one we saw in the newspapers?" the man responded.

"Yes, this is the one," Ephraim said.

"But . . . but Goering is your enemy, he is my enemy. He . . ."

"That's why we took his plane away from him. Now it is for all Germans to enjoy. What could be better? How about it?"

The man looked at the face of his friend who declared all sorts of bad things would surely happen. He ignored him while grinning from ear to ear.

"Okay?" Ephraim asked Hannah. She nodded, her face full of a smile as she climbed from her seat. Moments later Ephraim and his new passenger were aboard and she started the propeller, then watched as they headed for the other end of the airport, lifted off, and just missed the trees. The man was probably having kittens she thought, and he'd come back with the thrill of his life.

Fifteen minutes later the plane came in low, dropped just past the trees and landed in the field. It came to a stop in the same position as before. The farmer had a very large smile and was quickly out of the plane, trying to encourage his friend to go. The older gentleman backed away, his head shaking vigorously in the negative. Finally his friend turned to Ephraim and shrugged, then they picked up their tools and disappeared in the woods along the river.

Hannah quickly climbed on the wing and let herself into the seat of the plane. She had her belt and goggles on when the plane skipped across the field, bounced into the air, and lifted above the trees. The evening sun glistened off the clouds in reds and oranges and Hannah couldn't remember anything so beautiful. As they swept north and east she laid her head back and simply let the swift fresh air wash over her, enjoying this island of peace and beauty in an otherwise gray and stormy sky.

When she opened her eyes again she could see the dusty cloud that marked Berlin. They were nearly there, their moment in the sun ending quickly. She wanted Ephraim to turn the plane around, keep going, fly on for as long as the little yellow bird would carry them. But they could not. She closed her eyes once more, burning the day's feelings into her mind so that she would never lose them.

The biplane banked left and rushed toward the ground. As they came to a stop and the propeller fluttered and then stood still, she wiped away the tears from her cheeks. Her heart hurt with the knowledge that their time together was nearly over.

* * *

Hannah, Rachel, and Zohar arrived for the concert fifteen minutes early. Hannah had returned to the apartment with just enough time to take a cold shower and dress while Rachel told her about Tappuah. Hannah received the news with mixed emotions. Their falling in love so quickly did not bother her. She understood perfectly what Tappuah was feeling, but having to leave one of her new sisters behind nearly broke her heart.

They found their seats and Hannah looked for Ephraim. He was in the concert booths above and on the far side from her. She found him looking at her while Colonel Mackland was trying to tell him something. She gave him a smile, then looked away. It was hard to be in the same room and keep her distance.

Joseph appeared and took a seat next to Rachel. She noticed that Rachel put her arm through his as he told her something that seemed to excite him. Rachel gave him a congratulatory smile then leaned toward Hannah and told her that Joseph had been hired by the Americans to work in their intelligence service as an interpreter. His Russian was proving invaluable. Hannah tried to look happy while feeling that another one of her sisters was slipping away.

She concentrated on the program in her hands. The Americans had done this first class. Their visiting politicians should surely be pleased. She looked around her. The theater was in top condition, everything repaired, all the right people in their places. Even General Zhukov was here, his entourage taking three private boxes and half a dozen of the rows in front of them. It seemed the Russian had gotten over the loss of Rolf Bauer rather quickly. Inside he must be boiling. It made her smile.

Andrik came on stage to loud applause. He greeted all, especially the dignitaries, then took up his position in front of the orchestra. She saw Gunther with his cello and Tappuah at the piano—flushed, frightened, excited.

It began. The music reverberated off the walls and pounded their senses with its beauty. It had been so very long since she had heard an orchestra! She had forgotten how wonderful the sounds were, how they reached every emotion, tingling her spine with the thrill of brass and violins and percussion and piano. Tappuah played with fervent emotion, her hands moving across the keys with such speed and accuracy that it left Hannah in awe. She could see the passion in Tappuah's face, her eyes wide and full of wonder. When the last note echoed from the walls Hannah stood with all the others to applaud again and again the sounds of music that seemed almost out of this world.

As Andrik presented a bouquet of flowers to Tappuah, Hannah could see the love in their eyes and she stopped worrying. They would be all right in Berlin. They would build lives here as they helped rebuild the city. Their music would lift and give hope to others. Tappuah had found her place and Andrik would protect her.

Hannah and Zohar left the building alone, Rachel and Joseph taking a separate route. They walked into a crowd of Berlin's most beleaguered who had heard the music and drifted here as if pulled by a magnet. Andrik had announced that more concerts would be held each night for the next few days and that there would be no charge for Berlin's survivors. They were the ones who really needed the music.

The streets seemed cleaner than usual and a few streetlights dotted the ruins. Hannah and Zohar walked back to Dahlem, passing through the area usually filled with black-marketeers. They had been closed down for the night by the military or by the music or possibly a little of both, and the two women traversed the center of town without incident. As they walked into their street, Hannah saw Ephraim sitting on the steps of their apartment. As she got close enough she could see he had an envelope in his hands and a strange look on his face. Zohar excused herself and went inside.

He handed Hannah the envelope. She opened it and pulled out the single sheet, then read it under the dim light from the entry. At first she wasn't sure of what it meant. She could not read English well. She read it again then realized that Ephraim had been reassigned to the Pacific. She felt weak and had to sit down. He sat next to her.

"I leave first thing in the morning," he said softly.

She had known it was coming, but why today? Why, when everything else had been so wonderful? Why today?

He took her hand and held it and she lay her head on his shoulder, their hearts aching. Both had known this was coming, but for the past few days both had secretly wished it away. Hannah was suddenly afraid. He would fly in combat again. She gripped his hand tighter. If she lost him now, if . . .

Ephraim knew what she was feeling. He had wanted this day to come, had prayed it would, but now that it was here he was painfully torn. Before there had been little to come back to. Over the last few days, that had changed. He put an arm around her shoulder. "It will be all right, Hannah. It will be all right."

Hannah felt a tear reach the corner of her eye. She turned into his shoulder. Now only God could grant her wish. "Next year in Jerusalem," she prayed in her mind. "Please let it be. Please!"

See Chapter Notes

CHAPTER 28

The next morning Hannah stood on the roof of their apartment building and watched Ephraim's plane take off from Templehof Airport. She watched until it disappeared, the sunrise on her right. She ran her fingers over the hard cover of his book. Its words were her only comfort now. She clung to them like a camp victim holding on to a crust of bread, afraid she'd wake up and find it all a dream.

As she returned to the apartment, then went out onto the balcony, Wally pulled up in his jeep. He looked up at her and gave a weak smile of condolence before disappearing through the front entrance. A moment later Zohar let him into the apartment and he handed Hannah an envelope.

"Ephraim told me that if I didn't get these he'd break my face. I picked them up from the British sector myself about twenty minutes ago. Ink's still not dry."

She hugged him gratefully. "He knew you'd want to get moving and he didn't like the idea of other GIs making a move on you." Wally grinned at Hannah's blush.

"Last bit of news," he said. He had received new orders as well. He was going home.

She congratulated him and he was gone, another piece of her new life suddenly missing.

Rachel joined her on the porch. "How are you doing?" she asked.

"Emotionally I am a wreck." She forced a smile, then paused before speaking again, her hands wrapped tightly around Ephraim's book. "I will be all right. He'll join me in Jerusalem, eventually. How about you, will you be coming to Jerusalem?"

Rachel smiled. "You mean will I stay here with Joseph? No. In an odd way he has helped me handle my return to humanity, but it is not meant for us to marry, not here at least. I will go with you to Jerusalem. It is time to be with our people. It is where I belong."

Zohar stepped to the door. "A message from the Jewish Agency. They need you to come right away. Something to do with children."

Hannah did not understand what it meant but nodded. A few minutes later she entered Dov's office. Though their relationship had been rocky at first, she had begun sending more and more Jews from the hospital to his offices and had learned to respect what he was trying to do against horrible odds. For his part, Dov had learned she was on his side even if she didn't always do it his way.

"Sit down," he said, a crease to his brow, but a smile on his lips.

"Your message said something about children," she said curiously.

"Mmm." He looked up, causing Hannah to look over her shoulder. Leo Krueger stood in the doorway.

"It is my fault, Hannah," Leo said. "We need your help."

He sat down in the chair to her left and pulled it over close to and facing hers. He took her hand. "Are you free to go to Jerusalem?"

She told him about Ephraim's transfer. It was hard to keep the tears away.

"Yes, I am ready to leave," she said. "He'll come to Israel and join me there."

Leo was genuinely pleased. "May God make it so. Now, as you know, many children died in the war and many of those who survived lost their parents. Some languish in refugee camps, others are in hospitals here in Berlin, in Frankfurt, and other places recuperating from the death camps. None of them have any place to go except Israel, where families wait to take them in."

She was still confused.

"Eight are being released from the hospital in the Russian sector. If we do not take them they will be sent to Russia."

"Then we must take them," she said. "Why is this such a problem?"

Leo looked at Dov who leaned forward to speak. "Leo found out about the children through an old communist friend of his who works at the Russian hospital. He has taken it upon himself to look into the matter and has discovered that none of the children have the necessary papers to get them out of the Russian sector and into this one. We have talked with the Americans and because of the large numbers of refugees coming every day they will not give them any such papers unless they have documents and transport to take them further. A destination outside Germany."

She was still confused. "You are talking in circles," she said. "I do not understand what this has to do with me."

Leo smiled. "Ephraim has many friends in the U.S. sector and they will provide the documents to get the children to Marseille. Now all they need is someone to take them."

She gasped. "Me? You want me to take them?"

Dov broke in quickly. "There is a home there, a hospital, for children. If you can get them there we can take care of them, and, eventually, get them to Israel."

Once again she was overwhelmed with the responsibility of taking care of others. "I cannot . . ."

"You are going there. You have tickets for you and your two friends now, and the Brits are supposed to get you the rest in the next few days are they not?"

"They . . . they were delivered this morning, but . . ."

"We will give you additional train passes for the children, and the Americans say they will get us papers to get them across the border into France. It will only be necessary to accompany them, that is all," Leo said reassuringly.

Hannah nodded slightly, her fears alleviated at least in part. "Are they strong enough to travel?" she asked.

"If they had to walk, for some it would be difficult, but aboard the train they should be all right." He was looking at his desk and she could see he wasn't telling her everything.

"You are a horrible liar, Dov," she said.

His head came up, and he took a deep breath. "Two of the children are small, under the age of eight. Neither will talk much. The oldest girl is sixteen. She is angry at the world, impulsive, and will survive at any cost. You will have to watch her closely. The others do not trust adults or anyone for that matter. You are right, I would be lying if I said they did not have problems."

Leo smiled. "They have come from the camps and the forests, Hannah. You know what they are dealing with as well as anyone."

Children. Few survived. Those who did had paid a horrible price physically, emotionally, and mentally. Then to be released and have no one to turn to, no family, no one who cared in the least whether you lived or died. It was more horrible for children than anyone.

"What do you mean by the forests?" Hannah asked.

"Some escaped, some were sent from the cities by their parents. Somehow they survived and now come back to us. We must help them," Leo said. "They have no one else."

"I will talk to Rachel and Zohar. If they agree, we will take them." She stood and left the building. She would find Rachel first.

See Chapter Notes

CHAPTER 29

A day later, Hannah, Rachel, and Zohar stood next to their suitcases in Dov's office as the children entered in single file, the smallest first.

Her name was Beth and she was a small seven-year-old. The next was a boy, thin, pale, with dark hair and blank eyes that reminded Hannah too much of so many in the camps. Mentally, the boy was still in the past—lost in the nightmare of survival. It had been months since his physical release. Hannah wondered if his mind would ever follow. When Hannah asked his name she was told it was David, then Leo said he hadn't spoken since leaving the camps. He was eight.

The next two were twins but not identical. Though they both shared auburn-colored hair and dark eyes, their body style was quite different. Margaret was thin, wiry and tall for her age, while her sister Madeleine, though also thin, was short and large boned. Her tendency toward being heavy was already beginning to return and Hannah could see that she had been eating very well since being released. Both had ready smiles and seemed to be adjusting fairly well.

"Hello," Margaret said, extending a hand. As Hannah shook it she felt the strength of the grip. "We are sisters," she said. "But if you want something done you ask me. I am the oldest and the most dependable."

Madeleine gave her a wicked stare before turning to smile at Hannah. "We will do whatever you say. We are obedient girls and cause no one trouble."

Hannah realized the two were a team, tough and knowledgeable about the rules of survival. She had seen it in the camps, had even been that way herself. *Yes sir, no ma'am. Right away. Whatever you say.* Feigned obedience. The rule of survival when dealing with their keepers.

The next was another boy. He had the eyes of a forty-year-old.

"He is new to the group," Leo said. "His brother is the boy, David, and we do not wish to separate them. He is also older. Seventeen."

"What is your name?" Hannah asked.

"Aaron. I am a survivor of Bergen Belsen. I do not need a woman to tell me what to do, or to get me to Palestine. I come only for my brother."

"Yes, he will need you for a long time. I was in Ravensbrück. Rachel and Zohar were at Auschwitz. We have learned that we survive better together. I hope we can depend on you to help us."

His eyes showed a slight sign of respect for their past, but then his face went passive and he tried to move past them to join his brother. Hannah stopped him. "I will let you come only if you agree to do as you are told by the three of us. Do you agree or do you stay behind?"

Leo was about to interfere when Hannah put up a hand to stop him. Though Aaron towered a good foot over her, she stood toe to toe and held on to his arm with a strong grip. "Do you agree?"

Aaron's chin went solid as granite and he was about to walk out when David fussed. Aaron looked at him, then back at Hannah. "For my brother, but only for him," he said stiffly. He walked to David and sat down by him, then took the boy in his arms. Hannah had mixed emotions. Aaron was filled with enough hate to kill half the Germans in Berlin and yet he had a corner of his heart reserved for the love of a brother. She could only imagine the turmoil that must be in his heart.

Anna and Sarah came next, their arms intertwined. Both were thirteen years of age, both thin, with dark hair and eyes. Anna had a deep scar across her cheek, and Sarah was limping.

"Hello," Hannah said. "Are you related?"

Anna shook her head in the negative. "We met in the forest. Sarah had been shot."

"And you have been helping her ever since?" Rachel asked.

Anna only shrugged. "She helps me too. I can't see very well. A beating in one of the prisons, before I escaped from the city. After we met we helped each other."

Hannah felt the tears but fought them back. "Is her injury healed enough for traveling?"

Anna smiled. "It won't get any worse. It is the way it healed, that's all. Maybe when we get to Israel . . . maybe they can fix it . . ."

"Yes, maybe they can."

The two girls seated themselves on chairs provided and the last girl stepped up to Rachel and Hannah. She gave Hannah a challenging stare. "I don't want to go. I can stay here and survive, and I don't need your help."

"Then why don't you?" Rachel asked, a cold tinge to her voice.

The air went suddenly icy but the girl didn't respond. Instead she dropped onto a chair and folded her arms belligerently across her chest. Hannah saw what Leo meant. This one was in deep trouble, her hate eating at her like acid. Her name was Naomi, the sixteen-year-old.

Dov came in and gave Rachel the necessary papers and tickets. She stuck them in a canvas bag the Gunthers had given them. Also inside were their own papers and Rachel's belongings. Hannah carried her and Zohar's personal items in a battered, old suitcase, Zohar's necklace safely hidden inside. She thought back to the day they had found it, to Sperling and to their attempt to keep the necklace safe even at their own peril, only to find out it was paste. It seemed so long ago.

Hannah noted that each of the children carried a knapsack of their own, their few belongings safely stored inside. Out of habit they all kept the packs clutched in a firm grip and had both arms around them, afraid that someone might suddenly take them, as everything else had been taken from them.

"All of you," Dov said, his eyes resting on the children. "Hannah Gruen is in charge and you must do as she says. It is very important for everyone's safety. The trains are overloaded, the stations packed with people coming and going, and if you do not stick together you could find yourselves unable to get to your destination and then to Israel."

Hannah watched her new charges. The twins nodded agreeably, Aaron looked away, and Naomi burned Dov with a hot stare of defiance. David hardly noticed anything was being said, and Anna and

Sarah seemed agreeable enough. Beth's reaction was to climb onto Hannah's lap and lay her head against her shoulder. It made Hannah melt inside.

"Any questions?"

"I don't want to do this," Naomi mumbled.

"Speak up Naomi," Rachel said, firmly. "If what you say is important it should be said so all can hear."

"I don't want to do this!" Naomi hissed.

"You want to stay here and starve then? Is that it?" Rachel asked.

"I won't starve," Naomi said.

"No? And how will you survive? Become a thief, a prostitute? These people are offering you a chance to go to Israel where you will not have to worry about such things. You are a fool if you walk away from it."

"I wont starve," Naomi repeated firmly, but said nothing more.

Dov spoke. "You will be taken to the train station by our people. You will have to change trains several times and you will run into border guards and others who will want to check your papers and tickets. You are on a group ticket and your papers are also in group form. Hannah and Rachel will have them, so stay close. Without them the authorities will have no choice but to remove you from the train and . . ." his voice trailed off. "Stay close to them," he finished.

All knew what he didn't say. They would be sent to a camp, or to a jail. They had all seen enough of such places.

"Good luck then," Dov smiled.

Hannah placed Beth on her feet, then stood and took the little girl's hand. She watched Aaron pull David up from the floor and the others leave their chairs and fall in behind Hannah, Rachel, and Zohar. All except Naomi. As they left the building she was still sitting there.

They were helped into the back of a truck, the tailgate lifted nearly into place when Naomi came down the steps and climbed in with the rest of them. She kept her eyes fixed on the unseeable, a hard, angry look on her face, but at least she was there.

Suddenly David started screaming and trying to get out. Aaron clung to him, talked to him, tried to calm his fears but he broke free and was over the back of the tailgate and on the ground running away before Aaron finally caught up to him.

Hannah immediately knew what was bothering little David and she quickly joined the two boys who were now sitting in the middle of the street, David curled up in his big brother's lap.

"It is the truck, isn't it?" Hannah said to Aaron as she knelt beside them.

Aaron nodded. "He was loaded into a truck when he was taken to the forest." He hesitated. "They lined everyone up next to trenches and shot them. I saw it. I followed them and I saw what they did. When they left to get others I ran to the pit and found David." A smile crossed his lips. "He had tricked them. Several soldiers were shooting and he fell forward as if he had been hit, then played dead." The smile disappeared. "He lay there, the blood of others running down his face. He has been this way ever since."

Hannah felt her heart ache as she ran her fingers through David's hair. "Let me take him." She started to put her arms under his frail body and lift. At first Aaron had a hard time letting go and David clung to him, but then Aaron sensed something in his brother that told him it would be okay. He let go and Hannah picked up the boy and started toward the truck. She held him tightly as his fear started to build again and he tried to struggle. Then it occurred to her to sing to him. But what? She could only think of a song she had heard her mother sing many times. How did it go? The words were Hebrew. It had been a long time since she had even thought of them, let alone sung the tune. She struggled to put together the words, then they came back to her in a rush and she began to sing in the language of her forefathers.

Slowly David relaxed and she was able to hand him up to Rachel and Aaron.

She climbed aboard and sat beside Aaron who held David in his lap. She kept singing and Zohar joined in. David stayed in the truck.

As they situated themselves to leave, a jeep pulled up and Wally hopped out, removed some boxes from the back of his vehicle and handed them to the driver and his companion who placed them in the back of the truck. Hannah went to the tailgate and knelt down so that she could reach his extended hand.

"Food and a few candy bars for the kids," Wally smiled. Their hands touched and Hannah thanked him warmly. She nearly choked on the last of her words; then the truck pulled away and she could only wave. As they turned into the main street Hannah wiped away the tears and began handing out the food to each of their little group. They began eating immediately and it was all she could do to get them to stop and stuff the bread, cheese, and fresh apples into knapsacks and suitcases. The insatiable appetite of a survivor would never allow this food to last, but she must try. As a reward for their obedience she let each eat one of the two Hershey chocolate bars.

Eleven anxious faces watched out the back of the truck as it worked its way through the ruined streets of Berlin. Things were being cleaned up. There were fewer garbage heaps in the streets now; carefully arranged stacks of old bricks stood next to ruined buildings in preparation for their use in rebuilding. People were everywhere, but there was less despondency and more purpose to what they did. The Americans had organized labor forces and were paying in food and the new occupation currency. Hope was returning.

A sudden chill went down Hannah's spine. Israel. Only a week ago it had seemed so far away, a distant dream, almost a fairytale one would read about but never see because it only existed in the mind. Now they were on their way. Even though her heart ached for Ephraim, the thought of Israel made her smile.

She was going home. A home she had never seen.

PART TWO
THE ROAD HOME

CHAPTER 1

The train was less crowded than when they came to Berlin but the depot was even worse, full to overflowing with people trying to find food and shelter. It was the middle of July and Berlin had become the center of movement for displaced persons trying to find either a way back to their old lives or a path to a new one. Hannah felt sorry for them. Many would go hungry, even starve during the next six months unless the Russians became more cooperative, freeing more German food for the German people instead of sending most of it east. She shuddered at the thought. The war was over and yet the victims continued to mount.

She shared a compartment with Aaron, David, Anna, Sarah, Naomi, and Beth who sat on her lap. The others were in the next compartment with Rachel. As she watched each of them mark out their territory and try to assert themselves firmly into a sort of pecking order, she realized that most of these children had known nothing but war, hiding, and survival of the fittest. Beth, the youngest, had been born only one year before the invasion of Poland, and Aaron, the oldest, had lived half his life fighting for food and kowtowing to prison guards just to stay alive. The amazing thing was that both had survived at all.

She watched Naomi. She had large, dark eyes set in a round face that had remained lovely in spite of the horrors it had been put through or seen. But the eyes were cold, distant, and filled with hate. Hannah had noticed that at the depot as they worked their way through the mass of humanity and rubble to find their train. It had been Naomi who refused to help anyone but herself. In fact, contrary to Hannah's instructions, she had disappeared, only reappearing as they boarded and she needed her ticket. Hannah saw that her coat pockets bulged slightly and knew that the girl had either been stealing food or begging for it, for none of the children had money of their own. Now as Naomi sat staring out at the countryside from her window seat, she gnawed at an apple while the other children watched and drooled. It didn't bother Naomi in the least. If anything, Hannah could see that the girl relished the feeling of superiority it seemed to give her, but then they had all been that way hadn't they? Time and kindness had helped her, Rachel, and Zohar get past it for the most part. Hopefully Naomi would be blessed in the same way.

"Can I have some?" Beth asked. Her head lay against Hannah's shoulder and her eyes were fixed on Naomi's apple.

Naomi gave a wicked smile and took a large bite. Several more bites and there was nothing left but the core. Then she popped that in her mouth as well and finished it. Hannah could feel the disappointment in Beth and held her more tightly, then thought of something. Removing a sack from her suitcase, Hannah opened it. "I suppose we're all hungry," she said.

She allowed them to each pull out one of the sandwiches delivered by Wally. Naomi was the only one who did not eat.

"Not hungry?" Hannah asked.

Naomi ignored her by looking out the window.

Hannah extended it to her. "Put that away for later."

At first Naomi turned away, and then her overwhelming need to survive took over and she grabbed the food, quickly jamming it inside her coat pocket as she turned back to the window, her face showing both anger and confusion.

"Where are we?" Aaron asked after he swallowed his last bite. They seemed to be passing through a town. Dov had told her their route, what cities they would pass through. There would be many small towns, but this was probably Leipzig. She told him so just as they pulled to a stop in a station much like Berlin's except smaller. As the train came to a stop, people passed by their compartment on their way to the exit while others boarded and anxiously peered through the glass door looking for a place to sit their war-worn bodies. Without thinking, Hannah started to put Beth on the seat beside her so as to send the signal that there was no room, but then she caught herself and held fast to Beth's thin form. She did not weigh enough to cause Hannah any hardship. Another could join them. She signaled to the next person who peered inside and slid herself closer to Aaron, pushing him toward David.

"Hey!" Aaron said, as the door opened and a thin and tattered man stepped inside. He stiffened at Aaron's exclamation and started to back out, an apologetic look in his eyes.

"Hush, Aaron!" Hannah said firmly while giving the man a welcome smile. "Please, join us," she said, pushing harder toward Aaron who reluctantly picked up his little brother and put him on his lap, while scowling at Hannah. After a brief hesitation then a grateful smile the man let himself into the seat beside her before hugging his own small bag of possessions to his chest. Hannah could see now that he was much younger than she had first thought, but war or the camps had taken their toll.

"He should go somewhere else," Aaron muttered as he squirmed this way and that in an attempt to show discomfort with his brother in his lap. "Crowded enough in here!"

Hannah ignored him as the train lurched forward and started from the station. Little David weighed even less than Beth and couldn't possibly be causing Aaron much grief. They all busied themselves with looking out the window until the battered city gave way to the war-torn and dusty countryside.

"Do you speak German?" Hannah asked the man in that tongue.

"Yes, but not very well. I am French," he stammered.

"Are you Jewish? Do you speak Hebrew?" she asked in that language.

There was deep relief mingled with joy in his face. "You . . . you were in the camps?" he asked.

She nodded.

"And the children?" There was a tinge of sad disbelief in the question.

"Some of them." She looked at her haggard group. "David and Aaron survived in the hills and forests." She looked at the boys next to her. "Aaron was a part of the resistance for a time, but was man enough to take care of his brother as well."

Aaron's ears perked up, pleased at the words. He knew Leo had told her of his past but he hadn't thought she cared much. Maybe he had been wrong.

"The war made many men of boys before their time," the new man said. "All of these have done well. Not many children survived."

"A blight on humanity, or haven't you heard?" Naomi said stiffly, but in fluent Hebrew.

It was the first time Hannah realized that Naomi knew Hebrew and she glanced at the others to find out if any of them also understood. "Do the rest of you . . ."

Anna and Sarah nodded and it was obvious from the look on Aaron's face that he did as well. Only the little ones did not and Hannah understood that. There had been no teaching of Hebrew in the camps and hiding places.

"It has been a long time," Anna stammered. "If we were caught speaking it in the camps they beat us."

Hannah nodded understanding. She had forced herself not to even think in the language for fear she might slip and say what she was thinking. She had watched as others had been beaten nearly to death for a simple exclamation of joy at finding a piece of meat in their soup!

"Where are you coming from?" Hannah asked their new traveling companion.

"Dachau," his voice was nearly inaudible. "I come from Dachau."

Aaron gave a snort of disbelief. "No one survived Dachau," he said critically.

The man did not reply. Like so many, he did not rush to discuss his experience.

The train passed through many other villages and towns, stopping at all to exchange passengers. They said very little to one another, some preferring sleep to conversation, others watching Germany disappear behind them, their eyes and minds taking in the movement of the masses of humanity that appeared at each station and along the roads next to the relentless iron rails over which the train carried relatively few to better places. Hannah soon realized that the further they traveled, the more the children talked and even smiled. Even Naomi was visibly relieved. Only their new guest seemed to change little, his tired, sagging countenance remaining as it had been when he had entered their compartment more than seven hours ago.

They entered the outskirts of Stuttgart as the late afternoon sun began setting outside their window. Rachel suddenly appeared at their compartment and quickly slid open the door and entered, her face pale and drawn.

"What is it?" Hannah asked apprehensively.

Rachel forced a smile and did an admirable job of deceiving the children that whatever it was it was minor, but Hannah had come to know her friend well enough to tell otherwise.

"Can you come with me a minute?" Rachel said evenly. "I can't get the lock on one of the suitcases to work."

It was a lie but Hannah quickly stood and placed Beth on the seat with a smile and promise to be back, then stepped out of the compartment and joined Rachel in the companionway. They inched their way through those standing and sitting on the floor as they worked their way to the rear of the car.

"What is it?" Hannah whispered.

They had reached the doorway to the next car, passed through, and worked their way through the crowded aisle to the rear of it, where Rachel came to a stop and pointed through the dirty glass. "The man sitting in the second row. Do you recognize him?"

The car was different than theirs. Like the one on which they had traveled to Berlin, there were no compartments, only rows of seats with an aisle down the center.

Along with the dirty window, the people standing and sitting in the aisle made it difficult for Hannah to see. She stepped closer to the window, peered through and stared at the man Rachel wanted her to see. As she did, her breath caught in her lungs. Quickly stepping back she turned away, leaning against a bare spot of window to her right.

"Sperling!" she said. How could this be? What was God thinking that He would make them face such a miserable piece of humanity again!

She tried to compose herself. It was nothing. Just coincidence! He did not know they were aboard. They could avoid him. There would be no trouble.

But what is he doing on this train? She looked back at where he sat, a large package in his lap. The seat next to him was filled with two small children who crowded against the window as if trying to avoid this small but evil man.

"What should we do?" Rachel hissed.

Hannah clenched her fists in an effort to overcome the fear this man seemed to thrust on her. "Come on," she said in controlled anxiety as she started back to their compartments. "We'll be in Stuttgart soon. There will be Americans at the station. We can tell them about Sperling and they will take him off the train."

Rachel seemed relieved, the color returning to her cheeks.

"Until then, keep Zohar in the compartment and draw the curtains."

Rachel nodded understanding as they came to their own car.

"You must not let on to Zohar or the others, do you understand?" Hannah said as they came to their compartments.

Rachel nodded again, took a deep breath and disappeared inside, quickly drawing the tattered curtains. Hannah said a little prayer of her own and then pulled the compartment door open to go inside. As she did, she glanced back the way she had come. What she saw caused her heart to stop beating.

Sperling stood at the other end of the aisle, his eyes glued to hers, an evil sadistic twist on his lips. He began pushing his way through.

Hannah froze. To go inside would endanger the others, to stay would mean a confrontation, and this time there was no guilt-ridden German industrialist the size of a small European car to keep Sperling from wringing her neck. He was there before she could decide.

"Well, well, the Jewess from the hospital," he said in German. The acidic hatred in his eyes made Hannah's skin burn.

"You left me with an empty suitcase," he said coldly.

"Oh?" The calm in her voice belied the hot turmoil that ran through her. "And I thought it was you who *stole* an empty one."

His eyes narrowed to thin slits, but then some grotesque thought caused his countenance to change. She had seen that look on the faces of the female guards when at morning roll call they had barked out a dozen names of women who were missing because death had caught up to them during the night, and the guards were glad to be rid of them.

"I'm glad you are aboard this train, Miss Gruen," he said. "In fact I cannot think of anything I would like more." With that he pushed past her and went on his way, disappearing behind two taller men trying to sleep on their feet.

Hannah stood riveted to the floor for a moment, regaining her strength while the cold words trickled through her mind like ice water. What did he mean? What was he doing on board this train? Suddenly she felt the impulse to follow him but her feet seemed frozen to the ground. Taking a deep breath, she forced enough strength into her toes to pry them loose and work her way toward the back of the train. As she neared the connecting junction of the two cars she could see him standing near the outside exit. He glanced at his watch nervously, then peered out the window of the door as the train began to slow. He reached for the handle that opened the door, released it, and was suddenly gone. The fool had jumped from the train? Was he afraid of something? Why . . .

It was then Hannah remembered. He had been carrying a package! He did not have it with him when he jumped from the train! With the adrenalin rush that only fear can produce, she turned back to their compartments, hoping she would not be too late.

* * *

The train was traveling just fast enough that the explosion knocked half a dozen cars off their rails and sent Hannah and her friends careening into the crowded station. People ran yelling and screaming for cover, trying to escape the crush of the large metal projectiles loaded with more passengers than they could carry. When the cars came to a metal-grinding halt, people were crushed or too wounded to free themselves. The fire created by the blast and sparks from metal on metal and concrete began to travel through the wreckage, a starving beast seeking prey.

Hannah found herself still conscious, lying flat on her stomach in front of Rachel's compartment. She pushed herself to her feet and began helping Rachel lift her group free through the shattered window, then fled to her own car where she found Aaron breaking out the remaining glass of their window, and Naomi screaming at Anna and Sarah to get moving through the opening! The man from Dachau had picked up Beth and was climbing to freedom with her cradled in his arms. Rachel suddenly appeared outside and took the frightened girl while Hannah directed Aaron to get out. She picked up David and then handed him to Aaron. As she helped Naomi jump free of the wreckage, Hannah was knocked to the floor by someone behind her, then trampled on by others as they lunged for freedom, the fire licking at their heels.

Half stunned, she felt the hot flames coming through the wall and ceiling and backed away as she struggled to her feet. As she turned to jump from the window she remembered their luggage and turned back, grabbing a suitcase and tossing it out, then another and another. As she reached for the fourth, the bag with their tickets, the flames drove her back and enveloped the bag. She tried again, felt the searing of her flesh, but made another attempt, then another.

"Hannah! No! Get out!" Rachel yelled from outside.

Hannah gritted her teeth against the pain as she reached again for the bag, but it was too late. Wedged in the wreckage of the overhead luggage rack it burst into flame and there was nothing she could do. Turning, she put a foot on the metal window frame and jumped. Rachel and Zohar caught her and quickly pulled her coughing and weakened body a safe distance from the flame-engulfed wreckage.

The others gathered round and as Rachel quickly counted heads, they widened the distance between them and the growing inferno. The little group found themselves surrounded by others of the same mind, and Hannah felt the chaos and the panic, heard the screaming for loved ones and the thunderous sound of destruction ringing in her ears until she thought her head would explode.

She felt the tug on her skirt and looked down to find a frightened Beth, tears running down her cheeks. Hannah picked her up and held her shaking body close as she looked around her, double-checking, making sure they were all there. She felt a sudden wave of relief roll over her, weakening her knees and forcing her to the pavement of the street, Beth still in her arms. The others gathered tightly around her.

"Anyone hurt?"

Hannah looked up to see the stranger from Dachau.

Anna spoke. "Sarah, her arm . . ."

Sarah was holding her arm while softly crying. The man knelt beside her and looked at the forearm with an experienced eye, then used his fingers to verify what he could see.

"It isn't broken, just badly bruised," he said.

With his usual skepticism Aaron spoke. "How do you know this?"

"I am a doctor," the man said, turning to Aaron. "My name is Cardan, Pierre Cardan, and I have been treating patients at Dachau. The soldiers broke arms, I fixed them. It is what I did and I know the feel of them. Is anyone else hurt? Even a scratch? They could become infected and cause serious consequences. Anyone?"

Hannah felt the sting in her hands and said so. He looked at them. "You are burned, but not badly. Rachel, find water, the colder the better." He looked directly at Hannah. "When it is brought to you, put your hands in it. It will help."

An hour later Cardan had used the contents of his small bag of bandages and ointments to help them, Hannah had soaked her hands as best she could in the pail of water Rachel had gotten from who knew where, and Sarah lay with her head in Anna's lap, pain etched in her face. Cardan disappeared in a sea of injured survivors.

They watched the flames subside, watched as the injured were taken away in American Army medical ambulances, and the dead were covered with whatever was available, to await their turn for removal and burial.

"Children, there will be no trains going through here tonight so let's find a more comfortable place. We need to get some sleep." She stood and started down the street. The others, too tired to argue, fell in line behind her. They came to a small park with thick grass and Hannah found a spot and gathered everyone around her. "Try to sleep," she said.

Like all victims of the war, the children had learned to sleep wherever they could and they curled up and shut their eyes. Sarah was the only one fully awake, the pain in her arm too much for her eyelids to overcome. Doctor Cardan had promised he'd return with some sort of pain-killer. Hannah hoped he was a man of his word.

Hannah lay down and Beth snuggled in next to her. Rachel sat next to them with her knees drawn up under her chin. Zohar lay curled up next to her and was already sleeping.

"You have found a new friend," Rachel said quietly.

Hannah smiled. "So it seems."

"The tickets are gone, aren't they?" Rachel said matter-of-factly.

Hannah nodded. "I will go to the authorities in the morning and see what can be done. Possibly we will have to return to Berlin. You will need to take some of the money they gave us and find food."

Rachel nodded, then lay down and closed her eyes.

Hannah was grateful that it was a warm night. She watched as others wandered into the park and staked out ground for themselves. She wondered how many strangers were in even worse circumstances than they were, how many would make this place their home because they simply couldn't go any further.

She saw Doctor Cardan in the glow of a night lamp and raised herself to speak quiet words that would help him find them. He came through the darkness, worked his away around several new arrivals, and joined them. He went to Sarah first and gave her the pills.

"How many were hurt?"

"Thirty-five dead, forty-three injured. Some of those won't last the night," he said sadly. "Good luck to you." He turned to her and handed her a small sack. "Pills for the girl's pain. The Americans had some." He gave her as pleasant a smile as the late hour and the circumstances would allow and then stood and headed back the way he had come.

"Thank you," she said to his back.

He waved a hand at her without turning around and was quickly out of sight. She found herself thanking God she had asked him to share their compartment.

She closed her eyes and tried to sleep but couldn't. She thought of Ephraim. She could only hope he was all right, that somehow he would survive the task he would be asked to do and they would be together again. Without him . . . she felt her mouth go dry and an empty hopeless feeling crawl inside her gut. How she wished he were here! She needed his strength now more than ever! How could she possibly get through this?

Little Beth turned over in her sleep and moaned. Hannah pulled her close, felt her warmth. She had to go on. Beth needed her to go on.

"She wasn't in the camps you know," Naomi said, from where she lay in dark shadow. "She ended up there at the end but only because her Nazi father had to run for his life and didn't know what else to do with her."

Hannah felt the hate ooze out of Naomi and she had to bite her tongue to prevent a like response. "It was not her fault that her father was a Nazi any more than it was your fault that yours was a Jew," she said calmly.

"She received preferential treatment from the commandant. She never went hungry, never had to sleep on the frozen ground, and yet you treat her like one of us."

"Was her way of escaping death anymore a sin than snatching bread from a dying friend in order to preserve your own life?" Hannah said evenly. She did not know Naomi's past, but she knew that few survived without hurting others. It was the guilt they all had to live with.

"Her father loved her enough to try and save her, a Jew. Thank God there were a few such men among the Nazis," Hannah said.

"He left her behind, Hannah, that is not the act of a saint!" Naomi said spitefully.

"Nor is it the act of a devil," Hannah said simply. She paused a moment. "Is Beth's survival what is really bothering you Naomi? Do you hate her because she lives, or is it your own survival that you find so horrible?"

"I don't know what you're talking about!" Naomi said, turning her back to Hannah.

"I think you do. There aren't any of us who weren't forced to hurt others and because of it we have constant dreams of those we stole bread from or pushed aside to get more food. We see their faces every time we look in the mirror and know that we survived and they didn't."

Naomi didn't move, didn't respond, and Hannah knew she was hurting.

"You forget, Naomi, I was there too, and I remember; I dream. I see those faces. Yes, sometimes the guards come back and beat me in my dreams but usually it is the old woman I turned away from because my heart had become as cold as those who stood over us with the sticks and whips. Or my sister who I couldn't carry anymore so I left her lying in the mud. I convinced myself she would get up and follow, that she leaned on me because of self-pity, not because she was too weak to do anything else. I turned away and when she didn't get up, the guard shot her. It will haunt me the rest of my life."

Hannah felt the tears come to the corners of her eyes and bit her lip to keep from crying, but it wasn't self hate she felt anymore, it was remorse—deep, heart wrenching remorse. She could only hope that God and those who had suffered because of her could finally forgive her.

"We all dream the same dreams, Naomi. All of us. If you think having a Nazi father was a bed of roses, talk to Rachel. Then maybe you will understand that Beth does not deserve the treatment you insist on giving her."

After long moments of silence Naomi turned onto her back. After a few minutes she spoke. "Do they ever say anything to you?" Naomi asked in a sad and quiet voice. "When they come in the night do they ask you why?"

Hannah's heart ached. "Yes, they ask."

"And what do you tell them?"

"Nothing." What did one say to the person you had let die so that you could survive?

Naomi bent her arm until her wrist lay on her forehead. She stared up at the star-filled sky without really seeing it. "Do you think . . . is it really them? In our dreams I mean."

"They have gone onto other things Naomi. Better things. They do not wish to punish us. It is we who punish ourselves."

Naomi rolled back onto her side and said no more. Hannah felt Beth move against her and snuggled closer against the cooling air. Was she right? Ephraim had said so, and she had felt the words warm her heart. Her father was in that better place, her sisters and mother. They were all right. Ephraim was right—it was the ones left behind who suffered.

The moon appeared above the wall, full and beautiful, its light cascading over them like a blanket. There was Beth lying in the crook of her arm; Naomi, David, and Aaron; Rachel with Sarah and Anna snuggled at each side of her rejuvenated body. Margaret and Madeleine were a few feet away, holding each other against the shadows of the night. All of them were safe, alive, and they must go on. They must live good enough lives that the dead would be pleased.

Hannah watched the round sphere climb in the sky, saw its silver glow cascade off trees and ruins, grass, and the cobblestone street. It warmed her against the chilly night and gave her peace. Her eyelids grew heavy, then she drifted into a restful sleep. Only Ephraim came to interrupt, smiling and laughing with her as they rode on yellow wings over the German landscape.

Tonight at least, the others didn't come.

See Chapter Notes

CHAPTER 2

They found Sperling's body three hundred yards down the tracks. He had jumped at the wrong time, hitting a sign-post and killing himself instantly. The man was such a fool. His self-appointed moment of glory had been nothing but an act of terrorism that ended in his own ignominious death. Hannah hoped his victims had been at hell's gate to torment him with his failure before the hot flames lashed out to engulf him.

Hannah sat in the waiting area of the American headquarters in Stuttgart. She had come to discuss their situation and try and get word to General Clay that all their papers and tickets had been lost in the fire and they needed to be reissued. In her head she knew they would do so, but in her stomach she felt empty—even afraid they would not.

At first the commanding officer, a Colonel Pittman, hadn't believed her, but when she had reviewed the meeting with General Clay and his British counterpart, Ronald Weeks, he had decided it might be best to at least check. That had been more than two hours ago.

The waiting area was crammed with people, both from everyday traffic of local people with local problems, and from last night's disaster. All of them were a haggard and tired-looking bunch, with little hope of things getting better any time soon.

Even Hannah's hope had been dealt a bit of a blow, but she had determined not to give up. Too many relied on her now and they deserved to get beyond this horrid place and have a chance at a new life. It might take them longer now, but they would get there. They must.

She saw the aide to the commanding officer coming her way. Finally. She stood as he instructed her to follow him and they entered the commander's office for a second time. He sat at a desk reading a stack of official-looking papers. When she was seated he put them away, sat back and looked, and decided how to say what he was thinking. She had the painful premonition that all had not gone as well as she had hoped.

"You have talked to the general?" she asked.

"General Clay cannot be reached, but I was referred to Colonel Mackland of Army Intelligence and he said you are telling the truth." He forced a smile. "And that we should take good care of you. According to Colonel Mackland you and your friends have helped us round up some of the Nazis still trying to run this country." The smile disappeared as readily as he had placed it across his lips and he nervously shuffled the papers on his desk. "Unfortunately it will take time to get your papers renewed. Especially those that allow your immigration to Palestine."

"I do not understand. The papers have already been granted; it is surely a small thing to reissue them."

His eyes remained on his paperwork. "Things are not quite that simple, especially in the case of the British."

"How long?"

"I don't know, possibly several weeks," He looked up. "We will do our best to get them for you, Miss Gruen, but it will take time."

She took a deep breath. "And tickets to Marseille, how soon can we be given new ones?"

"As soon as your new papers arrive. Until then all of you are to be taken to Tirschenreuth and housed there under the direction of the UNRRA."

Hannah felt the wind go out of her lungs. She had heard of both Tirschenreuth and the United Nations Relief and Rehabilitation Administration. Tirschenreuth was one of dozens of work camps turned into camps for displaced persons the allies were administering in conjunction with the United Nations. It was their way of dealing with the tens of thousands of homeless the war had left in its wake. She would not go there a week ago; she would not go now.

She stood to leave. "Thank you, Colonel, but . . ."

He turned around, his face firm as concrete. "You have no choice, Miss Gruen. You will find your group and your friends waiting for you outside. You will board the truck we have provided and you will be taken there now. When your papers arrive I will notify you, then you and your friends can carry on with your journey. The children will remain."

Hannah felt panic. "But . . . but I don't understand. Our papers . . . the children's papers . . ."

"Do not exist," the colonel said, "and you and they will be treated like any other displaced person without proper papers. You Jews will not be treated any differently than anyone else under my command, regardless of what you might have been through. Those are my orders and I will follow them to the letter."

It was suddenly clear to Hannah. This American was not like Ephraim or Wally. This one did not like Jews, and though he would not stand them up against a wall and shoot them he would not help them either, not when he had orders that would allow him to do otherwise. Her back stiffened.

"I want to talk to General Clay, immediately," she said.

"I told you, the general is not available. He was called back to the States to confer with the President and his cabinet."

"Then I will speak to Colonel Mackland," she said just as coldly.

Colonel Pittman's face hardened with anger. "That is not possible now. When you get to . . ."

She stepped forward to the edge of his desk. "Colonel, are you sure you want to take this position? Do you understand that I will go to Berlin myself if I need to? And that if you force me to do so I will make it as unpleasant for you as I possibly can?"

The Colonel seemed to soften a bit for a moment, then a slight smile crossed his lips. "You can try, Miss Gruen, but understand that if you circumvent me it will only delay your own departure for Palestine. I will make certain of *that*."

Hannah wanted to reach across the desk and strangle him but resisted. "Were you born German, Colonel?" she asked.

The question caught him off guard but he quickly regained his composure and answered. "No, of course not, I . . ."

"You should have been! You would have been a good Nazi." Hannah turned, left the office and slammed the door behind her. It was all she could do to cross the waiting area without her knees buckling. She was frightened. She could not go to the camps, and would not take these children there either! Not after what they had all been through!

But what else could she do? How could they escape? She pushed through the front door and into the fresh air, her mind a jumble. Why would he do this? Why would any American? She had heard there were anti-Semitic feelings in the States. Her father and the uncle who had lived there had spoken of them, but surely it would not come here! Surely even the worst Jew-hater could not continue such a path after seeing the camps!

She found herself suddenly surrounded by people and started to push them away before she realized it was Rachel, Zohar, and the children.

"What is wrong?" Rachel asked as Hannah tried to put on a pleasant face.

Hannah looked around her. There was a truck and several soldiers nearby; one of them was already moving in their direction. She must try to keep everyone calm until she could decide what to do. "Children, we're going for a ride with the American soldiers. Does everyone have their belongings?"

"Hannah, what is wrong?" Rachel asked again, but quietly. "What is going on?"

"Just help me get the children in the truck, then we'll talk. It's important that we keep calm, Rachel, please."

Rachel hesitated only for a second, then nodded. "All right," she said softly. All right."

David hesitated again and Hannah took him by the hand to give him comfort while Aaron climbed aboard. David then followed and Hannah breathed a deep sigh of relief. Once they were all inside, an armed soldier joined them and the tailgate was closed. The truck lurched forward and Hannah laid her head against the side and closed her eyes. They must get away, but how? How did three women and a brood of children stop a moving truck and disarm three soldiers so that they could run into hills and mountains unfamiliar to all of them and without the proper papers to go anywhere once they did? It was impossible!

Rachel leaned close. "Where are we going?" she said firmly.

Hannah told her. Rachel felt the hot anger well up inside. "I won't go there, Hannah! They will have to shoot me first! And the children—little David will die if he has to go through the gates of another camp!" She was near panic, the horror of the past making the thought of return unbearably frightening.

"I know, but what can we do, I . . ."

Rachel gripped her friend's arm firmly. "I will think of something, but I will never go back!"

They were outside Stuttgart and moving southeast. Munich lay in that direction. Hannah remembered now; Tirschenreuth was just outside Munich. She told Rachel, who nodded understanding but was deep in thought herself.

"I have a plan," Rachel said after a few more minutes. She told Hannah what they must do. Hannah thought it over, then agreed. It could work, and they were desperate. A moment later Rachel stood and moved to where Anna and Sarah sat. She checked Sarah's arm, then asked everyone to slide toward Hannah before sitting down next to the American soldier. A few minutes later they were carrying on a conversation. Hannah watched the rifle lying across the man's lap. At first his fingers clutched at it tightly, but as Rachel used her charms and moved a little closer the grip lessened until it was practically unattached to his arms. Soon Rachel had him talking about himself, the States, and his part in the war. Rachel moved closer, her shoulder rubbing against his, then a finger reached out and gently caressed the barrel of the weapon. Rachel's fingers moved back and forth along the length of the cold steel while listening, talking, laughing with her new-found friend.

Hannah leaned over to Naomi. "I need your help, Naomi, okay?"

Naomi had kept to herself that morning, the usual belligerence either gone or well hidden. There was no sign of its return now as the girl simply nodded at Hannah's instructions.

They traveled another mile, Rachel working her magic, Hannah waiting, Naomi watching, a slight smile on her face because she understood now that Rachel was not just flirting out of a sudden liking for this American.

As they left a small village and entered a forested area along a river it happened.

Rachel moved so quickly that the guard hardly had a chance. In less time than it took for Hannah to blink, Rachel grabbed the weapon, stood, and aimed it at the stomach of the soldier. He sat there in shock for only a second, then his face turned red hot with embarrassed anger and he started to stand as if to retrieve his weapon.

"Give me . . ." was all he had time to say as Hannah and Naomi slammed into him and knocked him to the floor. Rachel used the rifle butt against the back of his skull and the man went limp.

"Thanks," Rachel said with deep relief. She knew how to use the weapon about as well as the Israelites had known how to make bricks without straw!

Hannah ripped part of her skirt away and quickly tied the soldier's hands behind him as the children watched, stunned and curious. Why were their leaders and Naomi treating this American as if he were the enemy?

Aaron sat David down and took the gun. He pulled up and back on the bolt and found that the chamber was empty. Chagrined, he showed it to Rachel and Hannah.

"No wonder he thought he could take it back," Hannah said.

Rachel gave a weak smile as Aaron pushed the bolt forward, shoving a shell in place.

"There is the safety." He pointed at the small button near the back of the bolt. He pushed on it with his finger, first backward then forward. Hannah nodded her understanding of how it worked but had no desire to take the weapon.

"You keep it," she said. Aaron looked pleased.

"Now what?" Naomi asked.

Hannah turned to the children. "This truck is not taking us to Marseille, but to a displaced person's camp at Tirschenreuth." Everyone's face showed the dismay she had hoped for and Hannah quickly spoke again. "We must stop the truck." She told them what she wanted them to do, and even David's head nodded understanding. Moments later Anna and Naomi were pounding on the back of the cab. The truck slowed as Aaron prepared to present his weapon as a good reason for the two men to turn the vehicle over to them. As she noted the look on Aaron's face, she wondered if giving him a weapon was the smart thing to do.

When they came to a full stop Hannah felt sweat cascading down the sides of her face. What if the men refused? She couldn't shoot them! It was not their fault that their colonel was a fool! She shoved the thought aside. Aaron would have to shoot one of them in the leg or something if they forced her! They had no choice! Oh dear God, don't let them make him shoot!

She heard the doors slam, heard voices through the tarpaulin cover as the two men walked to the back of the truck.

"Hey, Grant!" a voice yelled.

"What's the problem?" The one on the driver's side asked.

Grant lay on the floor, conscious, but with another piece of Hannah's skirt stuffed securely in his mouth. He tried to mumble, but Beth kicked him hard and he shut up. Hannah smiled at the little girl's nerve but then concentrated on completing their task.

"Grant?" the voice asked again, this time with some nervousness attached.

Hannah nodded at Rachel and they quickly pulled the tarpaulin back. The two men stood at the tailgate, confused, then stunned.

"Hands up," Beth yelled, grinning. Her German only added to the two men's confusion.

"What the . . ."

"Put your hands up," Hannah repeated in English while stepping forward. Aaron pointed the barrel at the driver's chest. His hands shot up like they were attached to pulleys and Aaron had jerked on them. The other one hesitated, the instinct to fight back taking over. "I'll kill him before you can put a bullet in the chamber," Aaron said firmly. Hannah felt nauseated at the cold sound of the words and was praying the soldier would listen. The arms relaxed and Hannah felt relief cascade clear to her toenails.

"Throw the rifle into the gutter! Now!" Aaron said. The soldier did as he was told. Rachel jumped down, removed their sidearms, and then stood several feet behind them.

The children clapped their approval and Naomi quickly had the tailgate down.

"Take your friend out of the truck," Hannah said.

The two men stepped forward and pulled Grant from the floor and placed his feet on the ground. "We ain't your enemy, ma'am," the driver said coldly.

"No, but your colonel has decided to be."

The three men looked down at their feet, then at one another. One of them spat out a word that questioned the colonel's parentage. It was obvious they were aware of Pittman's aversion to Jews and didn't agree with it, but they said no more.

"Move over there, near those trees," she said. Aaron emphasized the statement with a motion of the weapon. They started to walk while whispering to one another.

"Aaron, give me the gun and see if you can figure out how to drive that truck," Hannah said.

Aaron hesitated only a moment, then turned the weapon over and started back to the truck.

"Stop talking," Hannah said, jabbing the gun into the back of the sergeant. He did. "Rachel, Naomi, rip some pieces of the tarpaulin we can use to tie these nice boys up."

"You don't have to do that, ma'am," The driver said. "That's what we was talkin' about before you jabbed me with that gun. You're right about this and we'll just sit here for a spell and wait until you have a few hours' head start, then we'll start walkin' back to Stuttgart."

"We've been to Tirschenreuth, lady," said the other one. "It ain't no place for kids if it can be helped."

The one called Grant still had the cloth in his mouth but nodded agreement.

"Take that out of his mouth," Hannah said.

"Thanks. You'd best get movin'," Grant said after wetting the inside of his mouth, a sour look on his face.

Aaron joined them. "I can't figure out the gears, and the gas gauge doesn't work," he said in broken English.

"The truck was filled up this morning, both tanks. That should get you into Austria a good piece, if you're inclined to go that way." He explained the gear system. "It's a little tough at first, but you'll get the hang of it," he smiled.

"Can we put our hands down, ma'am?" the second man asked.

Hannah smiled while nodding and lowered the gun as well, though the barrel remained pointed in their direction and the safety remained off.

Naomi joined them, strands of tarp in hand. She was disappointed when Hannah told her they wouldn't be needed. "We will take your helmets, shirts, and any papers you think might help."

The driver smiled, showing a solid set of yellowed teeth, probably from smoking cigars like that sticking prominently from his shirt pocket. "Corporal, you heard the lady. You too, private."

He untied Grant quickly and his two companions took off their shirts and stuffed them inside the corporal's helmet, along with some papers the sergeant had in his pocket.

"My, uh, helmet is in the truck, where . . ." Grant, rubbed the back of his head, glancing at Rachel. Hannah could see that he was still sheepish about being taken in so easily.

Hannah nodded, pushing the safety in place and taking the last helmet from the sergeant. It had papers placed in it. "Thank you, all of you," she said.

"No problem, ma'am. I was at Dachau when it was captured. I know what you have been through and colonel or no colonel, them camps is no place for people. The colonel, he don't understand. He came too late to understand. When I get back, I'll take him to Dachau, maybe . . . well, anyway, good luck."

She nodded and they started back for the road. When the children were back in the rear of the truck with Rachel, and Naomi and Aaron and Hannah were in the front, Hannah saw that the three men had moved into the trees and found a place to sit. Aaron ground the gears until he found one he thought would work, let out on the clutch and they lurched backward.

He swore in Yiddish and hit the steering wheel with his hand, his face red, then ground them again as Hannah heard the laughter from the trees.

"All the way right, and forward," yelled the sergeant.

"All the way . . ." Hannah started to say.

"Yeah, I heard him." Aaron said while shoving the stick and jamming it forward. He let out on the clutch a second time. As they finally started forward, Hannah waved to her former captors. They waved back, large grins on their faces. A moment later they disappeared in the thick trees.

"We should have tied them up and put them in the back until we were out of the country," Aaron said.

"We're in enough trouble as it is," Hannah replied. "Any idea what we should do now?"

Aaron smiled. "Not one, but at least we're free." His face grew serious, his hands twisting on the steering wheel. "I was going to take David and run the first chance I got. I'm glad I didn't have to." It was his way of saying thanks. "No camps, Hannah, not unless there just isn't another way."

She nodded agreement. She was sure the camps were different now that the Americans ran such places. The barbed wire was probably gone and the guards with the whips sent to prisons, but the barracks, the sickness, the black and incessant depression . . . the thought of such things made her wilt inside. Ephraim had helped her get rid of those feelings; she wasn't about to invite them back if she could help it.

They drove on in silence. They had to get to France, but how? The Americans were not going to take the theft of their truck lightly and they could only go as far as the gas would take them anyway. What then? Hannah didn't know, but they'd find a way. Even if they had to walk.

As they reached a junction, Hannah told Aaron to pull off into some trees, then handed him one of the shirts and a helmet. She put the shirt over the top of her dress and placed Grant's helmet on her head. They were starting to see American trucks and army personnel. From a distance she hoped they would be looked upon as a normal part of the whole.

She and Aaron went to the back of the truck to check on the children and let them out to stretch their legs. The response to their new attire ran from Beth's giggle to Rachel's laughing smirk. She suppressed it quickly when Aaron gave her a hard look.

They were sitting under a tree, reviewing the maps, when they overheard the twins, Madeleine and Margaret, speaking to one another.

"It's only a little ways from here," Madeleine said. "I am sure of it."

"No, you are wrong. It is closer to Zurich, not Munich."

Hannah stepped to the two girls who sat with their backs against the same large tree. "You know where we are?" she said, smiling.

"Of course; our parents brought us here many times," Madeleine said.

"She is wrong, it is not here, though it looks much the same, but further to the west, in the mountains around Zurich."

"What are you talking about?" Hannah asked.

"Our summer home," Madeleine said matter-of-factly.

"You had a summer home?" Naomi asked.

"Several, but this was my favorite," Margaret said.

"Not mine, not anymore," Madeleine responded.

"Why not?" Hannah asked.

The girls looked at one another. "Our parents took us there when things got bad in Berlin. We were safe for a while but then the local Nazi Bürgemeister and his police found us. At first they only questioned father and sent him home. It was then that he sent us to France."

"And your father, could he still be there?" Rachel asked.

"We were on the train, our parents waiting on the station's boardwalk waving good-bye as the train pulled away, when the police found them. We saw them taken away. Everyone who was taken away had been sent to Belsen."

Margaret added, "No one lived who went to Belsen, did they?"

"Where did you go in France?" Hannah asked.

"To an orphanage run by the OSE," Margaret said.

Hannah knew of the OSE, also known as the Society for the Health of the Jewish Population. It had been founded by a group of Jewish Russian doctors in St. Petersburg in 1912 to take care of Jews. That it had been founded at all was a miracle and attested to the tremendous influence of some Jews in Czarist Russia just prior to the first world war. Then catastrophe had struck when in World War I the eastern front completely destroyed the most compact Jewish communities in the countries surrounding Russia, and hundreds of thousands of Russian Jews had been forced from their homes by the traditionally anti-Semitic Russian army who were tired of what they were told was decadent Jewish influence. This forced the Czar himself to turn on the Jews and he issued his order of May 5, 1915, compelling 150,000 more of Hannah's people to leave their villages overnight. Among the displaced were entire orphanages. The OSE cared for more than 25,000 such children while joining with the American Joint Distribution Committee, a Jewish finance organization in the United States, and a special Paris Aid Committee in France to send food supplies and medical aide into Russia. After that they set up institutions for another ten thousand children. It was because of these events that many Jews joined the Russian Revolutionary movement to overthrow the Czar, only to have those Jewish Bolsheviks close to Lenin turn on them and have them thrown out of the country.

Ironically they fled to Berlin, Germany, which offered by far the most hospitable conditions for Jews in the 1920s. With the rise of Hitler in 1933, the OSE fled to Paris. With Albert Einstein as their figurehead chairman, displaced Russian doctors of Jewish heritage living in France ran a convalescent home for Jewish children under the age of six at Montmorency. During the war, hundreds of children were sent from Poland and Austria as the Nazis began their systematic destruction of a people. Hannah's father had thought of sending her and her sisters but they had refused to go.

"You were in Montmorency?" Hannah asked.

Margaret nodded. "When we arrived there weren't very many, but more and more came as the war grew. Then the Nazis came to France and we had to leave."

"We lived in a castle," Madeleine said. "The Germans nearly killed us there with their bombs so we had to go away."

"Where did you go?" Rachel asked.

"To Montintin," Margaret said.

"Some of the children couldn't go, they were sick," Madeleine chimed in. "The doctor told us we had to leave soon or we would be sick too. Diphtheria they said."

"And what was Montintin like?" Hannah asked.

"Another castle, but without beds or any furniture. We slept on the floors."

"The train ride was horrible," Margaret added. "People were hanging on the train everywhere, trying to escape the Germans. I don't know how all of us stayed together, but we did."

"Some were riding on top of the train and would fall off because of the choking smoke," Margaret added. "I saw them." She grimaced.

"Never mind, Margaret," Madeleine said a bit annoyed at the memory. "The train only went to Limoges. After that we had to walk. It was a long way. Twenty miles maybe."

"The French fascists were the worst, you know," Margaret said. "They were the secret police the Nazis used in the unoccupied part of

France. They wore black shirts and would come to Montintin in the night and take two or three of the oldest children away. We never saw them again."

"Our leaders knew it was only a matter of time before all of us were sent away. They tried very hard, even before we went to Montintin, to send some of us to the United States," Madeleine said. "But we didn't have anyone there to vouch for us, so we stayed. Then it happened. One night a truck came and took many of us away, young and old alike. We were sent to Auschwitz. When we arrived, only the strongest were kept alive; the others were sent to take showers."

They were gassed, killed, burned, destroyed. It made Hannah's heart ache with anger and frustration. Orphans. What harm could they have been to the Germans, to the French fascists?

"Can you get us to your summer home?" Rachel asked.

"Yes," Margaret said.

Madeleine stood. "Don't listen to her. She doesn't know the way. I told you before, if you want something done you should ask me."

"That isn't true; you are the one who is always getting lost."

Hannah felt a bit frustrated, but bit her tongue. "You say it is near Zurich. What is the closest town?" she asked Madeleine.

"Innsbruck," she said haughtily.

"Then we will go to Innsbruck, but Madeleine, you should listen to Margaret a little more. Innsbruck is closer to Munich than it is to Zurich."

Margaret's face lit up at Hannah's mild reprimand and she stuck her tongue out at her sister. Madeleine returned the favor and they both walked back to the truck ignoring one another. Hannah couldn't help the smile as she wondered how many times this little scene had played out over the years. She and her sister had been much the same. She shoved the thought aside. Now was not the time to get melancholy.

When they were on their way again, David refused to go in the back of the truck without Aaron so Rachel drove. "What are we going to do when we get to this summer house?" Rachel asked.

"If it is empty, we will live there until we can get in touch with the Jewish underground. Then we will go to Palestine."

"You and I and Zohar?"

"No, Rachel, all of us. We will all go to Palestine."

Rachel only nodded. It was the right thing to do. These children should never be left behind again.

CHAPTER 3

The truck sat under a canopy of trees a few hundred feet from the road. They had driven all night, skirting Munich and climbing through the mountain passes toward Innsbruck. Margaret had moved to the front of the truck so that she could show them the way. After traveling for an hour they had turned west on a road that headed toward Zurich. They now stood about halfway between the two cities. It seemed that both girls had been right, and Hannah was sure Madeleine would point that out when she discovered it.

Hannah had taken over driving during the night so that Rachel and Aaron could rest, but then they had arrived outside a small village where Margaret had become confused. She knew they were close, and directed them into a side road. Her hesitancy prompted Hannah to wait until morning. Driving into the wrong house could only lead to trouble. They had pulled off the road and tried to get a few hour's sleep.

Hannah, seemingly the first to wake up, opened the door and stepped to the ground, stretching. She heard thunder in the distance and glanced up at the dimly lit sky to find rolling, dark clouds. Rain was imminent.

She heard a noise from the gray shadows of the trees and froze, then saw Aaron coming out of the forest and started breathing again.

"You're up early," she said.

"I haven't slept more than a few hours since David and I began hiding in the hills." He spat at the ground. "The house is empty."

Hannah nodded. "Are you sure it is the right one?"

"Madeleine went with me. She's waiting for us to bring the others."

"Are there any neighbors?"

"Not close enough to worry about." He turned back and pointed. "The place is about five hundred yards up the road." He went past her and banged a hand against the tailgate, then climbed inside telling everyone to wake up. Hannah climbed back in the truck and started the engine as Rachel stretched herself awake. She wondered how much gas they had left but would measure it later.

The big truck lumbered up the road until they came to a gate on the right. Rachel got out and opened it, then they drove through acres of thick trees until the large house appeared in an opening. Raindrops splattered on the windshield as she braked to a stop in the cobblestone driveway and shut off the engine. The children were bounding over the tailgate and running up the stairs as the drops turned to a downpour, soaking her and Rachel before they could run to the covered porch.

As Hannah brushed the water out of her hair, she noticed Naomi with her face against a windowpane, trying to see inside. "How do we get in?" she asked.

At that moment, the door opened and Aaron stood in the opening. Apparently he had found a way.

"There are laws against breaking and entering," Hannah said with a smile.

"Someone should have told the Germans that." He stepped back and let everyone in before shutting the door behind them.

Hannah's eyes adjusted and she could see why the place had survived intact. There were pictures of Hitler and others on the walls and a large Nazi flag over the fireplace.

"They have ruined the place," Madeleine moaned. Margaret grabbed the first picture within reach and ripped it from the wall, tossing it angrily in the large fireplace and shattering the glass. Aaron lifted David high enough to reach the flag, tearing it off the wall. When the last of it had drifted to the floor, Anna picked it up and wadded it forcefully before tossing it in the fireplace. Madeleine retrieved some matches from a small table and quickly lit a fire, then everyone went through the place, methodically cleansing it of the demons the Nazis had left behind. There was an anger and determination in the children's movements, born of experience. They would never put up with anything that smacked of Nazis and their methods again.

When everything was burning, Hannah found herself staring at the growing flames, still feeling chilled. She rubbed her hands against her arms trying to dispel the goose bumps. Rachel put an arm around her shoulder and turned her to the window.

"Look, the sun is shining," she said. "Let's see if we can find some food, shall we?"

They went into the kitchen and began searching the cupboards. They were well stocked with canned goods. Next they went into the cellar and found barrels of flour, beans, and smoked meat hanging from hooks in the smoke room.

Hannah laughed lightly. Their luck was holding. The Nazi elite of this area must have taken over this place, stocked it with what was needed for the entertainment of their tight little circle and now she and her little group were reaping the benefits.

"I am surprised someone hasn't discovered this place by now," Rachel said.

"They might have, but they're still afraid. For Austrians the war is barely over. The people may still fear the Nazis and a reprisal of some kind."

"Or there is still someone around they are afraid of," Rachel said.

The statement made Hannah a bit uncomfortable but she shoved it aside. They would not stay long, and they would keep a sharp eye out. For now they needed food. She removed a smoked ham and Rachel dipped a small bucket into the flour barrel and carried it back upstairs. They quickly had an audience as everyone gathered, their bellies aching for something to eat. Hannah and Rachel took charge, assigning Aaron and David to see about wood for the stove. Zohar was to take Anna and Sarah and check the bedrooms, making sure there was linen on all the beds, and the rest were given duties in the kitchen. Hannah left Rachel and went outside to move the truck behind the house. As she stepped into the sunlight she felt a bit nervous, and carefully looked into the forest around them. Was Rachel right? Was this place still being watched by the Nazis? They must be vigilant and she must get to a phone and notify Colonel Mackland and Dov and make arrangements to get new papers. They could travel on to Italy and have them sent to the post office in Milan or somewhere.

When she parked the truck she saw Madeleine coming out of a detached garage, pale and shaken. She quickly hopped down and ran to her. "Madeleine, what is it? What's wrong?" She helped the girl sit down on the back steps of the house. Rachel, who had seen them from the window, hurried out the back door and joined them.

"What happened?" she asked, sitting down next to Madeleine who immediately turned her head into Rachel's shoulder.

Hannah was already crossing the yard to the garage. She opened the door slightly and peered in. The place was large, dark, and had the bittersweet odor of rotting flesh she knew from the camps that gave her a chill. As her eyes adjusted she saw that there was a car parked further in. A black car with a Nazi swastika hood ornament.

She felt the sudden urge to turn and run but pushed the door open instead, letting the fresh smell of sun and rain at least partially clear her nostrils. She went to the car. Unlike everything else in the building it had no dust, no cobwebs, its highly polished surface visible even in the shadows. Then she saw the form in the front seat and realized it was a man slumped against the door. She squinted. It was obvious he was the source of the smell, his skull caved in from what must be a gunshot wound.

Hannah turned and ran for the door, then bent over as she retched. What little had been in her stomach lay at her feet.

Rachel was quickly by her side, then headed toward the garage.

"Don't go in there, Rachel," Hannah said, reaching for her. "Not yet. Get Aaron and Naomi, find some shovels, and tell Zohar to keep the children away."

Rachel recognized the odor, and quickly went after the two oldest children. By the time Rachel was finished and she and the two teenagers stood at the garage door with shovels, Hannah had things under control.

She told them what she had seen.

"Serves him right, whoever he is," Aaron said coldly. "Let him rot."

"We can't do that and stay here," Rachel said. "His miserable carcass can still kill us with its disease."

Madeleine had finally gotten control of her tongue and spoke from the steps. "He is the local Bürgemeister. The one . . . the man who took our parents."

"What is he doing here?" Naomi asked.

"He probably confiscated this house, used it as a retreat for him and his cronies. When the war ended he couldn't escape and came here to hide. Then killed himself."

"A coward. They were all cowards. None of them could have survived what they put us through." Aaron spat on the ground beside him.

"You're sure it is the Bürgemeister," Hannah said to Madeleine.

"Yes, it is him. Ask Margaret if you want. He is the one my father feared the most."

Margaret started down the steps. "That won't be necessary Margaret. Whoever it is, he is quite dead." She looked at Naomi and Aaron, then Rachel. "It isn't pretty."

"Let's get this over with, Hannah," Rachel said.

Hannah nodded and turned to Zohar. "Prepare something to wash in when we're finished. A disinfectant in heated water if you can find it."

Zohar disappeared inside the house as Hannah and the others entered the garage.

Aaron took the lead, opened the car door and let the stiff corpse fall on the floor with a sickening thud. He grabbed a collar of the coat and began dragging him across the floor. Hannah had watched such methods used to haul the dead from their barracks each morning. It had sickened her then, and it sickened her now.

"Stop!" she commanded.

Aaron came to a halt, a lack of understanding on his face.

"We are not the Nazis, Aaron; even our enemies we bury with respect." She looked about her and saw a dusty, grease-spattered tarp on the workbench. Retrieving it she lay it out next to the body, then she rolled him into the center of it. Before putting the other half over him she stooped down and searched his pockets while trying very hard to control her queasy stomach. There was a wallet in the inside pocket, the keys to the car, and a handkerchief. She threw them behind her then covered the body. "Now, we will each grab a corner."

Aaron only shrugged and took a corner. It didn't seem much different to him but he was willing to follow Hannah's lead. It was a good sign.

The body was heavy and the best they could do was get it a few inches off the ground. They carried it into the forest behind the house and Aaron began digging a hole. Each of them took their turn until they had a cavity sufficiently deep to put the body inside. Then they covered it.

As they came back to the house Zohar had hot water ready and they began scrubbing themselves, all except Hannah. She took a bucket of the antiseptic and several cloths and headed for the garage. The smell had dissipated to a bearable level and she quickly began scrubbing down the leather seats of the car, then the carpets and the dashboard. They might need the vehicle and she wasn't about to sit in the Nazi's decaying filth. As she opened the back door to do the same, she found a briefcase on the floor. She shoved it aside until she was finished. Leaving the doors open she got behind the wheel and put the key in the ignition. It turned over weakly, then chugged to life. The gas gauge read half full. She let it run, recharging the battery while she opened the case and checked its contents.

Personal papers, letters to Franz Leibert, the man now rotting in the grave outside, from Hitler and from Leibert's wife. The first were letters of commendation for his work in "turning back the enemies of the Reich." The letter from his wife was dated only two months earlier telling Leibert that she was in Italy, safe and sound, and grateful. She hoped he would join her soon by the same route. Apparently he had decided to escape a different way.

Maybe not. She lay the briefcase aside and searched the car again, then the garage. There was no weapon. Someone had killed Herr Leibert and it made her even more nervous. Had it been vengeance, or the food and valuables in the house? If it was the latter why were they still there? It made her head ache.

She returned to the car and shut it off, then went back to the contents of the briefcase. In a separate section of the case there was a list of names. Enemies of the Reich. She let her eyes drift through the names, all of which had been crossed out. There was a category for "imprisonment" and one for "labor." She found Margaret and Madeleine's parents under a third category titled "extermination," the word *Juden* scrawled next to all but four of them. It was apparent to Hannah that most of these people had either been shot or sent to the death camps. She stared at the names, anger burning the nausea from her gut. These had been people with families and property. Men like Leibert had taken everything from them. Aaron was right; he had gotten what he deserved. Whether it was for greed or vengeance did not matter.

Rachel approached. "What have you found?"

Hannah showed her. "Margaret and Madeleine's parents are on the list meant for death."

Rachel saw where Hannah pointed. "We should tell the girls."

"When we're in Palestine." Hannah put everything back in the briefcase, closed it, turned off the key and got out of the car. They rolled down the windows and closed the car doors, then Hannah went to the rear of the car and opened the trunk lid. A suitcase. She opened it and found clothes neatly folded and in place and a stack of money. Reichsmarks. Worthless. She tossed them back, rifled through the clothing again, found nothing of value and shut the trunk lid.

"Apparently he was going to join his wife." She remembered the wallet and letter and retrieved them from the floor where she had thrown them. The wallet contained money as well, Swiss marks this time and worth something. She handed the bills to Rachel, found nothing else in the wallet and tossed it aside.

Opening the letter she read it aloud.

Kammerad,

Your guest will arrive in the next few days. Take good care of him and see that he meets his schedule.

"No signature and no name for his guest," Rachel shrugged. "Makes you wonder if he ever came here."

"Mmm. Except for the missing weapon."

"Missing?"

"I searched. There is no weapon. He didn't kill himself."

Rachel swallowed hard. "You think someone else got to him."

"Yes, but who and for what reason?"

"Hannah?" The voice came from the garage door. It was Zohar.

"We'll talk about this later. Hannah shoved the wallet and other items inside the briefcase, picked up the bucket and started for the door. "Coming," she said calmly.

They closed the garage door behind them, then Hannah tossed the cleaning water into the trees and left the bucket in the sun to dry. The children were on the porch eating, except for Madeleine and

Margaret who sat on the steps talking. Hannah washed herself thoroughly. Not because she thought she would get ill from Leibert but just because she felt dirty from coming in contact with the Nazi at all.

"Are you all right?" she asked the two girls as she dried with a towel.

They nodded but it was a lie. They were struggling. This idyllic spot was full of memories for them. Memories and the body of the man who they believed had seen to the killing of their parents.

"We will stay here only tonight. Will you be all right if we do?"

Again the nods. Again the lie. Hannah hugged them both. Rachel then handed her a plate with food. It was hard to eat but the ham tasted delicious and the fresh-baked rolls even better. Zohar was turning into a very good cook.

She looked at her young friend as she came from the kitchen door and put more rolls on each of their plates. She was changing. The frightened little girl at the hospital was sleeping through the night and seemed happy. Hannah also noticed Aaron seemed to be watching Zohar with particular interest. She smiled. Aaron was young, his hormones active. Zohar was getting prettier everyday. Why shouldn't he watch her?

Aaron saw her staring at him and blushed, then looked away. Hannah smiled, stood, and went in the house. No sense embarrassing him further.

They spent the day preparing beds, exploring the house and the gardens where they found that someone had planted a few hearty vegetables that were near maturing. Margaret and Madeleine brooded about until David discovered a basement closet filled with items that had been a part of the house before the Nazis had taken it for themselves. The two girls spent the rest of the day returning the items to their rightful places and making the chalet their home again.

Hannah called Aaron, Naomi, and Rachel aside and talked to them about security and why there was an outside chance that someone had killed Leibert to lay claim to this place.

"Then you think they might come back," Aaron said.

"I say we get moving. Tonight," Rachel said.

"It will be better to wait until tomorrow. I do not want to get on the road tonight and get lost or run out of gas. We have weapons; we can protect ourselves. Aaron you will take the first watch, then Naomi, Rachel, and myself. Every four hours, agreed?"

They nodded and all went about with their duties. Hannah watched Aaron check his weapon and then walk down the driveway and disappear in the edge of the trees. Rachel had another rifle and would keep it close the remainder of the day.

As the sun settled over the mountains to the west, the women and girls sat on the front porch in chairs and a swing watching David and Aaron kick a half-inflated soccer ball back and forth. David still wasn't smiling much, but it was good to see him active in a child's game he obviously had never played before. Naomi was sitting on a large rock near the road, the rifle in her hands. Hannah had tried to quell the apprehension she had about her decision to stay most of the day. She knew it was the right one even though she didn't know why. Still, the thought of someone coming made her nauseous.

Beth sat in the swing next to Hannah, her feet pushing them higher and higher, a delightful smile on her face. They played a game in which Beth would use her skinny little legs to push them higher and higher, then Hannah would put her own down and stop the swing at the apex. Beth would nearly slide out, grab for Hannah, and they'd both giggle and laugh. Then the sun disappeared and the mountains began to chill. Hannah called everyone inside. They gathered around the fire for a snack of more rolls and hot chocolate before the children went to their various rooms to sleep. Zohar, Rachel, and Hannah were left to watch the dying embers of the fire. Aaron had disappeared outside and was probably with Naomi.

"Marseille or Rome. Which offers the best chance of getting to Palestine?" Hannah finally asked. She had been thinking on the subject all afternoon and it was time to make a decision.

"If we go to France we have no guarantee of getting the children to Palestine for some time. The Jewish brigade is in Italy. They are helping refugees leave Europe. We can use all the help we can get. I say Italy.

"Zohar, what do you think?"

"I am not good at these things, Hannah. I trust you and Rachel will get us there no matter which direction we take."

Hannah smiled. "Then it will be Italy."

They sat in silence for a few minutes until Hannah sensed someone on the steps and looked up to see David standing there, his index finger in his mouth.

"What is it David?" she asked.

He said nothing but came down, ran the short distance to where she sat and hopped into her lap, laying his head on her shoulder.

She kissed him gently on the forehead and held him tightly, then started singing the song again. Zohar and Rachel joined her until he seemed to drift off.

The three women found themselves mesmerized by the soft final embers of the fire and the peaceful night surrounding them until they were startled by footsteps on the porch. Zohar scrambled behind the couch and Rachel was instantly across the room in an effort to get Private Grant's rifle from where it sat in the corner. Hannah placed David in the chair as the door opened and a man and a woman entered, Aaron and Naomi behind them, Naomi prodding with her rifle while Aaron kept one of the American forty-five caliber handguns ready.

Hannah found herself staring at an older couple who looked extremely tired and somewhat confused.

"Put the weapons away," she said to her three friends. They lowered the guns.

"Thank you," the older gentleman said with a good deal of relief. "Without a word he went to the shelf near the door, removed a kerosene lamp and lit it before hanging it from a hook on an over-head pillar. "There, that is better." He forced a smile as he looked at his captors. He was not as old as Hannah had first thought, but the gaunt look of his face had caused shadows that made it seem so.

"You have been here before," Hannah said. Even she hadn't known where the lamp was, nor would she have guessed to hang it on the hook mounted in the pillar.

"Of course. One remembers his own home. Even the camps cannot take that from him." He smiled.

Hannah felt herself suddenly weak in the knees. "You . . . you are . . . do you have two daughters, Margaret and Madeleine?"

The woman let out a slight scream, her hand going to her mouth to cut it off. "You . . . you know of our children? You have brought us word?"

Hannah wrapped her arms around the short little woman and hugged her as Rachel sat the gun in the corner and bounded up the stairs.

* * *

The celebration lasted until sunup. Madeleine and Margaret cried, screamed, ran around the house as if possessed, and their parents were forced to sit down as the tears flowed and they held their children for the first time in more than four years. The other children watched—envious, happy, hopeful. If it could happen to Margaret and Madeleine, couldn't it happen to everyone?

Zohar fixed them all some more to eat. No one turned away the food.

Hannah sat on the couch, Margaret and Madeleine curled up on the rug asleep in front of their parents. Their mother had her head on her husband's shoulder and was experiencing a peaceful sleep. Probably her first in many years. Their names were Emil and Lilith Silberman. Emil could not close his eyes, afraid he might wake up and find them gone.

"It is hard to believe," he said. "So many died and yet, our family, all of us survived. I must surely be dreaming."

"Then we are all having the same wonderful dream," Hannah said. She thought it ironic that without Sperling's madness and the wreck of the train in Stuttgart, then the cruel forcefulness of the American colonel they would not be here. She wondered how many years it might have been before this family would have been united if things had gone differently.

She sat forward. "How . . . how did the two of you survive? What happened after you sent the children to France?"

"My wife and I were interrogated for the second time the day we put the children on the train."

"By Leibert, the Bürgemeister," Hannah said.

"Yes, but how did you know?"

When she told him, his eyes saddened. "Herr Leibert was a decent man before the Nazis came. He and I were friends and our wives knew each other well, but that all changed when the Nazis made him their puppet. He became very cruel after that, and very greedy."

He took a moment to make his wife more comfortable by laying her down on the couch and moving to another spot, then went on. "I was a wealthy businessman in Germany, this was only one of several summer homes we owned, but I was also a Jew and after the night of the broken glass my factory in the Ruhr valley was confiscated, as was our home and all our property. What they did not have were the deeds to businesses outside the country and the numbers to my accounts in Switzerland, where they believed millions of marks resided. It was apparent they sent word to Leibert that he was to get that information from me. The interrogations started, then the beatings, and finally the threats. He even brought my wife in and put a knife to her throat." He looked at the frail lady whose head lay on his shoulder, a smile creasing his lips. "She defied him and swore she would never forgive me if I told him anything! Needless to say her fearless belligerence made him realize that taking her life would give him nothing. Then I saw a chance to free us."

"You made a deal," Hannah said.

"I told him I would give him what he wanted but only in Zurich, at the bank where the deeds were kept in a safety deposit box. I would give him one of the account numbers as a show of good faith. He agreed.

"The account was a small one, our personal household account, but it had enough money in it that Leibert's greed became a factor. He personally took us to Zurich."

"And you gave him the rest," Rachel said.

He smiled. "Only after my wife was set free and placed with friends who could protect her. After I knew she was out of his grasp, I took him and his guards to a small park across from the bank. I wrote the accounts down, gave him the key to the deposit box, and watched him cross the street to satisfy his greed. He returned a few minutes later, fighting mad."

"There was nothing there," Hannah smiled.

"The deeds were there, but they didn't matter—the property had already been taken from us, but the other cash accounts were empty. He demanded an explanation. I had been telling him all along that I was not the wealthy man he thought I was, that all my money was tied up in property and in my factory. I reminded him of that. He wanted to kill me, I could see it in his eyes, but we were in a public park. This was not the place. He put me back in his black car and started out of town. I went willingly. I knew all along that I would not escape. I was sent to Madenek, then Fohrenwald, and finally was liberated by the British at Belsen. After getting my strength back I returned to Zurich and found Lilith living in horrible conditions. She had no money, had never really gotten well from our imprisonment." He paused, his eyes sad. "I had hoped she would get to the United States. We have friends there, but without money . . ." He shrugged.

"Then you came here," Hannah added.

"Yes, we needed money before looking for the girls." He smiled as he stood and went to the fireplace. He pushed on one of the stones and it sprang outward, then slid to the side. Reaching inside he pulled out a stack of Swiss notes. "It will give us a fresh start," he said.

Hannah laughed. Leibert had been a fool.

He put the money back in its place and sat down. "Now, what about you, how did you get here?"

Hannah told him their story. When she told him about the fire and the loss of her papers his brow furrowed. He laughed when she rehearsed their mutiny and theft of an American military truck.

"You are a resourceful lady, Hannah Gruen, and we owe you a great deal for returning our daughters to us." He looked at his sleeping wife, then leaned forward. "You can stay here as long as you like and I will do whatever I can to help you complete your journey."

"Then you are not concerned about Leibert's mysterious death."

"Leibert had many enemies. There was a time I would have killed him myself." He sighed. "But we will watch just the same until we can notify allied authorities. It will be all right."

Hannah felt better but the pain in the pit of her stomach did not completely go away. She stood. "None of us slept last night so we wait one more day, then we go."

He agreed and she went to her bedroom. As she closed the door she saw that Emil Silberman's eyes were already closed. She undressed and climbed into bed, then got out again, closed the curtains against the rising sun and prying eyes and got on her knees.

She had a lot to be thankful for but she also realized they were in a tight spot and needed help. She didn't know how to contact the

Brigade, how to get them through Russian-occupied Austria, not to mention on ships that would take them to Palestine. She needed a little of Ephraim's faith and determination to find a way.

When she felt she would surely fall asleep if she remained on her knees any longer, she climbed back between the cool sheets and closed her eyes. She didn't know how but the way home would open for them. Feeling at peace Hannah drifted off to sleep.

It was the sudden sound of gunfire that awakened her.

CHAPTER 4

Hannah sat straight up in bed. She heard running in the other room and confused voices.

"What do you want?" It was Emil's voice and it was coming from the front porch. Hannah donned her skirt, then pulled aside the curtain slightly. The light of day made her squint at first, then her eyes adjusted and she could see several people in the front yard. All of them had weapons. Another fired in the air.

"You aren't wanted here Emil." A hat shielded the speaker's face.

"Henrie, the war is over."

"Not until all you Jews get the message," Henrie responded.

"There are only ten of you. Is that all you could muster for this welcome home?" Emil asked.

"Ten is enough."

"Mister, I think you should know you aren't the only one with a weapon." It was Rachel's voice from the living area. This could get very nasty, very quickly.

Hannah hastily pulled on her blouse and ran for the door that separated the two rooms. As she entered the living area she saw the children on the floor, Lilith's arms wrapped around Margaret and Madeleine, tears of fear cascading down her cheeks. Beth stood up and ran to Hannah who quickly ushered her back to the floor.

Rachel looked at Hannah. "I'll kill him before I let him in here, Hannah."

Hannah only nodded. They had to protect the children.

"We'll give you twenty-four hours," Henrie said to Emil. "I have the deed to this place now and you're going to get off one way or the other."

"We'll leave when we're ready, Henrie, not before," Emil said evenly.

"Then . . ." He didn't finish his sentence as the roar of an engine reverberated in the trees. Hannah got to her knees and peered out the window to see the American truck come around the corner of the house and aim its large hulk at the men standing in the lane.

"Americans!" Henrie yelled.

His followers scattered in all directions but Henrie froze just long enough that the truck caught him in the chest as it slammed to a halt. Henrie landed twenty feet away, flat on his back and semiconscious.

Hannah stood and stared at the truck, then at the trees where the last of the men was disappearing. She picked up Beth and joined Rachel and Emil on the porch. Aaron opened the truck door and got down. He had on the helmet and shirt Hannah had discarded in the front seat. He reached Henrie as the man was struggling back to consciousness. Emil quickly joined Aaron as he saw the boy also had the American-made forty-five handgun. He gently grabbed the weapon but Aaron jerked it away, an angry look on his face at having been challenged.

"If you kill him, all of us will be blamed and forced back to the camps," Emil said.

Aaron shoved the gun in his belt and turned back to the truck. "Tell him if he comes around here again I will kill him no matter the consequence," Aaron said. He then climbed back up into the driver's seat of the truck and put it in reverse, backing it away.

Hannah felt sad and grateful at the same time. Aaron had taken a decisive step against their enemy, but the hate that had surfaced scared her. Aaron was a time bomb and he had come close to exploding. Next time, someone like Emil might not be around to stop him.

Henrie tried to lift his head, shake the cobwebs away. "An American? What . . . is he doing here . . . How did you . . . Why are there American soldiers . . ."

Emil knew that Henrie's vision had been blurred by the blow just enough that he had only seen a uniform and hadn't understood what had really happened. It was something that could be taken advantage of.

"These people are protected by the Americans, Henrie. Don't come back here again." He helped him to his feet. "Now go, before they decide to haul you away to a prison."

Henrie, dazed and a bit frightened, stumbled down the lane, leaving his weapon behind. He turned back once, a mixture of anger and confusion on his face, then he disappeared in the trees. Hannah had the sudden thought that they hadn't seen the last of Henrie. When he thought things over and realized that one blurred soldier did not an army make, when the embarrassment of being soundly thumped became unbearable and his pride stirred up his hatred again, he'd return.

"How did he get the title to the house?" Rachel asked.

"My guess is he forced Leibert to sign papers, killed him, then rushed off to file them with the Austrian government. He received a new deed and came to claim his property," Emil said.

"Our being here is a threat to his plans then," Rachel said. "And he'll be back."

"Henrie is shrewd, but a coward when confronted, he will not come at us head on, but you are right, he will find a way."

Aaron came through the house and joined them, the shirt and helmet gone.

"Thank you," Hannah said. "But . . ."

"I meant what I said, Hannah. I won't let people like that push me around anymore. Ever." He glared at the trees through which Henrie had disappeared until he was sure his enemy was gone, then turned around and went back into the house.

Emil came up the steps and hugged his wife. She was shaking and sobbing. Emil tried to give her comfort as all of them moved back inside and each found a place to sit down.

Rachel stayed near the window, the rifle still in her hands.

Hannah blinked several times, even pinched herself to make sure she wasn't just having another nightmare. Would they ever be safe from such people? Had all the good in humanity been murdered by the Nazis? Probably, at least in Austria, which had been one of the first countries to actively try and get rid of Jews. At first they tried to deport them, but when other countries would not cooperate, they were some of the first to officially suggest a "final solution." One of the most diabolical was a man by the name of Heydrich, who eventually headed the extermination program for the Jews. It was obvious that the hatred was just as strong at the grassroots as it had been among the country's pro-Nazi leadership.

Hannah now realized that this idyllic, restful place could become their graveyard. Their very isolation could give men like Henrie the feeling they could get rid of them without a ripple of consequence.

"When you leave for Palestine we go with you," Emil said.

Hannah only nodded.

Zohar came from the kitchen wiping her hands on her apron. "There is breakfast ready. We must eat." She turned and went back the way she had come. Hannah inwardly thanked her young friend. They needed something to take their minds off Henrie and his rabble. Food was the greatest temptation that could possibly be offered.

She stood and took Beth by the hand. "Come on everyone, Zohar is right, we must eat." The others got up and joined her. After a Jewish blessing by Emil the ham was placed on the table and the children began eating. Hannah watched Emil and Lilith glance at one another, then Emil shrugged and used his fork to stab a piece of the pork and put it on his plate. He too had learned that one ate what one had, that kosher laws were not as important as staying alive. His wife followed his lead but Hannah noticed that both of them ate more of the potatoes and fresh bread Zohar had prepared than they did meat.

Spirits improved dramatically though Rachel kept the rifle at her side and Aaron stayed close to the window where he could see the front lane. Both were fighters, both would die rather than be terrorized by men such as Henrie—men created by Hitler and Himmler. She had to get them out of Europe. Soon.

The meal helped cleanse the air of fear and soon the smaller children went to their rooms to play and Hannah and Lilith helped Zohar clear the dishes, while Emil and Naomi finished the last of the rolls.

"You make a fine meal, Zohar," Emil said as he pushed his plate away. "I haven't eaten such food for a long time."

Zohar blushed and thanked him. "I am sorry about the ham. I know . . ."

"There will come a time when all of us can return to the way things were. For now . . . we eat, and thank God."

"If you still believe in God you are a fool," Naomi said stiffly.

The room went silent. Emil winced and looked around the room as if waiting for someone to disagree. His eyes settled on Hannah. "Is this what you have been teaching these children?" he asked.

"She has nothing to do with it. The camps taught us," Naomi responded. "Any Jew in their right mind discovered there is no God." She stood and left the room. The others went back to their tasks, an uncomfortable silence thick in the air.

Emil finally spoke. "What happened was God's will. He chastens us for our sins. We will do better now. We must try harder to please Him."

"It is that particular God Naomi has trouble with, Emil," Hannah said. "Innocent children were butchered by the Nazis. They had no sin and deserved no punishment."

"Then you believe as she does," Emil said.

"No, but the God you speak of is not a God I and many others can believe in." With that she left the room and searched for Naomi. She found her on the front porch in the swing. "May I join you?"

Naomi didn't answer but moved enough that there was room in the swing next to her. Hannah knew she could never explain what she had learned from Ephraim as well as he had explained it but she had to try. And she did.

Naomi listened, but said little, nor could Hannah read Naomi's body language enough to determine if she was getting through. There was absolutely no reaction, positive or negative. She just sat and listened, every part of her neutral, her eyes never leaving the mountains to the west.

Hannah sensed Naomi's aloofness. The girl was staying because she had come to respect Hannah, but she refused to hear. Hannah stopped.

"You're not willing to consider other options are you, Naomi?"

Naomi didn't answer at first and when she did the words made Hannah ache for her.

"At first I prayed constantly, Hannah. I used every ounce of my soul to cry out for help. Things only got worse. One day another woman, a believer, was found on her knees by one of the guards. She died from the beating. It was then God stopped existing for me. If He can't stop the wicked, of what use is He? If He lets the good die, why be good?" She stood and walked away, taking the steps from the porch. As she got to the bottom she turned back. "If He had saved that woman I—I think things would have been different. Just her, not all of us. I could have gone on praying if He had just saved her." She walked away.

Hannah felt empty inside. She had failed. Oh, how she wished Ephraim were here to explain it all! She had been just like Naomi—cynical, bitter, full of despair about God's desertion of her and her people—but Ephraim had changed all that! His words had touched her very soul and changed her forever. She had opened her mouth and only made things worse.

Hannah looked up to find Emil at the door.

"They will not come tonight; they must make sure the Americans are not here. Then they will come. Greed pushes such men to awful things. I stayed too long once, we all did. We should learn from that."

He sat on the railing of the porch. "I have enough money to bribe the guards at the border to Italy. Once there I have business associates who might be willing to arrange papers into Greece, or even directly to Palestine."

"It will take a good deal of money," Hannah said.

"I have a hundred thousand Swiss francs in the fireplace."

"That is your nest egg for starting a new life."

"There is enough for all of us to get a new start, in Jerusalem." He turned to go back in the house then glanced back over his shoulder. "Tomorrow. It won't take them more than that to find out we are alone. We should be gone."

Hannah nodded agreement and he disappeared inside. She was glad he was here.

After a few minutes she followed him, called everyone and gave instructions.

They would leave in the morning.

CHAPTER 5

Hannah woke at sunup to find Beth staring at her from the door of the room she shared with Rachel. She sat up. "What is it Beth?"

"Can we go for a walk? The mountains are so pretty and . . . and we won't see them again for a long time. Can we?"

Rachel rolled over. "She's right. Let's go up to the waterfalls Emil told us about last night."

After food and luggage had been packed the night before, and everything prepared for travel, everyone gathered around the fireplace for rolls and butter. Emil, Lilith, and their two daughters had begun remembering good times in their mountain retreat and had mentioned a beautiful waterfall only a mile up one of the valleys. It had sounded too wonderful; now they would see.

"All right," Hannah said, throwing off the covers. "Let's go for a walk."

Beth clapped her hands and Hannah had to shush her, telling her the others might like to sleep. It would be a long day. "Get dressed, but do it quietly."

The three of them slipped from the house. Rachel and Hannah wrapped shawls around their shoulders and Beth donned a sweater found in one of the bedroom closets. Rachel also carried her rifle.

"Is that necessary?"

Rachel shrugged. "You never know what kind of animal you might encounter in these mountains." She slung it over her shoulder by its strap.

They were nearly at the valley mouth when Aaron caught up to them. "You're up early," Hannah said. She knew he had sat up in the living area most of the night, a self-imposed guardian against Henrie and his stooges, though she, Rachel, Emil, and Naomi had also taken their turn.

Aaron smiled. "I couldn't sleep."

The air was fresh, clean, and crisp, filled with the smells of the forest. Pine and the mold of dead leaves and needles mingled with the scent of flowers, and a dozen other odors attacked their senses. They walked for nearly forty minutes before they came into an open valley and found the waterfalls pouring their cool liquid over a precipice high on the far valley wall. A pool of water as clear as glass lay at the bottom. They each lay on their stomachs and took in all they could of the cool liquid. Then they lay on a grassy spot and watched the sun's rays move down the valley wall as it lifted higher into the morning sky.

Beth and Aaron took off their shoes and waded up to their knees while Rachel and Hannah watched. Beth giggled and grew wide-eyed as a fish swam close by. Aaron tried to catch it for her and soaked his shirt to the shoulders. It was the first time she had seen him enjoying himself.

"This is what it should be like for them," Hannah said. "A slice of heaven."

"Is there such a place?" Rachel asked.

"Heaven? Yes, I think so now. I had stopped believing but Ephraim helped me understand, see it differently."

"When you're in love you believe anything," Rachel said, only half teasing.

"Yes, I suppose so," Hannah said with a smile. "At least it creates an open heart, but it is more than that. It has touched my heart." Hannah turned on her side and looked at her friend. "Your mother is all right Rachel. She's happy, growing, learning. She is lonely for you, worries about you, but knows you will see each other again."

"And my father?" The usual bitter tone was missing.

"I don't know the end for him. He was deceived, that must make a difference, but God is a good judge, a perfect one."

"Ephraim relies on the next life too much for his comfort, Hannah. I can believe only in what I see, what I know. Death is the only reward for the wicked. Obliteration from the lives of those they hurt."

"And that is enough for you?"

"It is all there is," Rachel said. "It has to be enough."

She sat up as Aaron finished pulling on his shoes, and headed down the trail. Hannah was disappointed once more. Why couldn't her friends feel what she felt? Was her love for Ephraim getting in the way and allowing her to be deceived? No, it was more than that. The problem was she simply did not have the ability to convey what she had come to know as Ephraim did, and it made her feel horrible.

"Look!" Beth pointed to a small deer as it leaped over logs and glided deeper into the forest. They watched as its lithe form darted away from them, then they continued their trek home.

As they stepped out of their wooded haven, Aaron, who was in the lead, put up a hand. They all melted to a quiet standstill at the sound of trucks and men's voices. Aaron signaled to get off the trail to the left and into some thick trees near the valley mouth. From there they took in the ghastly scene below. Two large trucks were pulled up in front of the house and soldiers were everywhere.

"The Americans!" Rachel said.

"They're searching the place."

Aaron pulled the revolver from its resting place and started toward the house. Hannah grabbed his arm and pulled back. "The Americans are not enough of an enemy to shoot them, Aaron. Stay put!"

"It seems Henrie has discovered our little secret," Rachel said pointing to a small group of civilians standing near the trees at the front of the house. He had gotten hold of the Americans quicker than expected. They must have traveled all night to get here.

They watched as the garage was opened and several soldiers went inside. One came back and called to another. Hannah recognized him immediately. The colonel from Stuttgart. Colonel Pittman. He had come for his truck.

He went inside the garage, returned a few moments later and barked an inaudible order. The garage door was closed and a soldier put down his rifle long enough to use a chain and padlock to secure it. The colonel strutted to the porch where Emil, Lilith, and the others waited. His voice was inaudible at first but quickly exaggerated to a shout in an attempt to bully Emil who simply stiffened his back and refused to respond. The wind carried the colonel's response to

Hannah's ears. They had no papers. They would be taken to a holding camp and processed there. Where was the woman? Emil said nothing.

Hannah knew he was speaking of her. She was the one he really wanted. She had opposed him and now he wanted to put her in her place. His pride had been pierced and he did not like being wounded.

She turned to Rachel. "I must go out there. You can come or stay here. They may stop looking once they have me, and you will be safe."

Rachel looked frightened, confused. "No, no, we stay together. We must. Even . . . even if we have to go to the camps. We must."

Hannah turned to Aaron. "You have a choice as well, Aaron."

Aaron's anger and indecision showed in the firm set of his jaw and the fire in his eyes. He was trapped again. There was David and there was freedom. He had always managed to stay out of the camps, had even killed to stay free and now . . . now he was being forced into them by an enemy who was supposed to be their friend! He wiped sweat from his brow, then stood and tossed the gun into the woods before starting for the house. Hannah breathed again as she reached for Beth's hand and followed. Rachel dropped her weapon and fell in beside them.

They walked into the clearing as half a dozen soldiers rushed to surround them. Hannah felt rage build in her as they approached the steps where a haughty Colonel Pittman waited for them. Even worse was Henrie and his friends standing near the edge of the woods enjoying the whole scene.

She stepped toe to toe with Pittman and lifted her hands and straightened her arms. "Where are the shackles, Colonel? You always need shackles for such a dangerous lot."

His face went red, but his jaw remained defiant granite. "You're under arrest for the theft of a military vehicle and will be returned for trial."

"All of us? Even the ones who had nothing to do with it? Even the children?"

"As I told you, my orders are to take them to the camps where they will be processed and sent back to their countries of origin."

"Yes, I've heard your orders. It is the reason we stole your truck in the first place, and if we have the chance we will steal another. Anything to keep you from sending us back to the butchers who destroyed our families and still want to destroy us." She looked at Henrie. "Look at them. Vultures. Ready to feed on the spoils after you haul us away from here. They are probably Nazis and you do their dirty work, let them rob and steal from us."

"This is not your property," the Colonel said. "It belongs to that man over there. It was sold to him by the local Bürgemeister who died of some illness."

"And you believed him. You are a fool, Colonel." Hannah grabbed his arm and pulled him toward the garage. "Come with me. I will show you Herr Leibert, your Bürgemeister."

He pulled back and was about to bark an order when Hannah turned on him. "Leibert was also a Nazi. He had the owner of this home, who is standing on its porch, arrested, and forced him to turn this property over to him. He then sent him to the camps."

"I suppose you can prove—" The haughtiness was diminished.

"Yes, I can." She took him inside and retrieved the briefcase. She handed him the letters from Hitler but could see immediately that he could not read German. She took them back and read them for him.

"Leibert is buried in the back yard. We found him in that car in the garage, his head half missing from a bullet. You can dig him up and take a look if you want, but I warn you it is not a pleasant sight. Does it not seem suspicious that the man out there in the yard has a title belonging to a man who was murdered and left to rot here?"

The Colonel seemed shaken.

"It is time you recognized who the enemy is, Colonel. Those men watching you do this came yesterday and tried to scare Emil off his property with threats. We made him think your men were here, but you have told him otherwise and he has now lied to you in an effort to get you to do his dirty work. He thinks you believe as he does, and you are about to prove him right. Don't you see that by doing this you are telling them that what they try to do to us is all right, and what they did to all Jews was justified? You give them back their homes, their lives, their warm clothes and beds while you send us to camps that continue to deprive us of our right to a decent life. If you had half an ounce of courage inside that uniform, you would make them give up their homes and live in your camps for a year or two. You would make them face what they have done, show them that they committed horrible atrocities. But you do none of this. You close your eyes and you do their dirty work. Why, Colonel? Because of orders? If those are your orders then God help your country, for they are blind and inhuman!"

The colonel turned and looked out the window at the men on the far side of the clearing. He remained quiet for some time, then yelled for his sergeant.

The driver of the truck they had hijacked walked into the room. He gave her a quick apologetic look before the colonel turned to him and he stiffened to attention. "Put those men under arrest."

The sergeant gave a relieved smile, a sharp salute, and a "yes sir!" before turning back and giving the order. Hannah watched as the troops suddenly turned and surrounded a surprised Henrie and his friends.

"Thank you," Hannah said, humbly grateful. She sat down, drained.

"This will take time. We will need your testimony and that of your friends, especially the man who owned the house. My only request is that you go to the camp at Salzburg with us until we can determine all the facts. It will only be temporary, until your papers come, and we can get new papers for the children, but I need you to cooperate."

Hannah breathed deeply. "Very well. Until our papers come."

"The camp is actually at Ebensee, outside of Salzburg. It has a detention center for prisoners of war as well as a camp for displaced persons. These men can be put there until we are finished with them while getting written affidavits from you."

"And you can obey your orders to take all Jews to DP camps for processing," Hannah said.

The colonel gave a wan smile. "Yes, that too." He turned to Hannah. "You have my apology. I never fully realized . . ."

"Apology accepted," she interrupted, helping him hang on to a bit of his pride. "What about this place?"

"I'll leave some of my men here. Leibert is on our Most Wanted list. We thought he had escaped. We will need to remove the body and verify it is him, and the manner of his death. After we complete the investigation, I'll withdraw my men and the owner can either return or sell it. There should be trustworthy local authorities in place by then who can help him, either way."

They walked out onto the porch in time to see Henrie being forced into the back of one of the trucks at gunpoint, screaming. "This is my property. Don't you see the Jews use you Americans, like they use everyone. They are the trouble with this world! They . . ."

The sergeant took a soiled hanky from his pocket and shoved it in Henrie's mouth.

"The man really is a fool, isn't he?" Pittman said. "He really believed I was with him on this." His face darkened. "He was close to being right."

Emil gave Hannah a big grin and Aaron shook his head in disbelief, but his smile revealed that his faith in humanity was at least partially restored.

As the trucks with their newly acquired prisoners lumbered out of the clearing and disappeared, Zohar ascended the steps and announced that breakfast would be ready in a few minutes. Hannah looked at the colonel, who nodded agreement, then went to give his remaining soldiers their orders. Hannah gathered her chattering group around her and told them what had happened.

They sobered some when she revealed what must happen next. No one was anxious to go back to the camps.

CHAPTER 6

The camp was like all such camps, discreetly tucked away where it would not be a constant reminder to the population of deaths they knew took place daily under the Nazis. It had not been a death camp, one meant specifically for extermination, but was a labor camp. Jews and political prisoners had been brought here to work. Hannah didn't know what was made here, but knew that like all such camps, its main purpose was to keep Hitler's war machine running at full tilt while concerning itself very little with the number who would die while doing so. For Jews it would have been a cold and heartless place where their lives meant nothing, and death from starvation and endless cruelty would have been a daily occurrence at the rate of dozens, even hundreds.

On arrival, they passed through open gates and pulled up to what Hannah knew was the administration building. As they unloaded, she noted that the towers and most of the barbed wire had been removed. People could walk away but had no place to go or lacked the strength to get there. They stayed because the Americans offered food and medical care. Some stayed because they waited for the conquerors to give back their homes and their dignity. It was a dream. The Germans were getting the homes; they were not.

Once she was out of the truck with little David by the hand, they were all ushered into the commandants office where Colonel Pittman was filling in the camp commander on who his new guests were. As Hannah stepped forward Colonel Pittman turned and gave her a smile.

"I'll see to the interrogation of the Austrians. Major Stevens will take care of you." He extended a hand to shake. She took it. "Thank you again. I mean it," he said.

She nodded and he went out the door.

Major Stevens cleared his throat, then spoke in adequate German. Hannah was glad she didn't have to interpret. "Let's all sit down, shall we?"

Hannah motioned to the others and each found a seat, some on the floor. The camp commander noted this action and it added to his understanding that this woman was in charge and would be the one with whom he would have to deal.

"First of all, my name is Bob Stevens, my home is in the great state of Arkansas, I am not Jewish, but I am on your side. The colonel has told me about your situation and that you will most likely be leaving us soon. We'll make your stay as comfortable as possible."

Hannah sensed his sincerity but still felt apprehensive. She did not want to be here, and from the look on the faces of each of the others, they were feeling the same way. "Did he tell you about our papers?"

"He did, and he asked me to follow up. I will do that first thing in the morning." He smiled. "Believe me, if you are a friend of General Clay's, you are a friend of ours." He glanced at all the others, his eyes coming to rest on Emil. "I assume you are the owner of the house?"

Emil nodded, then stood.

"We will get you back to your home as soon as the colonel finishes his investigation," Major Stevens said.

"It is not home now. We wish to go to Palestine, eventually."

"Hmm. The wish of almost every Jew in this camp. Unfortunately, for you, it will take time and I have so few beds that you may find it better to return there until arrangements can be made."

Emil only nodded, disappointment on his face. He sat down and took his wife's hand while wrapping one arm around Madeleine, who sat next to him.

The major smiled at them. "We don't see many families here. Your story must be a bit miraculous."

Emil nodded. "Yes, I think that would be the proper way of saying it."

"When we leave, they will go with us," Hannah said.

"They won't have papers."

"We will find a way, but if they want to go, they will go," Hannah said matter-of-factly.

The Major smiled, then stood. "Come here after breakfast in the morning. We'll see what we can do for your group."

Hannah looked at Emil, then the others. They were exhausted, hungry, and their eyes begged for sleep. "Where can we get something to eat, and do you have any beds?"

"We are very crowded here and most of our guests are not Jewish. We . . ."

"We will not be put with our enemies!" she said forcefully.

"Now hold on, let me finish. We have a separate row of barracks for those of Jewish heritage and there are beds there."

"With lice or without?" Zohar asked, then put a hand to her mouth as if the words had escaped by mistake.

Hannah grinned. "It is a valid question."

"Without. We run a clean camp, Miss . . ."

"Gruen, Hannah Gruen."

"We run a clean camp. When I arrived we had the Germans in the surrounding villages come and clean. They are more repentant and come often to bring extra vegetables and fresh eggs. They don't complain if our tenants raid their gardens once in a while either."

Hannah was a bit shocked. "You . . . made them face what was going on here?"

"They already knew, but chose to ignore it. Let's just say we helped them face their ugly past. There will be good heavy blankets on your beds. We requisitioned them from the surrounding area as well." He sighed. "But there are still many problems. Even with the increased generosity we are unable to feed everyone adequately, and some . . . well they are just too far gone to make it. Some commit suicide, unable to live when they find they have no one left." He paused a moment. "You have regained your health much faster than most, Miss Gruen, both physically and mentally. All of you have."

"We were much luckier than most, Mr. Stevens." She stood. "Thank you. As you can see, we are hungry and very tired. Where can we get some food?"

"The kitchen is in the center of the complex. One warning, Miss Gruen. There are thieves here, and there is still hatred. Your people should stick together and stay in the Jewish section of the camp until we can get you on your way."

She nodded, her face grim. She was not looking forward to walking through the gates of this or any other camp; in fact she hadn't been in such turmoil in a long time. Emil led the way out and as she reached the door she turned back. "We will leave this camp no later than seven days from now, Major, whether you have papers for us or not."

He nodded as she closed the door. He could see that she meant what she said.

He hoped he could change her mind.

* * *

The children were pale with fear, huddling close to her and the other grownups. Hannah gave them the best comfort she could, but felt near suffocation herself. They pushed through the crowds of beleaguered and still hungry people to find the kitchen. There was food—hot, filling, and tasty—and it helped to waylay some fears. If there was one thing camp inmates had learned to equate with kindness, it was good food.

Next they went to their barracks. Emil, Aaron, and David were shown the men's barracks while Hannah and the rest went into the women's. Lilith resisted and Emil looked forlorn, then frustrated and angry as the soldier leading them said it was the rules.

"It is a rule that needs to be changed," Emil said. He turned to Lilith and promised he would look in on her and the children before going to sleep.

Hannah and her group were shown four large scrubbed bunks with mattresses, warm blankets, and soft pillows, and Hannah felt her own panic level subside to manageable levels. Possibly they could endure this for a few days. A very few. Lilith and her two girls took one bunk, Anna and Sarah another, Naomi and Zohar the third. Rachel, Beth, and Hannah thought of asking for a fifth, but after seeing nothing else available decided that it would be better to keep Beth between them.

It took nearly an hour for Beth to finally fall into a listless sleep between her and Rachel. When she did, Hannah slipped away to get some fresh air. Though the Americans had changed things significantly, she still felt terribly trapped and overwhelmed with her own feelings and flashbacks.

As she stumbled down the steps, Hannah breathed deeply of the night air but it did little good, the smells and sounds of the camp doing nothing to take away the weight of anxiety on her chest.

She passed a forlorn Emil coming out of the men's barracks and gave him an encouraging smile. He forced one in return that said he, too, was suffering and afraid, and would be glad when it was over. Then he went to a window of the women's barracks and called for Lilith.

Looking around her, Hannah saw that the camp was alive with people even though it was near midnight. It was obvious to her there were many who could not stand to sleep inside, preferring the cool evening air of the outdoors to the menacing shadows of the barracks where so many had lived and died in fear for so long.

After walking a short distance, Hannah placed her back against the wall of the barracks and watched and listened. People spoke of the past, the distant past mostly. Of homes and families before the war, of how things had been, of fond memories. She heard few talking about their experience in the camps. She supposed it was too early for that. Such large, open wounds healed slowly and needed no salt poured into them just yet. She knew that speaking of them would have to come, but it was still in the distant future, even for her.

She heard a woman ask, "Have you seen anyone from Krakow?"

"No, no one, I am sorry. No one." The loneliness of the words spoken made Hannah's heart ache.

The sound of an argument came from around the corner of the building and she walked to where she could see and hear more clearly. Several men stood a short distance away and were speaking in Yiddish. The argument was religious and concerned support for two different Rabbis that had come to the camp. It was heated, each side defending their position of who should take supremacy in religious matters. It made her remember how it had been in Warsaw; allegiances to different Rabbis ran deep and were often the cause of great rifts in the community. Such allegiances hadn't ever totally disappeared in the ghettos or the camps. Men cared for the Rabbis before they cared for themselves. It shouldn't surprise her that now, after freedom to worship had been reestablished, new disputes would ignite out of the ashes. It had been so since the dispersion at the destruction of the temple! Why should Hitler bring it to an end?

She turned away with a hint of a smile. Some things would never change. She didn't suppose that was all bad.

She remembered good and happy moments of Passover celebration, weddings, and community. They were as much a part of her as her flesh and were good memories. Though her religious beliefs were changing she would always remember the past, the good. Always.

She walked until she came upon a small group nestled around a fire built of logs they must have gathered from the nearby forests. She couldn't help but stop and warm herself against the growing night chill. *If only there had been such fires in the camps*, she thought. But none were ever allowed. Another sign of change, and as she looked at the flickering firelight dancing across the faces of the others she could see that it was a change they relished.

"You are new," said one, looking at her with the eyes of a critic.

She nodded.

"And well fed," said the woman. "What are you doing in a place like this? Slumming?"

"I was at Ravensbrück, but have been free for nearly four months now," she said defensively.

"It is obvious they fed you better there than here," said another.

"I was taken to a hospital, the Americans . . ."

Guilt turned Hannah away from the fire and she started back for their barracks. Guilt. She had felt it because she had survived and others hadn't; now she felt it because she had found food, and friends, and love, and these people were still on the edge of starvation and hatred. If she admitted it she even felt it because she was walking away from her old faith. Would there ever be a place where she didn't feel guilt?

Out of the darkness a familiar voice spoke to her. "Do not worry about them. They are still bitter."

She turned to see Doctor Cardan, his face lit up by a light hanging from one of the buildings, another change by the Americans. "But who can blame them? This isn't exactly what God promised His chosen people, is it?" he continued.

"God didn't choose it for them. Hitler did."

"An astute observation."

"It is the guilt I feel that worries me, not their bitterness."

"The result of Hitler's work I suppose."

"The root of the evil at least." She started walking again and he fell in beside her. "What are you doing here Doctor? I thought you would be on the next train to your French home after that night of misery in Stuttgart."

"I have gotten on the train many times since leaving Dachau. I never seem quite able to pull myself away from all this." He smiled. "After all, the pay is good, the perks so extensive, how could one go back to the pittance a country doctor makes?"

The smile avoided reaching the eyes where a deep hurt seemed to linger. Was it because, like all Jews, he no longer felt he had a place in this world? Was that why he didn't go home?

"You are going to work here then?"

"Yes, for a while at least. Who knows, maybe tomorrow I will get on the train, go home. Who knows?"

"Why here, why not Tirschenreuth? It is closer to France."

"Reputation. This camp is what we would call progressive. Major Stevens has a gift for helping people."

"He will need more than a gift to succeed here."

"He seems to find what is needed. A good-hearted scrounger fits in well in a place like this."

"Do you have a place to stay?" she asked.

He pointed at the nearest barracks. "Above average accommodations. Only two to a bed."

"Ah, ours is just next door."

He noted it with a slight nod, then spoke. "How are your hands?"

She had nearly forgotten the constant sting of the burns inflicted when she had tried to get their paperwork out of the train. She lifted them to the light. "Still a little red, some peeling, but nothing to worry over."

He took her hands and looked at them carefully before letting them go. "Yes, they will be fine." There was silence between them. "You are good with people, Hannah. You could be a big help here."

"Thank you, but the children . . . We leave in the next few days for Palestine."

He looked around them at the dozens of people. "That all could be so blessed, but until they are, someone has to take care of them." He pointed to another building. "That is the hospital, or something called a hospital. The major supplies it as well as he can, but the injuries doing the most damage lie unseen, where bandages do no good. That is where the real help is needed. It is where you are needed." He smiled. "I must get to my patients."

They said good-bye and she watched him until he disappeared through a door of the barracks turned hospital, then she turned and walked to her own building. Doctor Cardan's problem was like Zohar's—even after the camps he still had a heart.

She found Beth and Rachel in the bunk. Both seemed to be sleeping, and she tucked the blanket tightly around Beth before unfolding her own and getting comfortable. She closed her eyes against the shadows and pulled her pillow around her ears to avoid the sounds of this too-familiar room. An hour went by as she prayed for sleep that would not come. Finally she removed Ephraim's book from the suitcase she now shared with Rachel, and, blanket in hand, went outside. There was a light near the steps and she put her glasses in place and began reading.

Her mind drifted a little at first but gradually the words took hold and gently soothed her fears.

She had been concentrating on the Isaiah chapters of late and had come to what seemed to be the prophet Nephi's summary of them. He spoke of Jewish captivity in Babylon and then their return. She read of the coming of Christ and the Jewish rejection, then of their dispersion. What gave her the most comfort, enough comfort that she had read them over and over again, were the words which stated that, though they would be scourged by many nations for the space of many generations, there would come a time when they would believe in Christ as Messiah, and because of it would be reconciled to God. Was this that time? It was for her, but would it be for others? It was very clear that acceptance of Christ was at the core of reconciliation and yet for many, Christ had been at the very center of the persecutions against them. Were they ready to see the Christ she had come to know?

There were so many stumbling blocks to such acceptance. Most Jews believed not in a single man as Messiah anymore but in a

Messianic age, a time of political and spiritual strength when they would be restored to world domination and leadership and peace would reign among them again. The Zionist movement, started more than fifty years ago, was built on that concept. A political Messiah. A state that could bring about their Messianic age, but she knew now that there was much more to it than that. The gathering to Israel by her people was only a beginning. Beyond any physical gathering was a gathering to Christ as Messiah. A gathering to God.

It depressed Hannah, but she did not think her people were prepared for any but the first. They wanted freedom from persecution, a place of safety, and Palestine offered it. Without Ephraim and his book she would have wanted nothing else, either.

She found it ironic. Even a physical return would have been impossible without persecution. Even before the two great wars of the twentieth century, the Zionist movement was born of persecutions in places like Russia and Romania. Why would one want to return to a desolate land of sand and rock when you had nice homes and good lives in the idyllic mountains and valleys of Europe? Though she now understood that God did not cause such persecutions, He had not stopped them either. For Him not to do so required both the merciful God of Ephraim's description—a God who took care of the martyred in a better life—and a God who had great purposes in store for the remnant who had survived. A purpose with eternal consequences. And, according to the book in front of her, a purpose that included Judah's acceptance of Jesus of Nazareth as their Messiah.

She closed the book and stared at its brown cover. No, her people were not ready. At least, not most of them. Not yet. But this book was true, and in it God made promises that Hannah *knew* he would keep, even though she did not fully understand how He would do it, anymore than she understood completely why there wasn't an easier way for her people to come back to Him. Some things simply required faith.

"You're up late."

Hannah looked up at Rachel, then slid over and made room. They had read the book together before. Rachel usually listened without comment.

"You've changed," Rachel said.

"We all have."

"No, it's different with you. You seem more settled than the rest of us."

"Don't let appearances fool you. I am just as frightened and confused as anyone."

"Maybe, but you're confident now. You believe in something more. Because of it we all feel safe with you." Rachel paused. "Some of it was Ephraim, I think, but some of it is what you read in that book, isn't it?"

Hannah looked at the brown cover. "Yes, it is."

"How can you be a Jew and a Christian at the same time? It is an anathema to me, Hannah; I do not understand it. I was Christian and they taught us Jews were evil. Surely, you are not thinking of becoming . . ."

"I am becoming, Rachel. I can't help it. Something deep inside tells me Christ is the Messiah, but Ephraim's church, his faith, are not the same as what you knew. You saw what it was like when we went to Ephraim's church. You felt it, I know you did. Was it the same as what you felt when you were young and a Lutheran?"

"No, it was not the same, but I was young. I did not understand anything, not even the ceremony they put us through. It was all just ritual and held no meaning for me. I . . ."

"What did you feel at Ephraim's church?"

Rachel thought a moment. "Peace, I suppose, but that doesn't mean those who belong to his faith would not turn on us in a moment. You heard his words; some in that congregation had persecuted us. He knew it and we both know it."

"But he also denounced it, as does his church. Of course there will be individuals who do not live their beliefs, who are carrying bias and hatred for others. That is true, but it was never condoned by Ephraim's church and never would be." She took a deep breath. "Besides, it is not that which made me a believer. It is . . . something . . . something I feel." She shook her head. "I cannot explain it. It is in here." She pointed to her chest. It was so difficult to put it into words! "What Ephraim has taught me, what this book teaches me gives me hope and renews my faith in God. I still have questions, and I know it will take time to get them answered, but I *know* there are answers now. I know it!"

"And the answer to all this?" Rachel waved a hand over what they could see.

Hannah spent the next half hour trying to tell Rachel what Ephraim had told her. It was frustrating but she stammered through it as best as she could. When she was finished they were the only ones still moving about in the dimly lit paths, though many lay about asleep, still unable to go inside.

Rachel didn't speak for a few minutes as she tried to digest what Hannah had told her. "I hope . . . I hope you are right, Hannah," Rachel said softly.

"Our return to Israel was prophesied thousands of years ago, Rachel. God saw this horror, warned us of it in our scriptures as well as in Talmud. It has come. This book tells us why and even gives some idea of what the future holds. We must come to Christ if we want the full blessings God can give us. Not the Christ of most Christians, but the Christ of this book." She placed it in Rachel's hand. "Read it, then tell me you do not believe it is given of God."

Standing, Hannah went up the stairs, leaving Rachel alone. She got inside her blanket and let Beth instinctively snuggle up close before she said a prayer, closed her eyes, and went to sleep.

* * *

Rachel thumbed through the book and thought about what Hannah had said but was torn by two pasts, both of which had caused her such pain. She had sworn she would never believe again, could never believe again. The Christ of her past, at least the religion that preached of Him, had deserted her and her mother. She had cursed them for it every day she had lived since then. How could she possibly go back?

She stared at the book without really seeing it, her mind filled with the memories of being beaten by guards and shunned by Jews while waiting for her Church to come and rescue them; the sight of her mother praying to Christ and saints for relief that never came. She shook her head as tears cascaded down her cheeks and turned into sobs that racked her body.

After a few moments she regained control again and closed the book before getting to her feet. No, she could not believe again. The pain was too much. Though what Hannah said was different, even inviting, she just couldn't go back, not now. She stood and went inside. Maybe never.

See Chapter Notes

CHAPTER 7

Hannah found Emil at breakfast. She told him to get his suitcase, then they found a private place and she gave him his money.

"I will keep it in the major's safe, but we are still in this together, Hannah. I hope I never see that house again."

As he turned to go back to the administration building, she went to the kitchen and got in line to receive food, watching as people devoured what they had and looked for more. Even Hannah still found it hard to keep from shoveling her food in as if it would suddenly disappear. She had thought she had it under control, but here, in this camp, the old habits pushed to the surface as quick as weeds in an untended field.

When finished, she resisted using her tongue to wipe her plate as so many others did, and quickly threw it in the stack meant for washing. It made her heart ache when a skeleton of a woman grabbed it and licked it as clean as if it had been scoured. She quickly walked away as if to leave it all behind.

Emil grabbed her arm and told her Major Stevens would like to see her, then got in line. There were more people in the space between buildings and she had to dodge and twist her way through the mass of humanity to get to the Major's office.

She presented herself to his secretary in the outer room of the building and he said she was expected and should go in. Taking a deep breath she turned the knob and entered, closing the door behind her.

Stevens stood behind his desk, greeted her, and pointed to a chair.

"The man named Henrie Waller is on our list of escaped Nazis. He was one of the main officers at Dachau. Two of his friends were involved in camps as well. The rest are still being interrogated. Their discovery and imprisonment for war crimes will be good news to anyone with a stitch of human decency in them. Colonel Pittman said to convey his thanks, but that he'll still need your testimony about finding Leibert. It seems the last man to have been seen with the Bürgemeister was Henrie Waller."

"It will be a pleasure."

"Now, would you tell me why you would have papers from General Clay?"

For the next half hour she told him about Rachel and her father, Ephraim Daniels, and even the weasel Sperling.

"It seems to be your lot in life to hunt Nazis," he said.

"A more noble work doesn't exist," she said, "but right now all I want is to get my friends and the children to Palestine."

"I'll contact General Clay's aide in the next hour. We'll have your paper work sent and a message delivered to the Jewish representative in Berlin giving them instructions on how to get you new papers for the children. It shouldn't take more than a week to get everything replaced." He sat back, his hands locked behind his head. "You are very lucky to have such papers. Palestine is a long way off for most of your people. The British still haven't opened the doors for legal immigration. How can you get visas for the children?"

"Emil has money. If such things can be bought, we will buy them. If not, we will find another way."

"Yes, I believe you will." He was tempted to tell her that his information indicated there was a route set up to the south through Italy, but that would wait. No sense getting her all stirred up until her papers came. Besides, he had no details, just rumors that passed through the camp as often as refugees, and a few memos that crossed his path from HQ telling him to discourage Jews headed in that direction. Just the latest efforts by the British in their attempt to plug a leak in their dam upstream of Palestine. He had ignored it as best he could, hoping the dam would break and drench the stubborn English. But, that was a personal feeling, not an official one. His duty kept his mouth shut. At least for now.

"He called aloud to his aide who immediately appeared at the door. "Have Mrs. Benson come in here, will you?"

He nodded and left.

"Lucille Benson is American and one of the UNRRA people. I want you to meet her."

"The United Nations Relief and Rehabilitation Administration? Why should I meet her?"

A short woman with a robust figure and dark circles under her tired eyes came in, smiled at both of them and listened while Stevens made the introductions. "Miss Gruen will be here for a week or so. She and her friends, for the most part, have turned the corner, so to speak, and I thought you might be able to use her services."

Hannah was a bit put out at Stevens' audacity but let it go. Keeping busy would probably be best for all of them.

"Then you have lived in the camps."

"Yes, Ravensbrück."

"You have recovered quickly." There was no animosity in the remark, just admiration.

"The body can rebound a lot faster when you give a person hope, Mrs. Benson."

"Indeed. You speak English very well but you are Polish I think," Lucille said. "Do you speak Yiddish?"

"And German, some Russian, along with Hebrew."

Lucille looked pleased. "We have no one on staff who can speak Polish, Hebrew, or Yiddish. That alone could be very helpful. Are there others with you who might want to help? We will pay all of you."

"I will ask."

"Good. Those who wish to be of service can join me in my office across from the waiting area in an hour. Will you come?"

Hannah nodded.

"Good." She gave Stevens a thankful nod and left.

"Thank you," Stevens said.

"She may not like what we tell her," Hannah sighed. "I hope both of you understand that we will leave when our papers come and I would hope you would not delay them."

Stevens ignored the slap. "You have something to offer, Miss Gruen. I hope you won't hold back either, even if your stay is a short one. After all, you said it yourself. The body rebounds a lot quicker when there is hope."

Hannah smiled. "You should be a politician, Major Stevens."

He sat back. "I'll take that as a backhanded compliment. Give it your best shot, Miss Gruen. What have you got to lose?"

Hannah stood without answering the question. For her there was a great deal to lose. She didn't know if her own hope was strong enough to lift others. In fact, having been in the camp for less than a day she found herself already feeling their despair, and she was afraid it might become her own for a second time.

Very afraid.

* * *

Hannah had not been surprised to find Rachel, Emil, and the others a bit apprehensive about helping in the camp. After all, she had those feelings as well, possibly even more so. They had agreed to come and when she told them the UNRRA would be open to their suggestions, Emil had relished the chance. He had something to say about separate housing for the married.

Her small group sat in a semicircle of chairs facing Lucille Benson's desk. Next to the UN's chief administrator were the rest of her UNRRA staff, three on each side. They had notepads and pencils and had started taking notes after Lucille had asked the group what they thought could be done to improve morale in the camp. Emil had made the first suggestion and all pencils had come to a sudden halt. From the look on their faces, Emil had dropped a bombshell.

"You don't understand," said one of the UNRRA officials. He was the one from Australia, his thick English accent difficult to understand, requiring Hannah translate for her friends. His name was Adam.

"Putting couples together will only overcrowd us and . . . and . . . well, having sex in a barracks situation . . ."

"They are already . . . uh . . . having sex in the barracks," Emil said. "When everyone is outside they are inside. They pull blankets over them and are as discreet as they can be, but . . ."

"The rest find a place in the woods," Naomi added. "If you don't believe it, go for walk tonight." She smiled.

The children and Lilith were red faced, Aaron grinning. Lilith quickly gathered up the younger ones and left the room, nervously promising that they would return when the subject of schools was discussed. She gave her husband a look that showed both displeasure and joy, and Hannah couldn't help but smile that Emil was fighting as much for his own conjugal rights as he was for anyone else's.

"We do not have enough room, there are no facilities to handle the deliveries of new children in the hospitals, no place for them in the barracks. We have no clothes for babies and food is scarce. Why on earth would you want to bring new children into a place like this anyway?"

Emil sighed. "The babies will come whether you are ready or not. They want babies! They want to know that they can still love and be loved and that children are still possible!" He took a breath. "All of us have been deprived of affection for more years than we care to remember. We have had nothing but hate, hate, hate, and we are starved for its opposite. This desire is nearly uncontrollable. You see it in children who snuggle up to women who are total strangers, begging for love. You see it in a young woman who, starving for it, will fall in love with the first man who shows her any affection at all and give herself to him simply because she feels something she has not felt for years: love, tenderness, and the passion that these bring. And finally, you see it in married couples like Lilith and I who have longed to touch one another as we did once. Lilith was in every dream I had while I was in the camps. The thought of her kept me alive. To separate us now is, well, forgive me, but it is inhuman." He leaned forward, his elbow on his knee. He enunciated each word. "You do not know what it is like to go without affection. You take it for granted, but everyone in this camp knows. If you want to help us, you will give those of us who are married the chance to share these feelings as privately as possible, because we will share them whether you turn a blind eye to it or not. It would just be nice if you let it happen with dignity." Emil sat straight. "As to your argument about space. You are now putting two people to a bunk, so moving couples into some barracks should not be an issue of crowding. Not very much at least."

The UNRRA officials were all looking at the floor, or their notebooks, or out the window, their faces flushed. Emil's frank discussion of a subject most cultures said very little about had caught them off guard. It had Hannah looking at her hands along with everyone else, but she knew Emil was right. She remembered how Ephraim's attention, his love of her, had changed everything. She remembered, too, the almost uncontrollable desire to touch, to feel his arms around her. She had dreamed of more and only Ephraim's strength had kept them from going even further. Oh, how she ached for him, even now!

"You are promoting illicit sex instead of marriage," Rachel said. "Surely the rabbis are not happy about that."

Lucille nodded slightly. "No, in fact they have approached us about the problem but, uh, they were not quite so direct. We did not see, did not understand, we are sorry." She filled her lungs and continued. "New barracks could be built, small rooms created for couples."

"The costs . . ." the Australian said weakly.

"The Nazis were fanatics about stockpiling lumber," said another. "The Army can requisition what we need."

"But the locals are using . . ." Adam said.

"The locals can wait!" Lucille said firmly.

Hannah happened to notice Aaron's face at Lucille's remark. He was visibly shocked.

"Aaron, could you get men to build new barracks?" Hannah asked.

"Huh? Oh, sure, of course. We will need tools, but . . . yes, we have the hands."

"Well then, Adam," Lucille looked at the Australian. "You and Aaron will head the project. Work closely with the rabbis and find out how many rooms we will need immediately."

"The rest of the camp will want the same thing," said Adam stiffly.

"If they are willing to build, to work for it, fine. Let them come and ask," Lucille said.

Hannah was impressed. Lucille Benson really did want to help.

"Now, to our next problem—schools," Lucille said.

Emil stood and opened the door. Lilith and the children returned. As she went past, Emil whispered something in his wife's ear that made her flush and give Lucille a smile before quickly going to her chair.

"The children will not come to school. We have them but they hide from us."

"Do you make them go with the non-Jewish children?" Zohar asked.

"At first, but then we organized schools just for them. Still they do not come."

"Who is the teacher?"

"I am," came a reply. It was the lady from Greece, who seemed like a kind and patient woman.

"What language do you know besides Greek and English?" Zohar asked. Hannah was intrigued by Zohar's sudden forthrightness. She had never seen her so focused, even passionate, for anything other than her cooking.

"None, but I use others to interpret. All of these are Jews."

"The children are afraid of you."

The woman was surprised. "Me? But I am not German, I . . ."

"The camps taught us that no one could be trusted, not even some Jews, but especially not any outsider who spoke through one of us. They were the ones who killed and butchered and imprisoned us. It will take a long time to change that. Until then, give them Jewish teachers. The very act of doing this will help them change their minds about you."

Pencils moved hurriedly across notepads as Zohar continued. "All Jews are not the same, and all of them have different ways of educating their children. The Orthodox and the Hasidic have different ideas about what is important. You must involve each group in the education of their children. This will have to be done by organizing a committee with the teacher as an important member."

When Zohar realized everyone was watching her, she flushed and sat down quickly.

Lucille looked at the other children, her eyes finally settling on Anna. "Is this true?"

Anna only nodded.

"Does being here make you nervous?" Lucille asked.

Again Anna nodded.

Hannah glanced at the other children. They all sat stiff with paler than normal faces. They were frightened. Though she had gotten over most of her own fear of others, everyone else had not. Without thinking, she had pushed them into a situation that scared them. But it was necessary wasn't it? How else would they begin to realize they could survive? Even Aaron was beginning to see that all mankind was not their enemy.

"How old are you?" Lucille asked Zohar.

"Nineteen," Zohar responded.

"And how do you know these things?"

"My . . . my father was a school teacher."

"Very well. Will you help us organize this committee?"

Zohar looked at the floor, her face flushed. For a moment Hannah was afraid her young friend might decline, that her fears might get the best of her. She had finally begun to confront them, and Hannah prayed that on the very edge of putting them aside she wouldn't give up.

"Yes, until we leave, but not longer." She glanced at Hannah as if seeking approval. Hannah breathed again and gave Zohar a bright smile and nod.

"Children, would you like her to teach you?"

All of them smiled and nodded.

Zohar stiffened, a surprised look on her face. "But I . . ."

Hannah held her breath until Lucille pushed on matter-of-factly. "You will have to be very creative. We have few supplies and books."

Zohar nodded only slightly in agreement. Hannah could see that she was scared speechless. Rachel sat next to her and took her hand, gripping it tight and smiling. "I'll help," she said. Zohar relaxed a little.

"We will need at least paper and crayons," Zohar said sheepishly.

The lady from Greece made a note on her pad.

"How many of those do you have?" Hannah asked.

The people across the room exhibited a questioning glance toward Hannah.

"How many note pads?" she said.

Lucille smiled. "Ione," she said to the Greek lady, "requisition all of these you can find, will you? They will go to the school."

Ione made another note.

With that the meeting ended but Lucille asked Hannah to stay. When they were alone she spoke. "That was very helpful. Please, feel free to walk through that door anytime and tell me what you think, and that goes for any of the others as well." She smiled. "You and your group are a breath of fresh air, Miss Gruen. We need fresh air in a place like this."

"You handled everything very well. It is not a new experience for you is it?"

"No, I was one of the first to come over. I worked at Bergen Belsen in the British Zone."

"Were there Jews there?"

"There were many and it was growing all the time, even though they haven't given them full DP status."

Hannah knew what that meant. Food rations were smaller for one thing, and the chance of getting visas to leave the country were nil. Refusing DP status was tantamount to saying they were Europeans, temporarily without a place to stay, but able to return to their own homes, and soon. "The British can't be serious about this," Hannah said.

"They are afraid of your people, Hannah. Afraid that giving them DP rights will force them to recognize that Europe is no longer the place for Jews. That would force them to open Palestine." She sighed. "At first I thought they would see their policy was wrong, even foolish, but I was wrong. My organization is trying to change their minds, pleading for the President of the United States and the world community to put pressure on British leaders, but too many powerful people in London have their minds made up."

Hannah ached with frustration. The British intransigence that helped create the camps in the first place was still with them. Even after the camps. If that was the case, nothing would change them. Nothing but Jews fighting their way to Israel and taking it by force. She and her people were being forced to fight.

"Help us, Hannah. Help us at least take care of these people properly. The Brits didn't like my constant haranguing so I ended up here. I am thankful now, thankful to be in a camp where the military authorities understand the seriousness of the problem and are willing to do whatever they can, but this is not enough. We need people like you and your friends to bridge the gap that lies between us and your people. Without that bridge, we will be fighting each other and more will die."

She lifted a handful of papers. "These are requests from five different rabbis. Requests for baking facilities for matzo, space for synagogues and mikvehs, and of course, more barracks for married couples. Rabbis don't take their wives into the forest," she smiled. "But each of them wants their own barracks and they want it first."

"It is all about power, you know that."

"The rabbi with the mikveh is honored; the one without loses face. Yes I know. For that reason they all go without. When they work together and come with a single unified request I will do my best to provide one for the community, but there is no one to bring them together. Zohar talks of a committee for education. Who will convince your rabbis to cooperate on such a thing?"

"Mikvehs and bakeries are long-term investments. You and the rabbis act as if you think these people will be here for months, even years," Hannah said.

Lucille's face saddened. "In June, just a few weeks ago, your Jewish Agency applied for 100,000 immigration permits. It is not half enough but they will be lucky to get even one percent of that amount. One percent, Hannah! It could be several years before the doors open for your people, in my country or any other. The wheels of politics and pressure move slowly. Your people are beginning to organize in other camps, but not here. They must fight for themselves!"

"Organize? For what purpose?"

"To live in dignity, to prepare for immigration, both illegal and legal. To become a force for change, a voice that will apply even more pressure on the allies. I want you to work here, with me, in this office. I have eight-thousand Europeans to get home and will not have the time or the ability to do what is needed for your people. You will have to do that."

"I have one week."

Lucille smiled. "Then take that week and find someone who can carry on after that. Get these people to work Hannah. Give them an immediate goal, something that will benefit them and help them remember who they are."

"I will try," was all Hannah could say. She left the office knowing Lucille was right. Building barracks for the married would get them thinking of more than food; building a school would help them remember that there was still a future. Hope would come only when they stopped focusing on the past.

She felt herself suddenly excited and quickly moved back into the camp. She thought about whom she might train. Doctor Cardan entered her mind but he was needed far worse at the hospital. Instead she would watch. Surely someone would rise to the surface in the next few days whom she could involve. If not, when it came time for them to leave, Lucille would just have to find someone else.

She did not realize how well Lucille had chosen.

CHAPTER 8

With Naomi as her assistant, they schemed, then worked from dawn until dusk organizing what needed to be done. Major Stevens found out quickly that he had uncorked a whirlwind that devoured everything in its path. The requisitions poured in and his soldiers worked long hours to round up and provide the materials needed. Aaron and Adam were at each others throats until Naomi lit into them. Things quickly changed. Naomi wasn't about to let two men slow down progress, and had no qualms about saying so, her assertive personality doing the rest. Hannah watched this transformation in pleased amazement.

Once unified, Aaron and Adam pulled together a sizeable work force who immediately went into the surrounding villages and farms to buy all the tools they could get their hands on. Emil willingly provided most of the money. On the third day, when the first lumber rode into camp on the back of three-ton army trucks, the workers were armed with everything from hammers to transoms.

Most of the men were still weak, unable to work more than a few hours, but many hands were available and the work continued every minute, sunup to sundown. Adam became the overall foreman on the basis that Aaron was only short-term. Aaron worked directly with the men, appointing overseers and job foremen from among those in the Jewish section of the camp who had experience in such things. Lucille had been right—the Jews listened to Aaron. They only listened to Adam if Aaron gave the nod. Hannah only hoped that when Aaron left, Adam would have their confidence.

Morale skyrocketed as men, women, and children watched the first walls of their new barracks go up, and the roof go on in only two days. The rabbis became more genial with a steep increase in requests for weddings, and the spirit of work breathed new life into their people.

In her new position as director of the Jewish section, Hannah handled the rabbis with a unique combination of finesse and directness. She was up front with them from the beginning, telling them she would accept no competition among groups, and that such a competitive attitude was contrary to the Torah and the will of God, citing scripture to prove it. They quibbled. She listened, then proceeded to repeat herself and say that she backed Lucille's decision to give them nothing until they started cooperating. As a sign of her determination she told them there would be no rooms for their personal use in the first barracks. They left in a huff, but one by one they returned and privately acquiesced. Calling them all together again the next morning, she elicited final agreements of cooperation and then assigned them rooms alphabetically and offered them a plan for a bakery all of them could use. They accepted and asked if they could plan a single synagogue for the camp. They were getting the message.

Meanwhile, on the first day Zohar and Rachel had asked for and received a small abandoned house with a leaky roof for their new school. Though nearly half a mile away, it was just the right size, and away from the bustle of the camp so that the children would not be distracted. It had a homey feel to it that both women thought would help the children feel at ease. While Aaron and a few of his workers repaired the roof, walls, and floors, half a dozen others were given paint brushes to paint. Women were assigned to clean the interior and make it shine. When they were finished, the only thing missing was desks. They went to the colonel but he had no solution. There were no extra desks.

"But we must have desks," Zohar said forcefully.

"The schools in Salzburg have some, but I cannot requisition them. Schools for children are to be untouched."

"Would they sell them?" Zohar asked.

"Possibly, but I cannot make such an offer."

Zohar nodded and left the building. A few hours later she and two soldiers pulled up in front of the new school with a load of thirty desks and a well-used chalkboard, chalk included.

Rachel and Hannah watched in amazement as they were unloaded and put in place. "How . . . how did you do it?" Rachel finally asked.

"The necklace," Zohar smiled.

"But it is . . ." Rachel bit her tongue.

"A copy?" Zohar chuckled. "Yes, so I discovered, but it is a good one, and enough to buy thirty desks."

"Are you sure, Zohar? We will be leaving and . . ."

"I am sure. My father was a teacher. If the children receive only a single hour of instruction he would be pleased."

Once more Hannah was amazed.

On the evening of day three, Zohar and Rachel organized the community education committee. Hannah thought they were going to have a war on their hands as the rabbis momentarily lost their spirit of cooperation, each presenting himself as the best possible candidate. Hannah told her two friends to reject them all. The rabbis licked their wounds while Rachel and Zohar selected three women and four men to serve.

Two of the women were lucky enough to have surviving children, while the third had lost her two boys to the Nazis' insatiable appetite for slave labor. She had come to the school on her own and had volunteered to help clean. It helped her deal with her own pain. Soon she was eager to do more. It was a good choice.

The first week came and went and even Hannah didn't complain when their papers didn't come. She was too busy during the day to run off to Stevens's office and knew it would do no good anyway. He would not keep them from her, she knew that, and at night she was too tired to care. They could wait another few days.

In the first few days of the second week the first building was given an interior, trenches were dug for drainage, and a septic system was designed by the Americans. Toilets and sinks taken from the now defunct Nazi factory the camp had serviced during the war were installed, while a second barracks was started. Hannah could never remember something so beautiful being built so quickly.

Only ten days from when the first nail had been driven, they celebrated the first couples moving in. Hannah took a quick tour with Emil and Lilith who showed her their new room. Though only large

enough for a bed and small dresser, Hannah found herself jealous of
the love these two would share in the privacy of their little piece of
heaven. If Ephraim had suddenly appeared, she would have settled for
a wedding canopy and half the space.

Paper for the school wasn't plentiful, but it was adequate. Crayons
were found by soldiers who went to Innsbruck on weekend leave.
They were delivered by Colonel Stevens. Zohar hugged and kissed
him with such exuberance that he blushed for nearly a week.

Zohar decided the children's first effort would be to draw pictures
of their experience.

"They must learn to talk about it," she said. "Until they do they
won't be able to face the future."

Hannah was amazed by her young friend's ability to see into the
hearts of her new students, but she was gratified at the same time.
Zohar was finally breaking free of her own dark past. The Nazis had
made her think she was nothing, could give nothing. She was discovering they were wrong.

The first drawings were dark but poignant. Bloody scenes of monsters
with guns so frightful that Hannah wondered how they had ever slept at
night. At the end of each day Zohar allowed them to "burn their memories" over a fire. Smiles soon returned to sad faces and the children began
playing again, laughing. After a few days the dark pictures were replaced
with drawings of open fields, sunsets, and other children playing games in
front of a building that distinctly resembled their new school.

When she had a few minutes, Hannah dropped in and sat at the
back of the room, taking it all in. The day after the barracks had been
finished she was there, watching as the children were reciting a traditional poem. Some were old enough to have learned it before the
camps and were teaching it to the others. One of the new girls recited
a line out of order and a playful argument ensued. Zohar was about
to set it straight when David burst into recitation of the entire thing.
When he was finished the room was so quiet you could hear the birds
in the trees nearly a hundred yards away.

David sat at his desk, a large grin on his face. "That's the correct
words," he said. "My mother taught them to me."

"Thank you," Zohar said quietly, then continued the class.
Hannah left, the tears flowing like someone had turned on a faucet.

That night Aaron was amazed at his little brother's voice—a voice he hadn't heard for nearly four years. As she watched Aaron try to blink away the tears, Zohar slipped up to Hannah. "My mother's necklace has already given us much, hasn't it?" she said.

Hannah, biting her lip against her own tears, could only nod.

* * *

Papers for Hannah, Rachel, and Zohar came on their twelfth day at the camp. They were sent by special messenger with Colonel Mackland's compliments. She double-checked the envelope in hopes that something might have come from Ephraim, but knew as she did so her hope was in vain. He was in the Pacific. It was a long way and he would not know where she was anyway. Still, she had hoped.

There was a little note from Tappuah.

It was late in the evening before Hannah could go to the school for a little privacy, and the dim light of the few bulbs they had hanging from the ceiling was all the light she had when she took out Tappuah's letter and read it.

She and Andrik were doing well. They were attending church and reading the Book of Mormon but Tappuah had her doubts, though Andrik thought that it was simply wonderful. There were paragraphs about the changes taking place in Berlin, especially about the fear of most Berliners that the Russians had come to stay and they would never have a free city. They had found a little apartment near the church and were settling in and, finally, she thought she might be pregnant. It made Hannah jealous. It was signed with all her love, Tappuah.

Hannah wrote a reply and prepared it using the address she had gotten for the new Church building before leaving Berlin. She would mail it in the morning.

She was tired and stood to leave, shutting off the light before locking the door behind her. It was a warm, pleasant night and she breathed in the fresh air and let it fill her senses. She was glad they had come here. Though frightening at first, all of her little group had been changed by the experience. They were more settled, closer to one another, stronger, even more determined.

She missed Ephraim horribly, but she clung to the last memories of a cold swim in a small creek and the warmth of his kiss as they stood in the shade of Goering's plane. It was such memories that held back the buckets of tears.

She had managed to complete the book a second time. She knew it was true. She supposed that some, including Rachel, never would. She couldn't understand it, but it seemed to be the way it was. Each person had their own traditions, beliefs, and traits. Some prevented an open heart. Her slate had been cleaned by the war and she had wriggled free of most of the hindrances all Jews might find hard to get past. And she had Ephraim to teach her. Everyone needed a good teacher. And an open heart.

"Just the person I am looking for," someone said as she entered the camp.

Hannah broke out of her thoughts to see Dr. Cardan standing a few feet away, smiling at her. "And for what reason would you be looking for me? It is late, my brain has shut down, I have no money, no food, nothing. What could I possibly do for you?" Hannah teased.

They continued walking toward the center of camp.

"I want to congratulate you," Cardan said in his French-English accent.

"For what?"

"Look at this place, these people. They are putting on weight even though food supplies haven't changed. No more suicides, and our death rate has plummeted."

"They only needed a purpose."

"Yes, and thank you for staying long enough to give it to them."

Hannah felt the blood rush to her face as they walked on in silence.

"Would you have dinner with me?"

Hannah stopped. "Dinner?"

Cardan smiled. "Yes, you know, dinner. The last meal of the day. But I wish to take you into Salzburg, to a restaurant. Get away from potatoes and cabbage soup, even if it does have a bit of meat in it," he grinned.

She was flattered. "Doctor Cardan, you should know that . . ."

"You have an American friend? Yes, I know, but this is only for dinner, a celebration and a thank you, that is all."

She hesitated. "I . . . very well. Dinner. Once, for friendship."

"Merci. Thank you." He turned and walked to the hospital.

She watched him disappear through the door. Another good man still haunted by the camps. Naomi had heard that he had been one of the doctors forced to experiment on prisoners at Belsen. He had thought of committing suicide rather than giving in to the Nazis' demands but decided he and the other Jewish doctors could do it more humanely than their German counterparts. They had tried. She knew his dreams must be worse than most. She turned away, and walked directly into Major Stevens' aide.

"Whoops, sorry, Miss Gruen," he said.

"Quite all right. Did you need something?"

"Yes, ma'am, the major would like to see you in his office. It is very urgent."

They walked quickly back to the office, a dozen thoughts running through Hannah's mind.

She entered the office and faced a grim Major Stevens. He asked her to sit, then handed her an official letter from General Clay's office.

She read the words, then read them again.

They were closing down the camp.

CHAPTER 9

The news spread through the camp like wildfire. They were to be dispersed either to their own hometowns prior to the war or to camps in their countries of origin: Poles to Poland, Germans to Germany, Czechs to Czechoslovakia. All but the Jews celebrated.

By far the largest number of the Jews were from Poland. None wanted to return home, and before an hour had passed, they had sent a group to tell Major Stevens that they would not go. They would commit suicide before they would return to be slaughtered by those who had been allowed to murder their families and steal their homes! With that they had gone back to their barracks. It was a night filled with denunciations, arguments, anger, despair, and even hatred. How could the Americans insist on such a thing? Because they hated them as much as anybody, came the angry reply! They had done nothing, they would do nothing! They must fight or die here and never return to Poland! They had suddenly forgotten that at least this American camp had saved them. Hannah found it interesting and curiously gratifying that the energy to rebel had been given to them here, but she decided now was not the time to point out the obvious.

Frustrated by the growing rebellion, Hannah and her small group went to the schoolhouse, alone, away from the anger that frightened all of them, to debate what they must do. She had never seen them as sad looking as now. She could not blame them. They had found purpose in their lives and they had become a family working together, helping one another. Now it would be taken away from them. Again.

"Why tear down this camp?" Naomi asked. "Surely it is working better than any other."

Hannah did not answer, though she had a good idea. The American government wanted as much of their army out of Europe as possible, both physically and financially. Soldiers were needed in the Pacific or wanted back in the States by a war-weary nation. The camps were a drain on money and manpower and must be consolidated. It was the politicians doing the thinking. Politicians who had never come here and never would. They had no understanding of what was happening. Major Stevens had told her just the other day of a remark reported by the press. A British politician had made the statement that the Jews should stop making a nuisance of themselves and go back to their homes and help rebuild Europe. The man's sanity needed checking.

"We were going to leave weeks ago. We have delayed too long. Now we go!" Emil said, standing behind his wife and putting his hands tenderly on her shoulders. Lilith patted one of them as if to agree even though Hannah wasn't sure Lilith was ready for such a journey. Of all of them, Lilith was still the least recovered.

"We still don't have any papers for most of you. We will have to wait for those, but they should come soon. If they try to send us away before that time we will go to Salzburg, find a place to live, and wait."

Aaron had been sitting near the back of the room deep in thought, but now he spoke. "We should contact the Brigade," he said.

"The Jewish Brigade?" Rachel asked.

"I have been asking the American soldiers and new people who come here to live about them. They are still in Italy and are helping many to escape, taking trucks as far north as Posen, in Poland. They have established camps and are sending illegals to Palestine. We should contact them, set up an escape route, and get everyone out of here."

Hannah felt her mouth drop open. She closed it to utter a shocked response. "Aaron, there are more than sixteen hundred of our people here. We could not possibly get them all out in time."

"Why not?" Aaron asked. "Because we have no papers?" He smiled. "Major Stevens will give you anything you want, Hannah, he loves you."

It was said in jest but she turned three shades of red as everyone laughed at Aaron's joke.

"He does not!" she quipped.

They all chuckled at her reaction.

"Try!" Rachel said. "Ask him! It would be worth a try!"

Everyone chimed in.

"All right, all right, but what then?"

"I will go south and make contact with the Brigade. They will help us. I am sure of it," Aaron said.

"But they are British Army," Emil said. "The rumor in the camp says the Foreign Office is telling their army to redirect Jewish DPs back into Europe, making it much harder to get out than it was even a few weeks ago."

Aaron smiled at his friend. "The Brigade is on our side now that the war is over. We are their people and if the British commanders won't look the other way, members of the Brigade go around them! The very survival of our people depends on them and they know it. They can do it. They are doing it, but you are right; it isn't going to get any easier as the British tighten the screws. We need to go now!"

"People in the camp are saying that we can no longer trust anyone but our own people. Maybe they're right." Naomi said. "I was beginning to think the Americans would help us, make things right, but it's just a game. A political game of chess and we're the pawns. This . . . this place is nothing more than a facade, a delaying tactic. We must go. The sooner the better," she said bitterly.

Hannah looked at Zohar, who nodded. "We must try," she said. "The children will surely die if they are forced back to Poland. We can't let that happen."

Hannah paced in front of the desks, looking at the pictures that Zohar and Rachel had hung on the walls. They were of stick figures with round heads and big eyes and wide smiles. Children running in the sun with grass at their feet and blue skies overhead. She remembered the first pictures—the dark rooms and prostrate forms, and whips in the hands of monsters. Zohar was right—they could not let them go back.

They walked back to the camp only to find the anger and chaos growing. Hannah hurriedly went to Stevens' office and was ushered in. Taking a deep breath she presented Aaron's plan for the Jewish section of the camp to go south. She mentioned the need to contact the Brigade but left their method out for the moment.

Stevens' brow was wrinkled in thought as she finished, his fingers tapping lightly on the desktop. "To Italy. All of them. And then to Palestine." The brow was wrinkled more than Hannah had ever seen it.

"Let me ask you something, Major. What do you think will happen to these people if you send them back to Poland?"

A deep sigh. "Just between you and me, fifty percent won't last a year under the Russians and Poles, and our camps will be overrun, creating a miserable state for them as well."

"Then our chances are better going south, whether you help or not; but with your help the percentages go up substantially."

More tapping on the desk. "It could save a lot of lives, that's for sure. Your people are stubborn folk, and rightfully so after what they have been through. Some of them probably will commit suicide if we don't get them out of here." The brow remained wrinkled, his blue eyes both tired and sad. She knew he was contemplating the pros and cons, but found it gratifying that he was giving it any thought at all. This was a good man as well as a good soldier. He took a deep breath. "Yes, we must try. They told us to send them back to their countries of origin. That is Palestine isn't it? At least, originally. To get them there our paperwork can show it to be Italy, Greece, or Turkey." He was thinking out loud now. "We might even be able to give transport partway. We shall see." He looked directly at Hannah. "But they will need a place to go. We can't just drop them off in the middle of Italy, or the British will send them to Poland themselves. You say this can be done through the Brigade. We should contact them by wire to make sure."

"If you send a wire, it will be the British leadership who will receive it. What do you think their response will be?"

"At the very least they will tie it up in red tape. The Brits can be the biggest bunch of foot draggers in God's creation when it fits their purposes," he said with a tired voice. "Yes, you're right. Someone has to contact members of the brigade personally. No sense taking any chances of having this snuffed out before it gets a bright burn." The tapping again. "It will have to be some of your people. I'll send a letter with them, give them papers to cross the borders. If I send soldiers, the Brits will hear of it and want to know what's going on. We'd have the same result as if we had wired them."

"Agreed," Hannah said. "Aaron, Naomi, and I will go."

He hesitated only for a moment. "Can't send a military vehicle either. You better take that Nazi car Colonel Pittman brought in here a few days ago. The one from Emil's house."

Hannah had seen it sitting near the gate. Lucille had explained that it had been confiscated by the government, brought here until it could be forwarded to Frankfurt or Berlin for military use.

"I'll have our mechanics give it the once-over tonight, take all identifying marks off it. Travel incognito, if you know what I mean." He paused. "My orders are to start shipping people out in four days. It will take three weeks to finish the job. I don't know if we can move better than sixteen hundred people across Austria to Italy in that amount of time. I will need every truck I can get my hands on and that may raise eyebrows. The closer your Brigade can get to us, the better. Tell them that, and try to find a place where we can deposit some of them for a short stay if we get caught in a pinch. Maybe several places." He leaned across his desk. "Well, young lady, you are about to lead the children of Israel out of a second Egypt and into the promised land. You'd better have a few miracles up your sleeve, because if you don't get them out of here I'll have to send them back to the flesh pots of Poland, like it or not. Understood?"

She smiled at his analogy. "Understood." She stood and went to the door, then turned back. He could lose his command for this and yet he was willing. "Thank you Major Stevens, for all of us."

He nodded and she left, racing back into the camp. There was a lot to do.

CHAPTER 10

They were on the road shortly after five A.M., traveling south through the mountains of Austria. It was a beautiful July morning, the valleys lush and green, while the highest of the mountain peaks were beginning to show the first sign of fresh snow. Winter was never far away in this part of the world.

They had spent most of the night making plans. The camp would be divided into sixteen groups of approximately one hundred people. Rachel, Emil, Hannah, Aaron, and Naomi would lead five of the groups, with Zohar shepherding Beth, David, Anna, and Sarah, while Lilith saw to her own two children. Eleven other men were selected and Emil would talk to each today. He would also talk to the rabbis and get their support while cautioning everyone to keep it quiet. If the gentiles in the camp heard of their plans, word might leak out and they'd be stopped before they could begin.

Aaron had determined that they could get as many as fifty people in one of the three trucks, which were large and sturdy enough to take their load across Austria in a single day. They might need a temporary camp along the border with Italy, but that depended on what the Brigade could do. They had all gone to bed excited, believing it could be done, but as Hannah tossed and turned and thought of all the problems that could crop up, she was worried. So much depended on finding the Brigade, and finding them able to help.

Naomi knew nothing about driving so that left Hannah and Aaron. While Hannah drove they crossed the line between the American and Russian sectors and were stopped half a dozen times by Russian sentries guarding the roads to villages and towns. Their papers were in order and they were let through, but it took time. Hannah found herself wondering how they could ever have made it through on their own, without the colonel's papers. She shuddered to think they might have ended up in a Russian camp instead of at Ebensee, and found herself thanking God for their good fortune.

Aaron took over driving duties just south of Fohnsdorf. When Hannah awoke two hours later they were stopped outside a small village, and Aaron and Naomi were buying fresh bread and cheese from one of the locals. The village was called Villach.

She quickly got out of the car and joined her two friends who, because of their limited German, seemed unable to communicate. She greeted the villager with a smile while letting Aaron continue the questioning. Over the last two weeks she had seen a change in Aaron. He was less prone to fits of anger and had learned the art of diplomacy as he and Adam had butted heads over several problems. He had become a leader among the workers, no small thing for a man of only seventeen years of age. And this was his idea. He should be given as much leeway as he needed.

The local seemed to finally understand Aaron's question.

"Ah, yes," he said, pointing. "The Russians are in the middle of the village, at the courthouse, but they have most of their men camped north of the city, near the new camp for prisoners and displaced persons."

"What did he say?" Aaron said a bit frustrated. "I didn't catch it all. What camp? Are there Jews there as well?"

Hannah smiled at the local, "What kind of camp is it?" she asked.

"They have German soldiers there as prisoners. It is a horrible camp. The Russians treat them badly. Other than Nazi soldiers they are mostly Cossacks who fought with the Germans. They don't want to go back because they know they will be sent to Siberia, so some have tried to escape. The Russians kill them."

"Are Jews still kept there? Hannah asked.

The man looked away. "They were once, but they have been taken away."

"Where to?" Aaron asked.

"I don't know. Soldiers who fight with the British took them. That is all I know."

"And where are the British?" Hannah asked.

"They are stationed at Tarvisio in Italy. It isn't far."

"Do you know what unit of the Army they belong to?"

"No, no, I don't pay attention to such things! Why should I? They and the Russians occupy our country. They are no better than the Germans, maybe worse. I leave them alone!" He spat, then turned away to busy himself restacking his bit of fresh fruit.

Hannah thanked him and turned back to the car. She told Aaron and Naomi his news.

"We should go to Tarvisio then," Naomi said.

"He spoke of soldiers who fight with the British as the ones who came to get the Jews. It must be the Brigade," Aaron said.

They loaded into the car and Aaron drove them toward the other side of town. As they passed through the city square they spotted the Russian headquarters building, and a small park where soldiers and civilians alike milled about. As her eyes scanned the crowd, Hannah wondered if any were Jews trying to get south. They all looked the same, their tired and emaciated bodies sagging from the war but still strong enough to get in line to receive some sort of gruel being handed out by the Russians.

"Stop!" she yelled.

Startled, Aaron jerked the wheel and pushed on the brakes. The car bumped over the curb and back, coming to a halt a few inches from the bumper of a Russian truck.

"Oy!" Aaron yelled. "What is the matter with you? What is wrong?"

"Sorry, but we have to find out how many of our people are here who need help."

"But how?" Aaron said.

"I have an idea," Naomi said. She removed a tube of lipstick given to her by Ione and stepped outside the car. She wrote the word "Shalom" on the window, then waited as Hannah and Aaron joined her.

After a few minutes a thin, pale young man saw the word and whispered something to his companion. They argued a moment, then the first turned and walked across the street.

"You are Jewish?" he asked in Hebrew.

"Yes, we are going to Tarvisio from Salzburg."

The man's grin made his face look even thinner. He quickly signaled to his companion who shuffled across the street as fast as his tired bones would allow him.

"My name is Milo, and this is Moshe," the thin man said.

Hannah introduced her group then asked, "Are there others?"

They turned and looked back. "We have been speaking in Hebrew and have drawn no attention. I think no, not here, but we have a group . . ." He hesitated. "They are too exhausted to come. We came to find the Brigade."

"They come here?"

"We needed food, so we stopped. Like you, we go to Tarvisio."

"But how will you get across the border?" Naomi asked.

"We will go at night," said the second as he shoveled the gruel in his mouth.

"Where are your friends, and how many are there?"

"In bombed-out railway wagons outside Klagenfurt. There are more than a hundred. We have walked here from Germany."

"We will find the Brigade and bring them here. Wait for us and you can show us the way," Hannah urged.

The two men looked at each other then nodded, their faces showing so much relief and gratitude that it nearly made Hannah cry.

"Right here," she said it again while opening the door and getting inside. Aaron and Naomi quickly joined her as Aaron lowered himself into the driver's seat. Naomi handed the two men bread and cheese as Aaron started the car and lurched away from the curb.

Hannah heard Naomi crying lightly in the backseat but said nothing. She was too busy controlling her own tears.

* * *

Using their American papers they crossed the border without trouble and were quickly in the mountain town of Tarvisio, Italy.

The place was overrun with people and soldiers but they saw no insignias from the Jewish Brigade until they neared the center of town.

"There!" Naomi yelled, pointing at a truck.

The truck was just pulling away from the British headquarters building and launched itself into a street that ran downhill to the south. Aaron turned the wheel, sped around the small park and fountain in the center of the square and followed. They passed through the town and were quickly in the country. Other military trucks passed them heading in the opposite direction as Aaron honked in an attempt to get the driver of the Brigade truck to pull over. As they came to a crossroads and the truck turned right, Aaron jerked the wheel, darted through the corner of a hay field, and blocked their lane of traffic in the road.

As Hannah jumped from the vehicle, two soldiers stepped down from the truck and came their way. She saw the white and blue insignia on their shoulders and wanted to kiss them. Instead she stopped and spoke in Hebrew.

"We are from a DP camp in Salzburg, Germany. We have a message for you from the commanding officer there." She removed the envelope from her pocket and handed it to the smiling driver.

He started to open it. "The Jews we see don't usually have their own transportation." He smiled. He looked past them at the car. Major Stevens' mechanics had not only removed the Nazi markings but had roughed up the smooth surface making it look old and worn. "Nazi car isn't it?"

"You have a good eye," Hannah said. "The owner has no further use for it."

He read the letter of introduction, his face sobering. "Follow us." They turned back to their truck and Hannah and her two friends ran to their car. Aaron backed out of the way and the three-ton truck quickly sped past them. Another mile down the road they exited into a military complex of barracks. As near as Hannah could tell it had been military from the start and was probably one captured from the Germans. After passing a dozen buildings they pulled up in front of one with a Jewish flag on its pole. She had never seen anything so lovely, her heart thumping with expectation. A new home. A safe home. For all of them.

The two soldiers waited for their guests to join them, then all five went inside.

After a sharp salute the driver handed the man behind the desk the letter from Stevens. He read it and set it aside, pointing at chairs. The driver and his companion turned and left at his order.

"My name is Reuven Givon. I am the brigade's rabbi. How many Jews are there at Ebensee?" he asked.

Hannah licked her dry lips. "Sixteen Hundred."

"And he wants help getting all of them into Italy?" he said with a disbelieving smile.

"It is either here or back to Poland," Aaron said.

Hannah explained the orders received only yesterday.

"Then it will be here, but we will have to make many arrangements for a group this size. You understand that the British are not as cooperative as they were even a few weeks ago. It is becoming more difficult to find places for refugees while they wait for transport to Palestine." He sighed. "And we are being ordered to leave for northern Europe. It seems we are doing too much good for our people, and the British leaders in London think they can stop it by moving us to Holland. We have only ten days before we will be on the road."

"But how will you continue to help?" Aaron asked. "There are thousands more to come!"

"The Hagannah is already sending men from Israel to take our place and we are asking some refugees to stay behind and help." He smiled. "The Brits only give us a chance to lengthen our reach."

"I'll be sure to thank them," Hannah said stiffly. "How soon can you take our people?"

He stood. "Go back to town, stay at the Inn of Santo Pietro near the center square. I will be in touch."

"There is a more pressing problem," Hannah said.

"More pressing than your sixteen hundred? It must be at a very critical stage."

She told him about the two men and their friends in Klagenfurt.

He nodded, "Yes, you are right. We'll arrange to get them tonight."

"We will go with you," Hannah said.

"That is not possible," he responded matter-of-factly.

Aaron stepped forward. "We go or . . ."

Hannah put a hand on Aaron's arm. "Very well," she said. "The two are in the town square of Villach. They will show you where the others are. We will go back to Tarvisio."

She tugged at Aaron's arm and Naomi followed them from the tent. They went to the car and Hannah got behind the wheel this time. She pulled away and was back on the main road before speaking.

"We will use some of our money to buy food. All we can get. Then we will find those two men and one of them will take us to Klagenfurt while the other waits for the Brigade. The refugees will have food in their bellies when the Brigade comes for them," she smiled. "It will be easier for them to travel that way, don't you think?"

Aaron and Naomi only grinned as they went back the way they had come.

CHAPTER 11

Tarvisio's market was in a square in the eastern section of town but they found it already closed. The sun was nearly down and everyone had gone home. They drove through the streets until they saw a small vegetable store, the owner just closing the door.

Naomi hopped out and stopped her while Hannah shut off the car, then both she and Aaron quickly joined Naomi who was having a tough time settling the upset woman's feathers. Things were instantly better as Aaron waved a handful of Emil's Swiss bills in front of her face. The woman grinned broadly, then speaking in rapid Italian, she signaled they could choose what they liked.

For the next ten minutes they emptied the place of every edible fresh vegetable they could see. Tossing them in the boot of the car, Aaron paid her generously as Hannah tried to ask where they could find bread and cheese. The woman finally got the message when Naomi acted the part of a mouse. With a laugh, the owner ran into the street and pointed north. "Plaza Verona," she said. "Il Pane. Il Pane," she said as she signaled with her hands as if eating.

"Il Pane must mean bread," Aaron said.

Hannah thanked the woman as they got in the car and drove north looking for Plaza Verona, the last rays of the sun cascading off the tops of the tallest buildings. Most of the war had bypassed Tarvisio, but there were a few signs here and there of battles fought and buildings either destroyed or missing their upper stories. Verona street was on the outskirts of town and the bakery shop was in the only building still fully intact. The place was already darkened but Naomi jumped out and started banging on the door. Aaron watched the apartment above, saw a figure come to the window and peer out, then disappear. A moment later the light came on in the shop and the door opened.

"Scusa," Aaron said. "Uh . . . Ila . . . Il Pane. Bread." He showed the Swiss money.

"Ah, you need bread," the shopkeeper said in German.

Aaron was relieved. "Yes, yes, as much as you have."

The man seemed to be measuring them, his small round eyes glinting in the light from his shop window. "And for three of you, you need this much bread?" he asked.

"There are others. They have traveled a long way and are very hungry," Naomi said.

"Hmm. Would they be Jews?" he asked evenly. Hannah found herself a little nervous. Not because of the question but because she could not read this man's eyes. It was if he had suddenly pulled a curtain over them.

Naomi stiffened. "Does it matter?"

"No, it does not matter." He paused, as if thinking. "I have only a few loaves here, but I know of another bakery, a much larger one. I will take you there." He turned and went back into his shop. "I will be only a moment."

Concern nagged at the fringes of Hannah's mind as a few minutes turned into ten, then fifteen. As she was about to express her concerns to Naomi and Aaron the door opened and the baker returned with several loaves of bread wrapped in a linen tablecloth and held tightly under his arm. For some reason Hannah felt a sudden urge to walk away.

"We . . . we've decided to forget it," Hannah said, "Thank you for your trouble, but . . ."

Naomi and Aaron turned to her, confused. "What? But we need . . ."

"Never mind. I am sure things will be fine". She walked around to the driver's side of the car. "I am sorry," she said looking at the baker, "but . . ."

He reached quickly inside the linen cloth and Hannah suddenly found herself looking down the barrel of a Luger, her nagging fears suddenly confirmed.

Aaron took a step forward as if to grab the weapon, anger filling his face. The baker pointed the weapon directly at his ribs.

"I will not hesitate to kill you, Jew!" he said flatly.

Aaron stopped. "Nazi pig!"

The baker gave a hard smile as he looked at Hannah. "You will drive. This young man will sit in the front and the girl in the back with me. If you do anything I don't like I will kill one of them. Do you understand?"

Hannah nodded, her mouth too dry to talk. How could this be happening? She got in as the others did the same. The baker told Naomi to sit on her hands and rapped her on the forehead with the barrel of his gun when she spat at him.

"Naomi! Do as he says," Hannah said firmly. Naomi did, then stared out the window in an attempt to keep control.

"Go left. The street will take you out of town to the east," the baker said. "It is in a small village, just a mile or two."

"Do you greet everyone this way or just Jews?" Aaron asked spitefully.

"Many of your people come here now. They try to get to your Palestine. The British are not agreeable, the Austrians are not agreeable. No one seems to want you. We do them all a favor by getting rid of you here."

They rode in silence through the growing darkness of the town's streets until they reached the fields just outside its stone houses.

"The war is over. You can't kill us all," Hannah said.

"My men and I disagree with you, as do many others."

"Werewolves, one and all," Hannah said.

Through the rearview mirror Hannah saw the wan smile. "The Werewolves are fools. There will be no Fourth Reich."

"But you continue to fight," Hannah said.

He shrugged. "There is little fighting in what we do. Most of your people are too weak to fight. We round them up, send them to our camps. It is easy enough."

"The camps have all been destroyed," Aaron said.

The baker only smiled. "Turn there, at the chateau."

Hannah turned the wheel and pulled the car into a lane. A steel gate lay directly ahead. Two men opened it as they arrived, and she drove through. In the rearview mirror she could see them close it behind her. She felt her stomach cramp with fear as she realized she had put Aaron and Naomi in a deadly situation. Another man with an automatic weapon stepped up to the car as she reached the large front door of the war-weary Chateau.

"Because you are no threat now that we are here I will tell you the truth," he said arrogantly. "Two factories were built by the Germans in the mountains north of here. Munitions factories buried deep inside of mountains and hidden behind legitimate businesses. The allies do not know of their existence and we intend to keep it that way. To do so we need laborers who will not be missed. Our people watch the borders, watch for people like you and the people you are trying to feed. You will continue to run our factories. Not for the German war machine this time, but for anyone willing to pay our prices."

"Slave labor. What a unique idea," Hannah said facetiously. "With the war over there isn't much need for munitions. Even cheap ones."

"There will always be war. It is a market upon which you can always depend. Get out," the baker demanded.

They did as they were told and were promptly pushed inside. They found themselves in a large entry with a winding staircase to their right and another room to their left. The cold steel of a gun barrel nudged Hannah to a door that led to the basement. Forced to take the stairs, she found herself in a room dimly lit by three candles on a candle stand in the center of a beat up table. Hannah gasped as the two men they had met in the square earlier appeared out of the shadows and she realized there would be no one to meet the Brigade and save those at Klagenfurt.

Two guards searched them a bit too thoroughly and Naomi shoved one hard enough that he fell backwards and hit the floor. His weapon came up to fire but the baker yelled an order, then hit Naomi with the back of his hand, knocking her head to the side. She stood her ground.

"If either of you touches me again it will be because I am dead," she said through clenched teeth.

"You are worth more to us alive, but remember, you can be replaced rather easily," the baker said coldly. He led his men upstairs, locking the door behind them.

Hannah turned to the two men from the square. "What happened? How did they capture you?"

"Two of them were in British uniforms with the Jewish Brigade patch on the shoulder. We thought we were safe." Moshe spat and Hannah's eyes had adjusted enough to the darkness that she could see both men had been badly beaten.

"Did you get to the Brigade?" Milo asked.

Hannah nodded. "They were going to pick you up and let you lead them to the others. Without you they will have no chance of finding them."

Milo's shoulders visibly sagged with the news. "They have questioned us and they will do the same to you. They want to know the location. They want the others." Moshe wiped his swollen lips.

"I do not understand this," Milo said, frustrated.

Hannah explained about the factories.

"The Nazi in a business suit. Makes you cringe doesn't it?" Aaron said.

"We have to get out of here. If they get us to their camps we will have no chance of escape, and no one to stop their madness."

With perfect understanding bred by the camps, they all began looking around the room. It was bare except for the candle holder and its half-used candles. After a moment's search Hannah noticed the window high in the wall. Though Hannah could see that it had no bars, it was too high to reach, even if she stood on another persons' shoulders. But three people . . .

"We will have to jump them," Moshe said. "There is nothing else we can do."

"Aaron, could you hold both Naomi and me?" Hannah said, staring up at the window. "If I could get through it I might be able to escape and bring the Brigade."

"I can try," Aaron said. He placed his hands against the wall and stepped back and out to get a firm base.

Naomi turned to Hannah. "It is I who must go. I am younger and faster."

"And I am older and smarter."

"She is right, Hannah. She is faster and speed will make the difference. Naomi must go," Aaron said.

"If they catch you, they will kill you," Hannah said to Naomi.

"They will not catch me unless they kill me," Naomi said firmly.

It was not a comforting statement for Hannah and she was about to insist on going when Naomi touched her tenderly on the arm. "I will make it," she said.

In their weakened condition Milo and Moshe could only give limited help as Hannah balanced herself on Aaron's shoulders and Naomi began her climb. She reached the window and could see into the courtyard, but the frame was of wood and swollen shut.

"Hand me the candle holder," she whispered.

One of the two men quickly blew out the candles and removed them, then handed the rough iron candlestick to Hannah, who handed it up to Naomi.

"Better hurry," Hannah said grimacing.

Naomi used the bottom of the candlestick to punch lightly on the wood. It gave, then sprung outward. A moment later she disappeared and Hannah jumped down, stood quiet, listening, hoping. Minutes passed.

The gunfire made Hannah jump several inches off the floor. There were voices screaming orders, the starting of an engine and the racing away of a vehicle while the sound of at least half a dozen running feet filled the courtyard, then slowly died in the distance. Then it was quiet again. Hannah prayed with all her might that Naomi had gotten away but the fear remained and pushed her mind into near panic.

The door at the top of the stairs opened and two men came quickly down, automatic weapons ready. A third man followed. It was the baker.

"That was foolish. If she gets away she will bring help. They must not find you here."

Hannah felt relief on one side of her stomach and a growing fear on the other. For the time being Naomi had eluded them, but she could see the near panic in the baker's eyes. He must get rid of them. She hadn't thought of such a swift consequence and it weakened her knees. "She knows about the factories. She will tell them. Even if you kill us, they will find our remains and you . . ."

"We will be gone" he said. "Take them!" He motioned to his two men.

They marched them out a back door and into a large open area behind the house where a high wall greeted them. There were no openings.

Hannah's breath caught in her throat as she realized death was only seconds away. She suddenly understood what it must have been like for little David as he was taken with his mother to be shot, then the anger in her welled up and she stopped moving. As the guard jabbed her with the gun she turned and slapped it aside, then pummeled him with her fists, knocking him backwards. "No! I will not let you just shoot me! Never!"

The man guarding Aaron turned to hit her with the butt of the gun but Moshe slammed his body into him and knocked him to the ground. Hannah grabbed the gun of her guard and jerked. It came free so easily that she stumbled backward, the weapon tumbling into the dirt. As she fell flat on her backside the baker raised his weapon and pulled the trigger but it misfired. Frantically jerking back on the automatic firing mechanism he tried to clear the chamber, but Aaron was already slamming a retrieved stone into the side of the baker's head. He hit the ground with a thud and didn't move as Aaron turned on the guard Moshe had knocked down. As he scrambled to get up, Aaron delivered a blow that rendered him unconscious, and he hit the ground nearly as hard as the baker. Aaron grabbed the weapon Hannah had dropped to the ground and aimed at the last standing Werewolf, who was so shocked by the sudden attack that he had done nothing but watch until Aaron's gun barrel was shoved up his nose. He threw his weapon to the ground, raised his hands and backed against the wall, crying for mercy. Hannah was scrambling to her feet as Moshe retrieved the weapon and Milo checked the baker for signs of life.

"He is still breathing, but his head is crushed. He will die," Milo said. The second man moaned and tried to get to his knees. Aaron was about to pummel him again when Hannah stopped him.

"He will make a good shield, don't you think?" she said.

Aaron hesitated then nodded slightly and Milo helped the man to his feet.

Hannah grabbed the baker's weapon but could only look at it, dumbfounded. Was it cocked, ready to fire? Where was the safety? Why hadn't it fired before?

"We must go find your friend," Moshe said.

"Yes, yes. Put them in front of us," Hannah said, regaining her wits. "Make them go in the chateau first. It is the only way to get to the car." She was jerking on the lever of the weapon trying to make it work. "How does this idiotic thing work?" The adrenalin was coursing through Hannah, feeding the wild anger in her. She would not be taken. Not again. Not Ever!

Aaron grinned and quickly showed her, then barked the order and their two captives hastened to the back entrance.

"Wehrmacht," one of them said, "Don't shoot!"

"Wehrmacht? You lying pig!" Aaron yelled. He slammed the gun butt in the middle of the man's back and he hit the ground like his legs had been suddenly blown away.

Hannah grabbed Aaron's arm and pulled him back. "Aaron, get control. We don't have time for this. The others must be after Naomi. She can only evade them so long. We have to find her!"

Aaron's eyes were glazed over but he nodded. Milo checked the Nazi on the ground. The blow had left him unconscious, possibly with a broken back.

"Move!" Aaron said to the last man. They went up the stairs and through the door.

The house seemed empty. They pushed the last Nazi out the front door into an unexpected silence. Aaron cautiously followed. Still nothing. Moshe and Milo grabbed the guard and quickly returned him to the basement, shoving him down the steps and locking the door. When they returned, Hannah had the car started and Aaron was in the passenger seat. The two quickly joined them and they headed for the gate. It was open and Hannah braked only when they hit the intersection. They looked left and right. She was breathing heavy, tired, but still pumping adrenalin.

"Look!" Aaron cried.

She squinted through the darkness and saw points of light in the field to the right. Electric torches! She gunned the car and turned the wheel. As they drew nearer the lights she pulled the car into the gutter and into a field of uncut grain. Her lights illuminated a man and she gunned the vehicle. He jumped too late and was knocked to the side. The other lights turned on them frantically and weapons fired. She swung the vehicle in a circle as Aaron and her friends fired back. Then she saw something move just on the edge of her lights. Naomi!

As they reached Naomi, Hannah slammed on the brakes, one of Naomi's arms hanging limp at her side, drenched in red. The two in the back pulled her inside as Aaron covered for them and Hannah hit the gas feed. They raced for the road, coming free of the grain so quickly that she didn't see the ditch. The car hit hard and came to a bone jarring halt. Hannah and Aaron both hit the windshield and were knocked unconscious. Moshe and Milo were propelled against the back of the front seat but remained conscious. Milo struggled out of the car and fired at the approaching enemy who were desperately trying to stop them.

His magazine emptied. Moshe threw Milo his weapon and he fired again. Bullets struck the car's backside and one hit Milo in the chest. He dropped against the car and slid down it until he was sitting with his back against the rear wheel.

"You . . . you must kill us dear friend," he told Moshe. "Get the woman's gun and shoot us! If they take us again . . . our friends . . ." He couldn't say more, the pain in his chest creeping up his body and grabbing his tongue.

Suddenly the field erupted with gunfire, and the flashing lights of half a dozen vehicles poured into the field. One of them stopped directly between the car and the enemy and half a dozen soldiers surrounded Hannah's group in a protective maneuver.

Milo fell over and rolled onto his back as the pain in his chest sent cold chills up his legs toward his heart. As he stared up into the light of electric torches, a soldier stooped down and checked his wound, then barked orders. The last thing he saw was a flash of light as it hit the patch on the soldiers arm.

It was the Brigade.

See Chapter Notes

CHAPTER 12

Hannah woke up the next day in time for lunch but hardly felt like eating. Her head throbbed and she could only think she had a concussion when half a dozen Rabbi Givons appeared at the foot of her bed.

"My friends. Where are they?" she asked, while grimacing at the pain that even that bit of talk created.

The six rabbis made a motion to her left. "Both will survive. The girl was shot, but the bullet went straight through her upper arm. The boy has a headache like yours and about two dozen stitches in his scalp. It seems your head is harder than his," Rabbi Givon said.

She sensed a smile but her blurred vision prevented her from being sure. Forcing her eyes to focus she saw only a frown. If there had been a smile it was gone.

"The men who were with us?" she asked.

"The man named Moshe is alive. The other is not," the rabbi responded.

She felt sick inside and didn't know what to say.

"You should not blame yourself. If you had not been there and helped them escaped, even Moshe would be dead."

It was little consolation.

"We have retrieved the others from Klagenfurt. They are in very bad shape. Some are here, in the hospital, some under the care of friends, most in a safe place we have built a few miles to the south," the rabbi said.

"And the baker and his men?"

"His body has been identified as a William Staub. He was on the list of Nazis who disappeared when Matthausen was overrun.

The other men were like him. Nazis who supervised the camps. None survived."

"There are others, aren't there?" Hannah asked. "Thousands in hiding, waiting to kill, to wipe out our people. The baker said they were organizing, preparing for the day when the Reich would return."

"The baker was alive long enough to talk to us before he died. The Russians will round up the remainder. When the Russians are through with them they will wish we had caught them instead," Givon said.

Hannah sensed that the baker had not died a comfortable death, nor had his information been freely given. Her emotions over such things were still mixed in a jumble of pity, hate, and satisfaction. She wondered if she would ever be free of the desire to see them all dead.

"How are you doing in your arrangements for the people at Ebensee?" Hannah asked.

"As you know, the British are no longer cooperative so we circumvent them. Two of our best negotiators met with people from the UNRRA in Italy. They are willing to make room for the people at Ebensee until we can get them to Palestine."

She opened her eyes quick enough this time to see the smile before it disappeared. "How soon can the UNRRA camps be ready to take them?"

"How soon can you return to Ebensee?" Givon asked.

"Now, today!" She threw the covers off and slid off the edge of the bed. Her head throbbed so hard she thought she might pass out and she leaned back.

"Maybe tomorrow," Givon said as he came to her rescue and helped her back into bed.

"Yes, you're probably right. What about the car? The last I remember, it was in a ditch."

"It is being fixed by the Brigade motor pool. It will be ready when you are. We will send two of our people with you. They know what needs to be done. They are also looking for family and think they might be found at Ebensee."

Givon turned to leave, then turned back. "Now you know why I told you it was impossible that you accompany us. For some people the war is not over. Especially the war against us. Stay put until you go back to Ebensee, Miss Gruen."

She nodded and watched him leave the ward. An Italian nurse came to the side of the bed and handed her a couple of pills. She stayed conscious only long enough to be helped to the latrine, then make a quick check on her friends in the next beds. Both were sleeping soundly. How had they survived the guns, the hate and desire of their Nazi captors to kill them? Only the element of surprise in their actions, which in turn had left their captors in shock that they had acted at all, had given them the advantage they had needed.

And Naomi's escape. The girl had come so close to death.

Hannah lay down, closed her eyes. She wondered how many would have survived this horrible, near-annihilation of her people if they had only fought back! It was hard to know and it didn't matter now.

She rolled onto her side as the drug gently caressed her mind, then wrapped it in darkness. They had survived. That was all that mattered now. All that mattered.

CHAPTER 13

Hannah, Aaron, and Naomi returned to Ebensee the next day. They were accompanied by two men of the Brigade, Lieutenant Danek and Sergeant Rabinowitz.

The reaction of her people as they saw the blue and white shoulder patches of these two Israeli fighters would be unforgettable for Hannah. An endless line of people passed by them shaking their hands, many softly touching the patch as if to make sure they weren't dreaming. Their own people had come to rescue them, to take them away from their bad memories and desperate lives, and they gave them an almost worshipful welcome. Rabinowitz and Danek were embarrassed but stoic in their acceptance of the attention given. Both were disappointed as well. The old woman Danek thought might be his grandmother and the old man Rabinowitz hoped was his uncle, were neither.

The two men were invaluable over the next few days, both for lifting the spirits of the Jews in the camp and for helping to prepare them for a journey that would tax many to the very limits of their somewhat renewed strength.

The UNRRA would make room at their camps in Bari and Brindisi, cities on the far southern tip of Italy. Therefore, the trip would be clandestine by necessity, long by nature. Every truckload would be at risk once cleared through the Russian sector and out of Austria, and if caught by the regular British army would most likely be sent back to Poland.

Sergeant Rabinowitz was careful to tell them that once they reached Italy there would be a few times when they would need to walk several miles through rough terrain, the trucks picking them up after clearing what Rabinowitz called "hot spots"—places where the British Army had large numbers of men and heavy patrols.

This worried Hannah. There were now women who were several months pregnant and having great difficulty because of their weakened, even changed physical condition. Doctor Cardan was afraid for them and for the fetuses they carried. Hannah had called the women together and discussed the options. None of them wanted to stay, the fear of being left behind so strong that no risk was too great in order to stay with their people.

The two Brigade members carefully trained each organized group. They showed them how to get in and out of the trucks quickly and without injury, emphasized the need to be extremely quiet and set up a buddy system that paired the strong with the old, ill, and expectant. They took two days in which daily calisthenics were required for everyone who could do so without further harm to their bodies. Hannah had watched as even the rabbis, the recovering ill, and new mothers worked hard to strengthen themselves in preparation for their journey. The spirit in the camp was electrifying—something Hannah would never forget.

* * *

The first four trucks left on July twenty-third. Hannah was in the lead truck with Zohar, Beth, David, Sarah, and Anna at her side. They had forty-three others crowded tightly in every available space. She had tears in her eyes as she watched Major Stevens and Lucille disappear from her life as the truck rumbled from the camp, then left it behind. As they passed the school, Zohar sobbed and even David's face was somber. It had seemed like so long ago that they had come here and yet it was only three short weeks. She held Beth close. They had become a family here. Then again, they were going home. All of them. What could be better?

The Brigade had made arrangements with the Russians and they were quickly passed through all checkpoints as they crossed Austria. They pulled into the woods twice to stretch their legs, relieve themselves if necessary, and enjoy the crisp mountain air. Then they quickly loaded and continued their journey.

Their first walk came at the Austrian/Italian border. They were unloaded from the American trucks in a valley that ran north to south, located a few miles east of Villach. The American truck drivers received hugs from their precious cargo before they returned to Ebensee. Each driver would make the journey four times in the next four days. As Hannah watched them leave she was greeted by a member of the Brigade who seemed to materialize out of nowhere. He led them on a strenuous walk along a well-worn trail that took them upward and around the crest of a mountain, then deposited them in fields on the Italian side of the border. It took nearly six hours and Hannah was glad to see the trucks belonging to the Brigade parked near a local farmhouse. She found Rabbi Givon waiting. Her told her that the Brigade would be leaving for Holland on July twenty-ninth, just enough time to get all of the Ebensee Jews into Italy.

After a few minutes of rest they were then loaded aboard the trucks once more and taken to Verona, where they spent the night in a monastery. At first all members of her group were apprehensive. Their Christian friends in Poland and Germany had watched as they had been hauled away to the camps, or they had participated in sending them there. But they soon discovered things were different in Italy. They had brought some food with them, but hot soup, bread, and cheese were provided by the Brigade and prepared by the nuns. Though it took some time to feed the nearly two hundred people and bed them down under the blankets each carried with them, no one seemed to mind. They were on their way to a goal they had only dreamed of. There would be few complaints.

The next morning found them on a road that traversed the middle of Italy. With the truck's tarpaulins in place, Hannah saw little of the countryside until they reached Bologna. She felt the cobblestone streets under the vehicle's wheels as they entered the town and heard the echo of the engine as it traveled through narrow streets. Then it came to a complete stop.

The tarpaulin was thrown back and they were instructed to get down, quickly. As they did, Hannah saw that their vehicle was the only one parked in the narrow street.

"Where are the others?" she asked.

"Each takes a different route. If one is stopped, the others can still get through." He saw the look of apprehension on her face. "We have done this many times. Do not worry."

They split up into small groups led by the man from the Brigade and three Hagannah operatives who were now riding with them. They were led through the city streets in different directions, each circumventing the British checkpoint and gathering together on the far side of the town where the trucks miraculously reappeared at the very moment they arrived at a predetermined place. After quickly boarding, each was handed a fresh orange.

"A gift from the local Jewish synagogue and its people," the Brigade leader said.

Hannah voiced everyone's surprise. "There are still Jews here?"

He smiled. "Though Bologna was emptied of most of its Jews by the Nazis, many went underground, protected by their Christian neighbors, and took care of what was left of the synagogue. When we entered the city we spread the word that Rabbi Givon would be holding a meeting that night in what remained of the building. Nearly three hundred came. Besides locals there were Partisans, weapons still in hand, and some refugees who had trekked across Europe in those early months. They had been hiding in caves and forests but somehow heard of our meeting. Since then the synagogue has been rebuilt and our people have been returned to their homes. Most will stay here. It is their home."

"They are fools," an old man to Hannah's right said. "No Jew is safe in Europe."

"Maybe. Italy has been different. Even here, when we came we could not find the Sifreh Torah in the synagogue. We put out the word and a young Italian scholar, a Catholic who had been friends to many Jews before the Nazis brought them to us."

"He probably stole them in the first place," the old man said cynically.

"No, but he knew of their importance, and when the Nazis came and his Jewish friends had to flee without even a moment's notice, he went to the synagogue at great risk and removed the Torah from their sacred niche. He hid them in his attic.

"He was honored by all Jews when he brought them back. They knew his heart was good."

The truck was back in the country and moving fast through the green hills of middle Italy. From what little Hannah could see through a crack in the tarpaulin she knew it was a beautiful place.

The Brigade soldier went on. "Over the months I have spent in Italy I have discovered many things about the Italian people. Though there were some like the Austrians and the Germans, the Poles and Lithuanians, many tried very hard to help our people. Some put their own lives at risk by hiding Jews, or by helping them escape by boat or into partisan enclaves. They continue to help us."

"And the Pope, I suppose you are pleased with him also?" the old man said with disgust.

"It is true, the Vatican did not react well concerning the fate of the Jews of greater Europe. The Pope never took a stand against Hitler until he knew for certain that the Nazis would be defeated, but he saved many here, in Italy. He warned Jewish communities when he learned of roundups."

"He could have done more. Much more," Hannah said.

"Yes, but most of us could have. We didn't. All of us must share some blame, but it is foolish to try and place all fault on one man's shoulders."

That night they slept in open fields on the banks of the Tiber river just outside the town of Terni. Food was waiting, and they ate and bedded down. Hannah was awakened in the night by a young expectant mother experiencing her first labor pains. Hannah sent a member of the Hagannah to locate a doctor, then helped prepare the young woman for delivery.

Doctor Cardan had trained each group leader on what must be done and how to deliver if there was an emergency. As Hannah helped the girl get comfortable, then asked for hot water, towels, and blankets, she strove to remember it all.

"I have never seen a birth before, let alone helped with one." The young girl who spoke was a member of the Hagannah sent from Israel to help her people. She and others like her were brought in on the same boats that took camp Jews to Israel successfully. Her name was Dalia and she was a Sabra—a Jew born and raised in Israel. She was strong, smart, a fighter. This was the first time since meeting her that Hannah saw any lack of confidence. It was normal. She was also frightened. Very frightened.

She had seen only one other baby born. It was just after she arrived at Ravensbrück. A baby was delivered in the barracks. They had no doctor, no nurse. There was no hot water, no clean blankets. Yet the child had survived. Then it had been taken away by the guards and killed. The mother had died as well—had just given up when the baby was taken. This time would be different. Hannah would make sure of it.

The child came just before three in the morning. No doctor had been found and Hannah and Dalia had delivered a little boy.

"He is very small," said Dalia, holding the child close to her chest.

"Premature by a month and he was conceived in the camps, even before we were released. He is lucky to be alive at all."

"But how . . . I mean the father . . ."

Hannah looked at the mother, making sure she was asleep. "Probably a guard," she said sadly.

Dalia's face saddened. "How can anything that comes of such a thing be so beautiful?" she asked both with sadness and awe.

"One of the real miracles of this life," said Hannah.

They stayed awake until the baby was slumbering, then they dozed off. When Hannah woke up she found the mother awake hovering over the child. The position was strange and Hannah suddenly realized what was happening. She jumped up, yelling for the woman to stop but it was too late. The child was dead—smothered by hate.

One more victim of Nazi atrocities.

* * *

Of the four trucks in her group, Hannah's was the first to arrive at the UNRRA camp outside Bari, Italy. Hannah immediately saw that their conditions would not be as good as those at Ebensee but could be improved and tolerable until they could leave.

UNRRA officials were quick to get them housed and Hannah found herself busy from morning until late night as her people continued to arrive. One week after Hannah stepped inside the camp Rachel arrived. Her group was the last and included Emil, Aaron, and Naomi, along with Emil's family. Conditions were very crowded, with four in most beds and no barracks for married couples. Emil and Lilith were separated again.

The British officer in charge of the camp had been convinced to "look the other way" because of the commanders friendship with Rabbi Givon and the Jewish leaders of the Brigade, and because he was convinced the Jews had suffered enough. That nearly changed as he found his camp inundated with more people than they could handle. Then the imported members of the Hagannah, twenty of them altogether, took over.

Using the system set up by the Brigade they started delivering lumber, nails, shingles, and other building materials needed to expand the camp and house the growing numbers. Aaron and the men of Ebensee used their experience, tools, and know-how to speed up the process. It wouldn't be long before married couples were getting their own rooms again.

The UNRRA leader received a letter from Lucille and approached Hannah about continuing her duties at Bari.

"You understand that we will be leaving soon," Hannah said.

He nodded. "Hopefully, all of us will have that luxury."

"Yes, hopefully."

They had found another friend. His name was Robin Crockwell. He was British and it made Hannah remember that governments weren't people. Some Brits were on their side.

On the first day of August Hannah was receiving several new truckloads of refugees sent south by the Brigade. As they moved north they found more and more people and began funneling them south. She was giving instructions to one of the drivers when a handsome young man in a Brigade uniform walked up to her and gave a sharp salute. It was Aaron.

She smiled at him. His hair was cropped short and his tall, thin frame protruded from both ends of the uniform, but the proud look on his face nearly made Hannah cry. She finished what she was doing and they walked.

"I didn't think it would take long to get you in and trained, but this has to be some sort of record," she smiled.

"I'm not really in the Brigade," Aaron said sheepishly. "Some of the men who were ready to demobilize did so before the Brigade went north. They turned their uniforms and papers over to a few of us refugees so that we can continue to openly help while getting military training and preparation from Hagannah leaders before we go to Palestine. The old owners of the uniforms either go home and rejoin the Hagannah there or stay and help with things here."

"I take it that you are going to stay in Europe a while," Hannah said.

"Yes. They want me to go back to Tarvisio. Our experience in Austria will help. In fact, Emil has turned the house over to us as a way station for refugees." He paused. "I need you to take care of David."

"It would be an honor."

He stood in front of her and took her hands, looking down into her eyes. "Thank you for taking care of us. All of us. We owe you more than just our lives." With that he kissed her on the cheek and strode away. She wondered if the pride she felt was what mothers felt for honorable sons. Surely it must be. It both broke and swelled the heart.

Later that day she met with the others in the group at a house in Bari. Emil had rented it.

"It will make more room in the camp. The Almighty knows they can use the extra room!" He grinned.

"Besides which you are tired of sleeping alone," Hannah said.

He laughed. "Yes, that too." His face grew serious. "We are a family. We should live as one, at least until we leave Europe."

"Agreed."

"Besides, it is only for a short time. I have other news," Emil said. "In ten days a small yacht will leave Bari for Israel. I have booked passage for all of us."

Hannah was only a little surprised that no one jumped for joy.

"I can't leave that soon," Zohar said adamantly. "We have a new school for the children and I can't leave now."

"But a third of your students are right here," Emil said, a bit frustrated.

"We're needed here," Naomi added. "We should stay a while."

Hannah looked at Rachel, who gave her an agreeable smile. She looked at Lilith who seemed torn as well.

"A few weeks," Lilith said with pleading eyes.

"Yes, just a few," Rachel agreed.

"Can you get your money back, put him off?" Hannah asked.

"I suppose," Emil said with a sigh. "But only a few weeks, no more, agreed?"

Everyone was smiling again.

CHAPTER 14

There were newspapers in Italy. British newspapers. Hannah made a special trip each morning to a local store in Bari, paid the small fee in lira, and kept track of the war in the Pacific.

As she worked to help refugees come and go she ticked off the days and events that would bring her and Ephraim together again.

During their escape from Germany, the Americans had conquered Okinawa and there had been a huge U.S.-British air attack on Tokyo. Hannah was sure Ephraim had been involved, and she prayed, making her prayers for him even more fervent.

Churchill had been defeated in elections on July twenty-sixth, and a new government elected. Though Churchill had been friendly to Jewish immigration, many in his government had not. They celebrated in the camp that night because the papers said that the new leaders would be more favorable to their immigration, but the jubilation was short-lived as over the next few weeks an even more intransigent Foreign Office seemed to take on an even stronger anti-Jewish tone. Hannah could only deduce that Britain's leaders had all lost their hearing. The screams of the Jewish people still waiting for help could be heard around the world. Apparently greed and power made people deaf and dumb.

As she was working in Doctor Cardan's hospital late in the afternoon of August 6, his new radio announced that the United States had dropped an atomic bomb on Hiroshima. Hannah was shocked and had to find a chair and sit down. How many more innocent people would have to die to get evil men to give up?

The next day she, Rachel, Naomi, and Emil helped prepare a group who were leaving that night. The Hagannah and former

Brigade soldiers now living as civilians, or still pretending to be British soldiers, had such illegal departures fine-tuned. At dark, a curfew was declared and the 242 people selected to go to Israel would meet at a designated spot just outside Bari. Hannah was to give them only an hour's notice, then see that they were on time. Latecomers were left behind. No one else would be allowed out of the camp so that word of the escape would not filter to the wrong people.

When word came, Hannah did her duty, sending out aides to notify those who would be going, then she hurried with them to the rendevous point. She counted off the last to arrive just as the convoy of trucks pulled in.

All Jews in the camp had gone through training similar to that given at Ebensee by Sergeant Rabinowitz, so they knew the drill and quickly loaded into the trucks in predetermined groups of thirty. Another five minutes and the convoy would be on its way to a beach unknown to any of their passengers, where a ship would be waiting off shore. The commandant at the camp would be handed paperwork in the morning indicating that they had gone on to Turkey, Greece, or other places. He knew better but said nothing. There were more people to take their place.

As Hannah watched the last truck being loaded she saw Aaron at the wheel. She quickly jumped on the sideboard and gave him a kiss. He looked well and happy, older and wiser than his nearly eighteen years.

As she jumped down she prayed he would make it through all right. She knew that it was toughest on the drivers. Bari was on the southeast side of Italy; the ships waited in out-of-the-way places off the northwest shores. The drivers had to traverse the land in between with nothing but their wits, extraordinary knowledge of the roads, American dollars for a few well-placed bribes, forged documents to protect them from prowling British MPs, and a few unfriendly Italian gangsters looking to make a living. If caught, they would be imprisoned by the Brits, delayed by the others. The second would force a return to the camps; the first would find the drivers in prison cells of their own.

She watched the trucks go and found it interesting that she had no regrets that they weren't aboard. It wasn't time. Not yet.

Word was received later that week that the boat had been intercepted and all on board interned in a camp in Israel guarded by the British. But at least they were in Israel. Earlier, the Brits had sent some of the Jews back but the outcry of world opinion had been so loud that they had stopped. Pressure was mounting; the Brits were bending but refused to break.

Hannah heard a week later that two more ships had left but one was stopped and all passengers were sent to a new camp on the Isle of Cyprus. The British were quickly giving the Jews a new enemy to hate.

* * *

On August ninth, another atomic bomb was dropped on Japan. This time it was Nagasaki. Six days later, after another large, aerial bombing campaign, the Japanese officially surrendered. That same night another group of refugees left Bari for Palestine. They arrived without incident.

Hannah found that if she sent letters to Berlin they would see them on to the Pacific, so she began writing Ephraim every day. She received nothing in return, but there was nothing to do but wait. She was not family, so she knew the army would give her no official information, but she did try to wire Colonel Mackland in Berlin. His response came three days later and was brief. He knew Ephraim was involved in the attacks on Tokyo but was in good health. He also knew he would be sent home in the next two months.

Hannah's longing for Palestine began again.

She also studied a book she had found in a library in Bari. It was written in English and was called *Articles of Faith*. Written by a man named James E. Talmage, it answered many questions and raised others. In fact she had a list of questions for Ephraim several pages long.

Emil came to her on September sixth, four weeks after Hannah's wire from Colonel Mackland and a few days after the Japanese formally surrendered aboard the *USS Missouri*.

"We were going to stay a few weeks. We've been here two months," he said. "You know it is getting harder. The yacht owner has made enough money that he doesn't want to take the chance anymore, half the Hagannah ships are getting caught, and the British interning our people. The Brits are stepping up pressure on the Italians to stop helping altogether and they're feeling it. Hannah, it's time to go home."

They called a family council that night. Aaron, Rachel, and Naomi were absent.

Rachel was taking Hagannah field and weapons training in the hills north of Bari but Hannah knew she was ready to go to Israel. Word had come from Aaron that the Hagannah was stepping up attacks on the British there, frustrated with their continued intransigence on the issue of immigration, and they were beginning to prepare for war. As much as it frightened Hannah she knew Rachel wanted to go.

Naomi had gone north. She was now a member of the Hagannah and like many others in the new Jewish army, she would go to DP camps in the north and lead small groups of Jews into Italy. Aaron was still with the Brigade, feverishly working to get as many into Palestine as possible while training others like Rachel. Hannah was sure Naomi and Aaron would not be going with them either.

Hannah told them she thought it was time to go to Palestine and asked for comments. Everyone agreed except Zohar.

"I must stay here. There is still too much to do. I will come when Aaron and Naomi do."

"Zohar, I think you should reconsider," Emil said. "They have successfully taken nearly five hundred orphans into Israel just in the last few months. They need teachers like you there as much as they need teachers here."

Zohar, ever the peacemaker, only nodded. Hannah knew her young friend still didn't want to go and the thought made Hannah chew on her fingernails.

"Then we are agreed," Emil pushed.

There was no celebration, but everyone except Hannah and Zohar seemed relieved. It was time.

The next day Hannah traveled by train to Rome to see the head of the Hagannah in Italy. After introductions and formalities were out of the way, the man she knew only as Raffi asked what they could do for her. She laid the tickets on the table.

"We wish to have passage on the next boat you send to Palestine."

He picked up the tickets. "Where did you get these?"

"They were given to us by the Americans and the British. They should be worth the ten places we need. Properly copied, they can bring others to Palestine."

"Very well." He put them in a drawer. "You must be ready tonight. There will be only the usual notification of one hour; if you miss the boat you have no further promise."

Hannah nodded agreement as she apprehensively watched their papers disappear in a desk drawer. Since getting them renewed by General Clay's office, they had comforted her with the knowledge that no matter what happened, she, Rachel, and Zohar could leave Europe. That comfort was suddenly gone. She groomed her nails with her teeth all the way back to Bari.

When she got back to the house, Hannah found that Rachel had returned. She took her aside to tell her they might be leaving that night.

"It is time," Rachel said. "I will tell my leaders, then return to help with the children." She left the house and ran up the street as Hannah gathered the others from their rooms, told them this might be the night and to get their things ready. There was reserved excitement as each hurried up the stairs to stuff their few belongings into the small packs Emil had purchased before they left Salzburg. Emil and Lilith were the last to arrive, sacks of groceries in their arms. They put them away with fumbling excitement then went to their room to do their own packing.

When Zohar came home from her school, Hannah took her for a walk and told her they would be leaving that night.

"So soon?" Zohar said, a tinge of dread in her voice.

"Will you go?" Hannah asked. "I know in your heart you do wish it."

There was silence as Zohar turned to face the lapping water as it hit the shore. "You say I am needed in Israel. Do you say it because it is true or because you don't want to leave me behind?"

Hannah smiled. Zohar had always been able to read her mind. "You are like a sister. I left two sisters behind. It is unthinkable to leave another."

"It isn't the same, Hannah." She turned and put an arm around Hannah's waist, moving her along the beach again. "I love you, but I must stay. I will come, you know that. It may be in a few months or a few years when these camps do not exist anymore, but I can do more good as a teacher here than I can in Israel. At least for now."

Hannah put her arm around her friend as tears welled up in her eyes. They walked along the sea for another half hour before returning to the house. Zohar told the others and David crawled onto the sofa next to her, snuggling under her arm. He remained there for some time, nearly changing Zohar's mind. Finally she took him upstairs to his bed, tucked him in, then left the house. There was much to do at the school, she said. The truth was she simply couldn't stand the thought of seeing them off.

Hannah watched from the front step until her friend disappeared down the street. With an aching heart she finally went to her own room to gather her things, then to read to keep her mind off her melancholy feelings.

An hour later she removed her glasses and rubbed her tired eyes. She heard the door open, then soft steps on the stairs. Rachel came through the door still breathing hard.

"I am ready, Hannah," she said as she starting removing her things from a single drawer.

"Get some rest if you can. I'll stretch out on the couch for a while." Hannah went downstairs, lay down and closed her eyes. It was more than an hour before her mind shut down and allowed her some much-needed sleep.

She awoke to the pounding on the front door and rushed to answer it as Rachel bolted down the stairs.

Hannah recognized the woman as the one who was on duty for the Hagannah. "You have one hour," she said, then turned and ran into the darkness.

Rachel ran upstairs and told the others while Hannah got the already-prepared letters she had written while on the train. There was one for Naomi, Zohar, and Aaron.

As she sat them on the table she thought of their experiences together. Memories came in a flood and washed tears down her cheeks. She loved them so very much.

She pulled a hanky from her pants pocket and wiped at the tears. She cried so easily lately!

The others descended from the upper floor, their faces somber but excitement in their eyes. It had finally come.

"I think we should have prayer," Sarah said.

The others nodded agreement.

They had been praying together for several weeks. It had been Rachel's idea one day after she and Hannah had read from Third Nephi. All had agreed but Emil who had continued to put on his newly purchased prayer shawl, gather his family around him, read from the Torah, then say prayer for them in the traditional manner. That had changed last week. He had brought Lilith and the children in when Hannah had gathered the others. After saying their prayer, Hannah had asked that he read from the Torah and pray after his manner as well. It had been the way of things ever since.

But there was not time for all of that tonight. They knelt and Rachel offered a quick but heartfelt prayer for protection. They scrambled to their feet, pulled on shawls and sweaters, turned off all but the small light in the foyer and closed the door, locking it before hurrying off to the rendevous.

They would never see this place again.

CHAPTER 15

The trucks traveled across country to Naples, then drove north. Several miles more found them on a dirt road that ended above a beach of the Tyrrhenian Sea. The moon was nearly full and as Hannah climbed from the truck and took Beth's hand, she watched the rays bounce off the waves where they broke against the shore. In the distance she thought she could make out a dark ship resting like a shadow on the glistening water.

They followed their Hagannah leaders down the trail, hurrying to the beach where small rubber rafts waited. Rachel picked up David and immediately climbed in. Hannah and Beth followed, then Sarah, Anna, and the others. Four rafts were full in less than a minute and a small motor-powered boat began towing them out. Reaching the ship in less than ten minutes, two of the rafts began unloading passengers up rope ladders hanging over the side of the small schooner. When the first two rafts were aboard or on the ladders, the motor boat pulled forward and Hannah stood to help Beth and the others get hold of the ladders. She scurried up as the motorboat towed its rubber rafts back to shore for another load.

Finally onboard, she was hustled below to join the others. There were bunks sandwiched together so tightly they made a camp barracks look roomy. Hannah helped Beth into the one nearest the exit, then Rachel lifted David into the one above. Anna joined Rachel, and Sarah stayed with Hannah, her bad leg preventing her from climbing easily to the top bunk. Emil and his family were next to them, Lilith looking tired. Hannah worried for her but it was too late to go back now. They were committed. Now they must endure.

The rest of the bunks quickly filled as more boats pulled alongside and all seventy-two passengers were aboard. Hannah felt a bit squeamish with the first movement of the boat, and as they hit the waves again and again it worsened. Others began losing their dinner and she could no longer keep her own down. The next six hours were miserable—the smell, dizziness, and constant retching nearly unbearable.

At mid morning, they were allowed on deck, and the sun and fresh air helped. All of them had been sick except David. He seemed to be born for a sailor's life and was the one who provided them with water and cleanup most of the night. Once they were above deck, Hannah gave him a much-deserved hug and both stood at the side of the ship, looking for land. They saw nothing but blue sea and distant haze.

They stayed above deck all they could that day and night, but a storm the second day drove them below and the seasickness returned with a vengeance. Hannah languished on her bunk, too weak to sit or stand. Even little David was unable to leave his bunk, the sheer tossing of the ship too dangerous for him and his skinny land legs.

The seas calmed midway on day three and Hannah was finally able to crawl up the stairs and join Rachel, sitting with her back against the outside rail.

"We gave up a cruise ship for this," Rachel said with a smile. "Insanity must run in the family."

Hannah felt miserable but coughed up a laugh. "But what a deal if you want to lose weight."

Someone yelled "land," and they managed to get to their feet to see the coast of mainland Greece on their left and one of its islands on their right. They were close enough to the island to see the white buildings along the shores and the slopes of an inlet.

"It is the city of Heraklion," the captain said from his perch behind the schooner's wheel. "Four more days to your new home."

Hannah felt better already.

After the island disappeared in the haze, Rachel sat down and Hannah joined her. David brought them both a cup of water and they were sipping some when Hannah saw Beth on the steps. She stood long enough to join them, then lay her head in Hannah's lap. They stayed there until the sun burned and they had to seek shade.

At mid afternoon, Emil gained enough strength to come above decks and offer them some bread and cheese. They divided it, then nibbled slowly until they were sure it wouldn't come back up again.

That night, they slept under the stars and the sea seemed to level out. For several more days they slept, basked in the sun, ate when they could, and finally saw the distant shore of Israel in the late afternoon of the sixth day. Shouts and excitement dissipated the sickness of even the most ill as the ship made contact with those waiting on shore.

Radios and small fishing vessels were used by the Hagannah to keep track of the British ships guarding the coastline. The captain was told that a British vessel was still in the area and to lower his sails and his anchor to wait far enough offshore that they would not be discovered.

Hannah got up and went to where he stood, binoculars in hand, watching the horizon.

"You have done this before," she said in English. She had heard him speak it before and knew he had a good grasp of the language.

He nodded. "Several times. This is the most dangerous part. The British know they are being watched by your Jewish friends, so they play a game of cat and mouse, sometimes suddenly appearing where they are not expected."

"And if they catch us?"

"They send you back to Europe or put you in a camp in Israel or someplace else. As for me, they will take my ship and put me in jail."

"Then why do you do it?"

He shrugged, lowering the binoculars. "Let's just say I do not like the British." He grinned. "And the money is good."

She knew the Jewish Agency was funding these shipments, knew that the figure was fair, but the captain was not about to get rich from hauling refugees across the Mediterranean.

He went on. "The Nazis were butchers. They destroyed everyone who refused to become like them. I had a wife and two children who were put into their miserable camps because I fought with the Italian partisans. When we overran the camp I found my wife and children nearly dead and saw what they had done to others, especially to the Jews. I try to make it right." He lifted his binoculars to his eyes again, scanning the distant shoreline. The radio crackled and a voice spoke in Italian.

The captain immediately barked orders to his sailors who scrambled to hoist sails.

"They say it is clear, but we are to be cautious. There is a ship unaccounted for. You and your people had better go below." His brow wrinkled with concern as he turned away to concentrate on getting the ship ready for a dash to shore.

Hannah yelled the order and everyone quickly ran for the entrance to the hold. Fear and somberness permeated the bunk room as all realized the uncertainty of the next few hours. Hannah couldn't bear to think they might not reach shore, but now knew it was a distinct possibility. She wondered about the captain. How strong was his desire to help them? Did it go deep enough that he would risk jail and the loss of his ship to get them to shore, or would he run? Worse, would he turn them over to the British and try to make a deal to save his own hide?

She couldn't stand being in the hold, unable to see, to know what was happening. Climbing from her bunk she left the hold and went on deck. The schooner was headed directly for land under all the sail that could be mustered, the canvas straining under the wind. Sea spray bounced over the front and sides of the ship as the sleek vessel bounced through the waves in an unwavering course for the coast.

Hannah heard someone yell and looked up to see a sailor atop the crows nest shouting something at the captain while pointing behind them. The captain turned and used his binoculars, then barked more orders.

Hannah went to the side of the ship and scanned the horizon. A ship. Distant, but under full steam and closing. The British had found them. She was grateful the sun was finally gone, the gray of dusk quickly enfolding them in its grasp, making them more difficult to see. But would complete darkness come quickly enough to prevent their capture?

Hannah could see the captain just above her, his jaw set like granite, the steel gray of his eyes glinting with expectation of the chase. This was no a quitter. He would get them to shore, one way or the other.

Hannah watched as the British ship closed the distance in a desperate attempt to catch them before dark. The schooner veered neither left nor right. There would be no frustrated, last-ditch, fruitless effort to lose their pursuer. The Schooner had only one goal—the shores of Palestine—and every inch of sail was stretched to its limits to make it happen.

Hannah prayed as she watched the distance between the ships close to frighteningly small proportions. They would never make it. Though the land was growing larger with each passing second, though the night was collapsing around them like an avalanche, the British were close enough to use their powerful lights and keep them in their sights, their bright rays glancing off sail and wood and revealing everything and everyone it touched.

She ducked as it swept across the decks then blinked off, the shout of a distant loudspeaker reverberating over the water.

"Hail the schooner," came the metallic-sounding voice. "Lower sail and prepare to be boarded by Her Majesty's Navy!"

Hannah felt sick inside and glanced up at the captain, who was now just a dark shadow against a sky quickly filling with stars. He made no attempt to answer, gave no order to lower sails, his eyes fixed on where they were going, the schooner flying across the water in a desperate attempt to get them there.

Hannah turned and squinted into the dark gray of night. There were even darker shadows of the shoreline and they were close but she could not tell how close. A half mile? A thousand yards? Possibly a good swimmer could get there from here if they tried, but for tired and sick refugees it was too much. They would drown. So close, and yet so far away.

She felt sick at heart as she heard the English voice bark another command. The tone was more threatening this time, but the captain did not respond, keeping his ship on a straight and steady course for shore. He was trying to buy time, trying to get them close enough for survival. He was trying to give them a chance.

The explosion of cannons carried across the water, then there was a splash across the bow. As the powerful searchlight flashed across the ship's masts and deck, illuminating the sea beyond, Hannah could see that the schooner had gotten them close, very close to shore. Then she saw the small craft in the water. She blinked as if they might be a mirage, an illusion, but they were real. Little ships bobbing with people yelling something she couldn't hear.

The captain's voice sounded behind her and she turned.

"Get them overboard! Now!" He yelled a second time. "You are here! Now you must go!"

Hannah's heart pounded to action and she ran down the stairs yelling the order while grabbing Beth.

"We can't swim!" yelled one.

"It's suicide!" said another.

But others scrambled out and Hannah heard the splashes as they went over the edge and hit the water.

"There are boats! Small boats, waiting for us!" she yelled. "They will save us! We must go! Now!"

Others ran past her and Rachel grabbed David's hand and was instantly up the stairs. Sarah and Anna, Emil and Lilith and their children were frozen with fear.

"Lilith cannot jump," Emil said sadly. "We must stay."

"And Sarah! She will surely drown!" said Anna. "Her foot, she will never be able to stay above water!" Her voice was desperate with fear and anguish. They were so close and now they could not go!

Hannah watched as the last of the others passed her and went upstairs. There was screaming and hollering, the pounding of the British ship's motors and the wailing of its sirens as it saw what was happening and desperately tried to close and prevent their escape. Suddenly Lilith got to her feet.

"I cannot go back, Emil! I refuse to go to another camp! We must try!" She started for the door, and Emil quickly caught up as both disappeared above deck.

"Come on Sarah," said Anna with new resolve, "I promise it will be all right. I will take care of you! Haven't I always?"

The two companions slid out of the bunk and as quickly as they could, hobbled up the stairs. Hannah followed with Beth and hurried to the edge, thankful to see that the sailors had lowered the ladders. Emil was helping Lilith over the side and as she started down he quickly joined her as Hannah peered into the water. She could see people swimming to endless small boats dotting the waves. Oarsmen were desperately trying to position their boats, and others pulled in swimmers or dove in after them. There were so many! So many trying to help them! It lifted her resolve. They could do this!

Beth was shaking and Hannah knelt down. "We can do it, honey," she said. "There are many boats and people anxious to help us."

"But I can't swim."

Hannah noticed that the British boat was coming to the side of the now-drifting schooner. They were about to board.

Hannah heard a voice and looked over the edge. It was Rachel. She was in a small boat, soaking wet but safe, David next to her, both looking up.

"Jump Hannah! Jump!"

"Beth, look, it's Rachel. She will get you if you go down the ropes. Now! Hurry!"

Beth nodded then climbed over the edge and started down. She seemed to take forever. Hannah kept one eye on her while moving to help Sarah and Anna. "Anna, you go first. The soldiers are almost aboard the ship and they will never let us go free. This is home. We must go! NOW!"

Anna climbed over the rail, put her back against it and launched herself away from the edge. She landed in the water and two men immediately went after her. Hannah helped Sarah climb as Rachel reached Beth and pulled her into the boat. She glanced over her shoulder and saw a British soldier come aboard, then another, then they were pouring over the edge, grappling with the sailors.

"Go, honey, go!" she said to Sarah.

Sarah jumped. Hannah didn't see her land. She was grabbed from behind. She broke free and ran along the edge of the rail. She was grabbed again, broke free again, ran further! She was near the front of the boat now but had no time to climb. She planted a foot and lunged over the rail. She felt her foot hit the rail and throw her trajectory off balance. She plummeted straight down, her head hitting something protruding from the side of the boat. Blackness engulfed her as she heard screams, a man hollering her name! She hit the water as unconsciousness swept over her and the heavy liquid pulled her down to the sandy bottom of the sea.

CHAPTER 16

The light filtered in around the edges of Hannah's vision, then brightened until it hurt her head. She put up a hand to ward it off and it suddenly dimmed.

She blinked several times at the figure who leaned over her, tried to focus, kept trying until she saw him.

She blinked. It could not be.

Then she blinked again.

She must still be unconscious. A dream.

"Hi," he said smiling that great smile.

"Ephraim?"

He leaned down and kissed her lightly on the forehead, water dripping from his hair. "You scared the daylights out of me for a minute. You sank like a rock. Had a devil of a time getting a hand on you."

She tried to sit up, and he helped her.

"What . . . how . . . you can't be here! This is . . . this is . . . Have I died and gone to heaven?" She grabbed him and pulled him close, his warmth caressing her until she thought she would melt. She pulled back long enough to look at him again, to make sure that knock on the head hadn't given her hallucinations!

She pushed his wet hair back from his forehead. "It is you," she said softly. "It really is you."

He smiled. "Can you get up?" She nodded, then he stood and gave her a hand.

"We have to get moving. The British will have their land patrols here any minute!" The man speaking was standing at Ephraim's side now, anxious to get away.

"Where . . . where is Beth, Rachel, the others . . ." she said looking desperately around her.

"They are already on their way," Ephraim said. "We'll see them later. Come on." They ran up the beach, Hannah leaning heavily on Ephraim, her head still pounding and causing a little dizziness. He stopped to let her catch her breath and she looked back to see the schooner outlined in the light of the British ship. There were no more small boats in the water. All were on shore and quickly being hauled to trucks across the beach.

When they reached the trucks she saw the captain of the ship, who helped her climb aboard.

"I hope you don't mind a gentile guest for a few months," he smiled. "Seems like a better option than prison."

Hannah gave him a smile. He ran to the next truck and climbed aboard as Ephraim joined her, and their truck sped off the beach and onto a dirt road. A few minutes later they were in the foothills of the Carmel range.

Hannah couldn't take her eyes off him and held tightly to his hand. "You are here," she said softly again. "How can this be?"

"I flew in more than a week ago," he smiled. "I made contact with the Hagannah and told them who I was, and about you. They were trying to locate you, but I had them looking in the wrong place. The last word I had was that you were still in Salzburg. In the meantime I've been meeting every ship, hoping that somehow you had found a way out."

Someone handed them a blanket and Ephraim quickly flung it around their shivering bodies. The air was warm but its movement chilled their wet clothes. As they snuggled close, Hannah felt her heart would surely burst. He had come back to her.

The thought made her tingle all over. She felt like a heavy weight had been lifted from her shoulders, the past disappearing in a jumble of expectation and hope. She would never let him go again. Never. As the truck traveled through the hills she looked up at the stars, then at the shadows of the mountains around them. Israel. She took in the smell of it, the wonder. The land of her forefathers. The land of David, the home of Jesus, her Messiah. Now it was her land.

She closed her eyes and thanked God as she squeezed Ephraim's arm. The past no longer seemed to matter. They would make a new beginning here. A new life.

"Hannah Gruen," Ephraim said in her ear. "Will you marry me?"

Hannah felt the tears spring to the corner of her eyes, forcing her to bite her lip for control.

"Will you?" he asked again.

"Yes," she said. "Yes."

She had finally come home.

EPILOGUE

Hannah was baptized a member of The Church of Jesus Christ of Latter-day Saints by Ephraim Daniels on May 15, 1946. Delwin Osgood and Matthew Baker, members from Provo, Utah, studying archaeology for a few months in Jerusalem, acted as witnesses. Others baptized that day included Elizabeth Derzhinsky, born January 6, 1938 in Kielce Poland, and David Schwartz, also age eight and recently of Berlin, Germany. Permission for the baptisms was granted by Church leaders in Salt Lake City in a letter dated February 1, 1946. Included in the letter were congratulations to Ephraim and Hannah Daniels on their marriage, dated January 22, 1946, and a brief statement of policy concerning their sealing to be completed on the same date of 1947. Papers were enclosed that would expedite that ceremony, as well as the adoption of David and Elizabeth under the laws of the United States, effectively making them citizens of that country.

Illegal immigration continued to move forward and thousands came to Israel, even as the British, their policy more intransigent than ever, interned others on the island of Cyprus, or forced them to stay in Europe. Those who were successful in evading British policy and rough seas would be badly needed in the storm gathering on the horizon over their promised land. Hannah, Ephraim, and their new family found themselves caught up in that storm, but in January 1947 they all flew to the United States for a temple sealing. They returned in March to find their country in turmoil. War was inevitable and the Jews, outnumbered, sorely underarmed, and badly equipped would need the determination born of their ordeal in the camps to survive another attempt to annihilate them as a people.

CHAPTER NOTES

PART ONE—THE SURVIVORS
CHAPTER ONE

At the end of the war, the Nazis continued to try and eliminate the Jews. As the allies overran their camps, they marched thousands of prisoners further inland to different ones in an attempt to continue extermination. Hundreds died on these forced marches, either shot by frustrated guards anxious to get to safety, or suffering death from exposure or sheer exhaustion. A few escaped, but they were the exception, rather than the rule.

Hannah's story is based in fact. Trains were used and prisoners died like flies as the Nazis scrambled to hide the evidence of their atrocities from advancing allied troops and the ever-present fighter planes of allied forces.

Representatives of The Jewish Agency (the presiding body of the Jews before they became a state) ordered the compilation of lists of survivors as soon as the allies permitted and were prepared to help. Such lists were used to try and find family members. Though inaccurate at first, eventually they became important to determining just how horrible the Nazi atrocities had become. Happily they were also a prime source for reuniting families.

As early as January 1943, even though it had been announced by the United Nations that more than two million Jews had been killed, a public opinion poll reported that less than half of the citizens of the United States believed the announcement. In 1945 when the war ended, seventy-five percent of the citizenry of the United States believed the Nazis had murdered many people, but most gave figures of less than 100,000. Even when the camps were entered by allied forces, the median figure was still a million or less. Most simply could not comprehend the genocide.

CHAPTER TWO

Most Jewish survivors were afraid to return to their homes, were refused the right to return, or simply did not want to return. As one writer states, "For many refugees, it was a miracle that they had survived. . . . They had seen their families murdered, or brutally kicked into Wehrmacht trucks bound for liquidation. They had been betrayed by those they considered friends and neighbors. They had been starved, hunted, and systematically humiliated. Many were unable to speak about what they had been through. Why should they want to return? (Morris Beckman, *The Jewish Brigade, An Army with Two Masters, 1944–45*, Sarpedon Press, 38).

However, some did make the attempt. "Henry Ohrenstein had survived four concentration camps and two death marches. At the end of the war, he did make his way back to his hometown, Hubricszow in Poland. Of the 8,000 Jews who had lived in the town, he found only five. The Poles who had taken over Jewish homes and property were worried that their rightful owners might have survived, and would return to claim what was rightfully theirs. Ohrenstein was told that three Jews did come out of hiding in the forests and claimed their homes back. The Poles solved the problem by killing them" (Beckman, 41). Ohrenstein left Poland and never returned. Scores of similar examples exist.

The Jews wandered Europe, waiting for justice at the hands of their rescuers. Instead they were left in camps while the general populace of Europe, those who had tacitly consented to their murder and even participated, were left alone. Governments played political games and though they brought some of the worst Nazis to trial, thousands simply melted into the chaos of postwar Europe and were never caught. How could Jews live in such a place? Most couldn't. They wanted out. It is a blight on the credibility of governments such as our own that more was not done to set them free, but it is also heartwarming to know that, as depicted in this story, the average GI helped when he could.

CHAPTER THREE

The fact that LDS soldiers participated in the war, on both sides, is well documented. A recent book put out by Covenant Communications called *Saints at War* is a great resource for documenting who some of them were and what their experience was like. However, I have never found a real-life example quite like Ephraim Daniels.

Entire books have been written about the Werewolf movement. I recommend *The Last Nazis, SS Werewolf Guerilla Resistance in Europe, 1944-1947,* by Perry Biddiscombe.

The underground movement was created to harass the allies while the Nazi leadership regrouped and prepared for another offensive. As Biddiscombe states, "The SS Werewolf organization served as the original model, which throughout 1944–45 sprouted numerous extensions and parallels as various bodies within the Third Reich sought to participate. In a manner typical of the internal organization of the Nazi regime, none of the bureaucratic sprawl was either integrated or coordinated . . . the collapsing Third Reich was a chaos of conflicting personalities, some determined to resist, others eager to compromise with the enemy, others content to drift aimlessly among the shifting currents" (19). The overall policy became one of "scorched earth," the destruction of domestic traitors and generally making life unbearable for occupying troops. But because of the chaotic organization, different groups made different decisions; one assassinating those whom they considered collaborators, while others blew up railroads, and still others had skirmishes with allied troops. Some shot German soldiers who were unwilling to fight any longer, even hanging them from lampposts as traitors, butchered fleeing innocents, and even made deals with the allies for protection. Because of this fragmentation, the Werewolf movement never materialized into any significant opposition although isolated cells continued for years. The most noted of these was the ODESSA (Organization of Ex Members of the SS), a clandestine organization set up to funnel money to Nazi leaders for escape, or to protect those who remained, ostensibly to prepare for the next Reich.

CHAPTER FOUR

The most powerful debilitating feelings survivors had to overcome were based in the guilt and shame of being a survivor. Many times, survival required men and women, even children, to do shameful things to others. They stole bread from the dying, took clothes from the dead, and even acted as kapos for the Germans, beating other Jews mercilessly in order to get more food and to keep from being sent to die themselves. Some removed the gold fillings from the dead or from skeletons, melting them into bars to be shipped off to Berlin to help feed the voracious war machine of the Reich. Such actions destroyed a person's feeling that they could ever be accepted again. After all, if they could not stand to live with themselves how could others?

Ella LingenReiner states in her book, *Prisoners of Fear,* "How was I able to survive in Auschwitz? My principle is: I come first, second and third. Then nothing, then again I; and then all others."

Kitty Hart, in her book, *Return to Auschwitz,* recalls: "Promotion was much easier if you could prove yourself a bully and a willing murderer along Nazi lines. Most of the great complex of Auschwitz and Birkenau was in fact run by the prisoners themselves, and it was hideous to see how readily one of your own people would turn against you in return for a few privileges . . . Some were as proud of their armbands . . . as of a military decoration . . ." When such people survived, the nightmares lingered for years, even a lifetime. Many took their own lives.

It was the innocent who usually died first. Kitty Hart remembers, "During the first six weeks many of the newcomers died, usually from shock. Large numbers of them from foreign countries had been literally seized in their homes, transported in appalling conditions to this distant camp, and thrown into the horror of it without warning. Mother and I had gone through what you might call an apprenticeship; on the run, in the ghetto, and in prison. Nothing could ever again take us entirely by surprise. We were hardened by now. But not so the dazed, stricken Jews of remote lands . . . they went down like flies . . . and received little sympathy from their camp hardened peers."

CHAPTER FIVE
The Jewish Brigade was the only military unit to serve in the British Army as an independent, national Jewish military formation.

The Brigade was made up of mainly Jews from Palestine and had its own emblem. The establishment of the Brigade was the final result of the Zionists' desire to participate in the fight against the Nazis.

Because of his fear that acceptance of such a unit would legitimatize the Jewish yearning for a national home, then Prime Minister Neville Chamberlain did not favor such a unit. As a result, symbols of Jewish nationalism were discouraged. Winston Churchill was much more pro-Jewish as more and more information about the Nazi holocaust came to light, but it was not until 1944, after six years of prolonged negotiations, that the Brigade finally came into existence as a single entity.

After training in Egypt, the Brigade, made up of approximately five thousand soldiers, participated in the final battles against the Nazis along the Italian Front. The brigade was finally stationed in northeast Italy in the month of May 1945 where they came into contact with Jewish survivors of the holocaust and began a miraculous effort to save as many as they could.

As the British government became more determined to stop immigration out of fear of offending Arab sensibilities and thereby losing their grip on the last great bastion of British imperial rule, they sent the Brigade to northern Europe, then disbanded them in the summer of 1946. However, this did not halt their efforts. They continued to send truckloads of refugees into Italy, or to help them reach the Mossad's Bricha agents, who then arranged removal. It should be noted that this was often tacitly assented to by British officers who disagreed with their country's policy.

The skills obtained by members of the Brigade were put to use in Israel's War of Independence and in preparation for that war, which is the subject of Book Two in this series.

CHAPTER SEVEN

The Christian response to what was happening to the Jews was mixed. Pope Pius XII has been accused of doing too little. Some strongly believe that he could have saved many more lives and even halted the extermination altogether had he chosen to take a public stand and confront the Germans—even threaten Hitler, Goebbels, and other Nazi Catholics with excommunication. At the very least, some argue, a public denunciation over Vatican radio would have shown mankind what was happening in the concentration camps of the eastern portions of Hitler's domain. Such actions were never taken, and as a consequence many Catholics in Germany believed that the church was supportive of the Fascist movement.

Most writers on the subject believe as Gunther Lewy and John Snoek. "Whether a papal decree of excommunication against Hitler would have dissuaded Hitler from carrying out his plan to destroy the Jews is doubtful. . . . However, a flaming protest against the massacre of the Jews, coupled with an imposition of the interdict upon all of Germany, or the excommunication of all Catholics in any way involved with the apparatus of the 'Final Solution' would have been a more formidable weapon. This was precisely the kind of action the Pope would not take . . ." (Bard, 446).

As Bard also states that, toward the end of World War II, "The most important escape route, the so-called "monastery route" between Austria and Italy, came into being. Roman Catholic priests, especially Franciscans, helped ODESSA channel its fugitives from one monastery to the next, until they were received by the Caritas organization in Rome. Best known was a monastery on Via Sicilia in Rome . . . which became a veritable transit camp for Nazi criminals. The man who organized this hideout was no less than a bishop and came from Graz: in his memoirs Alois Hudal subsequently boasted of the many top people from the Third Reich to whom he had been able to render 'humanitarian aide.'

"It is difficult to guess the motives of these priests. . . . It seems probable that the Church was divided: into priests and members of the religious orders who had recognized Hitler as the Antichrist and therefore practiced Christian charity, and those who viewed the Nazis as a power of order in the struggle against the decline of morality and Bolshevism. The former probably helped the Jews during the war, and the latter hid the Nazis when it was over" (Bard, 375).

Protestant reaction in Germany was not much better. As another author states, "The German churches were constrained by their history . . . most had supported Hitler's anti-Weimar appeals against godless Jewish Bolshevism . . . After coming to power the Nazis quickly created the 'German Christians,' which mixed folkish ideas with elements of the traditional Church, complete with racial clauses. . . . Although

Hitler ultimately intended to do away with Christianity, he was careful to hide his intentions for fear of provoking popular resistance early on. Many Church leaders were fooled by his pious facade, and thousands of Berliners flocked to the new Nazi faith" (Richie, 540).

The lack of any firm stand against Hitler by the major Christian religions of Germany gave the average member of the faith a clear conscience in their support of him. Though "Individual Christians rendered practical help . . . only a small minority of the Protestant and Orthodox Christians in occupied Europe risked their lives on behalf of the persecuted Jews" (Bard, 447).

Some German members of The Church of Jesus Christ of Latter-day Saints were supportive of the Hitler regime, and even preached their support from the pulpit, general instructions to the contrary. Max Zimmer, President of the Swiss Mission, says that the presiding brethren in the West German Mission were asking the Saints "to pray for the führer in their meetings and in their homes and regard him as a divinely called man who would prepare the world for the 'United Order.' Attempts were made to harmonize Hitlerism with Church doctrine and even to prove that the Nazi party was organized after the pattern of the Church . . ." (*Church News*, Nov. 24, 1945). Like many of their Catholic and Protestant countrymen, they would come to realize they had made a serious miscalculation, but by then many of them had given their lives or been devastated by material, physical, and economic losses. Nearly eighty-five percent of all Saints in Germany alone lost their homes.

I should point out that there were some instances of members supporting Nazi anti-Semitism, but they were the exception and not the rule. Arthur Zander, a branch president, was also a member of the Nazi party and displayed a sign outside the chapel that said "Jews are not allowed to enter." Apparently such men could serve two masters or were afraid of what might happen to their flock if they did not bow to the Gestapo in a visible manner. Because of Zander's new policy, one member, Salomon Schwarz, who was considered to be Jewish by members of the branch was no longer welcome, but the Barmbek branch took him in. Unfortunately, even though brother Schwarz was not Jewish he looked to be of that race and was eventually sent to Auschwitz (Holmes-Keele, 26–27).

Friedrich Peters recalls helping Jews. " . . . [In] about 1939–40 the North German Refinery approached our church, because they were very concerned about their Jewish employees. Under the aegis of our system for taking care of our members, we helped the Jews of the North German Refinery by—mostly at night when the streets were empty—loading their things on "Scottish carts" and then transporting them to the Hanover train station" (Holmes-Keele, 271).

In another article we read: "Most German Mormons . . . had seen many examples of the brutal treatment meted out to the Jews in the pre-war era, but they did not know about the holocaust." Some members tried to save their friends and "Max Reschke . . . rescued his Jewish friends the Scheuerenbergs, from a column being driven up the streets by armed guards and eventually got them over the Swiss border . . ." (Tobler, 85–87).

General Church leaders denounced the war from Hitler's first attacks on others, and very few months went by between 1940 and 1945 when the First Presidency did not appeal for the end of the war. However, like so many others, Church leaders heard the news of Nazi atrocities but had difficulty believing them. Therefore, no actual statement denouncing Hitler's treatment of the Jews was ever made public. For more in-depth information, read Tobler's article, "The Jews, The Mormons, and the Holocaust," in *The Journal of Mormon History*.

CHAPTER EIGHT

"When the second world war began, Berlin was its most arrogant, its most pompous, and its most dangerous. When it ended, forty-five million human beings lay dead, Europe was in turmoil, and the once prosperous capital was a ruin" (Richie, 475). When the Allied forces began the bombing of Berlin, "the air raid sirens wailed, people rushed to their shelters and waited in the cold for the distant sound of planes . . . Direct hits often crushed an entire building, trapping people under piles of smoking debris. . . . After incendiary bombs fell, rivers of phosphorous would run down the streets or drip from the shards of buildings, burning everything in their path and setting people on fire; civilians were often badly burned but there was little the overstretched hospitals could do. Even seriously wounded patients would be evacuated to the cellars, where the nurses would sit with candles burning night after night. . . . Sometimes the whole city was on fire. At times you could not differentiate between night and day. . . . Corpses were piled on street corners ready for collection but by the end there was no energy for niceties . . . (Richie, 529–533). Tens of thousands of people died in the two years after the end of the war.

The Russians got to Berlin first and laid waste to it. Stalin then ordered the city looted. He saw all German possessions as "reparations" for everything stolen or destroyed by the Germans on their march eastward.

Hitler, Goering, Goebbels, Himmler and many others had come into possession of huge collections of art stolen during the war. Working with Swiss art dealers they sold impressionist art (which Hitler said was decadent) or traded it for that which was more acceptable, usually the old masters of Europe, especially Germany. Hitler refused to let these works of art be taken out of Berlin until it was nearly too late. As a result, the communists of the Soviet Union discovered most of them and sent them east. Stalin wanted to create his own super-museum in Moscow. For a brief list of millions of dollars worth of such works found, see *A History of Berlin* by Richie, 610–14.

Americans were not beyond culpability either. Trials of American soldiers caught stealing such treasures from Germany were held and some convictions achieved, but many soldiers smuggled paintings and other items out of Germany without repercussions. Even today there is some dispute about what generals requisitioned for the homes and headquarters in Germany after the war and why some of those items "disappeared." However, any acts of theft by western allies was small compared to that of the Russians. The Americans, French, and British were kept out of Berlin for more than two months after its capture so that the looting could be accomplished without interference. Most of Berlin's wealth was in Moscow by the time the Western allies arrived.

More important, the intentional delay of allied troops gave Stalin more time to put in place German communists to run the city. As Richie states, by the time the allies arrived, "Every important organization in every district of Berlin, including those ear-marked for American and British occupation, was now under Soviet control."

By the time the western allies arrived, "The German capital was in a far worse condition than any . . . expected . . . . Far from being put on its feet it had been stripped, ransacked and terrorized, and all who saw it were affected by the sight of the hideous wreckage and the grim, starving people who greeted them" (Richie, 629, 631). The treatment of women by the Russians is notorious. They were raped incessantly, forced into work details, and generally treated in a sadistic manner. It was not until 1947 that there was a call for a concerted effort to improve "honor and dignity" among Russian soldiers in Germany. By then the damage had been done. Venereal disease was rampant, and the birth of illegitimate children very high.

Because of the conduct of the Russian troops, the Western allies were received as liberators and soon floods of refugees began flowing into their sectors looking for food and help, nearly overwhelming them. It would be from this mass of humanity that the Americans, French, and British would find new leadership with which to rebuild Germany, but it would not be an easy task. In fact, as the Russians saw that the German people were more receptive of western democracy, they did everything within their power to force their former allies out of the city. Their efforts would culminate in the great airlift to save liberated Berlin just a few years later. After that unsuccessful attempt to starve the west out of Berlin, the Russians dug in and cut off relations—an act that led to the division of Berlin and the beginning of the cold war.

CHAPTER THIRTEEN

From 1933 to 1936, as things worsened in Europe, 174,000 Jews went to Palestine, most of them accepted legally by the British. As a result of this influx, tensions between Jews and Arabs escalated and Arab attacks on the Jewish population took place. The British reaction to a displeased Arab community was a renewed imposition of restrictions on immigration that turned a flood into a trickle.

The MacDonald White Paper of May of 1939 set a total quota of only 75,000 immigrants for the following five years. With the promulgation of this White Paper, growing danger from Hitler's new policies toward the Jews, and the threat of all-out war, the Zionist leadership declared illegal immigration the primary means for opening the gates of Israel to their people. On the eve of World War II, the Hagannah established the Mossad LeAliyah Bet (illegal immigration), which became the main body involved in bringing Jews to Israel.

Because of their efforts, by the end of 1939 thousands more Jews had been brought to Palestine, most of them illegally, but many more thousands were left behind. Even as word of ghetto atrocities and pogroms reached London, the British refused to increase quotas and even sent some captured illegal vessels back to their places of origin. Because of this continued intransigence based on the premise that the Arabs would declare war on Britain, thousands of Jews who could have been saved ended up in the death camps of Hitler.

During the war, some sixteen thousand illegal immigrants arrived by sea and another 4,000 by land. This immigration was conducted under the most tragic circumstances, but it demonstrated the resolve of the Yishuv to bring the immigrants to Palestine, and the fierce desire of the immigrants themselves to reach the country. Illegal immigration in this period laid the foundation for the great waves of post-war illegal immigration.

"From the end of World War II until the establishment of Israel (1945–48), illegal immigration was the major method of immigration, because the British, by setting the quota at a mere 18,000 per year, virtually terminated the option of legal immigration. Sixty-six illegal immigration sailings were organized during these years, but only a few managed to penetrate the British blockade and bring their passengers ashore. The British stopped the vessels carrying immigrants and interned the captured immigrants in camps . . ." (MFA article, p. 6 of 10). Even when the world community demanded change they turned a deaf ear—a condition that would remain or worsen until May 14, 1948, when the State of Israel was proclaimed.

It was the Mossad, under the direct authority of the Hagannah, the Jewish underground Army in Palestine, who continued to organize illegal immigration from Europe. Their main offices were in Paris, France, but they sent agents (usually drawn from remnants of the Zionist and pioneering youth movements, former Jewish partisans and ghetto fighters who struggled against Hitler) into all areas where an organized escape needed arranging. They were known as the *Bricha*, or escape, and their job was formidable.

In May 1945, the Merkaz Hagolah (Diaspora Center) was established in Italy to help smuggle refugees out who found their way to that country. They worked closely with Bricha and with the Jewish

Brigade, but the movement would not be able to reach into the heart of Germany and Austria for several months. Refugees strong enough to make the journey came to them, but most waited for rescue in Displaced Persons camps. Those who managed to get to Italy were put aboard ships bound for Palestine as soon as such vessels were available. Until then the Brigade and Mossad-Bricha built facilities where they could recuperate. The very worst ones were put in hospitals.

The United States immigration policy was not much better than that of the British. Little was done to increase immigration quotas to the United States before, during, and after the war. Though Truman sent representatives to view the conditions in 1945, he did not send a bill to congress until 1947. It did not pass. It wasn't until after the declaration of the official creation of the State of Israel by the United Nations that Congress finally passed a bill increasing immigration quotas from Europe. Unfortunately it had heavy anti-Semitic overtones that were not removed until 1950. Truman did strongly encourage the British to allow greater immigration to Palestine, but nothing more than a committee ever came of the recommendation.

It should be emphasized once again that some British soldiers who were still in Germany, Austria, and Italy did not agree with their governments' policy and many helped the Jews escape to French and Italian ports, from which vessels carrying illegal immigrants set sail for the coast of Palestine. Such men have been named "righteous Gentiles" by many Jews, and rightly so.

CHAPTER FIFTEEN

The involvement of German Industry in the Nazi war machine is well documented. Before the war began, industrialists donated millions of Reichsmarks to Hitler as he attempted to get elected and then throw out the Weimar Republic's leadership. Without their support the Nazi party simply would not have come to power.

During the war, German industrialists availed themselves of the "free" labor concentration camps offered. "The names of . . . prominent German firms appeared regularly in the SS records. . . . These included the aircraft companies like Messerschmidt, Junkers and Heinkel, automobile companies like BMW, and Daimler Benz, munitions companies like Dynamit Nobel, and the electric companies, Siemens, AEG and Telefunken" (Bard, 163). IG Farben, a chemical and pharmaceutical company, of which BAYER corporation had been the cornerstone, was one of the most noted companies. They had located a plant next to Auschwitz. The list goes on and on.

In recent years the news has been filled with reports about lawsuits brought against German companies that exploited slave labor during World War II. As one author states, "Contemporary scholars are continuing to learn about the extent to which Siemens, and every major German business in the thirties and forties, was implicated in the brutality of Nazi economic policies, most egregiously through the abuse of forced and slave laborers. Siemens ran factories at Ravensbrück and in the Auschwitz subcamp of Bobrek, among others, and the company supplied electrical parts to other concentration and death camps. In the camp factories, abysmal living and working conditions were ubiquitous; malnutrition and death were not uncommon. Recent scholarship has established how, despite German industry's repeated denials, these camp factories were created, run, and supplied by the SS *in conjunction with* company officials—sometimes high level employees" (Anti-Defamation League article, "German Industry and the Third Reich: Fifty years of Forgetting and Remembering," by S. Jonathan Wiesen).

Finally, Wiesen states, "Some businessmen, it is true, resisted the demands of the Nazi regime; some, like Oskar Schindler, protected Jews; some even allied themselves with the anti-Nazi underground. But there were relatively few such people. Greed drove all too many 'apolitical businessmen' to engage in odious conduct. . . . Undoubtedly, latent and overt anti-Semitism, anti-Slavic sentiments, and German nationalism also allowed some . . . to work with the regime out of a sense of patriotism, and without ever reflecting upon the moral boundaries they were crossing."

By the time the Third Reich went down in a blaze of ignominious defeat the industrialists had already taken steps to protect their profits and seek new leadership. However, most didn't escape the wrath of Allied bombs and Russian dismantlement of their factories which were shipped back to Russia where they would either be reconstituted or rust into decay.

CHAPTER EIGHTEEN

German soldiers were often sent to Siberia for slave labor, and thousands died there. One such case was Karl Heinze Schnibbe, a German member of the Church, who had been convicted of treason along with Helmuth Huebner, and another friend, Rudi Wobbe. Schnibbe's story is ironic. Convicted of treason he was sent to prison then taken to the front lines to fight the Russians in the last year of the war. He was captured and then sent to Siberia but was lucky enough to be one of the few who were eventually sent home. You can read his story in his book, *The Price*, printed by Bookcraft in 1984.

CHAPTER NINETEEN

The poem by Franta Bass is real as is its place of discovery. She did not survive the war. The art of the holocaust is documented on Internet sites and in museums. The picture described above was one painted by Leo Hass, who is similar to but certainly not the same as our character, Leo Krueger. Terezin was a real place and one of the propaganda successes of the Nazis. They convinced many wealthy Jews to purchase a place there with the belief that they would be safe and have special privileges. It was all a ruse and, eventually, nearly all who paid to go to Terezin were sent to death camps.

CHAPTER TWENTY

Of the Church at the end of the war we read the following: "By the end of 1944 the situation became desperate. . . . The members of the Church on account of the extension of the war are scattered in every direction, yet we maintain connections with them. . . . The attendance at our meetings has been drastically reduced . . . many of the brethren over fifty and under are being called to save the Fatherland. Reason is now insanity." Later in the same book we read, "The LDS losses in Germany were staggering during this tragic war. Almost every meeting hall of the Church was destroyed. . . . . In the East German Mission about 400 LDS soldiers and 50 civilians were killed. In the West German Mission, 150 members lost their lives, most of them soldiers. Three acting German Mission presidents were among the more than 600 Mormons who died . . . Included were also three district presidents . . . Yet the total number of Mormons in

Germany decreased only slightly during the war years, with 12,000 saints remaining. There had been sixty baptisms a year during the first half of the 1940's" (Scharffs, 116).

"When the war was over the first contact the German saints had with any American members was with the U.S. servicemen. (Missionaries from Church headquarters were not allowed into Germany for another three and one-half years.) Within three months after surrender, joint meetings were being held by Mormon occupation troops and German Saints. In many cases it was a tearful reunion with former missionaries who had served in the land that was now almost devastated. One of the first encounters occurred in Berlin, August 19, 1945" (Scharffs, 119). As you can see I have taken some license with the date. Ephraim and the mission president hold their meeting in June.

I have already referred to the story of Karl Schnibbe, Helmuth Huebner, and Rudi Wobbe. The quote from the pamphlet is exact as is the description of their fate. As Scharffs says in his book, "This incident caused more fear and anxiety among the members than . . . any other. . . . District President (Otto) Berndt was questioned for three days about the printing incident, but was released when he convinced the Gestapo that the Church was not involved in this crime. The books of the branches were constantly investigated by the Nazis. Members of the Church in the entire Hamburg area were in a state of near panic, fearing arrests at any moment because members of the court had said that these boys must have been inspired by their parents and leaders"(Scharffs, 103–104).

Unfortunately, all members did not view Huebner's act as heroic. As Scharffs says, "On the Sunday following the boy's execution, the mother and the grandmother of the slain Mormon attended a service in one of the Hamburg branches." Though the Saints had been cautioned not to say anything, one lady refused to keep silent, saying, "If I had a rifle, I would have shot him myself" (Scharffs, 104). Another sign that the Saints were frightened of the reaction of the Nazis is the excommunication of Huebner by worried Hamburg officials. Of course, the excommunication was accomplished by Arthur Zander, a Nazi, who was upset at Huebner's fight against the regime, so the motivation for the court may have been created by more than fear. The excommunication was reversed by action of leaders in Salt Lake City in 1948.

CHAPTER TWENTY–ONE

"De-Nazification and de-militarization policies were introduced with the intention of tracking down the worst Nazi criminals, but these proved inadequate and many thousands of important Nazis evaded justice. The task was made more difficult by the fact that most Nazis simply disappeared at the end of the war. Martha Brixus, a German, remembered: 'It was extremely embarrassing. No one was part of it any more. It happened very quickly. They suddenly were dressed differently, all uniforms gone, no insignia at all, and they'd all been "forced." . . . The turnabout happened so fast, it was a joke. I never saw anything like it. Even the Communist Otto Ackermann complained that given the way the Germans carried on after the war 'one would think that 90 per cent of them had been in the resistance'" (Richie, 634).

Nazis doctored their pasts and assumed false identities, either for purposes of escape, especially in the cases of well known leaders, or for the purpose of melting into the populace to avoid prosecution or, in some cases, to be put in place for a future revival of the fascist system. The intelligence organizations tried to ferret out such people but the process was nearly impossible. Only with the help of the citizenry were they successful, and the citizens of Germany were either directly involved or were not anxious to admit they even knew such people for fear of being tainted themselves.

And the allies were not beyond using former Nazis to rebuild a devastated Europe, especially the Russians. Nazi leadership, those who served directly under them, and those directly involved in camps, especially the death camps, were imprisoned when found, but many others in middle government were recycled into positions necessary for restructuring Germany. The allies considered it a "necessary evil."

Some very big fish did escape. Knowing the end was near, Eichmann, Bormann, Mengele, and many others disappeared. As mentioned earlier, the most noted organization for helping Nazis escape was the ODESSA (Organization of the Ex-Members of the SS). Argentina became the final destination of most of these men and many others. The German community in that country harbored them, and their lives there have become the subject of books and movies.

CHAPTER TWENTY–TWO

The crimes by industry depicted in this chapter are based in research. Even American industries were involved, usually without their knowledge.

"In the early days of May 1945 a special department of the Reichsbank, which administered booty from concentration camps, sent several crates of 'dental gold' to Aussee in the northwestern corner of Syria, dubbed the 'Alpine Redoubt' by Joseph Goebbels, Nazi propaganda minister. When the Redoubt was taken, the Nazi bigwigs were desperately retrieving the treasure they had hidden there." It is probable that the money was sent to accounts in Swiss banks.

"All in all, the fortune which the Nazis managed to hide and stow away is estimated at roughly four billion gold marks.

"Who was able to dispose of these monies, whose signature authorized the withdrawal of funds from accounts in Switzerland, Spain or Argentina—these are some of the yet unsolved secrets of the Third Reich" (Bard, 374). Some of these funds were controlled by those who created the escape route. Others were apparently controlled by men like Bormann, Eichmann, and Mengele.

Where did the money come from? Many think that political and religious considerations were the only motivation for the killing of the Jews. In reality that was not the case. "There was always the lure of the art treasures which might be stolen from Germany's neighbors. And it was never just a case of exterminating the Jewish race, but also one of Aryanizing Jewish assets, plundering Jewish homes, and prying gold from the teeth of Jews after they had been gassed . . ." (Bard, 374).

CHAPTER TWENTY–FOUR

When the Western allies entered Berlin, Stalin and his leaders did little to prevent incursions by Russian troops into sectors controlled by the French, British, and Americans. The American MPs were then forced to send them back and, on occasion, violence erupted.

As the animosity between east and west grew, the Soviets shut off communications and began to terrorize the population through a puppet East German police department. They kidnapped thousands as Soviet control intensified. Killings followed, and concentration camps reopened. The treatment of prisoners was brutal. By Christmas 1946 there were 16,000 prisoners in Buchenwald alone. After torture they were either executed or sent to the Soviet Gulag in Siberia. "In 1990 Bonn's Ministry for Intra-German relations estimated that over 240,000 Berliners and eastern Germans passed through the special camps in the years following the war." The Americans began protecting vulnerable Germans in the western sector, and when armed Russians entered and tried to seize Berliners they were arrested or shot by American MPs (Richie, 652). As you can imagine, even in its early stages this was no environment in which to leave American captives.

CHAPTER TWENTY–SEVEN

The allies requisitioned property for the comfort of their troops, but the Western allies were less possessive in this vein than the Soviets. Both encouraged the return of cultural arts, but the Soviets were very restrictive about what could and could not be done, much as the Nazis had been.

Men like Andrik in the book did exist, but they were the exception and not the rule. Most of those who were in Germany and heavily involved in the arts were Nazis, all others being banished from Germany and other countries controlled by the Axis. Artists were needed to lift the spirits of the people and the allies tended to wink at those who had been Nazis, only a few being put through de-Nazification procedures. The emergence of the Soviet Union as the new enemy meant abandonment of such procedures in all cases. But the most vile criminals and former Nazis were allowed to take positions of importance in the arts once again.

As Richie states, "The worst aspect of the sudden amnesia about Nazi Berlin was a sinister backlash against those who had left Nazi Germany and who now tried to come home. Refugees removed from their posts under the Nazis were not automatically reinstated if they returned to Berlin, and great musicians were never really welcomed back to Berlin" (Richie, 707). Some were even referred to as traitors. The end result? Berlin and all Germany became a cultural quagmire for two decades and, according to some sources, even longer.

CHAPTER TWENTY–EIGHT

The war in the Pacific would go on for months. Even though many American GIs who fought in the European Theater went stateside, some were sent to fight the Japanese who had attacked Pearl Harbor after making an alliance with Hitler and his Nazi government. The Second World War would not be over until the Japanese had surrendered.

"Inevitably children were among the prisoners at highest risk. Homeless, often orphaned, they had frequently witnessed the murder of parents, siblings, and relatives. They faced starvation, illness, brutal labor, and other indignities until they were consigned to the gas chambers. In relationship to adult prisoners, their chances for survival were usually smaller although their flexibility and adaptability to radically changed circumstances could sometimes increase the odds in their favor.

"Children sometimes also survived in hiding and also participated in the resistance (as runners, messengers, smugglers)" (Bard, 184-185). Some children were secretly kept by non-Jewish families at serious risk to themselves. Stories of the survival of children are numerous, but there are many more stories of their loss.

After the war, the care of orphans, both Jewish and non-Jewish was a project of extreme proportions. By August of 1945 there were 5000 in Berlin alone, and tens of thousands across Europe. Of course, the number of Jewish orphans was much smaller for obvious reasons, but there were still hundreds, even thousands, who had to be taken care of. The children of this story are based on the experiences of those who survived against odds most of us cannot even begin to understand.

PART TWO—THE ROAD HOME

CHAPTER ONE
"Train wrecks caused by the Werewolf movement included several trains derailed in 1945. In one case the saboteur steamed up a locomotive and ran it over the side of a blasted-out overpass onto an American armored column passing below. In June, an obstruction made of logs blocked the passage of a troop train at Gennep, in the British zone, and there were mysterious train derailments on 19 July and 13 August causing nearly 130 deaths and 110 injuries" (Biddiscombe, 69).

CHAPTER SIX

"As the Allies were taking Europe back from Germany in 1944–45, their armies 'liberated' the Nazi concentration camps. These camps, which housed from a few dozen to thousands of survivors, were complete surprises for most of the liberating armies. They were overwhelmed by the misery, by the victims who were so thin and near death.

"Thousands of 'survivors' died in the days and weeks following liberation; the military buried the dead in individual and mass graves. Generally, the allied armies rounded up concentration camp victims and forced them to remain in the confines of the camp, under guard for fear they would seek revenge on the German populace.

"Medical personnel were brought into the camps to care for the victims and food supplies were provided but conditions in the camps were dismal. . . . Victims lived in their barracks, wore their camp uniforms, and were not allowed to leave the barbed-wire camps, all whilst the German population outside of the camps was able to try and return to normal life. The military reasoned that the victims could not roam the countryside in fear that they would attack civilians.

"By June, word of poor treatment of Holocaust survivors reached Washington, D.C. President Harry S. Truman, anxious to appease concerns, sent Earl G. Harrison . . . to investigate the ramshackle DP camps" (Internet article, *Displaced Jews in Europe: 1945–51*, http//geography.about.com/library/weekly /aao51898.htm). It was Harrison's recommendations that began a change in the camps. The article goes on to say, "Jews became a separate group in the camps so Polish Jews no longer had to live with the other Poles, and German Jews no longer had to live with Germans, who in some cases, were operatives or even guards in the concentration camps. DP camps were established throughout Europe and those in Italy served as congregation points for those attempting to flee to Palestine."

Hannah and her group arrived in this camp about two months before actual changes began in most camps under the direction of the American military. However, some camps had already begun the process of change because of forward-thinking commanders and UN officials in those camps. Even then, the process of revamping a camp usually took much longer, but there were exceptions. What takes place in the following chapters did occur, for the most part, in other camps and are used here to help you understand the tremendous resilience of those forced to live under such conditions.

In 1932, Elder B. H. Roberts state: "Zionism is considered to have grown out of the persecution of the Jews . . . in such European countries as Russia, France, Germany, and Romania. It held its first general conference in August, 1897, in Basle, Switzerland; and since then has continued to hold annual conferences that have steadily increased both in interest and the number of delegates representing various Jewish societies, until now it takes on the appearance of one of the world's great movements" (Joseph Smith, *History of the Church of Jesus Christ of Latter-day Saints*, 7 vols., introduction and notes by B. H. Roberts).

Elder Roberts goes on to say, "Not to persecution alone, however, is due this strange awakening desire on the part of the Jews to return to the city and the land of their fathers; but the fact of the restoration of the keys of the gathering of Israel by Moses to the Prophet of the Dispensation of the Fullness of Times. Under the divine authority restored by Moses, Joseph Smith sent an Apostle . . . to the land of Palestine to bless it and dedicate it once more to the Lord for the return of his people. This Apostle was Orson Hyde, and he performed his mission in 1840–42. In 1872 an Apostolic delegation consisting of . . . George A. Smith and Lorenzo Snow were sent to Palestine. The purpose of their mission, in part, is thus stated . . . . *When you get to the land of Palestine, we wish you to dedicate and consecrate that land to the Lord, that it may be blessed with fruitfulness, preparatory to the return of the Jews, in fulfillment of prophecy and the accomplishment of the purposes of our Heavenly Father.*

" . . . It is not strange, therefore, to those who look upon such a movement as Zionism in connection with faith in God's great latter-day work, to see this spirit now moving upon the minds of the Jewish people prompting their return to the land of their fathers. It is but the breath of God upon their souls turning their hearts to the promises made to the fathers. It is but the fulfillment *in part* of one of the many prophecies of the Book of Mormon relating to the gathering of Israel"(Italics added).

In another source we read, "Anti-Semitism, tsarist persecutions and pogroms, Christian religious intolerance, and wars were taking place in the early stages of the gathering of Judah, but in and of themselves these factors were not sufficient to implant in the minds of the Jewish people the idea of return. Persecution and abuse had been their lot for centuries and had served only to further disperse Judah's scattered remnants.

"In his own way and for his own reasons, the Lord preserved Judah through the centuries from complete assimilation. Now the time had come in the divine plan for the Jews to go home. Their two thousand year dispersion was not to be reversed overnight, however. The gathering would take decades and would proceed in line with a well-defined, divine timetable, even into the Millennium" (*Jerusalem, The Eternal City.* David B. Galbraith, D. Kelly Ogden, Andrew C. Skinner).

However, this return is not the complete fulfillment of the doctrine of gathering referred to in scripture, but in my view is a necessary preliminary to it. In 2 Nephi chapter 2, the sequence of gathering is first to Christ and his Church and then to specific locations. (This is re-emphasized in 2 Nephi 10:6–7.) Though the Jews may set up political governments that will offer them a place of return, they must also be "gathered" into the gospel covenant and come unto Christ. Only then will the land become their inheritance and the place of peace and strength prophesied of in scripture. As Elder McConkie states: "But this gathering will consist of accepting Christ, joining the Church, and receiving anew the Abrahamic Covenant as it is administered in holy places. The present assembling of people of Jewish ancestry into the Palestinian nation of Israel is not the scriptural gathering of Israel or of Judah. It may be a prelude thereto, and some of the people so assembled may in due course be gathered into the true church and kingdom of God on earth, and they may then assist in building the temple that is destined to grace Jerusalem's soil. But a political gathering is not a spiritual gathering, and the Lord's kingdom is not of this world" (Bruce R. McConkie, *New Witness for the Articles of Faith*, Deseret Book, 519–520).

Although numbers of Jews will gather to Israel in unbelief and without the covenant, we see in the Book of Mormon that the greatest numbers will go there only after conversion to Christ. It is the responsibility of the seed of Joseph to take this message to them in preparation for that final great gathering, a subject further developed in other volumes of this series.

CHAPTER ELEVEN

The murder and attempted murder of Jews by those who still believed in Hitler's extermination policy are documented, but as Beckman states, "No one will ever know how many Jews were killed during their exodus from Europe . . ." (Beckman, 104), but the Jews were not all pushovers either. The Jews, "particularly the young had changed. The elderly had no chance of escape, but the young had witnessed death, had escaped it, and were not afraid of it. Now they lived only for the chance to kill Germans. It was all they thought about until they got to know of the Brigade. . . . Hard facts and rumors spread like wildfire at the end of the war. It became the goal . . . not only to reach the Brigade but to take with them every surviving Jew they could find. What they needed (to do so)—trucks, fuel, food, drink, clothing, blankets, medical supplies, cooking utensils—they took by force (Beckman, 102). As one survivor, a partisan fighter who found the Brigade in the month just before Hannah and her friends found it, says, "I want you to think of a man coming out of the camps or the forests in 1945, and all he wants is to get out of Europe where everyone he loves is dead, his whole people murdered, and they will not let him go. He comes out of camps and they put him back into camps . . . Those who do this to him, who do it after all his years of pain, are not the enemy who killed him, but those from whom he has the right to expect kindness and mercy and justice.

"He looks at the world and what does he see? . . . The Germans who killed the Jews are free and they have their jobs and their families. They are the mayors and the policemen and the Jews are homeless vermin . . . . What we learned in 1945 brought pain that never ends. We learned in 1945 that only the Jew cares about the Jew. In all the world there is no justice for the Jew, but only the justice that the Jew can take for himself . . ." (Beckman, 106). And thus the attitude of the Jews of today. "Never again."

The Brigade had been in Italy for several months by the time Hannah's group reached them. They had set up an organization to get refugees to Israel illegally and were working with Bricha to accomplish that goal. In every town of Italy they conquered, the Brigade found Jews needing help and they gave it to them. After the fighting was finished and the Nazis had surrendered, they knew that thousands more needed to be liberated in Austria, Poland, and Germany, and they began making forays into those countries to give what help they could. When given leave, instead of visiting tourist attractions, they went to the nearest refugee camp to help out. They introduced order where there was chaos, hope where there was darkness, and life where there was only the stench of death.

The account of the Ebensee Jews is historical, though I have changed some of the participants for the sake of my story. The camp was to be closed and its inhabitants to be sent back to their homelands. But 1,600 Jews refused, making it clear they would rather commit suicide than go back. That is when contact was made with the Brigade (Beckman, 122). While the details of the rescue are mine, many of these are based on true events.

The story of the Jews in Klagenfurt is also based in historical fact. The Brigade found them and, like so many others, took them to safe havens in Italy, then to Palestine (Beckman, 119).

SELECTED BIBLIOGRAPHY

1. Mitchell G. Bard, ed. *The Complete History of the Holocaust* (San Diego: Greenhaven Press), 2001.

2. Morris Beckman. *The Jewish Brigade, An Army With Two Masters 1944-45* (Rickville NY: Sarpedon Press), 1998.

3. Ezra Taft Benson. *A Labor of Love:* The 1946 European Mission of Ezra Taft Benson (Salt Lake City:Deseret Book Co.), 1989.

4. Perry Biddiscombe, *The Last Nazis: SS Werewolf Guerilla Resistance in Europe, 1944-47* (Charleston: Tempus Publishing Ltd.), 2000.

5. Livia Bitton. *I have Lived a Thousand Years: Growing Up in the Holocaust* (New York: Simon and Schuster Books for Young Readers, NY), 1997.

6. David B. Galbraith, D. Kelly Ogden, and Andrew C. Skinner. *Jerusalem, The Eternal City* (Salt Lake City: Deseret Book Co.), 1996.

7. Blair Holmes and Alan F. Keele. *When Truth Was Treason: German Youth Against Hitler* (Chicago: University of Illinois Press), 1995.

8. Alexandria Richie. *A History of Berlin* (New York: Carroll and Graf Publishers, Inc.), 1998.

9. Rosenthal Institute for Holocaust Studies. *The Vatican and the Holocaust: The Catholic Church and the Jews* (Columbia University Press), 2000.

10. Gilbert W. Scharffs. *Mormonism in Germany* (Salt lake City: Deseret Book Company), 1970.

11. Karl Heinz Schnibbe, with Alan F. Keele and Douglas F. Tobler. *The Price: The True Story of a Mormon Who Defied Hitler* (Salt Lake City: Bookcraft),1984.

12. Tom Segev. *Soldiers of Evil* (Jerusalem: Domino Press), 1987.

13. Joseph Smith, Jr. *History of the Church of Jesus Christ of Latter-day Saints*, 7 vols. Notes by B. H. Roberts. (Salt Lake City: The Church of Jesus Christ of Latter-day Saints), 1932–1951.

14. *The Seamstress: A Memoir of Survival* (New York: Putnam Press), 1997.

15. Douglas F. Tobler. "The Jews, The Mormons, and the Holocaust," *Journal of Mormon History*, 59–92.

16. Edith Velmans. *Edith's Story* (New York: Soho Publishing), 1999.

17. Isabel Vincent. *Hitler's Silent Partners: Swiss Banks, Nazi Gold and the Pursuit of Justice*, (New York: William Morrow and Co.), 1997.

INTERNET SITES:

1. The Jewish Agency for Israel at http://www.jajz-ed.org.il/

2. *A Teachers Guide to the Holocaust*, produced by the Florida Center for Instructional Technology at http://fcit.coedu.usf.edu/holocaust/timeline/after.htm

3. Children of the Holocaust at http://www.graceproducts.com/fmnc/main.htm

4. *Displaced Persons, Refugees, Holocaust Survivors*, a site put together by Dr. Stuart Stein at http://www.ess.uwe.ac.uk/documents/displaced.htm

5. *Encore Archive: The Art of Concentration Camps* at http://www.clal.org/e23.html

6. *Centenary of Zionism*: *Aliya and Absorption* at
   http://www.israel.org/mfa/

7. Jewish History Sourcebook at
   http://www.fordham.edu/halsall/jewish/jewishsbook.html